blue

praise for *Blue*:

"Take a trip with Lou Aronica that brings back your love of magic and everything it can make possible as you immerse yourself in his thought-provoking, creative novel, *Blue*...A story to remember and cherish, *Blue* and Lou Aronica have a few surprises in store that will leave you wondering "what if?" *Blue* by talented Lou Aronica will become a resident of your keeper shelf, a book to pull out and read again and each time you will find something more in its pages."
– Single Titles

"Author Lou Aronica creates a world that manages to be both surreal and tangible. Reading this book is like experiencing a lucid dream with depth and detail that play on all five senses."
– Blogcritics

"It doesn't happen too often (for me) where I read a book and tell everyone I know about it.And I mean everyone.*Blue* was such a book. This is a book that will delve into all the emotions you have and leave you wanting more. It is a story about courage, survival, loss, happiness and all the emotions in between.... This book is a must read, truly one of the best books I have read in quite some time."
– Review from Here

"*Blue* is enriched with great characters, a moving story line, and an author who will have you want to read more of his work. I could feel the anguish Chris felt for his daughter and wanting to spend as much time with her as he possibly could. The world of Tamarisk is full of intriguing people, who are almost as real as Becky. *Blue* is a five star read in my books!"
– Cheryl's Book Nook

blue

A novel by

lou aronica

THE
STORY
PLANT

This is a work of fiction. Names, characters, places, and incidents either are the product of the author's imagination or are used fictitiously. Any resemblance to actual events, locales, organizations, or persons living or dead, is entirely coincidental and beyond the intent of either the author or the publisher.

The Story Plant
Studio Digital CT, LLC
P.O. Box 4613
Stamford, CT 06907

Print ISBN-13: 978-1-61188-096-0
E-book ISBN-13: 978-1-943486-29-8

Visit our website at www.TheStoryPlant.com
Visit the author's website at www.LouAronica.com

First Fiction Studio BooksPaperback Printing: January 2011
First Story Plant Paperback Printing: September, 2013

Printed in the United States of America

For Molly,
who taught me a very real form of magic
I never realized existed.

acknowledgments

This novel was a very long time in the making, and many people helped, in a variety of ways, in the process.

My family—my wife Kelly, and my children Molly, David, Abigail, and Tigist—have always known what this story means to me and they've always supported it.

Early readers kept me on track. Special thanks to Peter Schneider, Keith Ferrell, Debbie Mercer, and my sister Fran Alesia for their encouragement and their comments.

Rick Levy and Lisa Tatum played a key role at a critical point in my taking this novel to a different plane. I wouldn't have seen it without the two of you.

Danny Baror and Scott Hoffman both threw themselves into this at vital moments, for which I am tremendously thankful.

Thanks to Barbara Aronica Buck—who, I want to make as clear as possible was not the inspiration for Polly in this novel—for designing the cover, and Brooke Dworkin for preventing me from making stupid editorial mistakes. If you find any stupid editorial mistakes, blame my obstinance.

Finally, I'd like to thank Ray Bradbury, mostly because all of us should, but specifically because he showed me first hand what a writer should aspire to be.

1

The soft whir of the DVD player was the only sound in the room. Chris sat on the sofa opposite the television, the remote control in his hand, though he didn't intend to use it. He would just let the machine continue fast-forwarding.

On the screen, the video record of his daughter Becky's life spun by. The smile he believed to be her first. Her masterpiece, *Still Life with Smeared Pureed Pears and Cheerios on Tray Table*. Her toddler form calming temporarily for a brief nap on his chest. The two of them running through the sprinkler. The perfectly orchestrated wedding service for her teddy bear and toy dog where Chris served as both best man and maid of honor. Her kerchiefed head at her sixth birthday party. Modeling her new coif when her hair returned once the treatments were over. His ex-wife Polly looking gaunt and tired—or simply angry about something—as she walked out of the auditorium with Becky after the second grade play. Back dives into the swimming pool at the resort in the Berkshires. Becky rolling her eyes at the camera during the school picnic. The forced laughter at the family reunion. The footage she took of him sleeping in the Adirondack chair on what would turn out to be his last full weekend at the house. Becky and Lonnie walking toward Becky's room in this apartment before they closed the door on him.

Hours and hours of motion sped by at a greatly accelerated pace. Like a time-lapse image of Chris's growing irrelevance in Becky's life.

Chris had watched the old tapes often over the past four years. He'd done so several times since he'd finally gotten around to digitally transferring them six months ago. It was something to do on Friday nights. The first time he heard Becky's preschool voice on the videos, he wept instantly. He missed that voice desperately, more than he'd even realized. He missed the way she spoke to him, how the sound of her saying the word "Daddy" defined everything that was right with the world. How she gave him every reason to believe that all promises could be fulfilled, all odds overcome. Becky's voice had been dismissive tonight when he called the house. She had plans with her friends and she was running late. He was no competition for her eyeliner, let alone the schoolmates who would soon be waiting.

To make things worse, Polly had answered the phone. Always a highlight. At least when her second husband, Al, answered there was the possibility he might say something funny. When Polly got on the line, she always mentioned some newly discovered financial obligation or suggested obliquely that their household purred just a little less smoothly when he called. A month ago, he hadn't phoned Becky at night for the first time since the divorce. He had been through a simply terrible day at work and he just didn't have the emotional energy. He missed calling twice more after that. If Becky had noticed, she didn't say anything about it.

The final images on the disc were less than a year old. His parents' visit from Florida. Polly let him have Becky the entire weekend, and they spent Saturday in Essex and Old Saybrook. He bought Becky a bracelet in a craft store and she dangled it on her wrist in front of the camera, laughing carelessly. Chris had hated seeing his parents go that Sunday. Maybe it was time to get them up here again.

The phone rang and Chris hit the pause button on the remote. On the television, Becky walked ten feet ahead of him down Main Street in Essex.

The phone call was from a telemarketer who wanted to give Chris the opportunity to buy vacation property on Victoria

Island in British Colombia. Chris had been to Victoria and thought it was beautiful, but he wasn't sure why anyone thought a person from Connecticut would want to own a vacation house on the other side of the continent. He politely declined the "opportunity." Pointless phone calls seemed to be the only ones he got at home. He'd been meaning for years to put his number on the nationwide no-call list for phone solicitations, but he just hadn't managed to do so.

The interruption left him feeling miffed and unsettled. He probably should have let the answering machine pick up the call, but he'd never been able to do that. Even if he had, the ringing still would have distracted him, taken the focus from his viewing experience.

He looked at the television screen showing the back of his daughter. For the first time, he noticed a woman coming toward the camera. He didn't recall seeing her there before. Probably because he was always looking at Becky. The woman was in her early twenties, pretty. Her face seemed somewhat familiar, though Chris couldn't place it at all. She looked a little like his niece Kiley; maybe that was it. Obviously, he had seen the woman every time he watched this video, but it had only registered on his subconscious. Chris picked up the remote, flicked the DVD player out of pause, and watched the image on the screen come to life at normal speed. The woman passed the range of the camera and disappeared.

A moment later, Becky turned and made a face at him that said "Don't you think you've used that thing enough today?" A few seconds after that the picture faded and the screen went blue.

///

"Two more stops and then ice cream," Al said, sounding more like an eight-year-old than an adult. Becky thought it was hilarious that he couldn't go more than an hour without some kind of snack. She had no idea where it all went. He actually seemed to be in pretty good shape for an old guy.

"I definitely need to go to American Eagle," she said.

Mom gave her a thumbs-up. "We also have to go to Papyrus to get something for Patricia's birthday."

Becky's best friend Lonnie raised her hand as though she were in Honors English. "That's right next to The Body Shop. I absolutely need to go there. If I don't get some new lotion, my skin is simply going to flake right off of my body."

"That's more than two stops," Al said in something very close to a whine. Becky grinned.

Mom leaned across and kissed Al on the cheek without breaking stride. "The ice cream will wait for you, hon. They keep it in freezers so it doesn't melt."

"If we have to go to three stores first, then I'm getting two scoops." He whirled and pointed at Lonnie. "And you're not getting any. It's bad for your skin."

Lonnie laughed and threw her package-laden arms around Becky. "That's okay; Becky will share hers with me."

"No, she won't," Al said, still pretending to be upset, "because I'm eating hers, too."

Mom patted Al on the arm and turned toward Lonnie. "You can have ice cream if you want, Lonnie."

"Thanks, Mom." Lonnie had been calling Becky's mother "Mom" since she and Becky were in Brownies together, but it still brought a little sparkle to Mom's eyes every time she said it.

They made a left and headed toward American Eagle. While she was reluctant to admit it, Becky felt as if she could use a little break herself, even though she wasn't in the mood for ice cream. They'd been at the mall for a few hours now, trying on shoes, browsing the bookstore, buying some new shirts for Al, a spring jacket for Mom, a couple of birthday presents, and a half dozen things for Lonnie. The only thing that Becky had gotten was a copy of the new Neil Gaiman novel, which she'd been dying to read. That was enough for her. She always liked shopping a lot more than she liked buying.

While the rest of them looked like they could go at this all day and night, what Becky really wanted to do was sit down. Not that she would ever mention this. The teasing from everyone else would be endless and merciless. In this family, marathon shopping was a point of pride and this wasn't one of the places where Becky felt like standing out from the crowd.

Before they could rest for a little while, though, she really needed to get some jeans. In the past month, several of her pants had crossed over from well-worn to ratty. She could barely wear them in public anymore, so the situation was bordering on an emergency. They turned into American Eagle, and as soon as they did, Becky knew she'd come to the right place. She always had luck here, and within minutes she had chosen several pairs of pants to try on.

"Not those," Lonnie said, pointing to one pair in her arms. "They're too cutesy."

Becky held up the jeans. They didn't look cutesy to her. "They are?"

"The teal piping on the pockets? Come on, Beck, you're not eight anymore."

Becky examined the pants again. "I like them."

Lonnie shook her head. "Wear them at your own risk."

Becky glanced over at her mother. "I'm going to try all of these on."

"We'll be here waiting for you," Al said. "Dreaming of Mocha Chip Explosion."

Becky threw him a smile. Al was such a goof. He was actually kind of fun to shop with, though, and he had really, really good taste even if he didn't want you to know that he did. It was kind of hard for her to believe that, at fourteen, she still enjoyed going shopping with her mother and stepfather.

Becky had to wait a couple minutes to get into a dressing room. The mall was extremely busy today and this particular store was rocking. While she waited, she looked around the room, her eyes landing on the terrific-looking guy behind the counter (she was pretty sure he was a senior in her school, not that he ever would have noticed her) and then the girl with the great clothes who worked the floor. Maybe she'd get a job here when she was sixteen. It wouldn't be a bad way to make some money, and there had to be some kind of discount involved.

Once inside the dressing room, Becky hung up the jeans she planned to try on, took off her sneakers and pants, and reached for the pair with the teal piping. She had no idea why Lonnie thought these were too cutesy. She thought they looked stylish, maybe even a little edgy. Lonnie could be very narrow-minded about fashion sometimes.

As Becky bent to try on the jeans, suddenly, out of nowhere, she nearly tipped over. The dressing room seemed like it was spinning on her. She threw an arm out to catch herself on the wall, but the lurching continued.

Her head swirled and she couldn't focus on anything.

For a few moments she couldn't do more than hold on to the wall, and then she slowly lowered her body onto the floor, feeling light-headed and a little nauseous. A second wave of dizziness washed over her and she leaned to the side, trying to take deep breaths.

This one was worse than the other times had been.

A moment later, the disorientation faded. But it was still a few more minutes before she felt steady enough to stand up. She did so only long enough to sit again on the bench in the room. She cupped her face in her hands and tried to calm her breathing, using a technique she'd read about in a book. Eventually it slowed down and she felt something like normal.

Becky didn't want to think about where this was coming from. They had been shopping a long time. She hadn't eaten much for lunch. She probably just needed to put her feet up and chill for a while. She stood carefully, thankful that she no longer felt faint, and stepped out of the pants that were halfway up one leg. She was nervous about bending down again, so she picked them up with her foot, grabbed them, and put them back on the hanger. Standing as upright as possible, she put the pants she'd worn to the mall back on and exited the dressing room, taking one more deep breath before opening the door.

"Nothing?" Lonnie said when Becky returned to the front of the store empty-handed.

"You were right; that one pair was too cutesy. The others just didn't fit right."

"That's too bad. You usually do really well here."

"Just not my day."

Al walked over with Mom. "I'm trying to convince your mother that I would look great in one of those hoodies over there."

"Trust me, hon," Mom said, "you'd just look creepy."

Al frowned and seemed about to say something when Becky said, "Mom, I'm really wasted. Do you think we can head home?"

"Ice cream first, right?" Al said hopefully.

Becky just closed her eyes. She wanted nothing more right now than to lie down on the couch and watch television.

"Al, we have ice cream at home," Mom said, observing Becky closely. "Come on, let's get going."

Becky felt relieved, but she hoped she hadn't just turned this into a big deal. On the way to the parking lot, Mom put an arm around her. "You all right? You look a little pale."

"Just used up. I'll be okay."

"You sure?"

Becky nodded. "I'll be okay."

They got to the car and Lonnie and Al (who'd taken the ice cream thing extraordinarily well) started blabbing at each other about the woman giving perfume samples at Nordstrom. It had been a running dialogue throughout the day. For some reason, they seemed obsessed with the way the woman had said, "May I scent you with Chanel?"

As Al drove out of the parking lot, Mom turned and patted Becky on the hand. Becky sent her what she hoped was a reassuring smile. Mom patted her hand again and then turned frontward to make sure Al kept his eyes on the road. He wasn't always the best at that.

As they headed toward home, Becky realized she was

feeling fine again. She knew she would.

It always passed after a little while.

///

It was terrible and thrilling. With every step Miea took into the planting field, she grew more certain that something was very wrong here. At the same time, though, she couldn't help but feel a bit of excitement at simply being in this place again. To be doing something instead of presiding over everything.

She knelt to examine the cancerous blond spots on a cluster of leaves. She ran a finger over the deep green striations on another set. She understood what it all meant and this weighed upon her.

Yet the smallest part of her felt somehow lighter. Some reachable part of her mind felt the faintest measure of buoyancy at simply returning to a place where she could be close to the earth. She felt sense memories of the thousands of days of her youth spent planting, nurturing, and cultivating, and especially the liberating summer out in these very fields, perpetually dirty, wearing the grime as casually as her colleagues did, thankfully unaware of the changes that waited only months in the future.

The lightness evaporated and the full gravity of her current function returned. Miea was too young to recall the Great Blight clearly, but there were reminders everywhere. In the bleak pigment sculptures of Naria Solani. In the discordant tone poetry of *The Age of Wither*. In the dozens of volumes of history and analysis and revision that had been solemnly committed to the page in the years since. What she did recall from that time was the clipped exchanges between her parents, the way they'd challenged, questioned, and criticized each other as their world teetered. Miea had felt uncomfortable being near them, unaccustomed to seeing them act this way together. She remembered wishing desperately that there would be less tension, that her home could have the harmony she'd always believed was there.

Then suddenly it was so. The Blight was gone. Without

explanation. Within two seasons, the ebony loam of the fields had spawned shoots as azure, indigo, and cerulean as ever before. Miea assumed that her parents had never forgotten how close everything had come to falling apart and probably always remembered that they'd nearly alienated each other forever. Things had never really seemed the same between them after that. Regardless, life on the other side of the Blight had been prosperous and promising.

But now these blond marks. These green veins.

"This does not necessarily signify anything," Thuja said gravely.

Miea turned to face the craggy minister of agriculture, more than four decades her senior. He hadn't wanted her to come here. He'd tried to use his considerable influence to prevent it, failing to understand how much Miea needed to see this herself.

"That's difficult to believe."

"Diseases—minor ones—happen all the time. Especially out here in the far reaches. We discover their causes and we cure them."

Miea tilted her head. "And what is the cause of this particular disease?"

The man averted his eyes. Surely, he hated having this kind of confrontation with someone so young. He was just going to have to deal with that. "It is early. We will find it."

Miea let her fingernails skim the dark earth. The soil was so rich, so moist with the nutrient-filled morning rains that distinguished the territory of Jonrae. It was difficult to imagine that something destructive thrived here. It was even more difficult, though, to deny her instincts.

"If there is any chance to cut this off before it begins to spread, we must."

"We have people working every daylight minute. Farmers, scientists, specialists." Thuja spoke more quickly than he usually did. A clear indication that, despite his words, he was nervous about what they'd found here.

"I want biweekly reports."

Miea saw Thuja recoil ever so slightly at her tone of voice. Then he nodded with studied deference. "It will be done."

"And I will return here in the near future."

Thuja made a show of glancing around him. "That might not be the most productive thing. I do not mean you disrespect, Your Majesty, but I believe your presence makes people nervous." He smiled professionally and extended his hand to help Miea stand. She looked away from him, turning toward a shrunken vine.

As she did, she remembered her mother's outrage at her decision to spend months in these fields. "The entire summer?" Mother had said. "Spend a few days if you insist. Spending the entire summer is ludicrous. There are other things to do. Other places you need to be."

"But no place else I *want* to be."

Her mother had frowned and walked away. Once again, Miea hadn't been sure where that left their conversation. At dinner that night, her father had spoken with her about her planned summer in Jonrae and her mother hadn't objected. Maybe Mother had realized how much the trip meant to her. Maybe she hadn't understood at all. It was one of many things left forever unresolved.

Miea held a withered leaf between her thumb and forefinger. Was it possible that she'd sowed the seeds for this plant herself? This cluster of vines could easily be four years old. The field supervisor, forever favoring her, had assigned her duties as close to the gatehouse as he could without his soft treatment of her making her angry, so she'd always worked near where she now stood. The thought—of all of it: her days in the fields, the skittish supervisor, the diseased plant, and her lost mother—threatened to bring tears to her eyes. Tears that she could not let fall. She wouldn't allow Thuja to see her cry, and it would be wrong to let the others see it.

She bent to kiss the leaf. To will some of her spirit into its blue planes.

The leaf came off in her hands.

Miea bowed her head and closed the leaf in her palm. She

shut her eyes tightly and silently whispered a plea for strength and answers. Then she placed the leaf gently on the dirt. She rose, not wishing to make eye contact with Thuja, but finding it impossible to avoid the worried gaze of his associates.

She had been a child during the Great Blight, aware of the disturbance in her household, but ignorant of the larger and more portentous implications for the world around her. She was not a child any longer. If the Blight returned, what else would be different this time?

"We need to go," she said quietly, nearly to herself.

///

It was not the ideal moment to listen, but Gage listened anyway. The equilibrium was tenuous at best right now, and there was much Gage needed to do, but listening was essential. Listening was the future. Listening allowed stories to begin.

From the depths of focus, Gage centered and settled on the island world, stretching through the expanse to listen. Gage damped the shouting—so much shouting—and magnified the whispers. Gage knew that shouts maintained stories. Whispers, however, started them. The whispers deserved acknowledgment and attention.

As always, there were hundreds of whispers. Some were too soft to hear. Others—many, many others—said nothing. Still others said something powerful, something plaintive, but said these things too late. The shouting drowned many more even though Gage had damped the shouting.

Nevertheless, Gage would gift all of the whispers. Few would understand the gift. Even fewer would take the gift and imagine with it. Sometimes, though, there were surprises.

Gage's focus deepened. When Gage focused on the new stories, on the possibility of the island world, Gage felt an enriched sense of meaning and purpose. It didn't matter that so much promise went unfulfilled. What mattered was that the promise continued to exist.

From this deeply focused state, Gage heard two whispers. They spoke together with different voices. One voice was young. The other longed for youth. There was much consternation here. Confusion. Defiance. They knew their story was the wrong story. They sensed that their true story together had not begun. This was unusual insight. Insight worth encouragement. If they understood this much—that they were waiting for a new story—they might do something with the inspiration. Gage had listened to others in this moment with the same potential, but something sparked here.

From the deepest place in focus, Gage imagined a gift and presented it to the two whisperers. Gage would return to these two, would focus on them again. There was reason to believe they would enrich the gift. If they did, a new story could emerge. A story meant to be.

Sadly, not a simple one.

2

The traffic crawled over the narrow bridge that connected Moorewood and Standridge. Chris was going to be late getting Becky again. First there had been that interminable conversation with Jack in the hall about "belt-tightening" and now there was a backup on the bridge. This part of Connecticut was never supposed to get crowded. As more and more businesses moved into the state, though, more and more people considered this area to be within reasonable commuting distance of those businesses. Hence the ever-present congestion going over the bridge, and another night when he would show up later than he said he would.

Becky never complained about his being late. Was that because she understood that traffic was a problem? Lonnie's father came home from this direction every night, so maybe she'd heard from her best friend how tough the trip could be. Either that, or it didn't really matter to Becky when Chris showed up. She never really complained to him about anything anymore.

Chris had moved into the apartment in Standridge exactly four years ago today. He'd wanted to live as close to Becky as possible, but he didn't think he could handle staying in Moorewood. At least in Standridge, he wouldn't run into someone who knew Polly and him every time he went to the supermarket or the post office. Even now, he still felt awkward with these kinds of encounters, knowing that while exchanging small talk with him, most were thinking, *Polly threw him out*. It wasn't until his marriage had ended that he'd realized that nearly all of their Moorewood friends had actually been Polly's friends and that he had been tagging along all these years.

Four years later, Chris wasn't any less confused by the sudden end of his marriage than he had been the day it happened. Of course he'd thought about splitting up with Polly. They'd fought nearly every day after Becky got sick. Before then, they'd been able to get past their differences of opinion, but Becky's leukemia had divided them in nearly every way.

Chris knew he never would have sought a divorce, though. It wasn't just a matter of "staying together for the kid." It was that he didn't want any nights away from Becky. He knew that she was closing in on her teen years and that she wouldn't want to spend nearly as much time with her family as before, but he wanted her to know that he was always available. That spontaneous moments could still happen regularly between them. That he would be as cool when she was an adolescent as she had thought he was before. He needed to be around all the time in order for this to work.

Polly obviously had no such concerns and certainly no concerns at all for him. Admittedly, they'd separated emotionally long before they separated households. He couldn't remember the last time he'd savored an evening out with her or longed for a night alone with her. Polly was often in bed less than an hour after Becky, while Chris read or watched a sporting event on television. The other option was to talk, and talking was usually disagreeable.

There had to have been a time when they liked being with each other, didn't there? He had vague recollections of loving Polly's company, of being fascinated by her opinions, and even more fascinated by her touch. He'd once called Polly his "big love," hadn't he? There was a time in their relationship when he missed her so much when they were apart that he ached physically. He was sure of it.

As with so many things that happened before Becky got sick at age five, though, these memories were indistinct. From that point on—and he remembered this vividly—Polly and he never seemed to be on the same page. They argued about treatment and about whether or not they should visit different specialists. They argued about how much to tell Becky and about how to handle her. They argued about his being too optimistic and about how to address the terrible dreams that woke Polly in the middle of the night. When Becky went into remission, they even argued about whether they could trust in it or not.

By that point, they didn't need a life-threatening illness to spark an argument. They could disagree about the weather.

"I can't be like this anymore," Polly had said to him one night. She'd gone up to the bedroom a half hour before, and Chris had been surprised to see her back in the den. He didn't respond beyond looking up from his book.

"Being in this house with you is painful to me," she said, sitting across from him.

Chris put the book down. "Would you like me to disappear?" he said sarcastically.

"That wasn't the exact solution I had in mind."

Chris laughed nervously. "What?"

"Who are we kidding, Chris? If you can honestly tell me you're happy with us, then I'll check myself into an insane asylum."

"I'm not happy with us, Polly."

"Then why are you still here?"

Chris cast a glance toward Becky's room upstairs. "That should be obvious."

Polly looked off in the same direction and scowled. "That's not a marriage."

"It's a family."

Polly closed her eyes and said nothing for a moment. "It's not my idea of a family."

Chris took a deep breath. "Is there something you are trying to say?"

Polly's eyes locked with his. "I want you to move out."

Chris felt his skin prickle. "I can't move out."

Polly's brows narrowed and she tilted her head to the right. "I want you to move out. I don't want this to get ugly and I don't want it to get contentious. We'll share Becky. You can have her one night during the week and half the weekend."

Chris laughed at the surreal nature of everything Polly had just said. "You consider that sharing?"

"She needs a steady home environment. She has a lot of schoolwork and projects now. She can't be bouncing around all week."

Chris's anger built so quickly, he didn't even feel it coming. "Fine. You move out and I'll take care of Becky's 'steady home environment.'"

Polly leaned forward casually in her chair. "You know that isn't the way it would turn out if we went to court. I work part-time. I'm around to get Becky to school and I'm here when she gets home. My lawyer told me there was no way a judge would make you the custodial parent."

"You've spoken to a lawyer already?" Chris was surprised he could even get the words out of his mouth.

"I had to make sure I protected myself before talking to you."

"Protected yourself?" Chris stood up and walked toward the opposite end of the room before turning to face her again. "Who am I, a stalker? Did you get a restraining order as well? I can't believe you went to a lawyer before we even talked about this!"

"There's nothing to talk about."

"I am not just giving up on this household."

Polly stared at him for several seconds before speaking again. "Chris, understand what I am saying. There is nothing to talk about."

The two weeks that followed were largely a blur. Hiring his lawyer. Searching for a new place to live. Forcing himself not to talk to Becky about this because he didn't want her to know how upset he was and because he couldn't trust himself not to betray his fury at Polly. Long sessions with his closest friend, Lisa, talking about nothing else. Making the final arrangements to leave, including the grossly unsatisfactory temporary custody agreement that ultimately became the official custody agreement. Breaking the news to his daughter and trying to bear up while she alternately sobbed and vented her anger. Then, finally, driving off in his car, looking into his sideview mirror to see Becky lift a hand and mouth "bye." He made it out of the neighborhood before he pulled into a parking lot and cried uncontrollably, seeing that one syllable form on her lips repeatedly, feeling a little more powerless and a little more like his life had ended every time.

And if he was going to be honest with himself, life—at least the life that he most loved—did end on that day. Life with Becky was always about instantaneous discovery and little gems of time. Now it was all about plans and captured moments. Pick her up for dinner every Tuesday night. Pack as much as you can into three out of every four weekends that ended at 4:00 on Sunday. Try to maintain some level of continuity and relevance through phone conversations and the occasional e-mail message. He'd quickly become a guest in his daughter's world. Even a few months before the divorce, he never could have imagined this.

The traffic stayed heavy all the way through town, only breaking up when he was a few turns from the house. By the time he pulled into the driveway, he was nearly a half hour late. He got out of the car quickly and walked to the front door. It still felt strange to ring the bell for entry to the house he'd once called home.

Fortunately, Polly wasn't there. She'd gone out to dinner with Al.

"Mom said to remind you that she needs the check for my orthodontia bill," was literally the first thing Becky said to him.

"Is there a reason I can't just pay the orthodontist directly?"

"You're gonna have to take that up with her."

Becky grabbed her spring coat and then held the door open for him to leave before pulling it shut behind her.

"I'm sorry I'm late. The traffic around here has gotten truly insane."

"No big deal. I was on IM with a bunch of my friends."

They got into the car and Chris leaned over to kiss Becky on the head. She leaned in his direction for a second and then back toward the passenger door.

"I was thinking Chinese for dinner," he said. "That okay with you?"

"Sure, wherever."

"The Rice Noodle?"

"Sure, that works."

Chris headed back toward Standridge. The Rice Noodle had opened the week after he moved into the apartment and it was one of the first restaurants he'd visited with Becky after the split. They'd over-ordered ridiculously that night, but Becky seemed to like trying everything—he was just thrilled to see her eat considering how sullen she had seemed as the split happened—and he had taken her back there often since.

"Okay day in school?"

"Nothing special. Geometry quiz. We're reading *The Odyssey* in English."

"Ugh, I hated it."

Becky wrinkled her nose. "It's been around for a couple thousand years, Dad. There must be something to it."

"There's a lot to it. That doesn't mean it's fun."

"Seems okay to me. I read the first couple chapters this afternoon. I can see how so many other stories came out of it." Becky shrugged and Chris couldn't tell whether she was shaking off the conversation or just his contribution to it. "Do you have anything new on the iPod?"

"The new Urgent album."

Becky turned to face him, though Chris couldn't make out her expression while keeping his eye on the road. "You like them?"

"You turned me on to them."

"I did?"

"You don't remember? About six months ago, you and Lonnie played songs from their last album in the car all day."

Becky nodded. "Huh . . . yeah. Anything good on this one?"

"Yeah, there's some really good stuff. You haven't heard it?"

"Nobody really talks about them anymore. I didn't even know there *was* a new album."

"Put it on."

Becky waved a hand. "Maybe on the way home. What else do you have?"

Chris pointed to the car's stereo system, which controlled his iPod. "Whatever you want. I just did a big download, so there's a bunch of new stuff."

Becky scrolled through Chris's "recently added" playlist. "Arcade Fire, I'm impressed. Death Cab for Cutie, good. Who's Tim Buckley?"

"Singer-songwriter from the seventies. He had a son he barely knew who went on to be the Next Big Thing in the nineties. Both of them died mysteriously and very young."

"How weird. Worth listening to?"

"Some of it is very good. Give it a try."

"I'm kind of in the mood for something a little harder. Wow, you have some new stuff from Crease?" Becky started the player. The car instantly filled with distorted guitars, thudding bass, and more anguish than any twenty-one-year-old singer should feel. Chris had connected with this band the first time he heard them and he found their new music especially stirring. Conversation was now impossible, but at least Becky approved of his taste in music—most of it, anyway.

When they got to the restaurant, they found it virtually empty. This was surprising even though it was a Tuesday night because The Rice Noodle had become the gold standard for Chinese restaurants in the area. The only other occupied table had a woman and two children, whose ages Chris guessed to be six and four. About five minutes after Chris and Becky sat down, a man wearing a tie and a shirt with rolled up sleeves joined the other party, sweeping his little son up and dangling him upside down. This caused the kid to squeal and the mother to good-naturedly scold the incorrigibility of the pair. Chris watched the entire thing while Becky studied the menu.

He turned back to her. "What do you want to order?"

"I can't really decide." She shut the menu and put it down. "I wasn't really in the mood for Chinese food."

"You weren't? Then why'd we come here?"

"You seemed to be in the mood for it."

"I did? All I did was suggest coming here. We could have gone anywhere else."

"It's no big deal. Can we get something steamed and maybe a noodle dish?"

"We can leave if you really don't want this."

Becky looked around at the many unoccupied tables. "No we can't, Dad. Let's just order. Whatever you want is fine."

Chris stared at his menu, confounded. He never had an effective response for the times when Becky got this way. How did parents break through to their kids when they put up these walls? He wondered if she did the same kind of thing with Polly. If his relationship with his ex-wife had been even slightly different, he'd have been able to ask her. He couldn't acknowledge communication breakdowns like this to Polly, though. Too much ammunition.

Once they ordered, the food arrived quickly. Becky didn't seem to have much of an appetite—for food or discussion. After trying several conversational gambits—schoolwork, friends, telling her about his job, trying to get her to suggest something they could do over the weekend—Chris realized he had been rolling a boulder uphill. They finished eating quietly and it was he who flicked on the iPod when they got back in the car.

"Thanks, Dad, it was great," Becky said when they arrived back on Polly's driveway.

"It was?"

Becky seemed genuinely surprised that he'd challenged her like that. Her face registered something between hurt and confusion, and then flicked back to casual.

"Thanks a lot, Dad," she said, reaching over to pat his arm before pushing out the door.

Chris watched Becky bound up the steps of the porch and enter the house. She still walked with a bounce, something she'd done from the time she was a toddler. He hadn't noticed it earlier in the evening.

She disappeared behind the front door. Chris noticed that he could still feel the touch of her hand on his arm. In every other way, though, she was entirely gone for the night.

///

"How worried should I be about this?" Miea said to the man Thuja had sent to brief her.

"It's an insect, Your Majesty."

"And this particular breed of insect exists only in Jonrae."

"Yes, Your Majesty."

"And it feeds on the plants that are currently dying there, which means this insect is therefore dying itself."

"Yes, Your Majesty."

Miea leaned back in her chair. Her neck was stiff. She needed a back rub. She'd welcome some good news even more. "Then I suppose I should be extremely worried about this."

"The minister told me to express his very strong belief that there's no cause for serious alarm, that—"

Miea held up a hand. "It is not necessary to placate me. And I have no interest in partial truths or vague assurances."

The man bowed his head slightly. "Your Majesty, I am telling you everything that I know."

"I'm sure you are," Miea said patiently. It wasn't this man's fault. Still, another conversation with Thuja was necessary. She needed to let him know that she expected those he sent to brief her to have as much information as Thuja had himself. She knew such a conversation would ruffle the minister. However, there was absolutely no room to spare feelings in this situation.

The man left a few minutes later after one more failed attempt to ease her mind. That his intentions had been good was as obvious as the fact that he was entirely out of his depth. Still, the man seemed genuinely worried about how this news would affect her. Why were so many people so quick to equate her youth with delicacy?

Miea could handle the news. She was sure that nothing would come to her as a devastating shock at this point. She was not, however, at all sure what she could do about the news. If indeed a new blight was upon them—and she cautioned herself not to jump to this conclusion—was she equipped to address it? Was anyone?

She had a few minutes. Time enough to make herself a cup of argo. The kitchen staff would of course be startled and maybe even a little miffed by her appearance, as they were every time she did this. They'd never become accustomed to seeing her there preparing her own beverages, even though she'd done so nearly her entire life. Miea started down the corridor, but as she did, she found Sorbus, her personal assistant, walking toward her carrying an ornately carved stone tray upon which he held a wooden argo pitcher.

"Good afternoon, Your Majesty," he said, tipping his head forward. "I thought you might like a bit of warm brew before your next meeting."

Miea did her best to smile. She really hated being waited on. There were times when it was necessary, of course, when appearances demanded it. However, she really was entirely capable of getting her own drinks. "Thank you, Sorbus. I was actually just planning to visit the kitchen myself."

The man laughed as though Miea were teasing him with absurdities. "That's really never necessary, Your Majesty."

Miea rolled her eyes. There was no point in trying to explain this to Sorbus or anyone else on the staff. She followed him back to her chambers and allowed him to serve the argo, thanking him again before he left. She sat back and sipped the hot drink, still bubbling as the petals of ingenito at the bottom of the cup released their flavor. This was the first quiet moment she'd had since sunrise. The first opportunity for an uncluttered thought.

The first real chance to mark the day.

Four years ago on this day, Miea hadn't awakened at sunrise. She had late classes and chose to sleep in before meeting Dyson for a mid-morning breakfast. The night before had simply been the most romantic evening of her life. She'd thought their plans for the evening were going to involve quizzing each other on the upcoming natural ethics test, but Dyson had something entirely different in mind. Borrowing a vehicle from a friend, he'd driven her nearly an hour away from the university to a tiny restaurant near the Perrot Arch. Under a canopy of kaibab leaves, lit only by the glow of the stars, a waxing moon, and the incandescence of flitting mianuses, they'd eaten the delicate creations of the woman who had prepared every meal here for the past thirty-seven years. A wispy foam bearing the essence of adria. A subtle white stew of cream and lidia broth dotted with rich kunz root. The sweet airiness of a perfectly executed jactorres.

The food and the setting were hardly the things that had made this night special, though. For this was a different Dyson who had sat before her. They had been dating for several months, and he had always been kind, always entertaining, and he had always made her feel as though she were important to him. However, she also sensed that he had been keeping something back, that no matter how much they enjoyed themselves, Dyson wasn't willing to let go completely with her. She could tell from the moment's hesitation before he kissed her or the way his eyes clouded when they talked about the future. Until now.

"I've been kidding myself," he had said softly, just above the gentle chime of the okka music that played in the background.

"What do you mean?" she'd said, concerned irrationally that Dyson was thinking about breaking up with her.

Dyson had looked down at the table and then at his hands. He had smiled shyly at Miea and then looked off in the distance. "I've spent the last couple months trying to convince myself that I was okay with what we had. That I understood that your being royalty would someday come between us. I really thought I could live with that."

"Dyson, we don't know—"

He had reached out for her hand and Miea had stopped talking. "We have a great time, Miea."

"Yes, always."

"And we can talk."

She'd nodded, thinking back on the conversations that sometimes kept them up all night. "Yes we can."

He had squeezed her hand. "And when I touch you, and when I look at you, I feel—I don't know—otherworldly. It's like our contact exists on some other plane entirely."

Miea had no idea what to say, so she'd simply brought his hand to her lips and kissed it. He couldn't be breaking up with her if he was speaking like this. However, she had no idea what he was doing.

"And now I realize . . ." He had hesitated, seeming to consider whether he should say anything else. ". . . I realize that I truly have been kidding myself. Yes, I understand that your future is preordained and shouldn't include a botanist from Elcano, but it doesn't matter. I won't be able to let go of what we have. I love you, Miea."

Dyson's confession had so overwhelmed Miea that she was stunned speechless. Where had this come from? What had happened while she wasn't watching that caused him to acknowledge this depth of feeling?

"You didn't want to hear that, did you?" he'd said, seeming to withdraw a little.

Miea had pulled his hand toward her again, holding it tight against her cheek. "I did. I absolutely wanted to hear it. I just didn't *expect* to hear it."

"I need for you to know."

Miea had gotten up from her chair at that point and crouched next to Dyson, pulling him into her embrace until they stumbled and landed together on the ground. Their waiter instantly rushed over to ask if everything was okay.

"Everything is as okay as possible," Miea had said. She'd turned to look into Dyson's bright, beseeching eyes and kissed him more passionately and more openly than she ever had before. This time, there had been no hesitation from him at all. Miea hadn't spent a great deal of time thinking about romance when she was growing up, but this sensation was much more than she'd ever imagined.

"I love you, too," she had said, and they'd kissed again before gathering themselves up and sitting back at the table. Miea had wanted to hold Dyson close to her. She had wanted to stare at him from across the table. She had wanted to watch him enter the room repeatedly. She had wanted to be alone with him and she had wanted to be right there, showing off their love in front of the entire world. She had wanted anything that included Dyson, realizing only now how long she'd felt that way.

In the morning, they had a picnic breakfast in a meadow on the edge of the university. They said little as they ate, but things were different between them now. Miea felt as though a part of herself had blended into Dyson, that there was a piece of her that would forevermore be with him, just as some of him would forevermore be with her.

"We could skip class," Dyson said, seemingly drunk with the early spring sunshine, though maybe he was drunk with something else instead.

"I wish I could. But you know if I skipped even a single class it would cause a royal scandal."

He laughed. "It must be excruciating to be perfect all the time."

She kissed him teasingly on the lips and then again on the bridge of his nose. "Absolutely excruciating."

He held her and Miea could feel the warmth of his breath on her neck, the lean muscles of his arms. What would it be like to disappear into this forever?

After a moment, Dyson shifted her body away from him and began to gather their things. "Come, my perfect love; our professor awaits."

Reluctantly, she rose with him. They walked down the hill arm in arm, and Miea pondered throwing caution to the wind and taking the entire day off with the man she loved. Her parents would certainly hear about it. Her mother would frown and her father would toss off some observation about the responsibility of their birthright. That really wasn't too much of a price to pay, and it wasn't as though she intended to adopt a reckless lifestyle. Just a few more hours of leisure with Dyson, then back to school tomorrow.

She abandoned the idea as whimsy, and they entered the main courtyard to the School of Natural Studies ten minutes before their Propagation and Perpetuation class with Professor Liatris. As they did, Miea's roommate, Camara, hustled up to them, flustered and out of breath.

"Miea, I've been looking everywhere for you. Have you been to the administration building yet?"

"What are you talking about?"

"They sent half a dozen of us out to search for you. You haven't seen anyone?"

Miea put a hand on her friend's shoulder. "I have no idea what you are trying to tell me."

"You need to go to the administration building."

"Why?"

"I don't know why. I only know that they said you needed to go there as soon as we found you."

Miea glanced over at Dyson. She could tell from his expression that he realized the school wouldn't summon her to the administration building casually. "I'll go right now," she said apprehensively.

Dyson touched her arm. "Do you want me to come with you?"

She shook her head. "You have to get to class. I'll see you after." She kissed him lightly and turned so quickly he didn't have a chance to kiss her back.

Administration was a short walk away. *We've gone to war,* Miea thought. Troubles with the Thorns had been escalating for months now, and the last time her father had come to visit, he'd told her that he feared that tensions between the nations might get much worse. Certainly, this would mean dramatically increased protection for Miea, maybe even a bevy of personal guards. Dyson wasn't going to like that. *She* wasn't going to like that.

Dean Sambucus was standing outside of the building. It was obvious, as Miea got closer, that he had been waiting there for her. As soon as he saw her, he ushered her into a private office. Sitting there alone was Amelan, her parents' chief aide.

A chill ran through Miea when she saw the man. *He wouldn't be here if we were at war. He would be involved in the planning. This is about something else.*

"Hello, Miea," he said. "Please be seated."

Miea sat down tentatively as the dean left the room. The air was still. Were those red rims around Amelan's eyes? "Is everything okay?" she said, knowing that "okay" wasn't a remote possibility.

"There's been an accident." He bowed his head and shook it slowly. When he looked up at her again, Miea knew without a doubt that Amelan had recently been crying. She suddenly felt light-headed. "There was a motorcade this morning out on the Ridge. The king and queen—I'm sorry, your parents—were headed up to Gunnthorn to meet with the prime minister of the Thorns in an effort to begin negotiations on a treaty. As they crossed the Malaspina Bridge, the bridge buckled."

Miea threw a hand up to her mouth. She closed her eyes, willing this conversation to be part of an elaborate nightmare.

"I'm afraid the entire motorcade was lost."

Miea's eyes flew open. "Dad and Mother."

"I can't begin to tell you how sorry I am, but they are gone. The bridge was more than a thousand feet above the water."

Miea lowered her head on the table and sobbed. Sobbed for a period that seemed to go on endlessly and yet wasn't nearly long enough. At some point she felt a hand on her back that she assumed to be Amelan's, though her sense of grief was too all consuming to confirm it. *My mother and father are gone just like that. Without a warning. Without a good-bye.* Eventually she lifted her head. The world was out of focus through her tears.

"You need to come back to the palace with me. The entire country will learn about this tragedy in the next few minutes, and they will be shocked and devastated. They need to know that our future is secure. They need to see you, Your Majesty."

Your Majesty. How many times had she tried on that appellation over the years? How many times had she imagined what it would be like to sit on the throne and receive her subjects? However, never once had she imagined doing it before she turned twenty. And always it was with her aging parents at her side, teaching her how to govern their kingdom.

"Your Majesty."

The title felt unnatural. As though unintended to fit her.

"Your Majesty."

The investigations had gone on for some time. After each report, Miea ordered another. There had to be a reason why this had happened. Bridges didn't just collapse. Something—someone—had to be to blame. If not the Thorns, then some other faction. It was impossible to imagine that a disaster of this magnitude was simply happenstance, even though study after study had suggested that.

"Your Majesty."

Miea felt the warm wooden cup in her hands, smelled the effervescent ingenito. Slowly it registered that a voice was calling to her. Here. Today. Four years later.

She looked up. Miea's eyes adjusted to the present.

"Your Majesty, the ambassador is here," Sorbus said. "I've put him in the meeting room."

"Thank you."

"Do you need another minute?"

No, I need much more than another minute. Much more than you or anyone else in this kingdom can provide me, Sorbus.

"No, thank you. Please tell the ambassador I'll be right there."

///

"He didn't mention it?" Lonnie said when Becky called her a few minutes after her father dropped her off.

"Not a word."

"Do you think he forgot?"

"My father? Not a chance. He knew what day it was. And he had to know that *I* knew what day it was."

Becky would remember the details of that day forever, she was sure of it. The entire weekend had been so crazy; starting from the time her parents sat her down Saturday morning to tell her they were breaking up. Dad had a new place in Standridge already, so they certainly weren't asking her opinion. Their basic message to her was that she should just shut up and accept it. That attitude from her father was nearly as shocking as the news itself. Still, she'd followed him around all day while he tried to pretend that everything was okay—even as he packed his stuff into boxes—and when she decided to just come right out and ask him for some kind of explanation, he just said a bunch of empty things. *Everything will be okay. Sometimes the road goes in unexpected directions, Beck.* Really, Dad? Could you make it a little more obvious that you think I'm too young to handle what's actually going on? She remembered being angrier with him than she'd ever been before. She should have forced him to understand how she felt. She just couldn't do it, though, and that made her even more furious.

Of course, she knew her parents didn't have a great marriage. That was pretty hard to miss. She couldn't remember the last time she'd seen them hold hands or kiss, and sometimes they were unnecessarily harsh with each other. But she hadn't expected them just to give up. That's not what people did if they really cared about their families.

And for her father to pretend that everything was going to be fine when any idiot knew that it wouldn't was just plain insulting. At least her mother had the decency to show that she was upset. Dad walked around like he'd been whacked on the head with a sledgehammer, but whenever he saw her, he smiled and talked to her about what they were going to do together the next weekend. What was with him? He hadn't even put on this much of a show when she was sick.

Watching him drive away that Sunday afternoon was one of the saddest experiences of her entire life. She started crying as soon as his car disappeared and her mother held her for what seemed like hours, letting her get as much of it out of her system as she could. Eventually they went inside and played Scattergories in the den while they ate Girl Scout cookies for dinner. Later that night, when Becky asked her to explain what had happened, her mother told her straight out that she and her father had been having serious problems for a long time. She didn't try to pretend that she didn't know what led to the breakup the way her father did. At least her mom took her seriously.

By the time Dad called that night, Becky's anger with him was over the top.

"Hey, babe, was the rest of your day okay?" he said.

What did he think? "It was okay."

"It's almost bedtime, right?"

"Yeah, I guess I'll be going up in a few minutes."

There was a long pause on the phone then, and Becky wondered what her father was doing. Was he just planning to sit there like this? Was this his idea of being with her? Finally, he said, "Wanna do a story?"

"A story?"

"You know, we can do a story on the phone like we did that time I was away on business."

Becky couldn't believe he would even try to suggest this. "I don't want to do a story, Dad."

There was another pause and then her father said, "Okay. We can wait until next weekend."

Becky felt her throat tightening. "Not next weekend, either."

"What do you mean?" His voice seemed a little shaky when he said this, like maybe she had gotten through to him a little.

"I don't want to do Tamarisk stories anymore." Becky said. She could feel her own voice wavering, but she got the words out.

"Babe, I know things feel very confusing right now, but . . ."

". . . Dad, stop. Don't treat me like a little kid. I'm not a little kid."

Her father's voice was quiet when he responded. "I know you're not, babe."

"I'm done with Tamarisk, Dad."

Another long delay. "If that's the way you feel right now, it's okay."

Becky gripped the telephone tighter. "That's the way I feel, period." She felt her eyes watering and she knew she was going to have a tough time keeping things together. "Listen, I have to get to bed."

"Okay, babe, you go. I love you."

"Yeah, love you, too, Dad."

Becky started crying again as soon as she got off the phone. And when she lay down in her bed and thought about what she had said to her father about Tamarisk, she cried some more. But she wasn't going to change her mind. Everything was different now. That meant that Tamarisk had to go.

Now, on the fourth anniversary of that terrible day, her father was still acting like everything was okay—even though it was so obvious that *he* wasn't okay, that he hadn't really been okay since he left.

"So why do you think he didn't say anything?" Lonnie said.

"He probably doesn't want me to think about it. He probably thinks he's protecting me or something. Can you believe that?"

"Have you ever talked about it?"

"Yeah, of course we've talked about it. I mean, it's kind of hard to make believe it didn't happen for four whole years. But he never gets into it with me. He never tells me what he's really feeling. He never tells me his side of the story. And, you know, I always thought we were pretty good at talking before this. But he's like Ghost Dad or something now. He's there but he's not really there, you know what I mean?"

"No idea."

"That's because you've been living the world's easiest life for the last fourteen years. Have you even gotten a pimple yet?"

"We aren't talking about my pimples—and yes, I have gotten some—we're talking about your father."

The phone felt heavy in Becky's hand. "I don't want to talk about my father anymore."

"Sounds like he's not the only one avoiding the subject."

"Give me a break, okay? You know I have an especially hard time on this day. My mom is off on a hot date with her new husband and my dad is a zombie. Is there really anything more to say?"

"No, I guess that really says it all."

Becky suddenly felt very tired. "Amazingly, it does. Look, I'm gonna go to bed. This day is definitely through for me."

"I could probably sneak out of the house if you need me to."

Imagining Lonnie slinking down from the roof of her house gave Becky the closest thing to a smile she'd had in hours. "We'll save that for a real crisis. I'll survive tonight."

"Are you sure?"

Becky closed her eyes. When she did, she caught the expression on her father's face when she'd turned to get out of the car earlier. She'd missed it before. He seemed like he was waiting for something.

"Yeah, I'm sure. I always do."

3

The whispers were quiet. The shouting less enraged than usual. Gage settled into this moment of temporary equilibrium. Moments such as these always passed quickly. The equilibrium never lasted. Not everyone was fit for the universe as it was. Unfortunately, Gage couldn't remake the universe. That was far beyond his capacities. All Gage could do was gift and imagine.

One whisper rose above the others. It was familiar in some ways, but with a different timbre. Gage had not centered on this particular voice before. It was a weary voice. One that had suffered a shattering experience. It was the voice of age on youth.

Gage concentrated on the voice more carefully. There was more to her story. Significantly more. A sense of disconnection. This story had ended before it properly began.

With astonishment, Gage realized that this voice was the direct product of an earlier gift. That happened exceedingly infrequently. Never before in this way. In the face of this extraordinary embellishment of a gift, however, there were dangers. Profound dangers. This voice—in fact the provenance of this voice—was in significant trouble. Mortal trouble.

The whisperer stopped whispering. Too much pain. Too much repression. It did not have enough resources to continue the story, though continuing the story mattered more to her than anything else.

Gage gifted the whisperer. At the very least, this would provide a semblance of serenity. Maybe more. Maybe a way to reconnect with the source, a way to continue the story.

When the opportunity arose, Gage would gift with the bridge. The two would need to cross it on their own, though. They would need to find their own way to harmonize their whispers.

Until then, Gage would continue to listen.

These stories held so much promise.

///

Lisa liked going to bars. Since Chris liked Lisa, considered her his dearest friend, he went to bars with her. For him, places of this sort had outlived their usefulness when he graduated college. Did he really need someone else to pour a drink for him? It wasn't as if his glass of Cabernet was being prepared in any way. If he could choose from a wider selection of wine, he would never choose the one he was drinking now, if he could choose the music, he would certainly choose something less overplayed, and a chair with a back would have been nice. Lisa enjoyed going to these places, though, for reasons she'd never made clear in all the years they'd known each other. Therefore, they went.

"I really think it's possible I could make my mother's death look like an accident," she said wistfully.

"You think that, but the crime scene investigators would get you."

She slumped dramatically. "You're probably right. Damned technological breakthroughs."

"Besides, I don't think her calling you three times a day is justification for murder."

Lisa threw her hands above her head. "That's because you don't have to take the phone calls. Try listening every day to a twenty-minute summation of last night's TV shows. Try listening to her petty complaints about her friend Millie over and over and over again. Try listening to her word-by-word recollections of the conversations she has with the produce guy at Stop & Shop. You wouldn't rush to judgment so quickly then."

Lisa made an elaborate show of draining her glass—she was drinking Cosmopolitans tonight—and putting it back down on the tabletop.

Chris laughed. "Your mother calls me 'Honey.' She can do no wrong as far as I'm concerned."

"I need a new best friend."

Lisa signaled the waiter for another drink. She put both elbows on the table and leaned toward him. This pose made her look easily twenty years younger, especially in the dim light of the bar. Chris often wondered what Lisa had been like as a college student. She seemed perpetually in her late thirties, even though they'd met when they were in their mid-twenties.

"What's new at work?"

Chris sighed automatically. "A woman on my staff who's on pregnancy leave called yesterday to tell me she's decided to be a stay-at-home mother, a guy came into my office today to tell me he's being sexually harassed, and management has decided to limit salary increases to two percent this year. Have I told you lately how much I love being an administrator?"

"You should've taken that spot in Rhode Island."

"It was the wrong place at the wrong time."

"It was the right job."

"In the wrong place at the wrong time."

"The job in Westport, then."

"It was a start-up. The risks were too big."

Lisa patted his hand. "You do know that their stock has gone through the roof, don't you?"

Chris pulled his hand away and gestured with it. "Yes, I know their stock has gone through the roof. Unfortunately, my crystal ball was in the shop the day they offered me the job, so I couldn't see a year into the future."

Lisa shook her head, glanced around the room, and pretended to concentrate on the song playing through the sound system. Chris simply focused on his only-adequate wine.

When Lisa's new drink arrived, she clinked her glass against his, drawing his attention. "So you never get a chance just to *wriggle* anymore?"

"Wriggling" was Lisa's pet name for genetic engineering, which Chris had done for fifteen years before being kicked upstairs two years ago. "I haven't wriggled in centuries. Nope, a Ph.D. in Botany is really only good for one thing these days: budget reviews."

"You didn't have to take the promotion, you know."

"I shouldn't have taken the promotion. But I did. That ship has sailed. Let's not have this conversation for the second time in five minutes."

"Hey, at least you can *get* a promotion in your job. I'm stuck in the same spot until I retire."

Chris smirked. "Yeah, tough spot. You sold two multimillion-dollar homes last month, right? As long as you continue to cater to high-end, recession-proof clientele, you get promotions all the time."

"But no sexual harassment cases."

"You could always start one."

Lisa snorted. "You haven't been down to the offices lately. The only thing I could start is an *asexual* harassment case."

Chris laughed in spite of himself. "Speaking of sex, what's the latest with Ben?"

"I think he's in Melbourne tonight. Either that or Taiwan. He touches back down on this continent sometime next week. I think he has a drive-by past Connecticut scheduled before the end of the spring."

"It's the perfect relationship."

Lisa rolled her eyes. "Yeah, perfect. We've been together for nearly three years and I think we've spent less than a hundred days in the same place."

"And you never fight and the sex is great."

"True on both counts."

"What's the downside?"

"The downside?" Lisa looked around the room and leaned forward farther, as though she was about to impart a state secret. "I think I love him."

This was a surprise. In all the years they'd been friends, Chris had never heard Lisa say she was in love with anyone. "Really?"

"I'm probably just kidding myself. But I miss him more all the time. I've been making him stay on the phone with me longer and longer lately."

"Like mother, like daughter."

Lisa reached across and punched Chris on the arm. "That was totally unfair."

Chris rubbed his arm. "So what are you going to do about these . . . feelings?"

"What *can* I do about them?"

"Tell him?"

"And screw up what we have? I don't think so. No, not a chance." She looked at Chris as though he had three heads. "So I assume since you haven't said a word about Patty that your date with her went the way your dates usually go."

Chris cringed at the mention of the latest woman Lisa had fixed him up with. She'd been doing this since a few months after the divorce. Lisa seemed to have an endless supply of women for him to meet and an equally large supply of optimism about blind dating in spite of Chris's gruesome track record. "I'm afraid so."

"What'd you do wrong this time?"

Chris pretended to be offended. "Why do you automatically assume it's me screwing up these blind dates?"

"Are you actually asking me that question?"

Chris knew not to pursue this. "She seemed really nice. She likes books, she likes sushi, and she has beautiful eyes. I thought things were going pretty well for a while there."

"Until . . ."

"Until I got sad."

"You got sad? Amazingly, I haven't heard this one before."

"There was the thing with the anniversary."

"Ah yes, the day that will live in infamy."

Chris shot Lisa a look to say that this wasn't something to screw around about, and she threw up her hands as if to acknowledge that she'd slipped.

"We should just remember next year not to do something like that around this time," Chris said. "I'm not very good with it."

"Sweetie, you have to get past it at some point."

"I am past it. That doesn't mean I can't mark it in some way."

Lisa nodded very slowly. Chris wasn't sure if this meant she was acknowledging his point or reproaching him. "How was Becky when you saw her that night?"

Chris shrugged. "Who knows? I might be the last person on the planet capable of answering that question."

"Teenagers are tough."

"It wasn't going to be like this with us."

"Actually, it probably was. From everything I've heard, it doesn't matter what your relationship is like with your kid before she becomes a teenager. Once she's there, all the wires get crossed. I know what you mean, though. You guys clicked."

"Excellent use of the past tense."

Lisa reached out for his hand again, but this time she squeezed it. Chris squeezed back and made a moment's eye contact with her. How many times had she propped him up over the years, when Becky was sick, when things had started to break down with Polly, when he moved out? There really was no substitute for old friends.

"You know, for some reason I still think about that fantasy world you guys created," Lisa said. "What a great way to spend time with your kid. Sometimes, I'll be showing a house, and I'll walk into some kid's room and it makes me think of the two of you telling stories together. That was an amazing thing."

It was unquestionably an amazing thing. The inspiration for it might have been the rightest moment Chris had ever experienced. It was a week after Becky's first chemotherapy treatment and the five-year-old had been visibly frightened and confused. She had trouble sleeping and he had already spent several nights up with her trying to find some way to comfort her, some way to ease her mind. Chris had never believed Becky was going to die—his failure to "take her illness seriously enough" was in fact one of the things he and Polly had been fighting about at that point—but he couldn't think of any way to imbue his daughter with the same confidence.

On their fourth night up together, Chris sat against Becky's headboard with her head on his chest, their usual position. They hadn't spoken for at least a quarter of an hour, but Becky was no closer to sleep than she had been when her shuffling in her room had woken him up an hour or so earlier. He hated that this was so scary and disorienting for her. He wished he could simply tell her she was going to be okay and that she would believe this. Her body was telling something different, though.

At that moment, an idea came to him, as though delivered by some otherworldly FedEx guy.

"Let's make something," he said, a little surprised by the sound of his voice after the lengthy silence.

"I don't think I can really do that right now, Dad," Becky said wearily.

"I don't mean make something with our hands. I mean with our minds. Do you want to?"

"Make something with our minds?"

"A story. Not just a story, though. We'll invent a whole world to put the story in."

Becky pulled back and looked up at him. They'd made up stories before, often on long car rides, usually based on characters from one of the books they'd been reading at bedtime. What he was suggesting here was something different, though, and he could see from her expression that it intrigued her.

"How do we do that?"

"We just start," Chris said, sitting up slightly. "Right now. What kind of world is it?"

Becky thought for a moment and then brightened, her eyes looking bluer than they had in months. "Let's make it a kingdom. Like in that book we read the other day."

"King or queen?"

"King *and* queen. Together." She put a hand to her forehead for a moment. "And they have a teenage daughter who is very smart and who makes them very proud."

Maybe something like your cousin Kiley who you adore? Chris thought. "Is there magic in this world?"

"Tons," Becky said broadly. "All over the place."

"Cows?"

Becky laughed out loud. He hadn't heard that in a while. "Cows?"

"It's an important detail. Are there cows and pigs and birds in this world or are there different creatures we never saw before?"

"How about flying pig cows?"

Chris chuckled. "We could do that."

"And talking fish."

"How would we hear them underwater?"

"They don't talk when they're underwater, Dad," Becky said as though everyone on the planet knew that already. That she was animated enough to scold him was a huge thrill for Chris.

"Right, of course. So they're walking and talking fish."

"They don't walk. They roll. Well, not roll, really. They just sort of flip around to get where they want to go."

The conversation continued until Becky, yawning, lay her head on Chris's chest and fell asleep. The next night at bedtime, they continued inventing pieces of the world, so caught up in this exercise that they didn't begin to make up a story until the night after that—which was the first night that Becky slept through in more than a week.

They called the kingdom Tamarisk—named after a tree Becky loved from one of the picture books on plant life Chris had bought her—and it evolved in numerous ways over the years. As Becky got older, the fish stopped talking and she replaced flying pig cows with creatures of sheer imagination with names that Becky seemed to take particular pleasure in determining. When she was nine, she decided that there should be an internal logic to the naming process. Chris came home from work one evening and she handed him a list of rules governing all Tamariskian nomenclature. However, some things about it had never changed. The same king and queen still ruled over the land, they still called the nemesis to the south The Thorns even though this didn't follow the naming rules, and the sophisticated, beautiful, gutsy, and brilliant teenage princess still starred in most of the adventures.

Rather than becoming less important after Becky had gone into remission, the nightly visits to Tamarisk became more of a highlight to the day. If Becky had a sleepover or Chris had a business function, they found some way to hook up over Tamarisk even if only for a few minutes.

Then, with a suddenness that was more shocking than the end of his marriage, it was over. The day he moved out, Becky declared that she would never tell another Tamarisk story. Chris was certain this was part of her reaction to the divorce—he sensed a kind of hostility in her that day that he'd never experienced with her before and couldn't fully understand—and that in time they would go back. It had never happened, though, and the years of creation between them took on a mythical status, as though it was legend rather than real life.

"It *was* an amazing thing," Chris said with the kind of shrug that indicated he was anything but reconciled about this.

"Life is long, sweetie."

"What does that even mean?"

"It means that our relationships go through movements. Like in a symphony. You're in a fugue period right now with Becky. That doesn't mean that a month from now, or three months from now, or three years from now you won't be someplace else with her entirely."

"What if the fugue is the last movement?"

"It's not. Even you don't believe that."

"Let's say I don't want to believe that."

"If it's important for you to make that distinction."

Chris looked at Lisa and chuckled. She glanced down at her watch and said, "I'm sorry, but we're all out of time for your bitching tonight. The rest of the evening will be dedicated to my issues and you telling me how fabulous I am."

Chris pantomimed prostrating himself to Lisa. "As you wish, milady."

4

Cam Parker was truly a gorgeous guy. He was the kind of guy you could look at for a really long time and not find a single thing wrong with him. Yeah, he knew it and, yeah, he definitely posed way too often, but that didn't take away from the fact that he was beautiful. And he was especially beautiful to Becky when he was talking to *her*.

"The guitar sound is just so hot. It's all—" Cam tore into an air guitar lick complete with sound effects, his face contorted like a rock star's onstage. Yep, he looked pretty great doing that, too.

"The electric stuff is great, but the acoustic stuff is a little derivative, don't you think?"

"I think it's brilliant. Who is it derivative of?"

Becky cocked her head. "You don't hear acoustic Pearl Jam or Guns N' Roses in their stuff?"

Cam got a dumb-but-cute expression on his face and said, "I don't know what you're talking about."

Becky's first thought was that he was blowing her off. Then she realized that he really might not know what she was talking about. She sometimes forgot that few of her friends had had as much of a rock-and-roll education as she'd had.

"Whatever," she said, not wanting it to seem like she was challenging him. "Are you going to the battle of the bands Friday night?"

"No question about it. Thunderclap is going to kick every

other band's ass."

Becky thought Thunderclap was pretty lightweight, but she decided not to mention it. "It should be a good show."

Cam leaned across the cafeteria table. Even as she felt herself blushing, Becky took note that he looked especially good from this distance. "Maybe we can hang out there," he said confidently.

That worked for Becky. She was about to tell him so when she saw Cam's expression change and then noticed the drop of blood on the table. Her hand flew up to her face as she realized that the blood was coming from her nose. Grabbing a napkin, she excused herself quickly and ran out of the cafeteria toward the nearest girls' room. Passing two students she didn't know, she slipped into an empty stall and latched the door behind her. She replaced the napkin with a wad of toilet paper and leaned her head back as far as it would go.

This couldn't be happening. It had been possible to explain away the dizzy spells. But if she was getting bloody noses now as well . . . she could barely think about it. She hadn't had a bloody nose since she was five. Back before the chemotherapy did whatever it was supposed to do and she got better. Yes, she knew that, technically, she was in remission and not cured, but after a while, you could be pretty sure you beat the thing, couldn't you?

Becky remembered those horrible chemotherapy sessions: how they made her vomit up her entire insides, how they made her feel like jelly, how she sometimes couldn't get out of bed the whole day. All of her hair fell out, she had black circles under her eyes, and everyone looked at her like she was the sorriest human being in the universe. Becky didn't remember all the specifics from that time—it was nine years ago, after all—but she would never forget how she felt. And she would definitely never forget how much she hated how she felt. She didn't want to have to go through that again. Maybe this really was something else—though it was getting harder and harder to sell herself on that idea.

"Beck? Beck, are you here?"

It was Lonnie. She'd been sitting next to her in the cafeteria, though Lonnie was as preoccupied with Brent as Becky had been with Cam.

"Over here," Becky said, unlatching the stall door for her and then replacing the toilet paper in her nose with another wad. The bleeding was definitely slowing.

"What's happening?" Lonnie said when she found her. "You ran out of the cafeteria—Cam said you were bleeding."

"I'm fine. It's almost stopped."

Lonnie latched the door closed and sat on the floor. "Your nose is the thing that's bleeding?"

"It's nothing. People get nosebleeds. Was Cam totally grossed out?"

"I don't care about Cam, Becky. And you shouldn't be thinking about him right now, either."

Lonnie knew all about the nosebleeds, along with every other symptom of childhood leukemia. Friends since preschool, Lonnie had often come over to play in Becky's room when she was sick, and they'd talked about her disease several times over the years.

Becky leaned her head forward and removed the paper. The bleeding was done. She looked at her friend and saw that Lonnie looked very worried. "It's really just a bloody nose, Lon."

"Are you sure?"

"Of course I'm sure."

Lonnie watched her carefully for several seconds, and Becky finally looked away.

"You're not sure, are you?"

"Can we talk about something else?"

"Are you gonna tell your mother?"

Becky's eyes snapped back to Lonnie's. "No. And you're not going to tell her anything, either. If this kind of thing happens again, I'll say something. Right now, it's just this one *isolated* nosebleed, and I'm not going to get too worked up about it."

"Beck, you can't mess around with something like this."

Becky stood up, threw the bloodied paper in the toilet, and flushed it along with the other piece, hoping Lonnie hadn't seen how much blood was there. "It's a bloody nose. Are you telling me you've never gotten a bloody nose?"

"You might want to try that line on someone who doesn't know you the way I do."

Becky touched Lonnie on the arm and their eyes locked for a second. In that instant, Becky felt like she was about to start crying and really, really didn't want that to happen. She turned away.

"If you have to know the truth, I picked it before I went to lunch and I guess I just dug a little too deep."

Lonnie punched her on the shoulder. "Are you trying to make me gag? Do you want me to spew all over you?"

"No spewing today. At least not near me. This is a new shirt."

Becky opened the stall and the two of them got out. Lonnie wrapped an arm around her.

"You're officially on twenty-four-hour watch," Lonnie said.

"I'm okay, Ma, really."

Lonnie smiled at her as they left the bathroom. Becky knew she hadn't really soothed her friend's concerns. Under the circumstances, it was kind of hard to be convincing.

///

Polly wasn't exactly a "getting your nails done" kind of woman. Her nails cracked with predictable regularity and she thought there were few things that made a person look less put together than chipped polish. Still, for the past several years she and Becky had gone to a nail salon together one afternoon every month. It had started as an indulgence for a cousin's wedding, but Becky seemed so tickled by the experience that it had become an ongoing thing. With Becky well into her teens at this point, Polly was glad to maintain as many rituals between them as possible.

As Polly pulled into the school parking lot to get her daughter—the complete experience involved picking Becky up in the car instead of waiting for her to come home on the bus, and stopping at Starbucks for a caramel latte—she saw Becky flirting overtly with a tall boy with scraggly hair. Becky leaned toward the boy as though she was magnetically drawn to him, presumably by the same magnet that kept her lips in a permanent smile while she spoke. When Becky saw the car, she patted the boy on the arm, waved at him, and ran over.

"Hey, Mom," Becky said brightly as she got in. She threw her backpack onto the rear seat and pecked her on the cheek.

"Hey." Polly gave a school bus the right of way and then turned out of the parking lot. "Did you have a good day at school?"

"Yeah," Becky said in a clipped fashion that suggested she wasn't being entirely truthful.

"Yeah?"

Becky waved a hand. "Yeah, yeah. It was pretty normal."

"Are you sure about that?"

Becky took a deep breath and her shoulders sagged. "Mr. Zales hassled us for the entire period about the history test we all bombed last week. It was ridiculous. I mean, isn't it the teacher's fault if the whole class fails a test?"

Polly's thoughts brightened as she remembered Becky's intensely conscientious reaction to getting a fifty-seven on the test. "It's definitely the teacher's fault. Though a few extra minutes of studying instead of texting might have helped a little, too."

Becky's eyebrows arched and Polly wondered if this was going to be one of those conversations that skidded off in the wrong direction over the slightest thing. Polly hated those.

Fortunately, Becky got past it quickly. "I aced my language arts essay, though."

"The one about culture clashes?"

"Yep."

Polly threw a proud smile at her daughter. "Nice job. That was an excellent essay."

"Ms. Kellerman thought so, too, obviously."

"Did anything else happen today?"

Becky shook her head animatedly. "Nope, nothing. Really, nothing at all. It was a nice, easy, normal day."

"So who's the guy?"

"What guy?"

"The guy you were mooning over when I pulled up."

Becky cackled. "I wasn't mooning over anyone. What does that even mean, anyway?"

Polly reached over and patted Becky's head. "It means making your interest more than casually obvious."

Becky's eyes narrowed again. "I didn't do that."

Polly grinned. "If that boy doesn't know that you like him, he belongs in a rock garden rather than a school."

"Give me a break, Mom. I wasn't that bad."

"I didn't say you were bad. You were definitely mooning, though."

Becky scoffed and looked in the other direction. Her daughter obviously liked this guy. She'd have accepted the teasing more jovially otherwise.

Polly stopped at a traffic light and let the silence extend between them. When the light turned, she said, "What's his name?"

"Whose name?"

"The boy you were . . . talking to."

Becky huffed and said, "Cam."

"Is he nice?"

"He's cute."

"Does that mean the same thing?"

"And he's nice."

"Sounds like a heck of a guy."

Polly pulled into the Starbucks parking lot and the two of them got out of the car. When they entered the café, Becky started swaying to a song that Polly didn't recognize. Polly loved watching Becky move. A study in grace and awkwardness. It was amazing how quickly the girl alternated between the two these days, but Polly knew that grace would prevail in the near future. Becky would definitely be a polished adult.

They ordered their lattes and sat at the one empty table in the shop.

Becky took a sip of her drink, recoiled from the temperature, and pulled the lid off to allow the coffee to cool. "It would be okay if Cam and I went out a little, right? I mean, assuming he asks me."

"As long as I knew where you were every single second," Polly said with a wry smile.

"Do you want to attach some kind of tracking device to me?"

"I think we'll trust your built-in tracking device to do the job." Polly tested her latte and then sat back. "Look, Beck, when it comes to guys, the best advice I can give you is to always keep your feet on the ground."

Becky arched one eyebrow. "Is that some clever way of telling me not to have sex?"

Polly chuckled and glanced away. Becky had never come at that topic so bluntly before. "Well, that, too, but that wasn't what I meant. What I'm trying to say is that it's important that you be realistic about boys. They can be a lot of fun as long as you always make sure you stay in charge of yourself."

"Did you always make sure you stayed in charge of yourself with Al?"

"Always. All the time."

Becky leaned forward. "Really? Even when he was totally cracking you up?"

Polly smiled at the memory of some of those times. "Yes, of course. Al is a very good man and he does seem to have an uncanny ability to make me laugh, but I've always kept my wits about me with him. That doesn't take anything away from our relationship, by the way. In fact, it strengthens our relationship because we know—at least I do—that we haven't based anything on fleeting emotions."

Becky tipped her head from one side to the other. "I'll have to keep that in mind."

"If you do that, you'll never need a tracking device—and

neither will I."

Becky took another sip from her coffee, determined it was safe to drink, and took a longer sip. "Did you do that with Dad?"

"Do what with Dad?"

"Keep your feet on the ground."

Polly took a second to think about her answer. Her thoughts flashed on the time she and Chris had snuck into the arboretum late at night and made love. On top of that, an image popped into her head that she hadn't remembered in years: Chris pushing her on a playground swing the morning after their third date. She hadn't been on a swing in years and she felt a bit odd doing it in front of a group of little kids and their mothers, but Chris implored her to kick her legs out to go higher—and against her better judgment, she did and she loved it.

"Not always, no. Certainly not in the early years. I think it's safe to say that your father was the one man I allowed to sweep me away." She thought about the sensation of flying that came to her when she closed her eyes that morning on the swings.

Then she shrugged. "Look how that turned out."

Polly caught the glimpse of a smirk on Becky's face before Becky took another drink. "The sweeping away part must have been fun, though."

"It *was* fun. Then it wasn't. The first part didn't compensate for the second, I'm afraid."

"And you think it's always that way?"

Polly nodded. "I don't think it's worth finding out if there are any exceptions to the rule."

Becky put the lid back on her latte. "That sucks."

Polly still hadn't grown accustomed to hearing phrases like that come from her daughter's mouth. "It doesn't, actually. It's just a fact of life that you have to deal with."

Becky turned away slightly, looking off at others in the Starbucks. "Sounds like tons of fun."

///

"So how do you know Lisa?" Chris said to the dark-haired, gray-eyed woman named Celia sitting across from him in the restaurant. They'd already covered weather and traffic and he figured they'd get to current events before their entrees arrived.

"She sold my house eight months ago when my marriage broke up, and we've stayed in touch. We talked last week and she told me she had a guy she wanted me to meet. I decided to take her up on it, and now we're here."

Lisa was obviously a full-service broker. Chris hoped she at least got Celia a good price for the house.

"Well, it's nice of you to come out to meet me. I find these things a little unnerving myself."

"I know what you mean," Celia said conspiratorially. "I promise I'm not dangerous, though."

Chris smiled. Lisa certainly had excellent taste when it came to women. Like so many of the others—a couple dozen at least at this point—Celia was attractive and bright and certainly seemed perfectly normal on the surface. It was unusual for Chris to leave one of these connections wondering what Lisa was thinking. Still, his blind dates rarely led to second dates.

"What do you do for a living, Chris?"

"I'm in the genetic engineering field."

"Really? That sounds intriguing."

"It was when I was actually involved in lab work. Back then, it was amazing on a daily basis. The idea of nudging the natural order of things to create something that still fit into the natural order of things was endlessly fascinating to me."

Celia's eyes grew wide. They were very pretty eyes. "You didn't work on humans, did you?"

Chris laughed. "No, nothing like that. Trees and plants. Altering strains to make them more resistant to disease, that sort of thing."

Celia leaned forward and said suggestively, "So you're not a mad scientist."

"At this point, actually, I'm not any kind of scientist. I'm a functionary now, a pencil pusher, a suit. I got kicked upstairs and now instead of doing the thing I love, I get to have a lot of meetings about other people doing the thing I love."

Celia frowned in a way that Chris interpreted to be sympathetic. "You can't go back downstairs?"

"The stairway doesn't run in that direction. I'm afraid the only way out at this point is through the window—and I work on the sixth floor."

Celia's expression changed. Her brow creased slightly and she sat back in her chair and looked around the restaurant. She studied the menu in front of her. "I'm surprised the waiter hasn't come to take our order yet."

They were onto top news stories after that: the president's latest speech, the economy, a remarkable rescue in the Arizona desert. It took them up to their entrees, and when the waiter delivered them, Celia looked at her meal and exhaled deeply. They ate quietly for a while, only asking each other if they liked their food.

"So, Chris, what you do you do for fun?"

"I used to like going for long drives with my daughter, but she doesn't really want to do that anymore."

"Does that mean you can no longer do them, either?"

Chris shrugged. "I could, I guess. It wouldn't feel the same without her."

"What else?"

"I like going to restaurants."

Celia looked down at her plate and smirked. He had no idea how to interpret that.

"And I like being outside."

"Camping, hiking, that sort of thing?"

Chris thought about this for a moment. "Not really. Just being outside, actually. Walking, taking in the air. I just like feeling the world, if that makes any sense. I haven't been camping since Becky and I—"

Celia examined him. "Becky?"

"My daughter."

"What were you saying about her?"

This wasn't the right place to go with this conversation. Chris couldn't say with any certainty that he knew the right place to go, but he definitely recognized the wrong one. "No, never mind. No, not camping and hiking."

The date was over maybe twenty minutes later. Chris walked Celia to her car, thanked her for spending time with him, and watched her drive off. There was no discussion about seeing each other again.

Why do I go on these things? he thought as he went back to his car. He was obviously awful at it. Yet he continued to allow Lisa to set him up. Coming here tonight, he had no sense of anticipation, no inkling that a new future was about to start for him. This date was a slot on his calendar, a meeting to attend. Celia seemed very pleasant, but he never for a second thought anything was going to happen between them.

Which brought him back to his first question: *Why do I go on these things?* He didn't have a satisfactory answer. He didn't have an answer at all. It was probably time to tell Lisa to take on a different lost cause.

5

"Your Majesty, the minister has arrived."

Miea looked up from her desk, where she had been focusing on the details of a diplomatic agreement with the Maurelle. She thanked Sorbus and reached for the folder of briefing documents Thuja had been providing her since her trip to Jonrae. The minister had requested this time to meet with her even though her next official briefing was only two days away. This made her both curious and apprehensive. Maybe he was coming simply because she had finally managed to convince the man how important it was to keep her fully apprised.

When Miea entered the conference room, Thuja stood to greet her, his tone grim but obsequious. She didn't notice immediately that there was another man behind him. However, when Thuja sat, Miea's knees nearly buckled.

"Your Majesty, I would like to introduce you to Dyson Specta. He has worked very closely with me for the past year and I've assigned him to be your direct liaison on all matters regarding my office. I promise you, he is at least as well-informed about our kingdom's agriculture as I am. Well, maybe *almost* as well-informed."

Thuja chuckled at his little joke, but Miea barely noticed. Her eyes held Dyson's for a moment and in this time she was back in the courtyard, catching a glimpse of his concerned expression as she kissed him and turned to go to the administration building. She hadn't seen him since then; she wasn't able to say good-bye before Amelan whisked her away. And after that . . . well, after that, nothing was as it had been before.

Gathering herself quickly because she wasn't sure what would happen if she looked at the man she once loved any longer, she turned and said to Thuja, "Thank you, Minister. I trust the information flow will be considerably better in the future."

"As indeed it must be, I'm afraid. Your Majesty, I've come with grim news." The minister looked down at his papers, though it was obvious he knew what he was going to say. As, sadly, did Miea. "The diseased foliage in Jonrae is spreading quite precipitously. Nearly two-thirds of the lolo plantings and a large percentage of chugach and gunnison have been devastated. Given the speed with which the disease is spreading and the near-total destruction of the afflicted plants, we must now assume that a blight is in fact upon us."

Though she had braced for the news, though she had anticipated it for weeks, Miea still found herself shaken by Thuja's words. "What do we know?"

Thuja turned to Dyson and the younger man spoke up. "Leaves and stems of all affected species exhibit green banding that lasts anywhere between ten days and two weeks. From there, the bands fade and necrosis sets in nearly immediately. The plants wither and die within days after that. Tests run on the root systems of dead plants indicate that the roots are being choked off, as though something invasive is choking them off."

Miea absorbed this new information. "What could cause something like this?"

She addressed the question to Thuja, still unsure of how to speak to Dyson. The minister answered. "That's one of many perplexing questions at the moment, Your Majesty. There are many possibilities, but we have run every conceivable test and have come up with nothing. There is nothing in the soil, in the air, or in any of the plants themselves to give us any inkling as to the cause of this disease."

"Just like the last time," Miea said softly. Both Thuja and Dyson bowed their heads. The cause of the Great Blight was one of the enduring mysteries, chilling in that its lack of a solution meant there was no way to prevent it from returning.

"We are seeking counsel from other departments," Thuja said. "It is possible that a different perspective will provide information we have overlooked."

"Meanwhile the blight spreads."

"I'm afraid this is the other thing we need to discuss, Your Majesty. We know from experience that if this blight goes unchecked it could reach all parts of the kingdom. We obviously can't allow that."

"But we also know from experience that attempts to contain the disease failed the last time."

"The kingdom chose to avoid certain measures last time," Thuja said gravely.

Miea narrowed her eyes. "What measures were those?"

"Your parents were steadfastly and vociferously opposed to the sterilization of afflicted areas, but—"

"Sterilization? You mean denuding the entire region?"

"If we sterilize the area, it is likely the disease will die in the process."

"But there are plants in Jonrae that exist nowhere else in Tamarisk. There are *living beings* in Jonrae that exist nowhere else in Tamarisk and cannot survive without these plants."

"That means they are likely to die anyway."

Miea could barely comprehend what Thuja was saying. She turned to Dyson. "Do you agree with this suggestion?" she said sharply.

Dyson seemed shocked that the question came to him directly. What was he thinking about any of this, anyway? He turned toward Thuja, who held up a hand.

"Your Majesty," Thuja said, "I have discussed the topic extensively with my staff. This is my recommendation to you."

Miea stiffened. "I will not authorize this today."

Thuja nodded his head sagely. "Every day we delay, the disease spreads. Soon you may be forced to make a decision even more difficult."

"Surely you didn't expect me to simply agree to this," Miea said without attempting to mask her irritation. "What data did you bring me?"

Thuja reached next to Dyson and picked up a folder. He handed it to Miea. "Everything is in here, Your Majesty. I don't think you will learn anything from this folder to contradict my recommendation. You must know I wouldn't make it if I believed there was any alternative."

Miea took the folder and stared down at it without opening it, as though willing some revelation to appear inside. "I will study this carefully. You will have my answer tomorrow."

Miea stood and Thuja and Dyson quickly joined her. "Thank you, Your Majesty," the minister said. He offered a shallow bow and moved toward the door.

Dyson passed directly in front of her. Their eyes met again for another instant. In that moment, Miea wanted to ask him to stay behind, to help her make sense of this briefing and maybe bridge the gulf of years between them. Then he, too, bowed—much more deeply than Thuja—and said, "Thank you, Your Majesty." With that, he turned away.

Miea felt energy seep away from her as the two men receded. Rather than returning to her office, Miea informed Sorbus that she needed to postpone her next meeting. She went to her chambers, still clutching the folder, sat heavily on her sofa, and closed her eyes.

Thuja wanted her to sterilize the area, to eradicate all life from the region. To wipe the chapleau and the seapowet from existence, all in the hope that doing so would save every other species.

Miea flashed again on her days working the fields in Jonrae. She had never felt closer to her land, never more in touch with the life force of her world. Now she needed to decide whether to snuff an irreplaceable part of that life force out forever.

Alone in her chamber, alone in her kingdom, alone in the universe, Miea searched desperately for some other solution.

///

For the first time in recent memory, Chris resolved to put everything aside.

She's fourteen. How many more days alone with her do you think you're going to have?

It was an inarguable fact that Becky was moving on, and even if he and Polly hadn't split up and even if things hadn't spiraled away from him in the ensuing years, Becky would still be moving on. There was nothing he could do and nothing he could ever have done to change that. Becky's world was a different one now, a world of friends and appointments and—imminently, though he shuddered to think about it—dates. Today, an all-too-rare confluence of events gave him an entire Saturday alone with his daughter. Lonnie was out of town, others were busy, no one was having a party or any kind of gathering that night, and Polly didn't throw him a last-minute curve. It really was just him and Becky for once. He wasn't going to screw it up.

The weather was gorgeous: low seventies, cloudless, the faintest breeze. It was an ideal day for a drive up the Connecticut River Valley. Becky loved the Colonial-era towns in that area with their mix of early American flavor and contemporary small-town independence. They'd spend the day exploring craft shops and antique stores, maybe walk along the river for a while, and grab something to eat in one of a dozen excellent restaurants. He didn't mention any of this to Becky ahead of time—it was nearly impossible to have a conversation of any length with her on a Friday night—but he knew she would be up for it.

"A drive? Sure, that would be great," Becky said as they pulled out of the neighborhood.

"We'll go up and walk around for a while, maybe have an early dinner someplace."

Becky took a deep breath, but didn't otherwise react.

"Is that okay with you?" Chris said.

"Yeah, yeah, it's fine."

"You don't have anything planned today, right?"

"No, nothing."

He frowned. "The way you reacted made it seem like maybe you didn't want to be away that long."

"No, no, it's fine. I'm just a little tired."

Chris was convinced that "tired" was code for something else. "Were you out late last night?"

"Not too late. I don't know; it was a crazy week at school. I'm just a little beat."

He wasn't going to do this if he was only going to be entertaining himself. "We can stick around town if you'd rather not make the trip."

Becky took a second before answering. "No, let's go." She hesitated again. "It'll be fun."

They didn't talk much on the ride up. Becky chose the music, something surprisingly quiet, and spent most of the time looking out the side window. Chris didn't want to think what he usually thought—that her attitude had something to do with him—but it was difficult to break this particular habit. Still, he fought through it.

Chris remembered a Saturday morning when Becky was seven years old. It had been a brutal week at work; the company was in the midst of reorganization and Chris needed to make some difficult decisions regarding the people on his team. On top of that, his relationship with Polly had gotten to the point where she often put him in a terrible mood before noon on the weekends. As much as he tried not to let Becky see this, he obviously failed on this particular instance because she called him on it.

"Did I do something wrong?" she said.

The question confused Chris. "No, of course not. Why did you say that?"

"You seem pretty angry. I thought maybe I did something."

Chris shook himself. This was the last possible message he wanted to send his daughter. "Absolutely not. I'm just upset about something at work."

"But you don't work on Saturdays."

Chris nodded. "That's true. But sometimes people take their bad weeks home with them. They shouldn't do that, but sometimes they do. I'll tell you what: Put your finger right here." He pointed to a spot in the center of his forehead. Becky did what he asked and he rewarded her with a huge smile. "Thanks. You just pressed my reset button."

"What's that?"

"It's something that fixes whatever is wrong and makes me go back to the way I normally am."

Becky touched his forehead again, grinned, and then touched her own. "Do I have one, too?"

"Yep, same place." Chris reached out and touched his thumb to her "reset button."

"But I wasn't in a bad mood."

"I was just making sure it was there."

After that day, while he still lived in the house, they pressed each other's reset buttons on several occasions. It didn't always work with Becky—especially if something had happened with one of her friends—but it always let her know that he knew something was disturbing her and that he was ready to help. He hadn't tried doing it in a very long time, one of many things his instincts told him to avoid. He wondered, though, if it might be called for today.

They parked in downtown Chester and visited galleries, shops, and the Artisans' Cooperative. As always, Becky seemed fascinated with the handmade objects, but she seemed almost too taken with them. More than once, he found her staring at the same thing for an unusual length of time. What was going on in her mind? Why didn't she feel she could talk to him about it? Here, of all places, in an easy setting away from their normal lives, was where Becky had always been most open with him, even recently. Not today, though.

"Want to go down to the water for a while?" he said as they left another shop.

"Do you think we can just leave?"

"Leave? Sure. Do you want to head over to East Haddam?

Or we could go to Old Lyme if you want. We haven't been there in a long time."

"I was thinking maybe we could go back to Standridge."

Chris checked his watch. It was just past two thirty. He thought they had agreed to spend the day here. "You want to go home?"

Becky wrinkled her nose. "Is that okay?"

Chris shrugged. "I guess," he said as he reached into his pocket for his car keys. They started to walk in the direction where they parked, Chris feeling thrown off by the abruptness of the change in plans.

The idea of a near-silent drive back to Standridge followed by Becky retreating to her room and coming out only for a quick dinner tore at him. For once, he knew with complete certainty that he hadn't done anything wrong here. If this day was slipping away from them, it was her fault, not his.

He stopped sharply. "You know what? It's not okay. What is going on with you?"

Becky seemed startled by the tone of his voice. She drew back on herself. "There's nothing going on with me."

"Look, let's agree on one thing, okay? I'm not completely unconscious. I'm actually capable of noticing when your head is somewhere else."

Becky looked down at the ground. "It's nothing, Dad."

Chris stared at the keys in his hand. "Nothing. That's exactly my point."

"What's that supposed to mean?"

"Never mind," Chris said, snapping the remote control on his key chain outward and unlocking the car doors from a distance. "Let's go."

"We can go do Old Lyme if you want."

"I don't want to go to Old Lyme. I was suggesting that for you, Beck. If you don't want to do it, then I don't want to do it."

"We can go, really. Come on, let's go."

"We're going home."

They spoke as little on the drive back as they did on the

ride there. The difference now, though, was that there was no longer a question about whether or not something was amiss between them. Chris felt dominated by his anger. At this point, he wouldn't have been able to avoid feeling angry if he had given it every bit of his effort. As was always the case when he got angry with Becky—as was still the case after all this time between them—he felt frustrated, cheated, and more than a little guilty because of it.

He took a quick glance over at his daughter and what he saw wasn't the object of his current scorn, but a tenderhearted girl wrapped in her own emotions, someone who certainly didn't deserve vilification and probably didn't deserve her father's recriminations even under these circumstances. She was a whole person, a good person, a person capable of exceptional levels of love. Just a brief scan of her face told him all of those things, things he'd known for as long as he could remember and rarely forgot even for a second.

He wanted to reach out to her. Yet he couldn't. When had he become incapable of telling Becky how he felt? This wasn't a new reaction. Only a newly acknowledged one. During softer days, Polly had once told him that she was impressed with the way he never let anything fester between him and Becky. If he sent her to her room, he went up five minutes later to talk to her about what had happened. If he sensed a breakdown in communication, he set out to repair it. How long had it been since that was true?

The playlist in the car ended and neither of them reached out to start another. They drove the last twenty minutes in silence. When they got back to the apartment, Becky headed toward her room.

"Is there anything in particular you want for dinner?"

Becky turned toward him. He wanted to understand her expression, but he couldn't even begin to do so. "Whatever you make is fine with me," she said politely. Then, avoiding eye contact, she went off to her room.

It was now 4:08. With the clock counting down one of the

rare days he had alone with his daughter, Chris sat on the couch in the living room by himself, entirely unsure how much more of this he could handle.

///

"What do you want from me?" Becky said forcefully. Now that the words were out of her mouth, Becky realized how long they had been in coming, how much she needed this confrontation. Even if it was only happening in her mind.

What *did* he want from her? What was the big deal about coming back to town early? Did she screw up some Master Plan of his? Was the world going to end because they didn't spend the whole day looking at trinkets? Maybe she should have told him that she felt her legs wobbling again. Maybe she should have let him know that she was worried about the stuff that was going on in her body. But that would have started an avalanche of him fawning over her that she wasn't ready for. And it shouldn't be necessary to tell him these things. It never *used to be* necessary.

Becky came out of her room when it was time for dinner. By that point, she was ready to forget about whatever had happened that afternoon and get on with the rest of the day. Maybe they could watch a movie together or something after they ate. But as soon as she saw her father's face, she knew that he hadn't forgotten about what happened that afternoon. He was still moping about it, still trying to make her feel guilty for having a mind of her own. And so they were right back in it again. She ate quickly, barely tasting whatever it was that he made for them. She didn't say more than three words the entire time.

"I'm gonna go read in my room," she said when they finished putting the dishes in the dishwasher. She wiped her hands on a towel and headed out of the kitchen.

"Becky," he said, stopping her.

She took a deep sigh and looked at him. "What, Dad?"

He threw his hands out from his side. "I give up."

"I'm sorry?"

"I give up. The ball's in your court now."

What was that supposed to mean? "If you say so."

"Do you understand what I'm saying?"

Becky shook her head. "Not really, no."

Dad looked right through her. He'd never seemed so far away from her before. "Maybe while you're reading you can go figure it out."

Becky felt the frustration well up inside of her. But rather than say anything, knowing if she did her father was likely to say something more hurtful, she just turned away.

You give up, Dad? Is this some kind of news? Didn't you give up a long time ago? She could point to the exact day, maybe even the exact minute. It took him a while to show that he'd given up, but there was no question that from the minute he and Mom split up, he was never the same to her again. There was always something going on, something that made him seem distant, confused, or sad. They had never been like that before. If that wasn't a form of giving up, then what was?

Becky sat on her bed and grabbed the book on her nightstand. But she didn't even bother opening it. Instead, she leaned back on her pillow and stared up at the ceiling. If this was the way her father was going to act, then fine. She wasn't going to let him get to her anymore. She wasn't going to spend any more time wondering why they didn't connect any longer. She wasn't going to try to pretend that the time she spent in this apartment with him was an okay part of her life.

What do you want from me, Dad? Do you want me to pretend that you and Mom didn't screw me up when you split? Do you want me to make believe that it's okay that nothing has been the same between us since you left? Do you want me to say that I understand why you aren't the same guy anymore? Do you want me to ignore everything that we once had together and tell you that what we have now is perfectly fine?

Sorry, but you're not the only one who's giving up.

Becky put her hands over her face and closed her eyes tight. How could her father possibly tell her that he was giving up on her? What kind of parent said that to his kid? Given everything else that was going on in her mind right now, this was more than she could handle.

You're giving up? What would you do if I told you I thought I was getting sick again? Would you run out of the house screaming and never come to see me again?

As soon as the thought came to Becky's mind, she knew how untrue it was. Dad wouldn't run away screaming, no matter what the last few years had been like. He would grab her and hold her as tightly as he possibly could. He would tell her not to be afraid, even while it was obvious that he was scared to death himself.

And he would do everything he could to help her and try to keep her spirits up. Just as he did the last time. Becky flashed back on those nights when she first got sick and couldn't sleep. Mom was great, but Dad was there with her every night, wrapping her in his strong arms and staying up with her. She was so confused in those early days. She had no idea what was happening to her and no idea what was going to happen next. But when he came up with the idea of creating a fantasy world together and Tamarisk came to life in her head, Becky suddenly started to feel better. She sometimes wondered if Tamarisk had helped her more than the doctors had.

Tamarisk and her dad.

She'd thrown one away and the other had given up on her.

And here, at the end of an uncertain week, when nothing at all seemed right to her, Becky felt an overwhelming sense of sadness. She missed her father. Desperately. She missed knowing that he was always there for her. She missed being able to talk to him about anything. She missed playing with him, pretending with him. But the saddest thing of all to her was that maybe it was too late to ever get it back. Maybe the things they'd once had together were gone forever.

Becky flipped over onto her stomach, squeezing her face into her pillow. She felt the tears run along the rims of her eyes, across the bridge of her nose, and onto the bed. And with the sensation of these first tears came a torrent. She cried as hard as she ever had before, choking back the sobs to keep her father from hearing her. Even though a part of her wanted him to see her this way.

She continued to cry. Longer than she thought possible. But she couldn't make herself stop. Every time she tried, she felt even sadder. Soon, she felt like she was all sadness and nothing else.

"I need something," she said softly, to no one in particular. She'd take just about anything at this point. Really, just about anything.

6

The folder sat at her side, offering no more options on its twentieth reading than it had on the first nineteen. The hour was late and Miea knew she should try to get some sleep. Like every other day, she had a full calendar tomorrow. This time, though, along with the items on her schedule, she had one other appointment she dreaded keeping—a conversation with Thuja where she gave him her decision regarding the sterilization of the fields in Jonrae.

Still, as late as it was, going to bed was pointless. She certainly wouldn't sleep and her thinking wasn't likely to be any clearer lying down than it currently was sitting in this chair in her anteroom.

When she was a little girl, Miea sometimes found her father sitting quietly in a chair in his chambers. He would be looking off in the distance, seemingly focused on nothing and everything at the same time. He obviously didn't want to be disturbed and she would creep out of the room hoping he hadn't noticed her. One time, though, when she was eight or so, he called out to her as she made her way through the doorway. She turned back in his direction and said she was sorry to bother him.

"No need to apologize," he said. "I was just trying to gain a little perspective."

"Perspective?"

"Yes, at least a little. It has been a trying few days and I thought maybe I could make sense of some things if I looked at them from a new angle."

Miea stood next to his chair and looked out in the direction he'd been looking. "Is this the new angle?"

Her father laughed. "That really was just a turn of phrase. What I'm doing doesn't actually have anything to do with angles."

Miea tried to focus on the spot where her father focused until she interrupted him again. "Has it helped?"

He touched her on the head and nodded slowly. "I think it has a little. You know, at some point you realize that every resolution leads to new complications, but I have some new thoughts about this particular problem."

"So you've 'gained a little perspective'?"

"In a manner of speaking, yes. Maybe I could gain a little more if my daughter would join me in a game of Kem."

Miea leaned back in the chair in her anteroom and thought about the four-dimensional board game with shape-shifting pieces. Maybe that's what she really needed now: someone with whom to play Kem. Certainly, she'd gained all the perspective she was likely to gain from staring off into space.

Had her parents ever had a decision this significant to make? She knew they hadn't sterilized during the Great Blight. Had they ever seriously considered it, though? Had the king and queen ever been forced to think about eradicating the scourge by dooming several species to extinction? It had turned out not to be necessary then. Would Tamarisk be as lucky this time as it had been the last? If it wasn't, where would the extinction end?

Maybe she could discuss this with her father. Since he died, Miea had "spoken" to him numerous times, talking to the picture of him she kept in her office and imagining his responses. It always helped—some times more than others—and Miea believed that it kept her close to his spirit. She'd never discussed anything this portentous with him, though.

Miea leaned her head back and closed her eyes. If she were going to have a conversation of this magnitude, she needed to clear her mind of everything else and focus on her father's face, voice, and wisdom.

"I need something, Dad," she said softly.

Miea studied the darkness. Slowly, her father's image emerged. It was only his head and it seemed rather inchoate, but Miea recognized it for what it was. As she felt his presence, Miea began to feel lighter, as though she were becoming weightless, as though her chair wasn't actually holding her any longer. Yet as disorienting as this feeling was, she knew she shouldn't open her eyes. Something told her that she needed to allow herself to feel this new sensation fully. A part of her was floating now, even though she was certain her body wasn't moving. She surrendered entirely to this non-space. She felt warmed. Peaceful.

"Hello, Brightness," her father said in his syrupy baritone. He'd never called her "Brightness" before, but Miea liked the nickname.

"I miss you, Dad," she said plaintively.

"Missing enriches."

"It also hurts. I'd gladly trade this 'enrichment' for more days with you."

"Our story is longer than this, Brightness. Our story is eternal."

"I know." Miea believed that, though it didn't make her feel his loss any less severely.

Her father tipped his head forward and Miea felt a warm wave wash upon her. He smiled and Miea smiled in response. For a long moment, they remained this way. Miea had rarely received this much comfort trying to feel her father before, and she longed to bask in it. At the same time, though, she knew that she needed more than his support.

"We have a problem in Tamarisk, Dad."

"There are profound dangers."

"It's like the last time, and we don't know anything more than we did then. We never knew what stopped it the last time. Now Thuja wants me to sterilize Jonrae to keep the blight from spreading."

"That answer enriches nothing."

"I know that. Of course, I know that. I know it in my soul. Unfortunately, I don't have any other answer."

"Imagine and embrace, Brightness. Don't eliminate."

As peaceful as she felt, as comforted as she was by her father's presence, as certain as she was about his message, something about this conversation with her father felt off.

"Dad, you don't sound like yourself."

Miea had always assumed that the conversations she had with her father came from her memory of him. Why, then, was she "hearing" him differently now?

The image dimmed for a few seconds and Miea feared it was going to fade away. Instead, when it had become nearly invisible, it reanimated with more vibrancy. Miea swore she could detect the scent of her father's shaving cream.

"Hi, love."

Miea felt her face warm and her eyes water. "Hi, Dad."

"Thuja is not a fool. He is actually extremely good at his job."

"I know he is, but—"

"—He's very limited in his thinking."

"That's a gracious way to say it."

"That's an accurate way to say it. Thuja and his people can be very helpful to you in this crisis. They understand the land. However, they need to know that you make the decisions. Make it clear that you'll consider any reasonable suggestion but that the chain of command stops with you."

"I can't let him sterilize Jonrae."

"Absolutely not. It was a bad idea during the Great Blight and it is a bad idea now. Tamarisk needs to remain whole."

Miea nodded, though she was relatively certain her actual body remained stationary. "I know, Dad. I know."

"An answer will come."

"I hope so."

"It will. It will come. Just remember to look at all the angles."

"Gain a little perspective?"

"Exactly."

"I'll try. I wish this were easier, but I'll try."

Her father tipped his head toward her again and Miea felt another warm wave. For more than a minute, the restorative energy flowed over her, though they shared no words.

Then he said, "Wait."

"What?"

"Just wait."

At that moment, her father's face shimmered into innumerable points of light and scattered into the darkness. Miea felt a few of the points pass through her own incorporeal form as they dispersed.

Everything was dark again.

Time passed.

Miea did what her father told her to do.

She waited.

///

Becky felt incredibly tired. The depths of sleep exerted a strong and, initially, unsettling pull on her. Given how she felt, she wouldn't have thought she'd be sleeping anytime soon. Slowly, she surrendered to the pull. She really had no choice—it was that strong.

"This meeting will enrich."

Becky heard the voice like it was inside and outside of her head at the same time. Now she was hearing voices, too? She was getting sick, her father was abandoning her, and she was going crazy—life just didn't get any better than this. Meanwhile, what did "this meeting will enrich" mean, anyway?

"Limitless imaginations create."

Gee, that made way more sense. If she was going to start hearing voices, it would be nice if the voices said something a little easier to understand.

Becky felt herself falling, even though she knew she was already lying down. This wasn't like going to sleep at all. Was this yet another new symptom, something else to worry about?

Was lying in bed going to become as unpredictable as bending over or moving too quickly?

Still, she didn't feel dizzy. In fact, she didn't feel out of control at all. It felt like she was headed somewhere. A tiny piece of her started to panic, but the rest of her found this fascinating. Maybe losing her mind wouldn't be the worst thing in the world. Maybe she'd enjoy being a crazy person.

Becky noticed something formless in the darkness. As she got closer—how was she moving?—the image began to come together. It was the back of a woman's head. A head with golden, lustrous strands of hair like her cousin Kiley's. The head turned and Becky saw the woman's face—and instantly she knew who it was.

Limitless imaginations create.

A part of her brain told her that it wasn't possible for this woman to be who she thought she was, but then another part of her brain reminded her that none of this should be possible.

The face looked at her. It seemed a little confused, a little unsure. Becky continued to move closer, her body—or whatever it was that she had out here—traveling entirely on its own. If she ever summoned the guts to tell Lonnie about this, it would make a heck of a story. Finally, she was mere feet from the face—just a disembodied face. It dawned on Becky that this should feel pretty creepy. But it didn't feel that way at all. What she felt was indescribable. Maybe that was appropriate, considering she'd never had an experience even remotely like this before. Had anyone?

"Princess Miea?" she said tentatively. Becky half expected her voice to sound as strange as this place was, but she sounded just like herself.

The face across from her seemed surprised. "You know who I am?"

"I guess I would know you anywhere. Even here."

The woman made an obvious effort to figure out what this meant. Becky noticed now that the woman was older than she imagined her. She'd always been a teenager in Becky's mind, but this Princess Miea seemed to be in her early twenties.

"Do I know you?" the face said.

"No, we've never met before."

"Then how do *you* know *me*?"

You've been in my head as long as I can remember, Becky thought. That wasn't a particularly helpful explanation, though. "I created a lot of stories about you, and about Tamarisk, and about the king and the queen, and about the bloat marshes, and the Rainbow Fair, and the dancepoodles—"

The woman's eyes opened wide. "You know about my dancepoodle?"

"Yeah, I kinda made it up. At least I thought I made it up. Now I'm not so sure."

The woman seemed sad suddenly. "I had a—companion, I suppose you would call it—when I was younger. It was a four-legged animal with pink, curly hair, and it performed the most entertaining dances. I loved that animal so much, but no one else remembers it—or the existence of dancepoodles at all. I've never seen one in the kingdom and there is no record of them anywhere. Except in my heart."

Becky wondered why she mentioned dancepoodles in the first place. She'd invented them when she was little and then uninvented them when she got older and decided that Tamarisk should be more exotic and that no one in the kingdom should own pets.

"I changed the stories," Becky said.

"The stories?"

"The stories I told about Tamarisk. I wanted them to be more sophisticated, so I got rid of dancepoodles." Becky tried to remember some other early creations. "And salmoladies—they were very smart fish—and caramelpetals, a really tasty flower."

"Caramelpetals," the woman said softly, almost nostalgically.

The woman closed her eyes for a long moment. She appeared to be meditating. When she opened them again, her expression had changed.

"You allowed us to happen," she said carefully.

"You think? Maybe. I guess." This was all so totally strange. Here she was, floating in space talking to the princess of the fantasy stories she used to create with her dad. Yet that wasn't the strangest part. The strangest part was that it didn't feel at all weird to be doing this.

"Are you a god?"

Becky laughed out loud. "I am definitely not a god. Just ask my father. I'm not sure he even thinks I'm a person anymore."

"But you brought us into being."

It was Becky's turn not to say something for a few moments. Had she actually created Tamarisk? *Had she actually created Tamarisk?* "I don't think that's how it worked," she said, not entirely sure why she said that. Becky noticed that the darkness around Princess Miea was starting to change. She thought she could make out parts of the rest of the woman's body and a bit of a room around her. Becky glanced behind herself, expecting to see some of her bedroom, but there was nothing there.

"There's a reason why this is happening," Miea said. "There's a reason why we've been brought together."

"This meeting will enrich."

"What did you say?"

"Something someone just said to me."

"Who?"

Yeah, great question. "I don't have a clue. Do you have any idea why this is happening now?"

The princess lowered her eyes, and when she looked up again, she had a slightly sheepish expression on her face. "No idea at all." She chuckled to herself and then added, "I've had the most awful day imaginable."

"Mine hasn't been so great, either. And now I'm hallucinating."

The princess's expression became more serious. "You're not, you know."

Becky looked into the woman's eyes for several seconds. It was like looking at someone she'd known her entire life.

"Yes, I know."

She did. Instantly. Though none of it made the least bit of sense.

///

Miea had been talking to the girl in this once-darkness for several minutes now. The girl's form seemed to be emerging, and Miea could see the outline of a bed around her. The girl didn't seem like a god. In fact, she seemed like one of the friends Miea had had in high school or college back before everything changed. The girl was definitely the one who had brought Tamarisk into being, though. Every instinct told Miea this was true. How else could the girl know about dancepoodles and caramelpetals? It was possible this was all an elaborate deception—after all, Miea had mentioned both "lost" things to others over the years—but Miea was somehow sure that it wasn't. This was what she was supposed to "wait" for.

"I'm not a princess anymore. I'm the queen now."

"The queen? But what about your mother and father?"

"Dead," Miea said, still surprised by how sad that admission could make her. "There was a terrible accident a few years ago."

The girl lowered her head. "Dead. That's horrible." She looked up then and Miea could see that this genuinely affected her. "That must be incredibly tough for you."

"The vexing thing is how I can't even begin to get over it. After all this time, it still hurts every time I think about it."

"Yeah, I know a little something about that."

"Your parents?"

The girl shook her head. "They're not dead. But sometimes it feels like the family we used to have is dead."

Miea couldn't understand what the girl was talking about, but it was obvious that thinking about it made the girl very upset. "I'm sorry."

"Thanks." The girl looked past her, focusing directly behind her. Miea wondered what she saw back there and she looked in that direction again, seeing nothing. "What is this place?"

"I'm not sure. I just wanted to have a conversation with my father—"

"—I thought your father was dead."

"He is. I wanted to have a conversation with him in my head, to imagine the kind of advice he would give me—and I found myself here."

"With me."

Miea smiled. "With you. What were you searching for?"

The girl raised her eyebrows and shook her head. "I didn't know I was searching. But now that I think about it, just before this happened, I asked for help."

"From whom?"

"I don't know. Anyone."

"Maybe there's something out here for both of us. Not that you could tell from looking around."

"I'm Becky, by the way. Do I refer to you as Your Majesty?"

Miea cringed. "It would be great if you were the one person I knew who didn't. And it doesn't seem appropriate under the circumstances."

"What *are* the circumstances?"

"I guess that's something for both of us to find out."

Miea noticed a glint in Becky's eyes then that she hadn't seen before. This wasn't at all what she'd expected when she closed her eyes to "gain perspective" in her chamber. Still, after one of the most perplexing days of her life, this kind of surprise was more than welcome.

"You can call me Miea."

"Thanks. I always loved that name."

"Thanks. I've always loved it as well."

"Are we in Tamarisk?"

Miea thought about this for a moment. "I don't think so. Maybe we're in the place that you come from."

"This is definitely not Connecticut. At least any part of Connecticut that I've ever seen."

"Then we're someplace else. A third place; a place where we could meet."

"Do things like this happen to you regularly?"

"Never before. But I'm glad it's happening now."

Becky smiled and the glint in her eyes grew. "Yeah, me too. Do you really think there's a reason why we've met?"

"I think there has to be. I suppose that's something we'll learn together."

Miea felt her form move farther from the girl. As the distance grew between them, she wondered if this was some sort of indication that this meeting was going to be their only one. At some point, the movement stopped, though. Becky was still visible, if only barely. Miea could see Becky's entire body now, lying on a bed.

As she watched, the darkness between them somehow became darker still. A dense black path connected her to her captivating new friend.

"Teach her about the path," said the voice that was neither hers, Becky's, nor her father's. The words meant nothing to her.

She looked at the lightless space that led to Becky.

Suddenly, she understood the voice.

"Before you leave," Miea said, hopefully loud enough for Becky to hear, "there's something else I need to tell you. Something that will keep us in contact."

7

Somehow, in his anger, Chris had managed to forget that Polly was coming by the apartment early on Sunday to pick up Becky. Only when the doorman buzzed his intercom at 8:30 did he remember that they had some outing related to Al's family. He thumbed the intercom to tell the doorman to send Al and Polly up, and then he went to Becky's room to roust her. She was fast asleep and in no mood to get up.

"Come on, you need to get going. You know your mother isn't going to want to stand around here waiting for you."

Not any more than he wanted to stand around waiting with her. Polly had only been to the apartment a handful of times—pickup and drop-off somehow had become his responsibility—and he was always uncomfortable when she was there. He imagined her scrutinizing his choice of furniture and every appointment in the living room, telling herself that it hardly compared with Becky's "real home."

Considering they had a child in common, he'd spent remarkably little time with Polly over the past four years. At school functions, they tended to position themselves on opposite sides of the room. At the middle school graduation party Polly threw for Becky, he absented himself after a half hour. If Becky wasn't ready when Chris came to pick her up, Polly would usually open the door for him and then leave him standing in the foyer to wait alone.

There had been that one time about six months after they

split that Becky insisted the three of them go out to dinner together. Becky made all the arrangements, including choosing the restaurant, and Chris waited fifteen minutes for the two of them to arrive, having stressed over bridge traffic with concerns that he himself would be late. The dinner was unremittingly awkward. Chris was still very angry with Polly and still teetering from her decision to reject him, and he found he had little to say other than asking about her family and a couple of the neighbors. As a result, he directed nearly all of his attention at Becky, using such stimulating conversation starters as, "So that math test you had last week turned out to be really easy, right?"

Now, ten minutes after Polly and Al walked into the living room, he didn't even have that option. He had no idea why it was taking Becky so long to get dressed. She didn't need makeup for this outing (though it was entirely possible that she'd still want to wear some), so this should have been a matter of simply throwing on some clothes, brushing her teeth, brushing her hair, and getting out here. She had to know how much he hated having to entertain her mother and stepfather.

"Do you guys want some coffee or something?"

Polly shook her head and looked off toward Becky's room. "We really need to get going. The drive is at least a couple hours."

Chris shrugged. "Want me to go prod her again?"

Polly smirked. "Will that accomplish anything more than it did the last time?"

Al walked over to the coffee table. "Monty Python. I love these guys." He picked up the box holding the DVD for *Monty Python and the Holy Grail*, the movie Chris had planned to watch with Becky last night after they got home from their drive—until things once again crumbled between them.

"Yeah, they're great," Chris said, moving toward the couch and Al, happy to be farther from Polly's increasingly impatient form.

"Are you a 'Knights who Say Ni' guy or a 'Killer Bunny' guy?"

"I didn't realize I had to be one or the other. To tell you the truth, I think I'm probably a Black Knight guy."

"It's just a flesh wound," Al said animatedly and then gazed at the box admiringly. "Truly great cinema."

"*Casablanca* and then *Holy Grail*."

"Don't forget *Caddyshack*."

"Right, of course."

"Did you guys watch this last night?"

"Didn't get around to it." Chris flashed on the evening's climax. Had he really told Becky that he was giving up? What kind of parent said something like that to his child?

"That's really too bad." Al looked over at Polly. "Polly just loves Monty Python, don't you, hon?"

Polly scowled at him. "Yes, they're up there with people who can burp the alphabet as standard-bearers for high art."

Al leaned toward Chris and said confidentially, "We've watched this movie six times together."

Chris chuckled and couldn't think of an appropriate way to continue this conversation. Clearly neither could Al, and silence returned.

Chris decided to sit down on the love seat. He looked at Polly. "You might as well sit for a few minutes. If Becky's trying to decide what to wear, I might need to make you dinner."

Polly rolled her eyes and walked over to the couch, clearly miffed at the indignity of having to accept this level of hospitality from her ex-husband. As she did, she called out, "Beck, today, okay?"

"I'll be right there."

A couple minutes later, Becky streamed into the room looking bright, in surprisingly good spirits, and utterly oblivious to any discomfort she might have caused her parents. Polly, Al, and Chris stood simultaneously as she entered, and the four of them made their way to the door. As they did so, Al playfully wagged a scolding finger at Becky and she punched him lightly on the shoulder. Chris felt a little pinprick watching the exchange.

Polly opened the door and moved into the hallway. Al joined her. Before Becky went with them, she pulled Chris on the arm, reached up, and kissed him on the cheek. After last night, that was enough of a surprise.

It wasn't the only one, though. With their heads close together, she whispered, "Dad, you're not going to believe this: Tamarisk is real." Then she kissed him again and bounded away.

The announcement so stunned Chris that he didn't think to ask her for an explanation until she'd gone down the hall. He just stood there, head tipped forward and staring out the doorway long after the others entered the elevator.

///

Chris couldn't remember the last time Becky had simply leaned over to give him an unprompted kiss on the cheek. It seemed that he always had to initiate the act these days, and even when he did, she responded with little enthusiasm. It was another one of those "teenager things" he might have been less perplexed about if he felt he was on steadier ground with his daughter. That made her actions this morning something of a real stunner. Had she been present during their conversation last night? How could she have heard what he said to her and responded the next morning so affectionately?

Then, of course, there was the mention of Tamarisk. It had been years since Chris last spoke to Becky about that place of their imaginations. She'd made it abundantly clear that she didn't want anything more to do with it and he'd quickly learned that it wasn't even safe to reminisce. A simple mention could earn her scorn, and if he actually tried to discuss it, Becky would criticize him for not understanding that she'd grown up and had moved on. So why did she raise the topic out of the blue this morning?

And what did it mean that she told him "Tamarisk is real" on the heels of the most distressing confrontation they'd ever had with each other? Was this some kind of response, some kind of coded message? Was Becky trying to juxtapose the current state of their relationship against the days when they'd invented dreams together? That was unlikely. It wasn't like his daughter to speak in codes. Still, if she wasn't making some kind of metaphorical statement, what, exactly, was she saying?

The simple fact that a peck on the cheek and a reference to their old stories could set his mind reeling underscored for Chris the absurdity of what he'd said to Becky last night. *I give up*. Why the hell had he even said that in the first place? He was angry and frustrated, of course, but he prided himself on never reacting out of anger with his daughter. He'd felt the need to say it, though; not to suggest to Becky that he was washing his hands of her (he hoped she hadn't interpreted it that way), but to tell her that he was resigned to allowing their relationship to be whatever she felt it should be. He was acknowledging that he couldn't control her and that he was ceding the fate of their future together to her.

There were two problems with this. The first was the ambiguity of what he'd said. She could have interpreted it too many ways, almost all bad. The second was that it wasn't true regardless of how she had interpreted it. He hadn't given up, and he couldn't allow himself to accept whatever Becky decided their relationship should be. He would have realized that this morning even if she hadn't kissed him on the cheek on her way out the door.

Even if she hadn't whispered, "Tamarisk is real."

No matter what any of it meant, it left Chris with some extra energy to carry him into the rest of the day. He'd seen a sparkle in Becky's eyes this morning that he hadn't seen in a while, and he knew in his heart that this sparkle wasn't about the trip she was taking to Al's brother's house. This had something, in some way, to do with the two of them, even if the nature of it remained a mystery. That meant a lot.

An entire free Sunday stretched out in front of him. Usually, an unstructured day intimidated him. However, today, driven by the sparkle in his daughter's eyes, the lightness of her kiss, and the playfulness of her mysterious proclamation, he saw these open hours as an opportunity. He'd make some more coffee, read the paper, maybe make a pass at the crossword puzzle, and maybe even watch that Monty Python movie after all. Perhaps he'd skip showering and shaving as well.

Eventually, the sunlight streaming through the living room windows beckoned him. He hadn't realized the weather was going to be so pleasant today. He decided to call Lisa.

"What time should I pick you up?" he said.

"What are you talking about?"

"It's a beautiful day and we're going to spend it together. What time should I pick you up?"

"Is it nice out? I'm still in bed."

"I'm not going to ask what you did last night. You still haven't answered my question."

"I'm sorry, sweetie, I can't come out to play today. I have an open house this afternoon."

"What time?"

"Chris, please don't be dense. I just told you I can't go out with you."

"I meant what time is your open house."

"Oh, that. Three o'clock."

"That gives us plenty of time to go out to brunch. Pour yourself into the shower; I'll pick you up at a quarter to twelve."

Lisa looked crisp and professional when she answered the door a short while later. Chris preferred the way Lisa looked when she wore casual clothes instead. Dressed like this, though, she certainly seemed like someone from whom he'd buy a house. She insisted on taking two cars to the restaurant so she could dash off if necessary to get to her showing on time, which made his picking her up in the first place superfluous. When she declined a Bloody Mary with brunch, he knew this real estate prospect had her a little more keyed up than usual.

"No drink? What kind of house are you showing today?"

"The four-million-dollar kind."

"Four million dollars? You have a four-million-dollar house to show today and you're having brunch with me? Shouldn't you be cleaning the grout in the kitchen tile with a toothbrush or something?"

"Yes, I probably should be, but you sounded irrepressible. I didn't want to try to repress you."

Chris smiled broadly. "Thanks."

"What's going on with you, anyway? You didn't get lucky last night, did you?"

"Don't be crude. I'm just in a good mood."

Lisa smiled and put a hand on top of his. "That's nice. Do it more often."

"I'm gonna give it a shot."

The waiter came by and, while Lisa ordered, Chris glanced around the restaurant. His eyes made contact with those of a young woman with lustrous golden hair. She smiled at him and glanced away a moment later. She seemed incredibly familiar, but he couldn't place who she was. She looked a little like Kiley—maybe he kept "seeing" his niece because someone was trying to tell him to call her. Was she a friend of Becky's? No, she was too old. One of her teachers? No, she was probably too young. Could it be someone new at the office? He didn't think so. Someone with whom he'd had a blind date? No, that was impossible because she wasn't scowling at him.

"What can I get you today, sir?" the waiter said, drawing Chris's attention back to his own table.

"A Mexican omelet with whole wheat toast, please. And some more coffee when you get a chance."

"I'll be back with that in a minute."

Chris took another sip from his cup and then glanced across the room again. The woman with the golden hair was talking animatedly with friends and she seemed a little different to him now.

"Someone you know?" Lisa said.

Chris shook his head. "No, it isn't who I thought it was."

Who did I think it was, though? Chris realized he didn't know—but that he somehow should.

///

They were finally on their way home. Becky had been looking forward to this trip for weeks—Al's niece and nephew were two of the coolest people she knew—but she couldn't help feeling distracted today. They'd be talking up in Kayla's room and Becky would find herself drifting away in the middle of the conversation. Back to that place—wherever it was—where she'd met Miea last night. That encounter was hands down the most bizarre experience of Becky's life, but it might also have been the most exciting. After all, it isn't every day that you discover the existence of another world—a world that you somehow helped create. And Miea was as great as Becky had always imagined her to be. She was regal and elegant without being stuck-up in any way. The thing about the old king and queen dying was tough, though. Miea looked so sad when she talked about them. Becky's heart went out to her immediately.

The whole experience left Becky with this little buzz the entire day, something like the way she felt when she ate too much sugar. She was revved up and feeling super-alert. She hadn't felt this sharp in a while, and it made her think that maybe the stuff with the dizziness and the bloody noses really was nothing more than a bad virus. If she were getting sick again, she would never feel this good ever, would she?

"Are you sure you're okay?" her mother said from the front seat of the car, tapping her on the hand at the same time.

Becky took off her iPod earbuds and said, "Yeah, I'm totally fine."

"You just seem a little, I don't know, gaga today."

"Gaga? As in Lady Gaga?" Becky said, laughing.

"No, not that Gaga. You know, *gaga*. Like your body is here and your head is in Southern California."

Not Southern California, Mom. "I'm great. Really. I'm just listening to some music. Maybe I'll switch to Lady Gaga."

"Did you have a good time with Kayla and Matt?"

"Yeah, of course. I love those guys."

Her mother seemed skeptical. "Okay. You didn't seem to

have as much fun with them as usual."

"We're kinda too old to run around the house now the way we did a few years ago."

That drew a smirk. "No kidding. I just—no, it's fine. If you say you're okay, I'm sure you're okay."

Mom turned back to the front of the car and Becky put her earbuds in again. What would her mother have said if she told her why she seemed so *gaga*? She'd probably have Al drive them to the nearest crazy house. Mom was great about most things, but some stuff just went right past her. Telling her that Tamarisk actually existed would be like telling her leprechauns had moved in next door.

Mom had never been big on the whole Tamarisk thing. She would smile when Becky talked about it and she even participated in a few of the stories, but Becky always got the impression that she did this to be a good mom rather than because it interested her in any way. That was totally fine with Becky. She wouldn't have expected her mother to have the exact same interests as she did.

Her dad, though, was crazy about Tamarisk. Of course that was the case—Tamarisk was his idea in the first place. But he didn't just seem to enjoy it because it was something he could do with her. He seemed totally into it. All Becky ever had to do to get her father's attention was mention something about some part of the kingdom—anything about it at all, really—and he was locked in. She probably could have called him out of meetings at work to talk about the king's peace summit with the Thorns or what the princess planned to wear to the upcoming luaka concert. He instantly became like a little kid when they created stories at bedtime, and there were more than a few occasions when Mom had to call up to him to remind him that Becky needed to get to sleep.

The expression on his face when Becky whispered to him that Tamarisk was real was classic. Becky knew that he wouldn't have any idea what she was talking about and that he would definitely want to talk about it further. That's why she told him on her way out the door. Let him try to figure it out for a while. It would serve him right for telling her he was "giving up." Of course, eventually she'd let him know what was going on. He'd really want to know. It would probably make his year. She could relate to that.

They ran into a ton of traffic on the way back, which made Becky incredibly antsy, but Al eventually got them home. Fortunately, it was late enough that Becky could just jump in the shower and then tell her mom she was going to bed.

Before they'd parted, Miea had taught Becky a method involving a kind of meditation that created a path between home and Tamarisk. Miea told her that she had it on "good authority" that the technique would work and get her into Tamarisk itself, not that place where they'd met last night.

Now it was time to try it out. Within minutes, she would be walking around in the world of her wildest imagination.

Before beginning the meditation, Becky got ready for bed. She blew her hair dry and put on her favorite sleeping T-shirt, an oversized one featuring Orlando Bloom as Legolas from the *Lord of the Rings* movies. She wondered if she was going to appear in Tamarisk exactly as she appeared in her bedroom. If so, she should probably dress more formally. She couldn't very well show up in a queen's palace in a T-shirt. At the same time, she'd feel really stupid putting on a cocktail dress to go to bed, and if her mother came into her room while she was doing this for any reason, she'd think Becky had lost her mind. She'd have to hope that whatever magic it was that allowed her to get to Tamarisk in the first place would allow her to look presentable when she got there.

Becky sat on the edge of the bed and focused on clearing her mind the way Miea had told her to do it. First, she had to visualize the events of the day and then imagine shutting off each one of them. One by one, her father's face, her mother and Al in the car, Kayla and Matt in Kayla's room, and the traffic on the highway appeared to her and she dimmed them back to the darkness. Then she had to lift herself onto the path. This required concentrating on the nothingness behind her eyelids in such a way that she could feel herself moving into it, as though her body were actually traveling into this dark space. Then, once she found herself moving, she needed to bring the vision of Tamarisk to mind. She needed to see Miea as she saw her the night before, and the land as she had always envisioned it. These images emerged from the blank space now and Becky could feel herself moving toward them. The temptation to open her eyes to gaze upon this other world was overwhelming, but Becky knew she needed to resist it. Miea had made it very clear that she would know when she was truly in Tamarisk. Only then could she stop the meditation.

But while the picture of the world became clearer—Becky had a very vivid sense of this place from years ago and it all came rushing back to her now—she didn't get the idea that she was there. In fact, she no longer felt the sense of movement. Instead, it seemed that she had only drawn a picture in her mind. It was an especially bright and especially detailed picture, but it continued to feel like a picture and nothing more. Maybe this was part of the process. Maybe this was some kind of barrier that she needed to cross. Becky kept her eyes closed, retained her focus, and willed herself through the barrier.

Nothing changed. After several minutes, it became obvious that nothing was ever going to change. Becky opened her eyes and saw her room and her things. She looked down to find Legolas looking back at her. She was certain she'd done everything Miea told her to do. She'd felt herself moving just the way Miea had said she would. But in the end, she wasn't any closer to Tamarisk than she had been when she was on the highway.

Becky felt the excitement she'd been carrying with her since last night drain away. Why wasn't she able to visit with Miea tonight? Did Miea need to do something on her end to make this happen? Maybe she'd been so busy with everything going on in the palace today that she hadn't had time to leave the door open or whatever.

Becky hoped that was the case.

If it wasn't, then last night was regrettably a once-in-a-lifetime event.

///

"The minister of trade is here for your meeting, Your Majesty. Should I show her and her staff to the small conference room?"

"Please tell the minister that we will hold our meeting in the garden, Sorbus."

"The garden, Your Majesty?"

"Is there something wrong with that? It's a gorgeous day and the goal of this afternoon's meeting is to exchange ideas. I think my ideas will come more freely in the garden than they would in the conference room."

For a moment, Sorbus looked at Miea as though he were worried about her. Then his eyes softened and he said, "I think the garden is an excellent idea. I'll set them up. Should I give you ten minutes?"

"No reason to keep the minister waiting. Tell her I'll be there in two."

Miea had woken up this morning feeling as though she'd slept for twenty hours. She could barely wait to get started on the day. Her schedule was full—when wasn't her schedule full?—but she found herself going from appointment to appointment with alacrity, spurred by the remarkable encounter of the night before.

Her name was Becky. She was fourteen years old, had shoulder-length brown hair, deep blue eyes, and a soft, round face, and she came from a place called Moorewood, Connecticut. Her very existence changed everything. Miea had asked herself any number of big questions about her world for as long as she could remember. The biggest one had always been the most impossible to answer: how did we get here? This wasn't the kind of question that most of her fellows were interested in pursuing. Even her father seemed baffled by Miea's fascination with it. To all of them, you simply accepted that you had a place in the world and let the larger mysteries remain mysteries.

Now Miea had an answer, though. At the very least, she had part of an answer. There was another presence out there last night—the thing that told her to wait and that showed her the path was definitely not her father. That presence had something to do with her meeting Becky; it even seemed to suggest that it was important that she do so. There were messages here she'd only begun to hear. What Miea knew already, though, was that meeting Becky opened her to a new way of looking at the universe. Knowing that there was a force out there that had willed her into being—even if that force seemed to be just a bright teenaged girl—suggested an order to the world that Miea couldn't be sure of before. With the knowledge of this order came a new sense of inspiration and, for reasons that weren't entirely clear to her yet, a new sense of optimism.

Therefore, Miea approached the new day with relish—no part of it more than the part she'd dreaded only the night before.

"Sterilization is not an option I am willing to consider," she told Thuja. The words of her father last night—that part of the conversation felt just like him—echoed in her mind as she said it.

The man lowered his eyes. "I'm very sorry to hear that."

"You shouldn't be sorry to hear that I refuse to order the elimination of several unique species in our kingdom."

"I'm sure you realize that isn't what I meant, Your Majesty. What causes me sorrow is that I have no alternatives to offer you. We have found no cause for the blight."

"But we will."

"If only I could be that certain."

"You *can* be that certain, Minister. I can't explain why I feel this way, but I know that an answer is out there. And I know that we will find it with minimal hardship."

Thuja seemed unconvinced. However, while Miea acknowledged that his concerns were legitimate ones, she urged him to push his staff further to find the source of the blight or at the very least offer a treatment that would forestall it without devastating ecological consequences.

"Your Majesty, I truly wish I could share your confidence," Thuja said as he prepared to leave.

"Try, Minister. Perhaps confidence is what we need most right now."

Miea moved to the garden for her meeting with the minister of trade with a healthy sense of resolve. However, the session started erratically. It seemed that the minister's staff was especially uncomfortable with being in such an informal setting with the queen. The goal of the meeting was to discuss ways to help the growers of bayless in their efforts to give the oddly-shaped and slightly sour fruit a larger consumer base. Miea listened to various members of the minister's committee present programs aimed at convincing the public that the fruit wasn't as ugly as it looked, wasn't so strangely flavored, and was nutritionally beneficial (though most popular fruits were considerably more nutritious). Their efforts were well-intentioned, but Miea couldn't imagine that any of them would help bayless growers make much headway.

Miea understood that it was her function to listen to the various campaigns, receive recommendations from the minister, and then comment on them. She wasn't in the mood to serve such a function today, though. Not when she felt so well and when the committee was so clearly missing the obvious.

"Children," she said, as one committee member sat down and another rose to give his presentation.

"Excuse me, Your Majesty," the minister said.

"Children love sour things—especially sweet sour things. The bayless isn't a particularly sweet fruit. To be honest, it isn't much of a fruit at all. It is also dreadfully ugly. I'm not sure why farmers cultivate these things at all, to tell you the truth. Better they were left to the wild to add character to the landscape. However, if farmers want to invest their energies in bringing this fruit to market, then they should devise a concoction—some kind of paste or chewy substance or beverage—that uses the bayless in a sweetened and disguised form and promote this concoction to children."

The minister of trade smiled at her. "Turn it into candy, Your Majesty?"

"I think that might be a better choice than trying to convince our fellow citizens that the bayless is beautiful."

The minister laughed politely. "I think it might very well be, Your Majesty."

"If this concoction is sweetened with haedrich, it will be healthful as well."

"That is a very wise notion, Your Majesty. I'll set someone to work on it immediately."

Miea not only felt that she'd contributed, but, having preempted the last three presentations, she'd actually put herself ahead of schedule for the day. As a result, she felt she'd earned a short time alone in the garden, sipping argo and enjoying the sunshine.

She wondered what Becky did for relaxation. Was leisure time an entirely different thing in the world the teenager came from? Miea had a feeling that there were far more similarities between Tamarisk and Connecticut than there were differences. Certainly, there had to be differences, though. What did Connecticut look like? Miea strongly believed that she understood how to bring Becky to Tamarisk, but was it somehow possible for Miea to travel to Becky's home as well? The thought was too fantastic for such a busy day.

Sorbus retrieved her from the garden and the rest of the afternoon was a jumble of diplomacy and problem solving. A state dinner followed this and consumed most of the night. Finally, feeling overloaded from a full day's encounters and tired of speaking so much, Miea sat alone in her chambers, sipping one last cup of argo. It was only then that she realized Becky hadn't returned. She had been convinced after last night that the girl would come to visit Tamarisk the first chance she got. Becky had as much as told her this when they parted. Still, she hadn't come.

Did her responsibilities keep her away? Maybe teenagers had much more to do in Connecticut than they did in Tamarisk. Perhaps Miea had done something to frighten the girl and prevent her from making the trip. That didn't seem to make sense given the way they spoke and who the girl was, though. Miea was certain the meditation process she described to Becky would get her to Tamarisk—the "voice" was so strong—but of course, no one had ever used it before. Was it possible Miea had made some mistake with the instructions she gave the girl?

If so, did that mean she'd never see her again? The thought left Miea with a surge of anxiety. She wanted to reach across the void to clasp Becky's hand this very minute.

They had so much more to do together.

8

Miea ran her hand over the replica of the Malaspina Bridge that she kept in her room. She had commissioned the model soon after she became queen, in response to the first report on the "accident" that claimed her parents. She'd demanded that the model be as accurate in every detail as possible to help her when she reviewed subsequent reports. While the artist who'd created the model did his job masterfully, the people who compiled the reports (more than a dozen in the years that followed) were less successful. Four years after the disaster, no one could tell her the definitive cause.

Sorbus entered her chambers. "Your Majesty, it is time for your meeting with the delegation from Gunnthorn."

"Please make them comfortable, Sorbus. I'll be there in a moment."

Miea returned to her office to collect a folder that contained her notes from the numerous briefings she'd received in preparation for this meeting. This was the fifth such meeting with the Thorns since Miea had become queen. Throughout history, Tamarisk had maintained a wary, uneasy relationship with their neighbors to the north. The tensions descended to war only once—over a small patch of fertile land more than a hundred years ago—but their coexistence had been dotted with skirmishes, subterfuge, and posturing. The cultural differences between the two kingdoms were profound: Tamarisk was agrarian, open, and progressive while Gunnthorn was industrial, repressive, and resistant to societal change. Most difficult for Miea (and every Tamarisk monarch who came before her) to deal with about the Thorns, however, was their compulsive need to intimidate. The leaders of the Thorns wanted all other kingdoms to fear them, even those with equal or greater resources and power. Miea knew there was a network of Thorn spies in Tamarisk gathering information about vulnerabilities and creating problems for the citizenry. The Thorns made little attempt to conceal the existence of this network. They were, however, so good at working themselves into the fabric of Tamariskian society that Miea's security forces had never succeeded in rooting them out.

The possibility of a damaging incursion from the Thorns always existed. That was why Miea pursued these diplomatic sessions. This one carried more urgency with it than most, however. As the search for a cause of the disease infesting plant life in Jonrae remained futile, Miea considered the very real possibility that the Thorns might have found an undetectable way to poison her kingdom. If so, no level of diplomacy would be enough to prevent an all-out conflict.

As she exited her office to walk toward the conference room, Miea found a teenaged boy in Thorn garb leafing through the pages of Sorbus's copy of her appointment calendar, examining each page carefully. Sorbus was nowhere in the vicinity.

"Excuse me," she said sharply.

The boy glanced up at her casually, bowed his head slightly in modest acknowledgement of her presence, and then continued to examine the book.

"Can I ask what you are doing?" Miea said with obvious annoyance.

The boy rubbed a page from the book between his thumb and forefinger. "This paper is extraordinary. Tamariskians are such master craftspeople. Even this appointment book is more elegant than anything we have in Gunnthorn."

The boy was admiring the book's composition? Unlikely. He was surely memorizing where she would be in the coming weeks. How could Sorbus have been so lax as to allow him to do this?

Miea walked up to the boy and peered at the page he "admired." The week after next. She'd boost security the entire week. She hated thinking this way and only really did it when the Thorns were involved. "I assume you are with the delegation."

The boy smoothed the page and took one additional long glance at it. Miea nearly tore the book from his grasp. At last, he turned to her. "Yes, I'm with the delegation."

"Then perhaps you should be *with* the delegation. Allow me to escort you."

"That would be very nice of you."

Miea walked with the boy to the conference room, silently fuming. Could this Thorn teen have been more arrogant? He had to know who she was. If he wasn't going to hide his obvious espionage, the least he could do was offer her some respect.

Thorn Vice Chancellor Capsicum stood to greet Miea when she entered the conference room. Of course, the chancellor wasn't here. He would never deign to journey to another kingdom.

"Your Majesty, thank you for your hospitality," the vice chancellor said. "Our accommodations last night were excellent as always."

We intentionally sequestered you to prevent you from doing any spying, Capsicum, but you probably already know that. "I'm glad you were comfortable, Mr. Vice Chancellor."

The vice chancellor gestured toward the boy who walked in with Miea. "I see you've already met my son, Rubus."

Miea glanced toward the boy, who now bowed toward her deferentially.

"I didn't know he was your son," Miea said, "but yes, we have met."

"Rubus has taken a special interest in Tamarisk. He practically begged me to take him along on this trip. I hope you don't mind."

"Your son is welcome in Tamarisk, Mr. Vice Chancellor. I

might only request that he remain with your entourage in the future."

Capsicum's eyes narrowed briefly and then he looked at his son disapprovingly. The boy would not meet his gaze. Clearly, he wasn't as skilled at deception as his father had expected him to be. Miea was sure he'd receive more extensive training upon their return to Gunnthorn.

The next half hour was an anticipated series of formalities: reviews of treaties, discussions about the levels of participation of each kingdom in an upcoming global conference, vague references to a revision in extradition policies. Capsicum lobbied for a reduction of Tamariskian soldiers on the southernmost border between the two kingdoms, claiming the Thorn villagers on the other side felt overwhelmed. Miea declined, noting Tamariskian military policy of respect for borders and choosing not to mention that the Thorn government had little concern for its citizens and only wanted the reduction to make it easier for spies to sneak through.

"Vice Chancellor, since we're speaking of borders, I'd like to discuss some abnormalities in Jonrae that concern me." Jonrae also bordered Gunnthorn, farther to the north. "Is it possible you are conducting experiments there?"

"In Jonrae, Your Majesty?" Capsicum said haughtily. "Jonrae is a Tamarisk territory."

"And easily accessible from Baranov."

"The border between Baranov and Jonrae is well guarded by your own soldiers, Your Majesty."

Yet I'm sure you could find a way to cause us harm if you chose to do so. "It is possible that an experiment held within your borders might still have unexpected consequences for Jonrae."

The vice chancellor shook his head. "There are no experiments going on in Baranov."

"Would you mind if I sent a delegation there to take some soil samples?"

Capsicum rose up in his seat. "I would mind exactly as much as you would mind if I sent a delegation to poke around

Tamarisk City."

Rubus leaned forward. "Maybe I could go to Baranov and prepare a report for the queen," he said. Unlike the other diplomats around the table, he obviously had no concerns about entering into a discussion between the highest ranking officials in the room.

"The queen is simply going to have to take our word for it," Capsicum said sternly.

"If there are abnormalities in Jonrae, there might be abnormalities in Baranov as well. We should find out."

The vice chancellor smiled, though his eyes remained dark. "My son is wise beyond his years." He turned to the boy. "Yes, Rubus; take a scientific team up to Baranov and come back with your findings. If there is something worth sharing with the queen, we will let her know."

The man and the teen exchanged a glance that Miea couldn't read. Of course, nothing would come of Rubus's "report." Just as nothing was coming from this diplomatic conference.

Other than Miea's increased suspicions that the Thorns had a very active role in the new danger facing her kingdom.

///

The pizza dough rose in the air and landed on the kitchen counter with an awkward *whumpf*. Dad had never been good at this part of the pizza-making process, but he insisted on doing it every time anyway.

"What's the point of the whole throwing-the-dough-in-the-air thing?" Becky said as her father retrieved it from the counter, patted it with flour, and tried again.

"Not sure, actually. Theatrics, I think."

The dough slipped off the side of his hand, but he caught it before it fell.

"This doesn't look very theatrical, Dad."

He smirked at her. "Certain things take practice. If you quit after a little failure, you never learn."

Becky didn't want to remind him that he'd been trying to do this since she was a little kid. "If you say so. I'll start shredding the mozzarella."

"Good idea. I should be ready with this in, I don't know, twenty or thirty minutes—assuming of course that I don't drop it on the floor and we don't have the start the whole thing over from scratch."

Dad threw her a sly glance and she rolled her eyes at him. He seemed to be in a very good mood. He had been, really, the entire week. He asked her more than the same two questions when they talked on the phone ("How was school?" "Did anything happen today?"), and he actually seemed to be listening to what she said in response. Their dinner together Tuesday night was relaxed. She got to pick the restaurant and they went for ice cream afterward and just hung out. They didn't talk much, but she didn't feel the way she usually did when they were quiet together—as though they were supposed to be talking but weren't.

Of course, that didn't mean that there still wasn't some weirdness there. The single biggest weirdness was that he hadn't said a thing to her about Tamarisk after what she'd told him last Sunday. Not a word. She was beginning to wonder if maybe he hadn't heard her. Or maybe he didn't understand what she'd said. Well, if he wasn't going to bring it up, she wasn't going to, either. At first, she didn't say anything more to him about Tamarisk because she wanted him to make some kind of move on this. It had been so long since he'd really tried to connect with her, and she was sure this was going to get him going—but he had to show her that it was important to him.

But now she had a different reason for avoiding bringing it up. It had been a full week since her "encounter" with Miea—and she hadn't been able to hook up with the queen again, no matter how hard she'd concentrated and how carefully she followed the directions Miea had given her. Becky knew that what happened to her had been real. But if it was real, why did it only happen that one time? She had one more thought and she was going to try it out when they went to bed tonight. She was anxious to do it now—actually, she'd been anxious to do it four hours ago—but she didn't think she'd be able to concentrate enough with her father roaming around the apartment.

For now, she'd think about pizza and shredding mozzarella. She glanced over to the kitchen counter. Her father had managed to stretch out the dough in some fashion, but he was repairing a hole in it.

"I'm thinking olives and garlic," he said while still bent over the brutalized crust.

"Works for me. Do we have any hot peppers?"

"Hot peppers? You don't eat hot peppers."

"I'm evolving, Dad."

He glanced over at her, a wry smile on his face. "Yeah, I think we have some hot peppers."

"Just a couple, okay?"

Eventually, they got to eat the pizza and it tasted great. Dad was really good at making pizza once he got past the "theatrics." After they cleaned up, they played a couple games of Yahtzee and then put the new Johnny Depp movie on pay-per-view. Becky was supposed to go to a party with Lonnie tonight, but she decided to stay home with her father instead. It had been a while since they'd had an easy Saturday together, and it just seemed like a good idea.

"Johnny Depp really is a smart actor," her father said as the movie played.

"He's gorgeous."

Dad looked sideways at her and she just grinned at him. "You really think he's gorgeous?"

"You don't?"

"He's not my type."

"You don't have a type, Dad. Yes, Johnny Depp *is* gorgeous. This is not opinion; it's fact."

"What do you mean I don't have a type?"

"Never mind. I want some dessert. What do we have?"

Dessert turned out to be an apple pie Dad had bought that morning, the movie turned out to be only okay by Johnny Depp standards (not that it mattered), and Dad insisted on watching the opening segment of "Saturday Night Live" before going to bed. But in the end, they'd made it through an entire day together without any tense or mopey moments. Becky wondered what her father was thinking, what had caused this shift in attitude. Whatever it was, she hoped he kept thinking it.

Now, alone in her room, Becky was finally able to test out her theory. About six months after Dad had moved out, Mom bought Becky a new bedroom set with a queen-size bed. Rather than just giving her old bed away, Mom asked Dad if he wanted it and he took it. It was certainly a step up from the ratty one Lisa had given him when he moved in here, even if it was only a twin. The thing about the bed that mattered now, though, was that they had created all the Tamarisk stories in this bed. Night after night, they added new adventures to the legend of Tamarisk. As strange as it seemed—though, really, how much stranger could anything be than what had already occurred?—Becky thought it was possible that this bed might be a "portal" of some kind to Tamarisk. She read that kind of stuff in fantasy novels all the time, and she was in this bed the one time she met with Miea.

Becky sat on the edge of the bed and went through the process in the same way she had every night since last Sunday. She closed her eyes and began to dim her memories of the day. Right after beginning, she heard the toilet flush in her father's room and needed to start over. As silence returned, she was able to concentrate completely on the darkness. She darkened the pizza dough and Johnny Depp and the intentionally lame song Al had sung at the top of his voice this morning. She darkened Lonnie's last-minute plea to come to the party and the text she'd gotten from Cam Parker saying that he was going to be there as well. She moved deeper into the darkness until it was entirely black and then called up the image of Tamarisk, of the palace, of Miea's face.

And she felt a tug. This was new, different from the sense of falling she'd had last Saturday night and much more of a sense of motion than anything she'd had since. It was like what happened when you drove through one of those automated car washes—all of a sudden you just got pulled along like you were on a track. Becky was definitely moving now, faster, though she still wasn't sure where she was headed. She still had the images of Tamarisk in her mind and she dared not open her eyes for risk of losing the connection.

Gradually, sounds of footsteps and distant voices and activity replaced the silence. Still, she kept her eyes shut. Then the pull stopped while the sounds became more insistent.

"So you've decided not to abandon us after all."

Becky opened her eyes.

To find herself in another world.

///

Miea had nearly stopped expecting Becky to arrive, the excitement and optimism of the beginning of the week replaced, methodically, by the diplomatic squabble with the Thorns, labor unrest within the Carpenters' Guild, and even discord on her own staff over the replacement of Sorbus's second assistant. Looming over all of it was the encroachment of the blight, claiming more vegetation daily. Thuja's team was not the least bit closer to discovering a cause or a solution. How foolish did the confidence she expressed a week ago seem to him now?

Miea had finished the day's appointments, and her secretary had just left her office. Remarkably, she didn't need to be anywhere this evening, a quirk of her schedule caused by the illness of a visiting dignitary. Miea wasn't exactly happy that a viral infection had afflicted the mayor of Cosmas, but she was relieved for the opportunity to take dinner in her chambers and then perhaps go to bed early. Rest would be good for her, if she could find some.

She had one last document to review. As she read, she felt the air in the room shift, as though someone had walked into her office unannounced. She looked up to find Becky sitting on her couch, eyes closed, and face rapt in concentration.

"So you've decided not to abandon us after all," Miea said jovially.

Becky opened her eyes and scanned the room dazedly. She looked at Miea and smiled broadly. "I did it."

"It seems that you did."

"It's gotta be the bed. Wow, this gets more bizarre all the time."

Miea had no idea what Becky was talking about. Regardless, the sight of the girl caused Miea's heart to lift. "It's good to see you again, Becky."

Becky had not stopped smiling. "It's great to see you as well. Is this really Tamarisk?"

"You're really here."

"Unbelievable. So all of it *is* real."

Miea walked over to Becky and touched her on the shoulder. "All of it. Would you like me to show you around?"

"Yeah, I'd love that."

At that moment, Sorbus stepped into the doorway. "Your Majesty, if you don't need anything more from me tonight, I'll be leaving."

"Have a good evening, Sorbus. By the way, before you go, I'd like to introduce you to a friend of mine. This is Becky."

Sorbus bowed slightly toward Becky and said, "It is a pleasure to meet you, miss." Miea could tell from Sorbus's expression that the girl's presence confused him; he probably wondered who she was and how she could have gotten into this part of the palace without his knowledge. Miea appreciated his concern, especially after the little episode with the vice chancellor's son. She would tell him about Becky tomorrow and hope that Sorbus would believe her. She didn't want to have the conversation now, though. Right now, she wanted to take her special guest on a little tour.

///

There was so much here that was just as Becky had imagined

it. And so much more that was beyond imagining. If someone had told her a couple of weeks ago that she would be strolling through a fantasy land with a princess—sorry, queen—she made up when she was a little girl, Becky would have smirked and said she was a bit old to believe in magic. But doing it was totally different from pretending to do it, and if this kind of thing didn't amaze you, you were in bad shape.

An intricately laid mosaic of multihued polished wooden tiles lined the corridors from floor to ceiling. Becky remembered the wood came from a tree called a plumas. The idea for it came when she misunderstood a project her father had been working on. Back then, she thought he could do anything with the trees he genetically engineered and she thought it would be fun if he made one that came in rainbow colors. She remembered being a little disappointed that he couldn't do anything that dramatic, but if he wasn't able to do it in real life, she could still do it here.

The people Becky and Miea passed along the way bowed to the queen and offered Becky puzzled looks. They couldn't possibly know who she was, could they? Maybe they looked at her strangely because of the way she was dressed, though she really wasn't dressed all that differently from them. In the early years of the Tamarisk stories, Becky dressed the characters in ornate clothing, very medieval, reminiscent of the Renaissance fairs she'd gone to every summer with her parents. In the year before she stopped creating these stories with her father, she changed her mind, deciding that Tamarisk would be a much cooler, much more contemporary place if everyone dressed in brightly colored nylon outfits, something like the warm-ups the UConn women's basketball team wore. Even Miea was dressed casually now, though the queen got to wear a special iridescent weave that was only made by one artisan in the territory of Odoric. Anyway, in jeans and an Abercrombie T-shirt (hadn't she taken this stuff off before she went to bed?), Becky didn't think she looked out of place here, even if it was obvious that people saw her as an outsider.

They made a left turn and went through a doorway outside.

Becky received an immediate sensory barrage. The colors were almost physically overwhelming. Of course, there was blue everywhere—Becky thought having blue leaves in Tamarisk rather than green was a fun twist—but so many other colors were totally new to her. Was this what aquamaroon looked like? Could that lemon-tangerine-melon bloom be the color she named juce? And what would you call the color of the flower over to the right, the one that seemed at once dark green, jet-black, and midnight blue?

As dazzling as the colors were, though, the sounds were even more amazing. Becky heard the deep bass rumbling of some animal nearby—maybe a mariton or a morongo. The rustling of the leaves in the wind had a percussive quality to it, almost like the playing of several musical triangles at the same time. Birds trilled in very deliberate patterns while some pounded with their beaks in a complex rhythm. There was shuffling, rustling, chirping, squeaking, and staccato notes, all coming from places she couldn't identify. And all of it seemed to be in sync and in tune. The result was something that seemed nearly symphonic, as though nature in Tamarisk performed one huge, endless concert. She never would have thought of this. Sure, she and her father came up with "voices" for the animals they created, basing many of them on musical instruments. But they never thought about tuning them together. Only one sound seemed to be off, something she could just barely hear in the distance. It was flat and sad. Was this something that sounded right to the citizens of Tamarisk? Did they even realize what their world sounded like?

Then there was the smell. Raspberries and chocolate. Two of her favorite smells in the world. The scent wasn't ultradistinct, but it was definitely there, just as she designed it. Becky wondered if an alien visitor—wow, she was actually an alien in this world—would have a similar explosion of the senses upon arriving in Moorewood. What would her hometown smell like or sound like to someone who'd never been there—or anywhere on Earth—before?

Without realizing it, Becky had stopped walking, feeling

more than a little bit dazzled. How many new things could she absorb at once?

"Is everything all right?" Miea said, drawing Becky out of it.

"Everything is very all right. There's just so much to take in."

"I suppose you'll need to come back often, then, to make sure you get every bit of it."

Becky connected with Miea's smiling eyes. "Yes, I guess I will need to do that."

They continued through the garden and walked to the edge, which overlooked a large glade that served as an entrance to a forest on one side and a long hill on the other. At the end of the hill was a town. Tamarisk City. While Becky had been very particular about the naming of everything here, she kept the name of the heart of Tamarisk simple in honor of New York City. They were very different places—Tamarisk City was busy but small—but they were both the center of their "kingdoms."

Becky watched a furred creature, one she couldn't place, hop three times and then take flight. It joined other birds in the Tamariskian sky, including something that looked like one of the huge passenger gulls she'd named waccasassa. There was wildlife everywhere out here, trudging along on cloven hooves, springing forward on long, elastic legs, rolling and tumbling to get to its destination. She was certain she could be entertained for hours simply watching this scene play out.

Becky heard Miea take a few steps away from her and she looked in her direction. The queen moved near a dense bush and extended her arm. Becky saw what appeared to be a feathered snout poke out from the bush to sniff the queen's arm. Then it pulled back and Becky heard scurrying from inside the bush. A moment later, the snout was back, followed by the elongated body of a hoffler, the feathered lizard Dad had invented years ago. The hoffler walked onto Miea's arm and then up her shoulder, nuzzling her neck.

"A friend of yours?" Becky said.

Miea laughed. "I'm not sure I've ever met this particular

hoffler before, but they're all very affectionate once they realize you aren't a mohonk intent on making a meal out of them."

Becky walked up to the hoffler and touched its snout. The animal pulled back instinctively, but then sniffed Becky's hand and rubbed the side of its long face against it.

"Now it's a friend of yours, too," Miea said. Becky couldn't help but chuckle, petting the hoffler on the top of the head.

Eventually, they went back into the palace through another door. Miea showed Becky her main conference room with tufted walls and wispy-yet-sturdy furniture made of winema (another of her father's inventions). Then she took her to a smaller room where the most essential meetings of the palace took place. A shell-like material that reminded Becky of fish scales covered the curved walls. The furniture was carved from a black-brown-green stone known as malheur.

"This is a very serious-looking room," Becky said.

Miea looked at her gravely. "Very serious things happen in it."

"Do you use it often?"

"Much more than I would like to." Miea made that statement sound especially grave, but she didn't say anything more about it.

After this, they went to Miea's chambers. Some of the touches Becky remembered putting in the princess's room were here—the inordinately high chair crafted in foamy payette, the portrait of Miea as a baby painted in extremely rare cibola dyes, the guessing board, a game whose rules changed every time you played and revealed themselves incrementally as you made each move. So was some of the furniture she'd designated for the king's and queen's chambers (which she supposed these actually were), including the chest-of-three-dozen-drawers and the comforter stuffed with the down of the elegant seney. Beyond this were knickknacks and furnishings Becky couldn't recognize, including a large model of a tall bridge and numerous pictures of people Becky guessed were Miea's parents.

They settled in the anteroom and one of the queen's aides

knocked on the door. Miea greeted her and then turned to Becky.

"I was just about to have some dinner. Would you care to join me?"

"Just something to drink, thank you. I already had dinner tonight." It dawned on Becky that it couldn't be the same time here as it was back home if Miea was just having dinner now and it was still light out. Maybe Tamarisk was in a different time zone (did that even make sense?) or maybe time ran entirely differently here.

Miea told the aide what she wanted to eat and then sat back in the sofa across from Becky. "What did you mean before when you said, 'It's gotta be the bed'?"

Becky leaned forward in her chair. "I tried so many times to get here in the last week. I thought I wasn't concentrating enough or that I'd forgotten part of what you told me to do."

"Or that what I told you to do wasn't correct in the first place."

"No, I really didn't think that was possible. It had to be something I was doing wrong. But no matter what I did, I couldn't get here. Then an idea popped into my head. When I met you in that place, wherever that was, I was in the bed at my father's apartment. I only sleep there on Saturday nights. I thought maybe it had something to do with the bed or the apartment or, I don't know, the paint on the walls. And you know what? It worked. I don't think I did anything else differently, but this time it worked."

This seemed to make Miea happy. "I really was beginning to wonder if you'd decided against coming."

"No, no, no, no, no. Not at all. I was getting pretty frustrated, if you want to know the truth."

"I'm so glad you made it now. I felt like we were . . . only beginning when we met out in that other place."

"Me too. And, man, if I had missed out on this, I would have been missing out on a lot."

Miea glanced around the room then with an expression that

seemed slightly melancholy. The queen's aide came back then with some sort of salad for Miea. She handed Becky a cup of lukewarm scarlet liquid. Becky sniffed at it carefully and then took a sip. The taste surprised her. Though the liquid was the consistency of water, it produced a thick, almost syrupy sensation on her tongue. It danced across her taste buds with a cinnamon-y/salty/spicy flavor. Definitely nothing she'd ever tasted before—and she wasn't at all sure how she felt about it.

"Do you like the barritts?"

"Mmm, just like Mom makes at home," Becky said with a grin.

Miea smiled at her. "I guess we have a lot to learn about each other."

Becky took another sip. She could imagine enjoying this. "And about each other's worlds."

Miea took a bite of her salad. "You say you sleep in the bed at your father's on Saturdays. How often do Saturdays come?"

Becky remembered that all the days had different names in Tamarisk, though she'd decided there should still be seven in every week. "Once every seven days."

"So we'll hopefully get to visit at least that often, then."

I wish there was some other way to get here. "Definitely then, if it's okay with you. And maybe—" she hesitated, knowing how much of a challenge this was going to be "—there might be a way for me to spend more nights at my father's so I could spend more time here."

Miea put her salad down and said, "I would welcome that."

How, exactly, do you plan to pull this one off, Beck? "Then I'll definitely see what I can do. I'd love to—"

Becky felt a sudden pull, almost as if someone had grabbed her from behind. She reflexively closed her eyes and the pull continued. *So this is what dirt feels like around a vacuum cleaner.* When she opened her eyes again, she was glancing up at the ceiling of the bedroom in her father's apartment.

What happened? Where did Tamarisk go?

Becky shut her eyes and tried to darken and send herself back, but she never felt any movement at all. Eventually, she turned onto her side and stared at the window in her room. Had she short-circuited or something? Did she need to reboot? What was Miea thinking about what just happened?

The taste of barritts was still on her tongue and she longed for the opportunity to finish her cup. Another night. She would definitely get back there another night. She was sure of it.

Becky closed her eyes and revisited Tamarisk in her thoughts.

Going there once a week was definitely not going to be enough.

///

Gage watched in wonder, spirit full, imagination approaching bliss. The bridge held, joining two worlds that were separate but not separated.

Surprise rarely came to Gage, but it manifested now. This was an extraordinary use of a gift. A maximal use of a gift. A potent reminder of the vitality of possibility, of the potential of imagination to reach beyond imagining. Gage centered on this thought for several long moments and felt the embrace of a warm wave. That, too, was exceedingly rare.

This new world provided new possibilities. New ways for Gage to imagine, to gift. Gage centered on the future of this world. It was expansive, defining, parameter evolving.

It was also clouded. The story here was not a simple one. Nor was it the one any of the participants foresaw. Gage could only postulate the future, but all indications were that the story here was costly, grievous. Maybe too much so for those involved.

Yet it was a story that needed telling. There was a path here that only gained completion through this story. It was a story Gage had no power to influence. Gage could offer gifts, but the story was now in the hands of the participants.

They needed to overcome the pain. They needed to surmount the grief. They needed to embrace the significance.

They alone would decide the fate of a world of possibilities.

9

Becky was sleeping especially late this morning, missing the beginning of a luminous spring day. Chris thought about taking his coffee and newspaper to the building's courtyard, but he decided to stick around and wait for his daughter instead. He spent a little time browsing an online plant encyclopedia, finding himself especially fascinated with the "known hazards" section of the site that likened eating a raw arum lily to the sensation of hundreds of needles pricking your mouth and also told him that dogs were especially susceptible to the toxins in the Aspen onion. After this, he downloaded a couple of songs and listened to them through the computer's headphones. It was during this time that Becky tapped his shoulder to let him know she was awake.

"Something good?" she said when he took off the headphones.

"Something from the eighties."

"Ah, Dad's feeling a little nostalgic this morning."

Chris chuckled and got up from his computer desk. "Actually, I've been working backward. I started with new stuff, but then, as you slept the entire morning away I wound up in the eighties."

Becky smirked at him. "It's not that late. It's only—" she peered around toward the clock on the cable box—"wow, it's after eleven o'clock."

"Remember when we used to tell you that you had to stay in bed until seven?"

"I can't believe it's that late. What are we doing today?"

"The first thing we're doing is eating breakfast. I'm starving."

"You didn't eat breakfast?"

"I was waiting for you."

"You didn't have to do that. I'm actually not super-hungry, but I'll definitely eat something."

They went into the kitchen and Chris opened the refrigerator and freezer simultaneously. He'd been planning to make an omelet, but if Becky wasn't "super-hungry," it wasn't worth it. He looked at her over his shoulder. "Bagel?"

"Works for me."

Chris took two foil-wrapped, sliced bagels out of the freezer and threw them in the toaster. He had a tendency to buy a dozen at a time at the bagel shop even if he was only going to eat a couple fresh. They were always good for days like these when he needed to change meal plans.

"So what *are* we going to do today?" he said as he took the cream cheese from the refrigerator.

"It's really nice out?"

"It looks beautiful. I haven't been outside yet."

"Want to go for a drive?"

Chris stopped unwrapping the package of cream cheese and looked up at his daughter.

"That was sort of a joke," she said. "Though we can if you want."

"We'll put it on our list of options." Chris went back to the package and then sliced a tomato.

"Listen, I have something to tell you," Becky said. There seemed to be a catch in her voice and this drew Chris's attention. "It's about Tamarisk."

He'd waited a week for her to bring this up again. "You mean, 'Tamarisk is real'?"

Becky rolled her eyes. "I can't believe you didn't ask me about that."

"I was too busy trying to figure out what it meant. You wouldn't believe some of the stuff I came up with."

Becky leaned forward against the kitchen counter. "It means *Tamarisk is real*. What did you think I was doing, speaking in some kind of code?"

Chris hoped he didn't look as embarrassed as he felt. "No, of course, I thought you meant Tamarisk was real," he said sheepishly. "What, exactly, does that mean?"

Becky pushed off the counter and spun animatedly through the room. "I mean it's really real. It truly exists. It's not just something in our imaginations."

Chris couldn't remember the last time he'd seen his daughter acting with so much vitality in this apartment. Probably the last time Lonnie had been here. What in the world was she saying, though? "Do you think you could clarify that one for me?"

Becky walked over and put an arm around his shoulder. "Dad, Tamarisk is a real place. All of that stuff we made up—and a whole bunch of other stuff—actually exists. I know. I've been there."

Chris screwed up his face. "You've been to Tamarisk?"

"Yep."

"When?"

"Last night."

Chris contorted his face into a mask of disbelief. "Last night? I guess I'd better get locks for the windows, huh?"

Becky pushed away from him. "I didn't go through the windows. I went on some kind of super-dark bridge. It was kinda amazing, actually."

"*Kinda* amazing?"

"You're right—it was *totally* amazing. Definitely the coolest thing I've ever done."

The bagels popped out of the toaster and Chris went to get them. "Is there a punch line to this somewhere?"

Becky looked at him quizzically. "What do you mean?"

It dawned on Chris for the first time that Becky wasn't engaging him in some elaborate joke or taking some nostalgic little trip of her own. She was actually talking about going to Tamarisk. It was certainly—at least probably certainly—one of those incredibly vivid dreams that you swear happened, but she seemed to be convinced.

"You went to Tamarisk last night?"

"When was the last time you had your hearing checked?"

Chris was befuddled. How does one respond when your teenaged daughter tells you she's traveled to an imaginary world? All he could think to say was, "Was it nice?"

Becky laughed loudly. "Yeah, it was really nice. It was like being in the middle of the most incredible movie you've ever seen. Except the best part was that we made a lot of this stuff ourselves. You won't believe what the hofflers actually look like—I touched one and it crawled all the way up Miea's arm."

"Miea, the princess?"

"She's queen now, but yes. Isn't this all just un-be-lievable?"

Chris nodded slowly. "Yes. Yes it is."

Becky cocked her head to one side. "You believe me, though, right?"

This had to have been one hell of a vivid dream. Becky was touching hofflers and interacting with a fantasy princess who had become queen. On numerous occasions throughout his childhood and, if he was going to be honest, even in his adulthood, Chris had dreamed of finding himself in another world, whether it was an alien planet or some alternate universe where the laws of physics were somehow changed. It was a favorite way for him to let his mind wander. When he created Tamarisk with Becky, he even imagined going there. He had a feeling, though, that his imaginings were never as real or three-dimensional as what Becky had experienced in her sleep last night.

"Yes, of course I believe you," Chris said, not wanting to diminish the gleam in his daughter's eyes this morning. She'd come to realize soon enough that this was merely fancy. For now, they could both enjoy her giddiness.

Becky smiled at him. "I knew you would. I can't wait to go back. There are a couple of hitches, though. I think I can only go for a certain length of time. Last night, I was in the middle of a conversation with Miea when I just got yanked back here.

My first thought was that I did something to lose the connection, but now I'm thinking that I only get to be there for a little while. The other thing is that I think I can only do it from here. I'm pretty sure it has something to do with the bed. We created the stories there and must have opened up some kind of, I don't know, doorway or something."

Becky's analysis of the situation struck Chris as funny and he gave out a little chuckle.

"What?" she said.

"Nothing. It's just a remarkable thing."

Becky watched him skeptically for a moment and then brightened again. "Remarkable doesn't begin to describe it. Anyway, this transportation issue is a little bit of a hassle. I've gotta be able to get there more than once a week. There's way too much to see and do there. That's why I've decided to talk Mom into letting me sleep over here on Tuesdays as well."

This was the most startling thing Becky had said yet. "Now *that's* a fantasy."

Becky's brows creased. "Why do you say that? Mom will do let me do it if I ask her the right way."

"Have you met your mother?"

"Dad, I'll take care of this."

Chris had no idea what this thing with Tamarisk was and what was really going on in Becky's mind to cause her to revisit it now. If she could somehow convince her mother to let her stay with him an extra night a week, though, Tamarisk would be real to him, too.

///

Becky was rarely uncomfortable speaking to her mother about anything. Mom could sometimes get snippy about certain things, but she never made Becky feel like she couldn't talk to her. However, the more Becky thought about it, she realized she'd never talked to her about anything like this before.

Becky had had many conversations with her mother about

the divorce over the years. Mom was good at letting her know what happened and about letting her explain how she felt. She turned out to be a much better listener than Dad, which Becky wouldn't have guessed ahead of time. But the one thing Becky learned pretty quickly to avoid was any conversation about how much she missed her father or how she wished she had more time with him. Mom got a little harsh during those conversations, saying things about Dad that Becky didn't want to hear, even if they might be true. Within months after the divorce, Becky learned that it was best to bring up Dad's name as little as possible and never talk to her mom about how she felt about him, even if she was really angry with him. After a while, this just became second nature—which made what she wanted to talk to Mom about tonight a lot tougher than most of their conversations. Especially because she couldn't tell her the real reason why she wanted to make this change.

Meanwhile, Mom had an entirely different agenda.

"I'm so glad your father brought you home on time today," she said as soon as Dad had driven away.

"Dad always brings me home on time, doesn't he?"

Mom shut her eyes and shrugged. "That's not really the point. I'm making your great-great-grandmother's chicken potpie tonight."

Becky still felt full from the bagel she'd had at eleven thirty, but she said, "Yum" anyway. Mom was very proud of her chicken potpie.

"I know you love it, which is why I thought I'd make it. But what I really want to do is teach *you* to make it."

Becky's ears perked up. "Really? One of your time-honored recipes?" Mom had always been a really good cook and her secret was making dishes that had been passed down from the generations. She'd even gotten a few from Dad's mother while they were married, including a killer pot roast.

"You're old enough. I think you're ready."

"Cool." This was actually pretty exciting to Becky. Mom often told her stories about learning to cook the classic family recipes from Grandma, how Grandma had learned from her mother, and so on. Becky knew she'd begin her "education" someday, but she figured Mom was planning to wait until she was a little older.

They went into the kitchen and got to work. Becky hadn't forgotten what she wanted to talk to her mother about, but she knew she could set it aside for later in the evening. This was much too special to complicate with something that could turn out to be tense.

The first step was poaching the chicken. Mom pulled out a piece of cheesecloth and then showed Becky how to fill it with different herbs and tie it with string.

"Congratulations," Mom said proudly. "You've just made your first bouquet garni."

"Wow," Becky said, dangling the packet between two fingers. "What do I do with it?"

"Throw it into that pot." Mom pointed to a pot of boiling water and Becky tossed the bouquet garni into it. Then they added the cut up chicken and left it to cook while they made the pastry for the crust. Mom pulled out the flour, salt, and butter and then filled a bowl with water and ice.

"We've been making pastry this way in the family forever. My grandmother used to make a big deal about using only butter. Lots of people put Crisco or some other kind of shortening—some people used to use lard—in their pastry, but we've always made ours with butter only and it always tastes the best."

"No trans fats, either," Becky said, recalling a conversation in health class.

"Right, no trans fats. Though your great-grandmother knew nothing about those. She just thought this made a delicious crust."

Mom showed Becky how to cut the butter into the flour and how to add just enough ice water to pull the dough together. Becky had baked with her mom lots of times before—cakes and muffins and that sort of thing—but Mom had always resisted letting her get involved with pie dough, saying it was "too precise" for a kid. She felt another little thrill as her mother showed her how to test the consistency and then wrap the dough into a ball.

As the dough chilled, Mom started them on the filling. "It's all about the roux."

"What's all about the roux?"

"The taste of the dish. Too light and it tastes pasty. Too dark and it's overbearing. The color is everything."

"Got it. What's a roux?"

Mom laughed and touched her on the arm. "One of the little secrets I'm going to impart today."

It turned out that a roux had something to do with flour and butter that you stirred for a very long time over low heat until it turned tan. Becky's legs started to ache from standing over the stove so long, but she didn't complain.

"Memorize that color," Mom said, pointing to the pan. "That's the color you want."

Becky tried to do exactly that. After all, if the roux was the key to everything, knowing this color was major information. Becky did her best to lock it into her brain. She wondered what they would call this color in Tamarisk, though compared to the colors she saw last night, this one was rather ordinary, even if it was so crucial.

The roux and the chicken became ready about the same time. Was this one of the family secrets or was it just coincidence? Mom took the chicken out of the pot to cool and then added a ladle of the broth to the roux.

"Mix this in until it thickens."

Becky did and then watched as Mom added two more ladles of broth. It was fascinating how the roux absorbed each. When this was done, Mom had her lower the mixture to a simmer and told her to let it cook for a little while.

"We have some chopping and peeling to do."

Chopping the carrots and the chicken was easy. Peeling the little onions was a lot harder for Becky, though her mother tore through them without any trouble. This was obviously one of those things that you got better at over time.

"Am I doing something wrong here?"

"Nope, they're a pain in the neck. When I was your age, I maybe got three done by the time your grandmother was finished with the rest. You're ahead of the game."

Becky looked down at the counter. There were five peeled onions in front of her. *Gee, I'm nearly twice as advanced as my mother.*

They threw the carrots, chicken, onions, and fresh peas into the soupy mixture on the stove and let this cook for a few minutes while they rolled out the dough and cut three circles to put over the individual casseroles.

"Now for just one more thing," Mom said, going over to the liquor cabinet. She pulled out a bottle and held it up. "Marsala wine. My personal addition. Your grandmother would groan if she saw me do this—even though she loves my chicken potpie—but I think just a little bit gives it another dimension."

Mom walked over to the pan, stirred it a couple of times, and then added a little of the wine. She grinned sneakily as she did it, like she was breaking the law or something.

"We're ready to go. Here, taste."

Becky took the offered spoonful from her mother and smiled at the flavor. There was something familiar about it. Nothing strange there, since she'd had this dish a million times. But that wasn't it. The taste was a lot like . . . barritts. How cool was it that they had a drink in Tamarisk that tasted like mom's chicken potpie? Of course, that would explain why the drink tasted so unusual to her at first. She'd keep that in mind the next time she drank something there.

Becky put the filling into the casseroles, topped the casseroles with the pastry, and put them in the oven.

When she turned around, Mom hugged her. "The long line of great family cooks continues."

The potpie was as good as always, and Becky enjoyed knowing that she'd had a part in it. The conversation at dinner focused on the "rite of passage" that took place in the kitchen that day, though Al also did five minutes on his first taste of a new flavor of Doritos that came out that week. As he went off,

Becky focused again on the conversation she wanted to have with her mother and decided she'd put it off until bedtime. Everyone—especially Mom—was in such a good mood.

After dinner, they went to the family room to watch "The Simpsons," "King of the Hill," and "Desperate Housewives" as they did every Sunday night. Then it was time for Becky to go to bed. When her mother came to kiss her good night, Becky screwed up her courage.

"Mom, I was thinking about something."

"What is it, honey?" Mom said, sitting on the side of the bed.

"You know how much I love being here with you and Al and everything, and I really love it that you're starting to teach me the old recipes, but I was thinking maybe it might be a good idea if I spent a little more time at Dad's house."

Becky was happy just to get the words out, but one glance at her mother's expression reminded her why they'd been so tough to say in the first place. Mom's eyes narrowed and her lower lip slid under the top one. She took a few seconds to speak, and when she did, she leaned toward Becky and made close eye contact with her.

"Why do you think that, hon?" She said it gently, but Becky could hear the strain behind her voice.

"I just think it would be good. He's, you know, my dad."

"He is, Beck, and I know you love being with him. But I think things run very nicely in this household. Don't you? I mean look at what we did together today."

What did that have to do with anything? "I was just thinking that it wouldn't be that much of a big deal if I slept over there on Tuesday nights. I'm with him then anyway, so it wouldn't make that much of a difference."

"Well, there is the matter of your schoolwork."

"I'm done with most of it before Dad picks me up. And I can do schoolwork there, too. I wrote an English essay at his place yesterday."

"It would mean getting up a lot earlier to get to school on Wednesday mornings. I'm not sure that's the best idea."

"That's easy. I'll just go to bed a half hour earlier."

Mom looked at her carefully. Becky could imagine what was going through her mind.

"You know, if your father wanted more time with you, he should have asked me himself. I'm going to have to speak to him about this."

Becky sat up in bed. The last thing she wanted was for this to become another difficult thing between her mother and father. "Dad isn't behind this, Mom. It's totally my idea. I swear it. I haven't even discussed it with him."

Mom's eyes got a little tighter. "If you say so, I believe you. I'm just a little confused. Our current arrangements have worked very well for a long time now."

"I don't think he has a whole lot going on over there when I'm not around. That's why I'd like to be with him a little more. I'm really only talking about Tuesday nights."

Again, Mom studied her. Was she trying to read her mind? Could she tell that there was some other reason that Becky was pursuing this now? "You really want this?"

"I do, yes."

Mom's lips tightened. "Your father is going to think he's won some great victory over me, you know."

"I don't think you have to worry about stuff like that, Mom."

"You don't know your father the way I do."

"But you're gonna let me do it, right?"

Mom seemed a little confused, as though she really thought a little thing like Tuesday nights was going to turn the whole world upside down. "You really, really want this?"

"Really, really."

Mom shrugged. "Okay, I guess." She chuckled. "I suppose if we have more time on Tuesday nights Al can take me to fancier places for dinner. He's just going to love that."

"Works out for everyone, then, right?"

Mom got up and kissed Becky on the forehead. "I always hate letting go of you."

"I'm not going anywhere, Mom."

Mom kissed her again and hugged their heads together. "You're my heart."

"Love ya, too, Mom."

When she pulled back, Mom looked a little sad, as if something terrible had happened.

She'd be fine, though. And Dad would be really pleased. And Becky would get more time in Tamarisk. She couldn't wait for Tuesday night.

///

Miea examined three leaf cuttings from a targhee bush located in Jonrae. Laid out on the conference room table, they illustrated a gradual progression toward death.

"What you're seeing here," Dyson said, "is the effect of the disease in its three stages. The first leaf shows the dark green banding that is the earliest symptom. The middle one—the one with the blond spots—indicates a plant seized by the toxins of the disease. As you can see, there is still a great deal of blue vitality to this leaf, but at this stage, the plant is very, very sick. The third leaf, the ash-colored one, is representative of a plant in necrosis."

Though she knew this story before Dyson told it, Miea's heart still ached when she heard it. She remembered playing chase-and-hide with her friends near the stand of targhee in the palace garden when she was young. Was it possible that this very stand would soon be as ashen as the leaf on her table? If that happened, what would it say about the condition of the entire kingdom?

"How long is the cycle from the first leaf to the last?" she said, her eyes still fixed on the doomed vegetation.

"About three weeks, Your Majesty. We've seen some hardier bushes hold off longer, but most succumb in this time."

She couldn't accustom herself to hearing Dyson call her "Your Majesty." When they had been together, he'd had several pet names for her—everything from "palace jewel" to "my-a

Miea." He seemed to devise a new one every time he saw her, as though he'd spent the night thinking only of this. During their recent briefings, though, she was simply "Your Majesty." The queen and her humble servant.

"That isn't much time."

"I'm afraid the news gets worse."

Miea looked up at him and caught his gaze. Dyson's expression was grimmer than it had been when he entered, if that was possible. Of course. This wasn't just a job for him. She didn't say anything.

"The disease has begun spreading at an accelerated rate."

"As it did the last time."

Dyson lowered his eyes. "As it did the last time."

Miea felt a surge of sadness. "Something must be done."

"Sterilization is still an option, Your Majesty, though at this point we would need to sterilize a wider circumference."

"Sterilization is not an option," she said briskly.

"Aggressive treatments were in fact used during the Great Blight."

"We used fungicides and chemical therapies. We did not obliterate an entire region and sentence multiple species to extinction. I cannot authorize that. I *will not* authorize that."

"By not ordering sterilization, you might be doing exactly that."

Miea felt her face burn and nearly responded angrily. Instead, she checked herself and said, "There are other options. We must find them."

Dyson looked past her and then down at the table again. He gently touched the bluest of the leaves. "Our foremost resource is life itself."

The reference made Miea's legs liquid. She hadn't heard that phrase in years. Any residual anger she felt from Dyson's earlier accusation drained away. "Professor Liatris. How many times did he say it that semester?"

"At least three times each class." Dyson looked up at her again and held her eyes this time. There was the hint of a smile on his face. It was the closest thing to warmth Dyson had shown, and it sent her back to her school days. To her days in love with the man standing before her. Sadly, her memory quickly drew her back to their last moments together.

"How many times did he say it the day I was called away?"

The semblance of a smile retreated. "None. The class was postponed. All classes were suspended the rest of the week."

Miea never knew this. Of course the kingdom had mourned and of course the university would mourn along with everyone else. However, Miea had been so overwhelmed with grief and premature responsibility that she never envisioned how the rest of her world had dealt with the tragedy.

"I should have known that."

"You had other things to consider."

Miea couldn't explain what she was feeling. It was a mixture of sorrow, longing, and regret she couldn't identify. "I should have contacted you. I should have let you know what was going on. Not doing so was unforgivable. The shock, though . . . I can barely describe it. Then there was everything that happened afterward. I felt stolen away, as though I had been jettisoned into someone else's life."

"You don't need to explain."

"I want to try, but I don't know if I can. One moment I was a university student—and your girlfriend. The next I was queen."

Dyson's expression hardened. Had she said something wrong? "As I said, you don't need to explain."

His voice was chilly. Miea couldn't understand why. "Dyson, you have no idea," she said softly.

"I obviously couldn't possibly. Your Majesty."

What had happened between them had clearly hurt Dyson, but why was he acting this way now? She was trying to explain, yet he was rejecting her efforts.

If he wouldn't allow her to do so, she wasn't going to beg him to let her. It had been a mistake to let her guard down like this. She couldn't allow the feelings of the distant past to make her vulnerable. Not when the kingdom relied so completely on her fortitude. For a moment, looking at Dyson had transported her to another life, another time. However, both that life and that time were gone forever. As was, sadly, the love the man standing here once had for her. They had a new relationship now. A relationship built on a common need to save their land from an insidious threat. This relationship superseded anything they might have shared in simpler days. As it must.

She looked down at the leaves on the table, picking them up and handing them to Dyson. "Thank you for the update. Please inform me immediately if there are any breakthroughs. Otherwise, I'll expect your next report in two days."

"As you wish, Your Majesty."

10

Chris still found it difficult to believe that Becky was spending the night. When he'd called his daughter last night, she'd mentioned it casually, as though she'd assumed it would happen all along. He was dying to ask her what her conversation with Polly had been like, but he thought that might be pushing it. Still, Polly could not have taken this easily. If she had, it would mean that all of his assumptions about her were wrong.

After speaking with Becky, Chris had gone out to the supermarket to get the ingredients to make shepherd's pie. It was one of Becky's favorite dishes and he could do most of the preparation the night before. Chris didn't usually cook on Tuesdays for Becky because of their time constraints, but if they were going to have the entire night, a home-cooked meal was definitely better than more Chinese food.

While they waited for the shepherd's pie to bake, they snacked on baby carrots and Chris helped Becky with her geometry homework.

"You're pretty good at this," she said after he helped her use the formula to calculate the surface area of a sphere. "Mom kinda topped out at multiplying fractions, so I stopped asking."

"Some of us had to take a few more math classes than others. I should be good right through calculus. I'm not making any promises beyond that."

Chris remembered how Becky used to save certain homework until he got home so she could ask for his help. It wasn't that Polly couldn't have helped her or even, in most cases, that Becky couldn't have figured out the work herself, but she seemed to like having him there for this. Every night after dinner, she'd show him the work she'd already done and what she wanted to run past him. Often, this simply involved him sitting at her desk with her while she worked, but occasionally he needed to provide actual assistance. He prided himself on never doing his daughter's homework for her, even though it would have been so much easier sometimes, especially when concepts were new.

The thought of how they once used to do this on a nightly basis ate at Chris, but he forced himself to concentrate on the present. Somehow, for some reason, he was getting the chance to experience this again, and he wasn't going to let old wounds get in the way.

Becky closed her math book and pulled out her biology text. "How are you with this?"

"I kinda work in the sciences, babe."

"In the *earth* sciences, though, right?"

"I still took three levels of biology in college. I'm pretty sure I can handle ninth grade."

Becky opened the book and the oven chimed.

"Dinner is ready," Chris said. "You want to finish your homework first or eat?"

"Let's eat. I love that stuff."

Becky didn't eat nearly as much as he had expected her to, but she seemed to enjoy what she had. He recalled that she wasn't "super-hungry" over the weekend and the thought came to mind that maybe she was starting to pay too much attention to her weight—she was slim by any reasonable standard, but he'd read enough about teenage body image issues to know that this didn't necessarily matter. He'd pay some closer attention to this in the future and talk to Becky about it if a pattern emerged. This kind of thing was uncharted territory for him—he'd never had much to do with Becky's adolescent issues—but tonight he felt that he would be up to the task. More importantly, he felt that his input might actually receive a hearing.

After dinner, Becky dispatched the rest of the night's homework quickly, leaving them time to watch an episode of "I Love the '90s" on VH1 before Becky's bedtime. 1999, the year of *Harry Potter*, Britney Spears, Mia Hamm, and Jar Jar Binks—and also the year when Becky had a *Little Mermaid* theme to her birthday party, dressed as a pirate for Halloween, and showed her first serious interest in the Beatles. Becky had been completely different as a three-year-old than she had been before. She was conversant and had opinions and she was so much better at doing things. She had favorite games, favorite books, favorite foods, and favorite things to do outside. She started preschool that year and came home a couple of days later declaring that Lonnie Cera was her "bestest friend in the whole world" and this turned out to be true. 1999 might not have been a high water mark for popular culture, but it was an unforgettable year for Chris as a parent. Back then, he remembered Polly commenting that Becky was growing up too fast for her. However, Chris thought she was growing up at just the right speed, and all of her new developments fascinated him.

Now, on the other hand, was an entirely different story. Now, there was no question that she had grown up much too fast. There were nostalgia shows on television about the year Becky started preschool. Were the songs released in '99 considered oldies now, too? Chris shuddered internally at these thoughts. He wondered if he was going to be this reflective every Tuesday night or if he would eventually become accustomed to this new arrangement and simply incorporate it into his life.

"Time to get to bed," he said, patting his daughter on the leg as the show ended.

"Are you gonna keep the TV on?"

"For a while maybe. I'll crash in another hour or so."

Becky stood up and took a few steps toward her bathroom. "How would you feel about reading or something instead of watching TV?"

"Fine, I guess. Why?"

"I might not be able to concentrate if the TV is on."

Chris stood with her. "Concentrate?"

"I need to concentrate really hard to do the meditation exercises that get me to Tamarisk."

Chris had temporarily forgotten that this was the reason Becky wanted to stay here on Tuesdays. "I can read if that would make it easier for you."

Becky walked over and kissed him on the cheek. "Thanks, Dad. I'm gonna go brush my teeth and stuff."

Fifteen minutes later, Chris was sitting on the couch with his book, the occasional turning of pages the only discernible sound in the apartment. When he had gone to kiss Becky good night a short while earlier, she had seemed extremely excited about returning to Tamarisk tonight. Still, in all likelihood, no matter how effectively she "meditated," she wouldn't be able to summon up the dream again. How was she going to feel about this? Would she wake up tomorrow morning disappointed, maybe a little crestfallen?

When she did, would she then decide that she didn't need to spend Tuesday nights at her dad's any longer? After all, if his apartment provided no greater access to Tamarisk than her mother's house did, what use was he?

Chris looked across his book and into the still living room. He loved that it was a weeknight and his daughter was sleeping in her bed here. He just hoped this wouldn't be the only time.

///

Becky opened her eyes when she heard the bustle around her. She was once again in Miea's chambers, but in spite of the sounds of activity, there was no one in sight.

It was a relief to be here again. The way she had been pulled back to her bed last time had her a little worried that something had gone wrong and that she was going to be cut off from Tamarisk completely. The meditation tools worked without a hitch tonight, though. This meant that now that her mother had okayed her staying with Dad two nights a week, she would get to make twice as many trips here.

Becky wondered where Miea was. She hadn't given much thought ahead of time to where she would show up in Tamarisk, but she kind of figured she'd appear in the middle of the action. She headed out of the chambers and into the hallway, where she ran into the man Miea had introduced her to the last time she was here. His name was Sorbus; Becky had created him as Miea's aide when she gave the princess some palace responsibility in the later Tamarisk stories. She wanted to call him Sheldon, though, because he looked a lot like Lonnie's grandfather, which was a little odd considering the outfit he was wearing.

"Hello again," he said cordially.

"Hi . . . I bet you're wondering what I'm doing here."

The man smiled. "Actually, Her Majesty told me a great deal about you after your last visit. She told me you might return to us again."

"Hopefully a lot in the future. That is, if Her Majesty doesn't mind."

"I think the queen would be very pleased by that."

Becky grinned and looked back toward Miea's chambers. "I suppose she's busy at the moment, huh?"

Sorbus nodded down the hallway. "She's having her weekly open forum with her subjects."

"The kingdom congress."

Sorbus smiled again. "Yes, of course you would know what that was." He seemed like a nice guy and Becky could tell from the way he talked that he cared a lot for Miea. "I'm sure Her Majesty would be happy to have you join her at the congress."

"Really? That would be great."

Sorbus gestured with his right hand. "Let me show you the way."

Becky and Sorbus walked through the same hallway Becky had walked with Miea three days ago. Instead of turning toward the garden, though, they headed in the other direction. As they got closer, Becky heard the sounds of a large crowd murmuring and shuffling about. Sorbus took Becky through a closed door and suddenly Becky was "backstage" at the palace great room. Members of the palace staff moved briskly through the space, looking very determined to get things done. Though this was like the most incredible vacation imaginable for Becky, she realized lots of people here had serious jobs to do.

Sorbus led Becky to the edge of the stage, which wasn't a stage at all but a huge, multitiered throne. Miea sat upon one ornately decorated chair while on the other sat two sashes, one of shimmering citrugrape and the other a shade of bronze that was bolder and more vivid than any she had seen before. Sorbus motioned for Becky to sit in a chair at the periphery of the throne, and when she did so, Miea turned and nodded to her with a sparkle in her eye before returning her attention to the subject in front of her.

Now seated, Becky had the opportunity to take in the magnificence of the great room. The ceiling was easily five stories high, and from the rafters bobbed glistening ornamental bubbles that popped when they hit the top, releasing a spray of smaller and more intensely colored bubbles that floated downward about a third of the way before beginning their ascent, growing in size, and repeating the pattern all over again. The walls in the hexagonal room were formed from a moldable crystal known as okanogan, and the hundreds of chairs that filled the floor were made from the same wispy winema she had seen the other day in the conference room. Between the lightness of the construction and the bubbles drifting in the air, it almost felt like the whole place was floating.

It was certainly bursting with life. Every chair held people dressed in various shades of the outfits she'd seen the other day, though several of them had taken to accessorizing them in surprising ways—with beads, twigs, a liquid-y/plastic-y substance that Becky didn't know, and with various combinations of the three. More than humans filled the room, though. In the early days of Tamarisk stories, Becky and her father had created dozens of species to inhabit their world and gave all of them speaking roles. As she got older, Becky felt that talking animals—even if they were animals of her own invention—were too childish for her Tamarisk. She took away their voices, but she left several with their intelligence and even, for some, very sophisticated forms of communication. These species inhabited the great room as well. The angular, hairy, watchful carrizo. The tiny, flitting bird known as the norbeck, which had four beaks and just as many eyes. The regal, graceful katmai, capable of remarkable dexterity from its six huge paws.

Becky was so caught up in her admiration of the wonders around this room that she didn't notice right away that the queen had concluded her business with the subject before her and had moved on to the next. A burly, weathered-looking man with a soft face bowed to her. He had a collection of young teenagers behind him.

"Your Majesty," he said in a gravelly voice, "this group of youngsters is without question the finest I have ever coached. I've been involved with youth speedcatch for nearly thirty years and, as you know, our little town of Ribault hardly has the resources to compete with the larger towns for the kingdom championship. But this year we did it—and against a powerful team from Pinzon—because of the dedication of these kids. It is a pleasure to present them to you."

The coach turned to face his team and the room broke into applause. Miea stood and, smiling broadly, opened her arms to welcome the team onto the throne. The kids—there must have been twenty of them—ran up and surrounded her while the coach followed behind slowly. An aide entered from the side carrying miniature versions of the bubble-things—Becky didn't know what to call them because she hadn't invented them—on a tray. The queen congratulated members of the team individually, attaching a bubble to each of their chests. When she did so, the bubbles started popping and reforming just the way they did on the ceiling. It was all very festive. When she reached the coach, Miea awarded him a larger bubble, which set off a more dramatic display that seemed to take him by surprise. The audience roared again.

"You probably don't know this," Miea said when she was finished, "but I had something of a junior speedcatch career myself. I'm afraid I wasn't much help to the palace team, though. You've done the kingdom proud with your accomplishments and the victory of tiny Ribault will not be soon forgotten."

Miea bowed toward the team, who bowed in return. The audience applauded loudly a third time and Becky found herself clapping as well. She wished she'd been around to see the tournament. Speedcatch, a game that involved running, throwing, and leaping while the opposition attempted to prevent you from doing the same, was a sport she'd created with her dad over the course of several weeks one spring. They'd even played a simplified version of it with some of the neighborhood kids a few times. Perhaps she'd get the opportunity to watch the professionals play it during some later visit.

The team made its way down from the throne and Becky waited for another person to step forward. When none did, Becky looked over at Miea, who had her eyes fixed skyward toward the back of the great room. Becky focused her attention in that direction, but couldn't see anything. At last, she noticed a little norbeck flying in spirals toward the throne. The norbeck circled the throne twice, flew up toward the ceiling, and then landed on an unoccupied chair in the front row, covering its head with its wings.

Miea, sitting again, grinned. "Your entrances are always quite dramatic, Ostrya."

An aide placed a wooden board on the chair and Ostrya landed upon it. It pecked the board with one beak, and then quickly turned its body to give two quick pecks with another beak.

"That's very kind of you," Miea said. Becky remembered that as a young princess Miea became fluent in the various communication methods of the nonhuman species in Tamarisk. She could obviously "talk" to Ostrya.

The norbeck pecked actively for the next several seconds, using all four of its beaks. Several in the audience murmured appreciatively.

"That's very impressive, Ostrya. I had no idea the symphony was that close to completion."

The norbeck pecked again, finishing this comment with a brisk rub of its right wing over its head.

"I'm sure you have been working on it nonstop," Miea said.

The creature pecked once, extended its left talon, and tilted its head.

"Yes, I would love to hear a portion. I'm sure everyone here would." Miea looked up at the crowd and the group applauded enthusiastically.

The norbeck pecked four times quickly and the room fell silent. From the ceiling behind Miea came a trilling chord. Then another came from the far end of the great room. Then another above Becky. Ostrya rose into the air and emitted three bold chords, using all four of its beaks to sound different notes in a voice that seemed like a combination of a flute and French horn. With this, dozens of norbecks appeared in the rafters, adding their voices to the symphony. The music was as much about motion as it was about sound, with notes and wild combinations of notes circling and diving around the room. At one point, a norbeck flitted a couple of feet in front of Becky's head to offer a series of quick arpeggios before flying upward again. Then, all at once, the creatures sounded in unison, offering four majestic chords (Becky thought she recognized them as major sevenths) before falling silent.

For a moment, there was no sound in the room. Then Miea stood and applauded and everyone—Becky included—stood and cheered along.

"That was magnificent, Ostrya," the queen said. "If the rest of the symphony resembles this in any way, the kingdom will soon have a new treasure."

Ostrya offered three quick pecks, once again covered its head with its wing, and then flew off briskly.

Becky felt emotionally charged by the musical experience. She loved music and had gone to more than her share of concerts, starting when she was very young, but the brief performance by the norbecks touched her in unfamiliar ways. It was almost as if she were feeling a new emotion, something that bordered on joy and confusion. It left her feeling physically heightened, the way she did after running or playing tennis. It took her a few moments to catch her breath.

As the room settled, a woman walked forward. She carried with her two husks of something that looked like corn.

"Your Majesty, my family has farmed the same land in Custis for five generations and it has never needed assistance from the palace before," the woman said solemnly. "But I'm afraid our latest hardship is more than we can bear."

Miea sat forward in her chair. "What has happened?"

"I've brought these to show you, Your Majesty." The woman peeled back one portion of the husk and the entire thing collapsed. Nothing was inside other than a few gray specks that fell to the floor. The woman peeled the second husk and the same thing happened.

Miea's expression shifted dramatically. She almost seemed frightened. "You say this happened in Custis?"

"Yes, Your Majesty."

"The farmland closest to the palace." Miea looked off to the backstage area Becky had entered earlier, though Becky couldn't tell what or who she was looking for. "Do you have any idea how this happened?" Becky saw that Miea was genuinely worried. Her reaction seemed a little extreme. There had to be times when crops went bad, right?

"I'm afraid I do, Your Majesty."

Miea seemed surprised by this response. "You do?"

"It's those disgusting vilases, Your Majesty. They get inside of our crops and eat everything, leaving only the husk. They are the most evil pestilence in the kingdom."

That sounded pretty awful to Becky, but the news seemed to relax Miea. She sat back and said, "I can understand your anger, but the vilas is not an 'evil pestilence.' This is how it lives."

"It lives by destroying my family's livelihood," the woman said bitterly before catching herself and adding, "Your Majesty."

Miea called upon one of her aides. "Please establish a subsidy for this woman and her family for the rest of the growing season. Also arrange for a team to go to her fields to extricate and redistribute the vilases." She turned back to the woman. "They cause no problem when they are sparse. In fact, they can be quite beneficial. Unfortunately, they occasionally concentrate in one location . . . and you have seen the results."

"Thank you for your help and generosity, Your Majesty." The woman bowed and walked away.

Miea looked to the side of the stage, nodded, and stood. "Today's congress is ended. I thank you all for coming and for sharing your thoughts, your contributions, and your concerns. Before we conclude, I would like to make an introduction."

Miea looked over at Becky and gestured for her to stand. "Becky Astor has come to visit us from . . . a distant land. I ask you all to welcome her. She is an important friend of mine and she will be traveling throughout the kingdom. Please look upon her as a valued member of the palace."

The crowd applauded. Becky wasn't sure what to do, so she offered a little wave, which immediately made her feel silly. She pulled her hand back to her side and watched as Miea approached her.

"Welcome back," Miea said. "I have a little time before my next meeting. Come join me."

///

Becky settled onto the sofa while Miea asked Sorbus to bring them some refreshments. Miea rolled her neck and arched her shoulders. She seemed tight and uncomfortable. Becky imagined it wasn't the easiest thing in the world to be the center of a large crowd for a long period—and Miea did one of these every week. Becky had always liked public speaking, but this was way beyond that. She wondered how well she would hold up under the same circumstances.

"That was a total treat," Becky said when Miea came to sit with her.

"It was a good congress today. I enjoy these sessions. They make me feel connected, and that makes me feel like I'm doing something."

"Aren't you doing something all the time?"

"In a manner of speaking. There are some portions of this role, though, where one considers it an accomplishment if you manage not to lose ground. Here I feel like we always move forward a little. I sometimes think that Tamarisk would be a much better place if I could just do a congress every day."

Becky nodded, though she wasn't entirely sure she understood what Miea was saying. Everything seemed to run so well here. "Well, I found the whole thing amazing."

Miea smiled. "I'm glad. That little piece of the norbeck symphony was quite impressive, wasn't it?"

Becky's eyes widened. "I'll say. I listen to a lot of music and I can definitely tell you I've never heard anything like that before."

"Ostrya is a remarkable composer. He deserves every accolade he receives. There isn't a human composer in the kingdom that can approach his inventiveness."

Sorbus came in and placed a carved stone tray on the table near them. He handed Miea a wooden cup, which she held up to her face in both hands, allowing steam and tiny bubbles to brush her skin. He then handed Becky a crystal glass. The smell brought an instant memory of her last time in Tamarisk.

"I ordered you more barritts," Miea said. "You seemed to like it."

Becky took a sip. The taste wasn't as surprising this time, of course, and she found she enjoyed it more. "I did. Though I definitely want to try everything."

Miea tipped her cup in Becky's direction. "Would you like some argo?"

"This is good for now, thanks." Becky took another sip. Yes, there were definitely flavors from the bouquet garni in there. It was exciting to think of how many discoveries—and rediscoveries—waited for her in Tamarisk. She wanted to see everything she'd imagined come to life. And just as importantly, she wanted to see new things, to feel that she was a part of this place.

"So what do you do when you aren't on queen duty?"

Miea chuckled softly. "I think I'm always on queen duty."

"But you must get time off. Even the President of the United States—that's the leader of the country I come from—gets to go to Camp David once in a while."

Miea nodded. "I'm afraid there's no camp for me. My last retreat was before my parents died. Since then, I haven't had much time off other than sleep and the rare evening to myself."

"That must be exhausting."

Miea took a deep breath and rolled her neck again. "You get used to it."

Becky couldn't imagine what it would be like to go four years without a single day off. She thought it was tough when she had a lot of homework on the weekends and couldn't go out until night. "Was it like this for your parents as well? Didn't they ever have time to spend alone with you while you were growing up?"

"It was different for them. They had each other and they each had areas of responsibility. I have more aides than I can count, but I ultimately have to make every decision. I've never felt comfortable just getting away from everything."

Becky put down her glass of barritts and pointed in Miea's direction. "It seems there's only one thing for you to do, then."

Miea tilted her head. "And what is that?"

"You need to find yourself a king."

Miea laughed loudly. It was the most girlish thing Becky had seen her do. In Becky's imagination, the Miea of her Tamarisk stories was an extremely confident teenager who still acted like a teenager. It was nice to see that she had some of this in her in real life.

"A king?" Miea said with astonishment in her voice. "As in a husband? Where am I supposed to get one of those?"

"Are you kidding? Did you look around the great room today? There were some gorgeous men out there."

Miea gestured with both palms forward. "Yes, there were. Believe me, I noticed. There always are." Her smile dimmed. "This kind of thing is very complicated for me, though. There's so much for me to do. I don't know how I'd ever begin a romance."

Becky felt sorry for Miea. It seemed like she had to give up an awful lot because she was queen. This wasn't what Becky had imagined for her. "So you've never been in love?"

Miea's eyes clouded over. "I didn't say that." The queen looked down into her cup and then held it to her cheek.

"Can you tell me about him?"

Miea looked at Becky with an expression that confused her.

"Am I asking too many questions?" Becky said quickly.

Miea watched her cup of argo again and said, "No, not at all. It's been a long time since anyone has asked me questions like these."

"Then tell me about him."

The queen smiled softly. "He was wonderful. We were wonderful together. And then events conspired."

She said this with so much sadness in her voice. Becky had talked to a lot of people about their relationships—friends and her mother, mostly—but she had never seen someone look as regretful when they mentioned an ex-boyfriend. Lonnie seemed to break up with a different guy every other week and sometimes she got very emotional about the splits, but when she did, it was like a baby crying after falling down. You always knew she'd forget about it in a few minutes. Becky got the impression that Miea was never going to forget about losing this love.

"Do you know what happened to him?"

"I'm queen," Miea said with a joyless laugh. "I know everything."

Talking about boys with Lonnie definitely didn't feel this way. Becky found this fascinating even as her heart went out to Miea. "Maybe you can hook up with him again."

Miea's face stiffened. "That's not possible."

"It could be."

At that moment, Sorbus returned. Becky hoped he was just coming to take the tray away, but he said, "Your Majesty, I apologize for interrupting, but Minister Thuja is here to see you."

Miea's expression darkened and she put down her cup. "Thuja himself?"

"Yes, Your Majesty. He says he has a report he wants to deliver personally."

Miea took a moment to gather herself and then she nodded. "Tell him I'll be right there." She turned to Becky. "I'm sorry, but I'm going to have to find out why Minister Thuja is here."

Becky had no idea what this was about, but anyone could have guessed that it wasn't good. "Of course. Should I just leave?" Becky realized she had no idea how to get back to her room on her own.

"Stay here as long as you like. Sorbus can have someone show you around if you're interested. I won't be back until late this evening. My leisure time is officially over for the day."

"I appreciate your spending it with me."

Miea smiled kindly and reached out a hand. Becky held it for a moment.

"I'm very glad I could," Miea said. "It was a true pleasure." The queen nodded toward the door. "I'm afraid I can't keep the minister waiting."

With that, she turned and left. It was fascinating to see how quickly Miea had jumped when Sorbus told her the minister was here. There had to be some kind of problem. Becky couldn't recall a Minister Thuja, so she didn't know what he was minister of.

She sipped the remainder of her drink and stood to go find Sorbus. She wouldn't mind spending some more time in the garden, or maybe even going out to see Tamarisk City. But as she took her first step, she felt herself being pulled in the other direction.

Almost instantly, she was back in her room. Feeling jolted, she sat up quickly, almost like waking from a shocking dream. Doing so made the room lurch and the dizziness caused her to lie back down again. Her head continued to spin.

That was the last thing she remembered doing that night.

11

Becky's Instant Messenger chimed again and she glanced over at her computer. monsterjam18? Who was that? She tried to think of who she knew with that screen name and her brain flashed through dozens and dozens of friends and associates. Finally, it landed on a guy she met a few months ago at Kayla and Matt's. Cute. Sophomore. Extremely tall. He seemed nice enough and they'd IM'd a couple of times, but something just didn't feel right about him. Maybe it was the screen name. monsterjam18. Not exactly her type.

For easily the thirtieth time today, Becky thought back on her conversation last night with Miea. What would the queen think of Mr. Monster Jam? Probably that he wasn't king material. She would definitely be right about that. But what about the guy Miea was once in love with? Becky really wished she could have talked to her about that longer. Miea seemed so sad when she brought up her old boyfriend. There was definitely some excess baggage there, some stuff she needed to take care of. Maybe when Becky got to know her a little better Miea would open up more. Maybe Becky could even help her deal with it. She was great at helping Lonnie through her various boy-related crises, though she guessed that Miea's was just a tiny bit more serious than anything Lonnie had gone through so far.

Becky looked back down at her history book. She was having a tough time concentrating tonight. She was feeling a little queasy, which was almost definitely because of the kielbasa Al made for dinner tonight. He could make toast taste bad, which was pretty funny, since he liked to eat so much. She really should have offered to cook since Mom wasn't going to be around. Or suggested they go out for pizza or something. Or maybe even suggested that she spend the night at her dad's instead. Al was great, but Dad was her father; didn't it make more sense for her to be with him when her mother wasn't around? Then she could have gone to Tamarisk and maybe had another chance to have a good talk with Miea.

All day, Becky wished she could have another taste of barritts, feel the softness of payette, or hear a symphony played by dozens of norbecks. She was missing Tamarisk terribly today, more than she had before. The more time she spent in the place, the more time she wanted to spend there. It made her senses tingle. It made her want to explore and discover. If only she could go there whenever she wanted. Maybe dash off for a quick visit during homeroom. Her body stayed here anyway; it would just seem like she was preoccupied.

She shook her head briskly. *Time to return to planet Earth, Beck.* She needed to focus on her homework, get her head into the industrial revolution. This Saturday night, when she next slept at her dad's, she might have the opportunity to run through the fields of Jonrae or mill through the shopping arcades of Pinzon. What was definite, though, was that she was going to have a history test fourth period tomorrow. While that wasn't anywhere near as appealing as the kingdom congress, she needed to give it all of her attention. She logged out of Instant Messenger—monsterjam18 would be devastated for all of four minutes—and started studying again.

About an hour later, her mother knocked on the door and stuck her head in.

"Hey, hon."

"Hey, Mom," Becky said, swiveling in her chair. Mom came in and kissed her on the forehead. "Did you have a good dinner?"

"The girls are great. It's always good to see them. We caught up on all the latest. Denise's daughter is dating a biker and

Denise smelled alcohol on her breath the other night." Mom leaned over and kissed Becky again. "You should be glad I go to these dinners every now and then. It reminds me how lucky I am."

Becky grinned. "Gee, Mom, you'd think you wouldn't need to be reminded."

"I don't, really. But this reminder comes with margaritas as a bonus. Everything okay tonight?"

"Yeah, everything was great. I've been up here studying."

"Was Al's dinner edible?"

"It was right up there with his best." Becky grinned to make sure her mother knew what she was saying.

Mom hugged her around the shoulders. "I really would leave something for the two of you when I go out, but he got so offended the first time I did that. He really thinks he can cook. Sorry, Beck, but I don't want to break his heart."

Becky waved a hand. "No big deal. I'm sure I'll survive. There was plenty of Pepcid in the medicine cabinet."

Mom sat on the edge of Becky's bed, which meant she intended to stay for a while. "So I haven't really seen you since yesterday afternoon. I'll need to adjust to this new Tuesday/Wednesday schedule. How were things with your father last night?"

"They were really good."

"He got you to bed at a reasonable hour?"

Becky rolled her eyes. "Yes."

"And he got you to school on time?"

"Mom, Dad's a grown-up, too."

Mom seemed for a second like she wanted to debate the point, but then she simply said, "I know he is. But your routine is important. He's not used to doing this, and I don't want you getting in trouble because your father can't get himself out of the house."

"Actually, he had to wait for me and I got to school ten minutes early."

"And he just dropped you off there? Did you have to stand

around outside?"

Becky laughed. "He waited with me, Mom. This is going to be fine."

Mom sighed. "I'm sure it will be. Did you sleep okay? You don't always sleep well there."

"I slept great. I can't remember the last time I woke up feeling so good."

That probably wasn't the best thing to say.

"What's that's supposed to mean?"

"It doesn't mean anything. I just slept really well and I saw some great things and I had a really interesting talk with Miea and—" As soon as the words were out of Becky's mouth, she couldn't believe she'd said them.

"Maya? Who's Maya? Does your father have a new girlfriend? If he does, it would have been nice to let me know that he was going to be introducing her to you."

Mom hadn't told Dad about Al until they'd been together for months, but that wasn't the point. "Dad doesn't have a new girlfriend."

"Then who is Maya?"

"It's nothing."

Mom looked at her suspiciously for a moment and then looked off, as if she were trying to remember something. "Miea was the name of the princess in that Tamarisk thing you used to do with your father, wasn't it?

Becky was surprised her mother even remembered that. "Yes, it is."

Mom leaned closer. She seemed to get taller when she did. "He hasn't convinced you to do that again, has he?"

Becky pulled back. "Dad's not involved with this. Except that I need the bed in my room there."

Mom screwed her face up. "What?"

You always tell me you don't want us to have secrets between us, Mom, Becky thought, plunging forward because she couldn't think of anything else to do. "You are not going to believe this," she said ultraenthusiastically. "I've figured out a way to *go* to

Tamarisk."

Mom leaned back. "Really."

"Really. I can only do it from the bed in Dad's apartment, though. That's one of the reasons I wanted the extra night there."

"So you could travel to Tamarisk."

Becky smiled broadly. "Isn't that amazing?"

"That's not exactly the word I would have used. Hon, you do realize that Tamarisk is a make-believe place that you made up when you were a little kid, right?"

"Yeah, I thought the same thing. But it's real."

Mom stood up and headed toward the door, patting Becky on the shoulder as she passed. "Either I've had too many margaritas or your father slipped something into your dessert last night. One of us is definitely not thinking clearly."

She stopped at the doorway, looked at Becky, and shook her head disapprovingly. Then she turned and went downstairs.

Becky wanted to smash her head against the wall. She couldn't believe she'd done something as stupid as simply blurting out Miea's name. Then she was dumb enough to compound it by telling her mother she traveled to Tamarisk. Almost anything would have been better, but she couldn't think of anything while they were talking.

Still, Mom didn't have to look at her like she was a mental patient when she said it. Yes, she could understand how it might sound a little weird—okay, a lot weird—but Becky wasn't the kind of person who said weird things on a daily basis. Shouldn't she get a little credit? And couldn't her mother consider the possibility—even for a second—that Tamarisk might just be real?

At least Dad believed her. He didn't think she was out of her mind. Her mom never understood stuff like Tamarisk.

Maybe Mom really would chalk the whole thing up to the margaritas. Maybe she'd even think she imagined the whole conversation. Fat chance. She was probably downstairs right now telling Al how her daughter had completely lost her mind.

Note to self: remember to use brains in the future. Becky would make sure not to mention Tamarisk to Mom again. Maybe this would just go away. After all, there was at least a tiny chance Mom would forget about the whole thing.

///

Chris's mind kept drifting back to geometry. Helping Becky with her homework last night had revitalized a long-dormant part of his brain. If he could again calculate the surface area of a sphere, could he also remember how to calculate a prism and a trapezoid? What about volumes and perimeters? He wondered what kind of math homework Becky had tonight. Had she needed his help? She didn't mention it when they spoke on the phone, but he should have let her know his consultation line was open twenty-four hours a day just in case.

Chris put down the book he was reading, the one he'd started last night when Becky asked him to be quiet so she could "concentrate." The novel began promisingly, but the last several chapters had failed to hold his attention. There was a time in Chris's life when he'd felt the need to finish every book he started, even if he wasn't enjoying it. He didn't feel that way any longer. If this one didn't kick in again after another chapter, he was shelving it.

There was no sound in the apartment. Last night at this time, Becky and he were remembering the scariest scenes from *The Sixth Sense* as they watched "I Love the '90s." It capped the best weeknight he'd had in a while. It was odd that something as average as watching TV with your daughter on a Tuesday could be considered a highlight, but it was the very averageness of it that made it so. He had been missing this; that much he had known already. He just didn't realize how much he'd missed it until he had a taste of it again.

Chris heard the metaphorical clock ticking ever louder. To him, parenting was a bell curve of milestones. When your child is born, each of her accomplishments seem to supersede the one before, and each makes you feel increasingly connected to her. Simple biological need gives way to interaction, which gives way to play, which gives way to meaningful conversation, and so on. The relationship deepens with each stage. At some point, though, you reach the top of the curve. Your child continues to grow, to become a fuller and more substantial human being, but your association with these events becomes more distant. She has meaningful conversations with her friends instead of you. She learns critical life lessons away from the house. She interacts more fully with the world and considerably less with you. She looks to her future and sees a place where you are something just slightly more elevated than a number on her speed dial. Of course, if you are divorced from her mother and only see her on Tuesdays and weekends, you descend the downside of the curve even faster.

The day Becky started high school, Chris started thinking about her going to college. Now, her freshman year was nearly finished. When it was, she would only have three years remaining before she left for good. She'd be home for the holidays and summers, but these would be nothing more than extended visits. Then, after she graduated college, who knew where she would wind up and how often he would see her?

There should be more of a warning signal that you're approaching the top of the curve and that you're about to head down, Chris thought. *If I'd known how close I was, I would have done something—I don't know what—to mark the occasion.*

He couldn't pinpoint when he'd hit the top of the curve with Becky, though he had a good idea. Was it the day he left the house? Was it a few months before or after? All he knew was that he was well along the slide down. When he reached the bottom, she would be gone. He couldn't imagine that he'd be any more prepared for this event three years from now than he was today.

Still, there was last night. Maybe all Tuesdays would be like that in the future. Maybe it was something to build on. Maybe life with your child wasn't a bell curve, but a waveform instead. Maybe you got to go back up again.

He went to the kitchen to rinse the night's dishes and put

them into the dishwasher, something he hadn't been in the mood to do when he'd finished dinner. He'd nearly had a bagel tonight, but forced himself to prepare a meal instead. It was a challenge because he was alone, but he felt compelled to meet it, in the same way that he felt it important to make the bed every morning even though no one other than he would see it messy.

The phone rang. He turned off the faucet and picked up the receiver.

"Hello?"

"You really must be kidding me."

Polly's "brusque" voice was unmistakable. It was the one he most closely associated with her. "What am I kidding you about?"

"You have your daughter—your fourteen-year-old pubescent daughter—talking about that fairy-tale world again?"

Becky had told Polly about Tamarisk? What was she thinking? "What part of that do you have a problem with?"

"What part of that do I have a problem with? Let's see, maybe it's the part about you not realizing your baby has grown up. Or maybe it's the part about your being so desperate to get any of your daughter's affection that you would exploit her sentiments. Or maybe it's that you have her so caught up in this that she actually thinks she's having conversations with elves and fairies."

"Is that really what bothers you, Polly?"

"You don't think that should bother me?"

Chris hesitated a second. He needed to slow the conversation down, to gain some traction. "I don't think that's the issue."

"Really. What do you think the issue is?"

"I think the issue is last night."

Polly's voice rose again. "You bet your ass the issue is last night. I spoke to Becky a little while ago and she told me that she's traveling to Tamarisk from your apartment. You don't think that I should find this a tiny bit upsetting?"

There was no hesitation this time. "I think what's bothering you is that she was here at all last night. After four years—four years in which you never did anything to clarify for our daughter that it was you who broke up our marriage—she has finally made a small step back in my direction, and that kills you."

There was a bitter laugh on the other end of the phone. "You really do think everything is about that, don't you? You really think that everything is about how jealous I was of the two of you and how I deliberately removed you from her life. Grow up, Chris."

Chris fought to control the tone of his voice. He didn't want Polly to think she was getting to him. "You know what? I was half expecting this call. I didn't know what it was going to be about, but I assumed you'd find some way to suggest that I was ill equipped to have Becky here during the week."

"If you're brainwashing her with that Tamarisk crap and you have her so deluded that she thinks she's traveling to other worlds in her dreams, then you're ill equipped, period."

Chris felt his blood rise. "Was that some kind of threat?"

Polly didn't respond immediately. "Chris, I don't need to threaten you. When Becky figures out what you're doing—and she'll figure it out all on her own—she will never be able to look at you the same way again. You might want to think about that before you take this any further."

Chris thought about telling Polly that Becky had initiated the conversation about Tamarisk. What would that accomplish, though, and what would he say if Polly asked him if he believed his daughter could actually go there? Becky seemed so convinced—she'd talked about last night's trip to Tamarisk nonstop this morning—that he was beginning to become convinced himself, as outrageous as it seemed. If he admitted this to Polly, though, she'd throw an even bigger fit.

He took a deep breath and simply said, "Thanks for the sage advice."

"I'm telling you, Chris, you're making a big mistake here. You can be as much of a smart-ass with me as you'd like, but this new tactic of yours will definitely backfire. And if I see it affecting Becky adversely, I'll respond as I see necessary."

Chris had to get off the phone. If he didn't, he would start popping off again and he'd almost certainly say something he'd regret later—not because he didn't mean it but because he absolutely meant it.

"I need to go, Polly. I was in the middle of something."

He thumbed the phone off and placed it roughly on the counter. He felt the jittery rush of adrenaline that accompanied every argument he had with his ex-wife. He could always count on her turning something magical between Becky and him into something ugly.

Really, though, what had Becky been thinking by mentioning this to Polly? Did this Tamarisk thing have her so completely caught up that she forgot herself? That didn't seem possible. She knew what Tamarisk represented to her mother. How had she expected Polly to receive it? Had she done this deliberately for some reason? If so, what was she trying to gain?

Chris thought about IMing Becky; she was probably still awake. The last thing he wanted to happen, however, was for Polly to walk into Becky's room while he was doing this and recognize his screen name. Maybe they could talk about it on the phone tomorrow night. Until then, he'd just have to take a few deep breaths and try to get his mind on pleasant thoughts.

This was something they'd have to deal with, though. If Becky was going to continue to "travel" to Tamarisk—whatever that meant to her—she would have to do it without her mother being aware of it. If Becky understood nothing else, he would make sure she understood that.

12

The last few days had been rough. Mom was giving her all kinds of strange looks though, thankfully, she hadn't brought the subject up directly. Dad had interrogated her about saying anything to Mom about Tamarisk and Becky really couldn't give him a good reason why she'd blurted it out. Meanwhile, Cam Parker was talking to her in single syllables and Lonnie was so infatuated with Dylan Spence—the latest flavor of the week—that she couldn't talk about anything else.

On top of it all, Becky had been having enormous headaches. She'd gotten one so bad while she was having dinner with Dad tonight that she'd thought she was going to throw up right at the table. She'd managed to make it through the meal, but she wound up canceling her plans with her friends for the night and going to bed early.

She took some Tylenol and laid down. She'd never before had headaches like the ones she'd gotten this week. If they kept up, she was going to have to tell her mother and go to the doctor, which was not exactly something she wanted to do. Realistically, though, she couldn't avoid the doctor forever. She had an annual checkup coming in a couple of months anyway. If there really was something wrong with her, everyone would find out then. The best she could do was hope to put it off for a little while. She was doing an okay job of dealing with the fear of the unknown. She wasn't at all sure she could deal with the known, though.

Lying down made the pounding intensify. She knew sleep would be the best thing for her, but she wasn't sure she'd be able to relax enough to get to sleep. There was also the matter of Tamarisk. Should she try to go in this condition? *Could* she go in this condition? If she tried to meditate, would her head just pop off?

She definitely didn't want to wait until Tuesday night to go back. Maybe the meditation would even make her feel a little better. Didn't people use meditation to *treat* headaches? Of course, when others meditated, they didn't zoom off to another reality (at least she didn't think so), but that was beside the point.

Slowly, all too aware of the throbbing in her head, Becky began the process. She needed to fight past the pain or she would never be able to get to her destination. For a short while, though, that seemed impossible. She kept at it, and eventually she was able to darken the headache the way she darkened everything else.

She opened her eyes in Miea's office. Once again, Miea wasn't there, and Becky stepped into the hallway to find Sorbus.

"A pleasure to see you again," the aide said.

"Good to see you, too, Sorbus. I guess the queen isn't around, huh?"

Sorbus's expression changed and he lowered his eyes. That seemed like a weird reaction. "She is going to be tied up for a long time today, I'm afraid. She'll be unhappy to learn that she missed you."

Becky nodded. She'd really hoped she'd have the opportunity for another talk with Miea, but she couldn't expect the queen to sit around waiting for her. Maybe that would be possible if Becky knew exactly when she was going to arrive, but she hadn't come close to figuring out the time thing.

"Her Majesty and I talked about what to do if you came when she wasn't available and she had a suggestion that might interest you. Have you ever been on a waccasassa?"

The question was like asking Becky if she'd ever been to

Alpha Centauri, but Sorbus wouldn't realize that. "No, I can't say I have."

"I can make the queen's available for you if you'd like to take a tour of the kingdom."

Becky's eyes brightened. "You could?"

"Her Majesty was very clear that you were to have complete access to all of her personal luxuries. After all, she rarely uses them herself."

Becky's fingers actually tingled. "I'd love to ride on a waccasassa. They're safe, right?"

"Oh, they're extremely safe. Please come outside with me."

They walked down the corridor and out to a large field. The colors and music of Tamarisk instantly impressed themselves upon Becky. Some of the sounds were different today—there was rhythmic banging that sounded something like a tympani, and the occasional appearance of something that sounded bowed—but the full effect was as symphonic as it had been the first time Becky stepped outdoors. A small biped creature with a flat face and a silky coat walked confidently up to her, reached out a paw to touch her leg, and then moved to a nearby rock to watch her. Becky grinned at it, but the creature's expression remained unchanged.

Becky noticed that her headache was completely gone. Obviously all she needed was a healthy dose of adventure to make it go away. *I'm going to get to explore. I'm going to get to discover. There's so much here for me.* She stepped toward the biped, intending to pet it, and it ran off in the direction of the palace.

She turned to Sorbus, who was saying something to another man. The man walked away, and maybe a minute later, Becky heard the air change with the flapping of enormous wings. Becky saw the shadow of the waccasassa before she saw the enormous bird itself. As big as it was, though, the waccasassa touched down on the ground incredibly lightly.

The gull-like creature was so much bigger than Becky had imagined, easily thirty feet in length and ten feet high. It had silvery-green plumage across its wings, an aquamaroon head, and mahogany tufts in the center of its back. It stared straight ahead, its long, shimmering beak pointed directly at the horizon.

"You can climb on whenever you like," Sorbus said, raising a hand in the direction of the megagull.

Becky regarded the bird. "Climb on? How? Where?" Becky realized the stories she'd created about waccasassa travel had left out quite a few details—like how you got on the things, for instance.

Sorbus directed Becky to the front of the bird. When they got there, the waccasassa lowered its beak and Becky noticed the numerous ridges that ran up its length. Sorbus gestured for Becky to use those ridges as a stairway. Grinning to herself, she walked up the beak and onto the bird's expansive back, settling into its center tufts. She looked around for a seat belt or something to hold her in before remembering that she'd designed the tufts to be sturdy enough to keep a person in one place.

"Do I need a helmet?" she said, calling down to Sorbus.

"A helmet? For what?"

In Connecticut, Becky wasn't allowed to get on Rollerblades without a helmet, but obviously in Tamarisk it was perfectly okay to fly on massive birds without them. "What about air pressure?"

"What about air pressure?"

Becky shook her head. "Nothing, never mind. Hey, if I'm going on a tour, do I get a tour guide?"

Sorbus turned his palms upward. "I would truly love to take you myself, but I'm afraid I can't today. Her Majesty might need me and we're a little short-staffed."

"How will I know where to go?"

"The waccasassa knows your itinerary. I think you'll enjoy the trip."

Becky laughed. "Okay, I guess I'll just wing it." She put a hand up to her face. "Sorry, I didn't mean that terrible pun."

Becky settled back. She was about to ask Sorbus how to make the waccasassa go when she felt herself moving forward. The bird took four huge strides and then leaped into the air.

Becky felt her stomach drop the way it did on a roller coaster and she instinctively closed her eyes, but as the bird began to glide, she felt more comfortable and began to look around.

From the sky, the landscape was decidedly blue. There were dots and patches of color everywhere, but they were like decorations on a vast blue carpet. It wasn't very easy to see because the waccasassa's back was so broad, but its body dipped with every movement of its wings, giving Becky a different angle from which to look. The palace was behind her and it was surprising how quickly Tamarisk City receded.

It didn't take long for Becky to grow accustomed to the feeling of being airborne. Flying in the open air was unlike anything she'd ever experienced before—actually, it was a little like her dizzy spells, but way more enjoyable—and she reveled in it. It was almost like she had wings herself. She knew people had dreams of being able to fly, but she'd never had one of those. If those people only knew what they were missing . . .

By the time they were in the air a few minutes, Becky could see nothing but forest. Not long after this, the landscape flattened and they came to a huge plain marked by deep black rows of soil and vibrant blue stalks of the local crops.

The waccasassa descended quickly. It seemed to Becky that it was descending *much too* quickly. Did birds have malfunctions? If they crashed, would the tufts save her? Maybe she should have insisted on a helmet. Could she actually get hurt in Tamarisk? Suddenly, she was very nervous, but when they were no more than a few dozen feet from the ground, the bird arched upward and stretched its wings wide to come to a feather-soft landing.

This was one very cool method of transportation.

The tufts supporting Becky had shifted and stiffened during the flight, and it took some effort for her to free herself. Soon, though, she made it down. She saw she was on a farm of some sort. The stand of crops she'd viewed from the air was in the near distance. On a hillside, large beasts that she'd named bonsals grazed lazily while chittering purismas pecked at and groomed them, and nearly round but incredibly agile pulgases hopped back and forth over the bonsals' hulking forms. The constant bouncing of the pulgases around the bonsals must have been annoying, because every now and then a bonsal would sit down, roll over, and attempt to kick at a pulgas without success—the big animals were much too slow. She felt bad for the poor, harried bonsals. She should have given them more dexterity, but she hadn't thought of it when she'd created their story.

The sound was different out here. If the sounds around the palace were like a symphony, here it was more like a folk song. The noises were simpler here and more ordered, and the "melody" was more basic. Becky could imagine humming the tune that nature made out here. The one constant was that discordant note. That same sound Becky had heard the first time she went outside in Tamarisk and heard again today near the palace was present on this land. It was out of tune with everything else and, if anything, louder here than it was near the queen. Maybe this was one of the ways that Tamarisk "invented" itself. Maybe Tamariskians had a slightly different sense of what sounded good—although what she'd heard from the norbeck composer sounded great to her. Mysteries were cool. She'd have fun trying to solve this one.

There was a wooden structure just down the hill from where she stood. Becky started in that direction and then turned back to the waccasassa. Did she need to tell it to stay? Waccasassas could be taught to go anywhere in Tamarisk, but they required special trainers to give them their directions. Becky had no idea how to talk to the bird.

"I'll be back in a few minutes," she said, almost certain the waccasassa—the only way she could get back to the palace—couldn't understand her.

As Becky got closer to the barn (it looked more like a big storage shed, but farms had barns, didn't they?), she heard a heavy shaking sound, something like marbles in a can, followed by swishing. The door of the barn was open and she saw a man banging the dirt-laden bottom of a large blue stalk against a crate and then plunging the stalk into a barrel of water and moving it around briskly. He repeated the process twice while she watched. After the second time, Becky noticed hundreds of tiny vegetables emerging from the dirt and clinging to the stalk. She'd come upon a microfarmer. There were very few of them in all of Tamarisk.

The farmer set to banging the stalk on the side of the crate again when he noticed her. Their eyes connected, and Becky felt for a second like she'd met the man before. When she looked at him again, though, she realized he didn't seem familiar.

"Well, hello," he said.

"Hello. I hope I'm not disturbing you."

"The only thing disturbing me is the dirt around these fenigers." He whacked the stalk a little harder and some more dirt came loose. "It's tenacious stuff."

He gave the stalk another whack and then plunged it back into the water with extra force. When he pulled the stalk out of the barrel, he examined the still-clotted cluster, scraping some more dirt away with his fingers. "I'm getting there. Very, very slowly, but I'm getting there."

He dug deeper with his fingers and pulled loose a narrow scarlet root. It looked a little like a carrot but it was a fraction of the size and it was twisted like fusilli pasta. "You like fenigers?" he said, holding the vegetable out to her.

"I've never had one."

The farmer looked at her disbelievingly. "You're not from around here, are you?"

"No, I'm not. But it's nice to be here."

The farmer nodded and then swished the plucked feniger in the barrel of water to clean off any remaining dirt. He handed it to Becky. "Give it a try."

"Thanks," Becky said, examining the vegetable.

"Little bites."

"Yes, I remember." She bit off the tiniest tip of the feniger—up to the first curl—and her mouth instantly filled with the taste. It was like she'd swallowed an entire plate of food at once.

The feniger was buttery like really good mashed potatoes, but a little spicy as well, as though it had jalapenos mixed into it. As Becky chewed—not the easiest thing to do considering the little size of the bite she'd taken—more flavors hit her taste buds. Something bitter like a green pepper and pungent like balsamic vinegar. Then the mashed potato flavor returned and stayed on her tongue after she swallowed.

"Wow," she said, looking up at the farmer.

"You got a good one?"

"I wouldn't know the difference, but I'm guessing it was a very good one."

Becky took another bite and the sensation washed over her again. She was suddenly ravenously hungry and she finished off the rest of the feniger in one shot. That was a mistake. Her hunger was instantly gone, replaced by a strong sense that she'd eaten the equivalent of an extra large pizza.

"Most people take it a little slower," the farmer said.

Becky put her hand on her stomach. She was stuffed. "I got carried away. That was silly."

"If you got a good one, I understand the temptation." The farmer grinned and then cocked his head. "So if you're not from around here, where are you from?"

"I live . . . near the palace."

The farmer nodded. "That's quite a distance away. Are you out here visiting family or friends?"

The flavor of the feniger still saturated Becky's mouth. She had a feeling it would be there for a while. "I'm just out for a ride."

"Heck of a trip. Well, it was nice to meet you. Enjoy the rest of your day." The farmer turned back toward the stalk and the bucket. "If you'll excuse me, I need to get back to work. I need to get the rest of these babies loose sometime before my hundredth birthday."

"Of course. I didn't mean to interrupt you. It looks like a tough job."

"Not tough, just slow. I really shouldn't complain, though. A regular farmer would need to harvest an entire row of normal vegetables to get the yield I get from one stalk. I remind myself about that every thirty whacks or so. Anyway, I'd better get back."

Becky started to turn and then stopped. "Would you mind if I gave it a few whacks?"

The farmer seemed confused by the request. "Your clothes are awfully nice—they certainly dress differently near the palace—I wouldn't want you to mess them up."

"Maybe just one whack?"

The farmer shrugged. "Sure, if that's what you'd like. I'll just take a little rest by the fence and you can whack away."

Becky smiled and walked over to the stalk, thanking the man. This was very exciting to her. She was going to *do something* in Tamarisk. So far, she'd had the time of her life, but she'd only been a spectator. Here, even if she harvested one little micro-vegetable, she'd be making a contribution. That felt very good to her.

The stalk didn't feel the way she expected it to feel when she picked it up. The bark was spongy and pliable yet somehow still rigid. She looked at the bottom of the stalk and saw mostly dirt and spidery roots along with a few curly ends of fenigers. She checked the crate the farmer had been banging the stalk against and noticed only a couple of vegetables at the bottom. How long had he been going at this? Was she holding a day's work in her hands?

"Do I do the water first or the crate?"

"Bang it a few times. Sometimes when you let it rest for a few minutes you can knock a bunch of dirt off in one shot."

Becky raised the stalk and tried to repeat the motion the farmer had made earlier. She hit the clod against the crate three times, but almost nothing happened. Didn't they have machines to take care of this kind of thing? She held the clod toward her and tried to free up a couple of vegetables with her fingernail. The dark black dirt was granular, more like salt than the dirt in Connecticut. Still, it clung to the fenigers like the thickest mud.

"You need to keep putting it in the water," the farmer said.

But wouldn't that make it more like mud? The whole process seemed futile to Becky, but she gave it her best shot. "How many fenigers are actually in here?"

"Dozens. Maybe more than a hundred. I'll have them all out by sundown."

Not if you let me do it, you won't. She whacked and dunked several more times, determined to have a little bit of success. Almost by accident, two fenigers came free and she pulled them from the root and threw them in the crate. Her arms felt strained, though it felt good—like she'd had a really active gym class.

She held out the stalk. "I think it might be better for me to leave this to an expert."

The farmer rose to his feet and took the stalk from her. "Your fingernails were getting smudged anyway."

Becky looked down at her hands. Why didn't the dirt just flake off? She thought about asking if she could wash her hands and then decided she'd rather not. "Thanks for letting me try this out."

"I'm happy for the help. Come back anytime. I can always use another set of muscles. Wear different clothes if you do, though. The soil in this area is different from the soil in most of the kingdom. It's great for microfarming, but not so good for nice outfits."

Becky stepped toward the entrance of the barn. "I'll remember that. Thanks again."

"Have a good time on the rest of your trip."

Becky waved and then headed up the hill. When she got to the top, she was relieved to see that the waccasassa was still waiting for her. What would have happened if the bird had flown off without her? Would she still have been pulled back to her bed at the allotted time the way she had on other nights? Or would she have been too far away for the signal (or whatever it was that connected her between the two worlds) to reach her, leaving her to figure out some way back to the palace—and then some way back home—by herself? Fortunately, she didn't need the answer to that question.

She climbed aboard the gull and settled into its tufts. She looked back toward the barn and saw the farmer gazing up at her. She could barely make out his face, but she saw enough to realize that the presence of the bird surprised him. Waccasassas probably didn't land in this area very often. She waved to him again and he waved back tentatively. *He probably thinks I'm rich or royalty or something. If he knew what I really am he'd be even more surprised.*

The bird was again airborne, taking a few quick, elongated steps and then leaping skyward. It felt a little weird to Becky not to have any idea where she was going, but she certainly felt safe nestled within the waccasassa (especially now that she'd experienced her first landing) and she knew instinctively that the gull would never put her in any danger. She closed her eyes and allowed herself to feel the sensation of soaring. This was nothing like flying in an airplane. She raised her hands upward the way she always did when she was on a roller coaster, and her sense of flight intensified. This place just seemed to have an endless number of remarkable experiences lined up for her.

The bird made a sudden, abrupt turn, as though something had called it. The waccasassa fully extended its neck and Becky felt a definite surge in speed. How fast could these things go? More importantly, how fast could they go and keep her from flying off into the air? So much for instinctive feelings! She couldn't fix her eyes on the landscape now. The air rushed by so fast that she found it hard to focus on anything. She had a feeling it wouldn't have mattered. The ground was probably whooshing past her.

A few minutes later, the bird slowed. Becky felt its body relax as the speed diminished, and by the time the waccasassa landed, Becky felt like she was riding a kite. She loved these animals.

Becky stepped down onto a field that was very different from the others she'd seen in Tamarisk. Lots of grays here. She didn't remember making anything gray in the stories she'd created—certainly not an entire field (or at least most of one; there were a few patches of blue). She stooped down to touch a plant. It wasn't just strangely colored; it was withered. The vine she held wasn't entirely dead—in fact, it seemed a little bluer up close than it had from a distance—and it hadn't entirely drooped, but no one would call it healthy. What happened to this place? Becky remembered the woman at the kingdom congress who complained about an infestation of vilases. Did something like that do this damage?

Standing here filled Becky with sadness. This wasn't the way Tamarisk was supposed to be. It felt wrong. Seriously wrong. At the same time, though, Becky felt a strong sense of motivation. Maybe it was because she'd just "gotten her hands dirty" here. She felt like she was part of this place now. That meant that if it needed help, she should do what she could to help it. She had no idea what that meant—or what the problem even was here—but she felt the need to try to fix it.

Becky looked up and saw a figure in the distance. The farmer of this field, maybe? He'd probably know what was going on.

As Becky approached, she noticed that the person she thought was a farmer was someone who seemed to be only a couple of years older than she was. He wore sunglasses and a hat, but even still Becky could tell he was really good-looking. Maybe even as good-looking as Cam Parker.

The boy was shoveling some withered plants into a bag. When she got closer, he stood up and walked toward her.

"Is this yours?" he said.

Becky didn't know what he meant right away. "The field? No, actually, I thought it was yours."

The boy took a few seconds to consider this. "I'm visiting," he said finally.

"Yeah, me too."

The boy looked back toward the bag. Becky got the distinct impression she'd disturbed him. When he didn't say anything more, she said, "My name is Becky, by the way."

The boy raised a hand in a half wave. "I'm Rubus."

"Where are you visiting from?"

Again, he didn't answer right away. "Another . . . part of the kingdom."

There was no way he was telling the truth. Was it possible he'd traveled here from another world as well? How strange would that be? "Do you know what happened here? I don't think these plants are supposed to look this way."

"Something got to them. I can't figure out what it is."

"Is that why you're putting things in that bag? Are you doing some kind of research?"

The boy's eyes flicked back in the direction of the bag again. "I, uh, yeah. That's what I'm doing."

Rubus either didn't like talking to girls or was nervous for some other reason. "Well, good luck with it. It'd be a shame if this farmer lost his field."

Rubus nodded, looked down at his hands, looked up at Becky for a long moment, and then looked out on the landscape. "It's a beautiful place, isn't it?"

Becky followed his eyes. Even this withered field seemed nice. It wasn't as much gray as it was silvery. "You're right; it is. I wish it were healthier, though."

"Not just right here. I'm talking about everywhere around here. So beautiful. So full of life. I don't know how they got all of this when what we wound up with was concrete and metal."

Concrete and metal? As far as Becky knew, there weren't any parts of Tamarisk filled with concrete and metal. Where did this guy come from? Some futuristic science fiction universe? The only part of this world that was mostly concrete and metal was . . .

"Gunnthorn."

The boy startled when she said the word. "What are you talking about?"

"You're from Gunnthorn?"

"What makes you say that?"

"Are you a spy?"

Rubus took a quick step toward her and for a second Becky

thought he was going to attack. Then he stopped, his shoulders slumped. "I'm not a spy."

"But you're from Gunnthorn."

"I didn't say that. And where are you visiting from?"

It was Becky's turn to hesitate. "I'm from . . . someplace just outside of the kingdom."

Rubus smiled at her wryly. "I guess we both have secrets, huh?"

Becky laughed. Something about the way he said that made her feel more comfortable. She had no idea who Rubus was, but he didn't seem like a bad guy. And he was *very* good-looking. "I'm not a spy, either."

"That's good. If you were a spy, I'd have to turn you in." He smiled at her again and then nodded toward the waccasassa. "Nice bird."

"Yeah. I'd offer you a ride on it, but I'm still learning how it works. I'm not sure how many passengers it holds."

"Too bad. I've never been on one. The view of this place from up in the air must be amazing."

Becky remembered that Gunnthorn had airplanes (well, something very similar to them) instead of passenger gulls, but that they weren't allowed in Tamariskian airspace. "You really like it here, huh?"

Rubus's expression got dreamy. "Here? I love it. I can just imagine what I'd do with land like this."

Those words from a Thorn made Becky a little suspicious. "Why don't you move here?"

He snickered. "Not so easy for someone like me."

"Why not?"

He looked down at his hands again. "My family wouldn't approve."

Becky thought about the conversation with her mother. "Yeah, I can relate."

"Parents can be difficult sometimes."

"Tell me about it. Mine have their moments. They're okay most of the time, though."

"I wish I could say the same. Listen, I have to get back to my . . . research. Maybe we could see each other again sometime, though."

Becky felt herself blush. *What's that? I don't blush.* "Yeah, I'd like that."

"Are you going to be here for a while?"

"I come and go."

"Me too. Can I look you up somewhere?"

Becky wrinkled her nose. "I'm not that easy to reach here."

Rubus seemed to think about this for a very long time. "That's too bad," he said. Then his expression brightened. "Who knows, though? Maybe fate will throw us together again."

"That would be cool." Becky lifted a hand in a mirror of his earlier half wave. "See you around."

He half-waved back. "I hope so."

Becky walked back to the bird, turning back once. Rubus was watching her. His eyes were still on her when she got to the waccasassa. When she turned toward the bird, she noticed that it was avoiding looking at her, as though it were ashamed of something. What was that about? Had the bird taken her someplace it wasn't supposed to go? It was kind of hard to believe that Miea wanted her to see this damaged field. Becky wished she hadn't taken away all the animal voices. It would be nice to ask the waccasassa what was going on. Instead, she climbed on the bird, and they took off.

They had another long flight where the bird did its supersonic thing again. Becky was better prepared for it this time, though. Eventually, they touched down in a long, blue field. As she stepped from the waccasassa, Becky saw nothing around her. Then, from a hill at her back, she heard the sound:

Step-crack.

Step-step-crack.

Step-step-step-crack-step-crack-step-crack-step-crack.

Poledisk! Becky laughed aloud and ran up the hill to gaze down at the other side. There she found a dozen teenagers playing another of the games she'd invented. Three kids on the offensive side circled around their teammate who was the launcher, protecting him while he prepared to launch the Frisbee-like disk he held. Meanwhile two other kids raced down the field, poles raised high, waiting to catch the launched disk. The six kids on the other side were defenders, holding their poles aloft and attempting to prevent the offensive team's efforts—or better yet capture the disk and go on the offensive themselves.

The launcher launched the disk just out of the way of a defender's pole and the disc arced down the field toward a receiver. He must have been a good one, because two defenders were covering him. In spite of this, he caught the disk and took off with it, keeping the disk spinning on his pole the entire time, as was required. Finally, one of the defenders was able to knock the receiver's pole with his own, causing the disk to fall to the ground, where the next play would begin.

Becky sat down on the hill to watch the action. These kids seemed pretty good at this. It must have been a pickup game, though, since there were no coaches around. Eventually, the first team scored, crossing the goal line on a play where the receiver nearly bobbled the disk away. Now the second team was on the offensive. Their launcher had a very strong arm, but he wasn't terribly accurate. His launches seemed to go all over the place, and twice in this series the defenders nearly intercepted him. Slowly, though, his team made its way down the field. Before each play started, the offense lined up and performed the same act to indicate that a play was about to begin, stamping their feet and smacking their poles together.

Step-crack.

Step-step-crack.

Step-step-step-crack-step-crack-step-crack-step-crack.

They of course had no way of knowing that they did this because Becky got the idea from her one year of Irish dancing classes.

The launcher's erratic launches threatened to kill his team's chances. His latest launch was so far off the mark that it landed a good twenty feet out of bounds. One of the receivers dropped her pole and trotted after it, looking back at the launcher with obvious anger. When she picked up the disk, she glanced up the hill and made eye contact with Becky.

"Hey," the girl said.

Becky waved. "Hey."

"What're you doing?"

"Just watching. Is that okay?"

The girl rolled her eyes. "As long as you like watching a slaughter. We're down by five."

"Ouch."

"Yeah. You like playing poledisk?"

"I've never done it."

The girl looked at her strangely. "You've never played poledisk?"

Becky wrinkled her nose. "They don't play it as much where I come from."

From the girl's expression, Becky could tell that this sounded weird to her, but the girl let it pass. She retrieved her pole. "Want to give it a try?"

Becky leaned forward. "You mean try playing?"

"Yeah. You can use my pole. Or maybe one of the extras. They'll probably let us play seven-on-six considering how much they're beating us."

Becky stood up. She was a little nervous about the idea of playing. After all, just because she created the game didn't mean that she'd be any good at it. "Okay. Yeah, I guess so."

The girl smiled and extended her pole to Becky as she came down the hill. The girl reminded Becky of someone, but she couldn't place it.

As anticipated, the other team was perfectly fine with the idea of playing seven-on-six. For the first several plays, Becky was one of the circlers, which was good because it didn't require much skill other than making sure to do the starting steps properly. She managed to keep the rushers away from the launcher, though ultimately the launcher's erratic performance killed the drive. When they switched over to defense, her teammates put

Becky on the line again. It didn't take much of a leap to realize that the kids on the line were the ones with the least talent. Considering that all of Becky's poledisk experience had come in the past few minutes, it was hard to argue against being lumped in this group. It turned out that she wasn't a very good rusher, either. She dropped her pole on the first play and never got anywhere near the action on the second. The other team's launcher got off a great launch and they were now only a few yards from the goal line.

On her way back after that play, she shrugged her shoulders and apologized to her teammates. They all seemed cool about things except for one guy, who just scowled at her.

The next play was amazing, though. Becky tried rushing again and found herself even farther from the launcher than she had been on the play before. As the launcher released the disk, one of Becky's teammates tipped the disk with his pole. Instead of launching forward, the disk went off to the side—right in Becky's direction. Not having any idea what she was doing, Becky stuck her pole up and caught the disk as it came toward her. She remembered that she needed to twirl the disk to keep it on her pole and she did so, frantically. Then she remembered that she was supposed to run with it. With the entire field open in front of her, she dashed toward the opposite goal line, twirling her pole madly as she did. She didn't want to look to see who was behind her, so she just ran as hard as she could. When she crossed the goal, she turned to find her teammates running up behind her and the other team shaking their heads.

"Your first score," said the girl who'd invited her to play, patting her lightly on the leg with her pole. *Caitlin Krieger, that's who she reminds me of,* Becky thought. Caitlin had sat next to her in third grade and they had done a couple of school projects together even though they never really became friends. Third grade was when Becky had invented poledisk.

"Totally luck," Becky said, grinning.

"Nice work," said the kid who'd scowled at her on the previous play. "You can stop twirling now."

Becky looked up at her pole and realized she was still keeping the disk aloft. She stopped twirling the pole and the disk dropped to the ground.

"Ready to try covering a receiver?" another kid said.

That sounded like fun and Becky thought it was nice that the kid was expressing confidence in her—even though the score she made was entirely accidental—but she wondered how much time she had left in Tamarisk tonight. It was probably best for her to get back on the waccasassa.

"Thanks, but I really have to go."

"Where are you going?" the Caitlin Krieger girl said.

"My ride is waiting for me. Thanks again for letting me play."

She said good-bye to the others, clicking poles with a couple before putting hers down on the sidelines, and then walked over the hill. By the time she got to the waccasassa, she could hear the sounds of the game resuming.

They were in the air again quickly. A few minutes into their flight, the gull swooped lower until it was maybe only a few dozen feet above the ground. It tilted to the left and Becky thought they were about to land, but the waccasassa continued on. The angle was a little uncomfortable for Becky and she shifted around to the degree she could. Doing so caused her to look down and she realized that the angle the bird was flying at gave her a clear view of the ground below.

And it was quite a view. Where much of the skyline near the palace and in the other places she'd visited today was blue with foliage and dotted with roads and villages, they traveled now over a huge expanse of water. Rolling waves of turquoise—a reflection of the Tamariskian sky—filled Becky's entire field of vision. Occasionally, Becky spied islands that seemed to be made of undulating plastic billowing in the wind, as though huge garbage bags rose up in spots from under the surface. Becky knew, though, that they were neither plastic nor billowing.

The bloat marshes. The waccasassa was taking her to one of the most exotic of all of her Tamarisk creations.

The bird dipped again and now they were practically skimming the water. Becky saw the waves flutter under them, surely a reaction to the size of the waccasassa and its enormous wingspan. She could feel moisture on her face as they got closer. At last, the bird righted itself and stepped down into a landing, its footing surprisingly solid on the roiling surface.

Becky stood up and looked outward. The island was so small that she could see water on all sides of her. The water wasn't the attraction here, though. She got down from the bird and took a few tentative steps forward. As she did, the smooth, glistening ground in front of her rippled first outward, then inward, and then sideways. A moment later, the earth swelled into a large bubble and the bubble rolled to the edge of the island before subsiding. As was true everywhere in Tamarisk, the sounds of nature were musical. Here, though, the sound was nearly entirely percussive—pings and chimes and snaps and booms.

Becky wasn't sure where to walk. At any moment, something could come along and trip her or send her onto her butt. Still, she had to explore. She moved in the direction directly ahead of the waccasassa's beak—was that north, south, some other direction entirely that only existed here?—and tried to anticipate the movement of the rolling ground. She wasn't entirely successful, slipping after only a few steps and finding herself on one knee just a few steps after that. She put both hands on the ground to prop herself up. When she did, a tiny ripple ran under her and stopped about a foot away from her left hand. Out popped the head of a slim, gilled red lizard Becky had long ago named a coweeta. It shook its head back and forth so quickly that the motion seemed a blur, and then it stopped and looked straight at Becky. Its eyes narrowed and it began to rise out of its hole. For more than a minute, it continued to rise. The coweeta was less than an inch across, but its body was dozens of feet long. Becky didn't move the entire time this was happening, watching as it stepped and stepped and stepped to her left. When the lizard's stubby tail finally emerged from the hole, it turned and began to walk back toward Becky. It made one circuit on the ground beneath Becky's arms and legs and then turned again and began to crawl up one of her arms.

Becky wasn't entirely sure how she felt about this. It was very cool to be interacting with Tamariskian wildlife this way, but this was a little like having a huge centipede crawling on you—a huge centipede with leathery skin and prickly little claws. Still, she didn't move. The coweeta rose onto her shoulders. *If this thing goes down the collar of my shirt, I'm gonna have to get it out of there.* Then it walked to her right shoulder—of course some of it was still on the ground at this point—and then down her other arm. When its forelegs reached the other side, the coweeta made eye contact with Becky again and then skittered surprisingly quickly back down its hole. When it was gone, the hole disappeared as well. Becky felt a series of tiny pinpricks everywhere the coweeta had stepped on her. It was very bizarre, but also kind of refreshing in a strange way. Maybe this was what acupuncture was like.

Becky finally got to her feet. As soon as she did, another bubble emerged from the right and continued to roll all the way to an edge of the island. This time instead of subsiding, though, the thing that created the bubble—a jornada—rolled its gelatinous body onto the island. The jornada was translucent, maybe six feet in diameter. It looked a little bit like a jellyfish and a little bit like a huge glob of rubber cement. Becky had no idea where to look when she looked at it. She remembered that the amphibious creature "saw" with the outer layer of its skin but that its vision really only identified heat patterns. It was impossible to tell if the thing was looking at her, though she knew it had to be aware of her. In fact, it was likely that it had come to the surface because she was here.

Becky was fascinated with the thing, but she wasn't entirely sure if she should approach it. She and her father had developed their creatures with a great deal of detail, but she couldn't remember all of them and they never worked out every single thing. What if one of the characteristics they hadn't worked out was that the jornada was highly poisonous or liked to attach itself to the bodies of humans and live there for several months? This made Becky hesitate for a moment or two, but ultimately the thing was just too interesting to ignore. She stepped forward, her footfalls of course challenged by the movement of coweetas, gwynedds, farallons, and whatever else lived under the surface.

She got within ten feet of the jornada when suddenly it melted. Its entire body liquefied and spread out, with some of the liquid pooling around her feet. *We definitely didn't think up that part.* Then, just as quickly, it sucked itself together and rolled back under the surface. Its bubble skimmed the "plastic" for a few feet and then subsided.

Did I scare it?

Was that its way of saying "hello?"

Becky bent down again to run her hands along the ground. So smooth. So elastic. Yet if she stuck a fingernail in it, it came up just like normal dirt. This was one of their more outrageous inventions.

She was about to explore further when the waccasassa trumpeted. This was the first sound she'd heard the bird make and at first, she didn't realize where it was coming from. The gull very quickly repeated itself, though, and Becky stood and turned in that direction. The waccasassa's beak pointed to the ground. When Becky didn't move toward it right away, it trumpeted again and then moved its beak downward.

I guess he's telling me we have to leave. Becky patted the dirt—which rippled outward—once more and then climbed back onto the waccasassa. The bird flew at much greater height this time and they seemed to be moving even faster than they had before. It was difficult to see much of anything at this altitude, so Becky closed her eyes and allowed herself simply to feel the sensation of flying. She felt the bird's dips and curves and opened her eyes only once when the waccasassa hit some turbulence.

She opened them again when she felt the bird descend, recognizing the outskirts of the palace, and then the palace itself. Her tour was obviously over. The bird landed gently in the same field from which they'd taken off. Sorbus was waiting for her and Becky wondered if he'd been standing there the entire time she was gone.

"Did you have a good flight?" he said when she stepped down.

"Amazing. Thank you so much for suggesting this."

Sorbus nodded. "It was really Her Majesty who suggested it. She's returned to her chambers, by the way. She has a few minutes before her next meeting."

"Do you think I can see her?"

"I'm sure she would like that."

///

Sorbus led Becky inside and into Miea's chambers. It seemed a little strange to Becky that Miea would be here rather than her office with only a few minutes before her next meeting, but Becky was just happy to have the chance to say hi. When she got to her room, though, Miea's expression seemed dark and her greeting just this side of polite.

"I'm disturbing you, aren't I?" Becky said.

Miea offered a little smile. "No, of course not. Sorbus tells me that you went for a ride on our waccasassa. Did you enjoy that?"

"How could I not enjoy that? Everything about this place is incredible—the people, the wildlife, the landscapes . . ."

Miea uttered a huge sigh and muttered, "Yes, the landscapes."

Becky hadn't seen Miea like this before. She'd seen her tired and sad, but this was something else, something that made Becky feel a little frightened. "What's wrong?"

Miea sighed again and gazed up at the ceiling. When she looked back down, she looked directly at Becky and it seemed to Becky that something had completely overwhelmed Miea.

"We may not have the landscape much longer," the queen said.

The words chilled Becky. "What are you talking about?"

Miea shook her head sadly. "I didn't want to burden you

with this. I wanted your visits here to be joyful and carefree. However, I'm too upset to put up a façade today, Becky. I've just been through the single worst meeting of my entire life." Miea sat up and leaned forward a little. She gestured for Becky to sit, which was good because at this point, Becky wasn't sure she could stand much longer. "Tamarisk is experiencing a terrible blight. It has destroyed numerous fields already and the disease is eating away at more of our land daily. Today I learned that the blight wiped out the niwot, an insect native to Jonrae. A creature that has existed throughout time is gone because of this pestilence."

Becky felt tears come to her eyes. "That's awful."

Miea closed her eyes and then opened them slowly. "It *is* awful. It is not, however, the most awful thing about this. The most awful thing is that the efforts of the most valued scientists in Tamarisk have brought us virtually no information about the blight. We have no idea what causes it. None."

"And if you don't know what causes it . . ."

". . . then we don't know how to cure it."

Becky couldn't believe what she was hearing. This gorgeous world, a world that had seemed so magical to her just minutes earlier, was in serious trouble. The blight had already killed one species here. Would it eventually kill all of Tamarisk?

"I think I saw a blighted field today."

Miea's eyebrows lowered. "You saw a blighted field? That certainly wasn't on your agenda. Do you know where this was?"

Becky shrugged. "I don't know where I was, but it was almost all gray."

Miea nodded. "That's what the plants look like in the final stages."

"I'm so sorry, Miea."

Miea reached out for Becky's hand and squeezed it. "I know you are. You can only imagine how sorry I feel myself. Much deeper than my sorrow, though, is my sense of helplessness. I refuse to believe that there's nothing to do about this. However, every day I get a little closer to believing just that."

Becky held on to Miea's hand. Her fingers seemed cold. "Is there anything I can do? I want to help."

Miea tightened her grip. "Who knows? Maybe there is. Thank you for offering."

"It's my place, too."

Miea's expression brightened the tiniest bit. "Yes. Yes, it is."

Becky flashed on Rubus's face in her memory. "There was a boy in the field with me. I'm pretty sure he came from Gunnthorn, though he didn't exactly say it."

Miea's eyes opened wide. "A Thorn boy? What was he doing?"

"He was putting plants in a bag. He said he was doing research."

"I knew it. I knew they were involved with this somehow. Becky, can you tell me anything else about the boy or about the field?"

"I don't know where we were. The waccasassa flew really fast to get there, though. Do the birds have any, I don't know, records you can access?"

"No, nothing like that."

"The boy told me his name was Rubus. I didn't get his last name."

This information seemed to confuse the queen for a moment. "The vice chancellor's son."

"That guy was the son of the vice chancellor of Gunnthorn?"

Miea glowered. Becky had never seen her look this intense before. "I think so. And we're going to confront him."

Becky wasn't sure what to say next. She looked up at Miea, but when she did, she felt a tug, as though someone was pulling at her from behind. She knew what this meant all too well. "I'll be back soon," she said quickly. She had no idea if Miea heard her, though, because she felt a strong jolt, then darkness, and then the firm presence of her mattress beneath her.

She was back in bed. The waccasassa, the bloat marshes, and all of Tamarisk were cut off from her for the night.

She thought about the blight and the boy she'd met who

might have helped cause it. She knew the reality of that tragedy would stay with her.

She looked down at her fingers and noticed they were clean. The Tamariskian dirt was gone from them. It wasn't gone from her heart, though. It would always be there.

Becky stared up at the ceiling and envisioned the queen's sad expression. She needed to do something to help Miea and Tamarisk. They meant too much to her not to do everything she could.

She couldn't lose this place now that she'd found it.

13

Becky was always beautiful to Chris. She had been beautiful when he'd held her a minute after she was born, even with a ruddy face and puffy eyes. She had been beautiful when she was a toddler with long wavy hair, an easy smile, and a permanently inquisitive expression. She had been beautiful when all of that hair was gone and her inquisitiveness had turned to worry. And she was beautiful now, walking into the living room at a little before ten on a Sunday morning. Still, Chris couldn't help noticing that Becky looked worn out, as though she were awakening from a wild night on the town. She seemed more subject to gravity, more weighed down. It was as though sleep hadn't refreshed her but rather debilitated her.

How much of this had to do with her "journeys" to Tamarisk? Was there something about this that was hurting her physically (even if she wasn't really going there; Chris still couldn't decide how to feel about this)? She definitely seemed more haggard in the mornings since she'd started talking about that world again.

"Hey, babe," he said as she sat down at one of the chairs across from him, rubbing her eyes. "You feel okay?"

Becky took a deep breath and then drew herself up. "Yeah, I'm fine."

"You look a little wasted."

"Nah, I'm okay. I think I might be getting a cold or something."

She gave him the faux smile he'd seen often the last few

years and not at all in the past few weeks. How was he supposed to interpret that? Did it mean that there was something more than a cold going on here? Did it mean that she didn't want him to worry about something? Did it mean that she didn't feel comfortable talking to him about whatever was bothering her? Since he didn't want to press it, he decided to take another tack.

"How's Miea doing?"

Becky's response couldn't have surprised him more if she had turned into the queen herself. Seemingly out of nowhere, her lips started quivering and her eyes filled with tears. One tear ran rapidly from her eyes to her chin. "Dad, something terrible is happening."

"Becky, what's wrong?"

She sniffled and then took another deep breath. Chris couldn't remember the last time he'd seen his daughter cry, and it unnerved him to watch her attempt to pull herself together.

"Becky, what is it?"

She closed her eyes, causing another tear to run down her face. "Tamarisk is in serious trouble. A blight is destroying everything. Species are dying. No one knows how to fix it."

When Becky was three, Chris had come home one night to find her weeping because Chester, her stuffed purple basset hound, had gone to the hospital. It turned out that one of her preschool friends had broken her leg and was in traction, and Becky had transferred her anxiety and confusion over this to one of her favorite toys. Was something like that going on here? Back then, Chris warmed up a can of chicken noodle soup for Chester and the dog was better within the hour.

"What kind of blight is it?"

"No one knows! They can't figure out anything. All Miea knows is that it's destroying the kingdom. She thinks the Thorns might even be involved."

"They'll fix it, babe. I'm sure they have a lot of people working on it."

"They have *everyone* working on it. But nothing's helping."

If Becky was imagining this, it was more vivid than any

flight of fancy he'd ever known her to experience before. There was no doubt in Chris's mind that this was entirely real to her. Even at their most creative moments of Tamarisk storytelling, he'd never seen her get this worked up over a dramatic turn of events.

The memory of those storytelling days gave him a sudden inspiration. "Maybe we can fix it."

Becky sniffled again and wiped at her eyes. "What do you mean?"

"Becky, you created this world. Everything in Tamarisk is something you invented."

"Not everything, not anymore. I told you; it's evolved."

"Okay, not everything. A huge amount of it, though. And everything you created is still there, right?"

"I guess. I mean, I haven't taken inventory or anything."

"Which means that if you created something new, that would be there, too, right?"

He could see the light coming on in Becky's eyes. "Like what?"

"Like a cure for the blight."

Her expression brightened. "You mean tell a new story?"

"That's what I was thinking."

She jumped up from her seat and hugged him, rubbing a tear across his cheek. "You're a genius, Dad. Why didn't I think of that?"

"Only because your own genius isn't fully developed yet."

She smirked at him. It was great to see that smirk replace the other expression on her face. "Right, that must be it. Let's go."

"Go where?"

Becky started walking out of the living room. "To my room. We have to do it the same way we always did, don't we?"

///

Chris would never forget the last Tamarisk story he'd told with Becky. It was the night before he moved out, the night before Polly and he finally revealed to Becky what was happening to their family. Chris had been so intent on keeping everything as normal as possible that he didn't want to suggest in any way that this night's story was going to be different from any other night's. Still, it was impossible to keep the tension that had been building in the household from creeping into their fantasy world.

The Thorns were Chris's invention. Before he suggested them to Becky, he thought a long time about whether introducing a "cold war" enemy was a good idea. Before then, Tamarisk had been relatively free of antagonists. There was the occasional thief or ne'er-do-well, and sometimes one of the nonhuman creatures acted aggressively, but there was nothing approaching a vast villainous force. The Thorns would create more conflict for their stories, but it would also steal some of the innocence from Tamarisk. Ultimately, Chris decided that it would give Becky a useful way of addressing—and even "controlling"—evil, and that this would be healthy for her.

In the days leading up to the last Tamarisk story, Becky had started a plot about the threat of war. The Thorns had started some border skirmishes and imprisoned a number of innocent Tamariskians as spies. In the final story, the king and queen of Tamarisk and some of their closest advisors debated the possibility of military action. They decided to embark on a diplomatic mission instead in the hope of saving lives. As the story ended, the royal entourage left the palace, doubtful they could strengthen relations with the Thorns, but feeling the need to make the effort anyway.

Chris never could have guessed then that the Tamarisk days would end this way. Even a few weeks after Becky's announcement that she was no longer willing to tell stories with him, he still believed they would pick up again. He even continued to think about new diplomatic forays that would create a sturdier peace with the Thorns. He had never gotten the chance to share them with his daughter.

Now, though, it turned out that the tense story of the king and queen's trip to Gunnthorn would not be the last one Chris told with Becky. There would be at least one more, though the circumstances were about as unlikely as Chris could imagine.

For full effect, they positioned themselves just as they had those thousands of times before. Becky lay under the covers, her head against her propped-up pillow. Chris leaned back on the wall next to her bed.

When my life passes before my eyes, Chris thought, *I'll see this image.*

"This is the continuing saga of the land of Tamarisk," Becky said, using the words that always prefaced a new story.

"A creation of Rebecca and Christopher Astor," Chris said, contributing his part of the introduction.

Becky smiled at him and then looked up at the ceiling. Chris knew from experience that she was gathering her thoughts for the story. He hoped the ceiling in the apartment had as many good ideas as the one in Moorewood had.

"These were dark days for all of Tamarisk," she said in a voice a half octave lower than her speaking voice. It made Chris laugh inside that Becky still did this, a product of her younger (and unsuccessful, though he never mentioned it) attempts to sound like a voice-over narrator. "A disease had descended upon the land, withering the vegetation, robbing delicate creatures of food and shelter. The azure/indigo fields had become tinged with gray. What had at first appeared to be a simple infestation had turned out to be something much, much worse. It was . . . a blight!

"More horrifying still, no one could discover its cause. The scientists delivered reports. Military leaders searched for signs of treachery outside the borders. The palace considered every option. This was the first time in the four years of the queen's rule where she felt entirely helpless."

Chris watched Becky tell the story, her brow furrowed and her voice somber. In spite of how seriously she was taking all of this, though, he couldn't help notice that there was also more drama and wonder in her words. Maybe it was because her language skills were so much greater now than they had been four years ago, but the Tamarisk Becky spoke about seemed realer than ever before.

It took him a moment to notice that Becky had stopped speaking. It took him another moment to realize—even though he'd been looking directly at her—that she was looking at him.

"Was that my cue?" he said.

"The helpless part is kind of a hang-up for me."

Chris leaned back and wrapped his right arm over the top of his head. It was his favorite thinking position.

You didn't leave me a lot to work with here, Beck. You already took out all the scientists and the military. Do I go with something spiritual? Something supernatural? Hey, maybe a teenager from another planet comes along and saves the day.

"It's a creature," he said brightly.

"Huh?"

"Something in the ecosystem they haven't considered. Maybe a migration pattern changed and one thing led to another."

"And suddenly the entire kingdom has a disease? That doesn't seem right."

Chris shook his head. "You're right, it doesn't." He resumed his thinking position. He stared off at the far wall.

"No, it's not a migration pattern. Or actually, it *is* a migration pattern, but not from one land mass to another. It's from one level to another."

"I'm completely lost."

"Some subterranean species of insect or something that has always lived deep below the surface starts moving up for some reason that I haven't figured out yet, and when it does, it starts feeding off of nutrients the plants on the surface need to survive. This species doesn't realize what it's doing, but it's starving everything else."

Becky's eyebrows arched. "That's pretty good. I mean, it could even be what's happening."

"Doesn't really matter, does it? If we say it's happening, then it is what's happening, right?"

Becky smiled. "I guess so. Tell it, Dad."

Chris remembered that it was never enough to talk about the story. They always had to tell the story in order for it to be an official part of the Tamarisk record. Chris sometimes found himself composing sentences for the next night's story while he worked in the lab.

"For weeks, as the populace despaired and the queen and her advisors puzzled, the blight went unchecked and its source went unidentified. Finally, the queen decided to take matters into her own hands. 'Take me to the fields of—'" Chris looked at Becky. "Where did they first find the blight?"

"Jonrae."

"'Take me to the fields of Jonrae,' she said to her advisors. Once in the fields, the queen looked out on the devastated landscape and dropped to her knees. Her beloved Tamarisk was shriveling in front of her. She ran her hands along the black earth and felt a sudden spark of inspiration. Quickly requesting a shovel, she began to dig. She had no idea what she was digging for, but she did so with all of her energy.

"'Your Majesty, let some of the field hands do this work,' one of the advisors said."

"'No,' said the queen," Becky said, immediately adopting the queen's role. "'I need to do this myself. There's something here. I know it.'"

For a moment, neither Chris nor Becky said anything. Chris figured Becky wanted to take over the storytelling, but she looked at him as though she were waiting for him to continue. "Back to me?"

"You know what's going to happen next; I don't."

Chris wasn't entirely sure that he *did* know what was going to happen next, but he hoped it would come to him if he just kept talking. "For nearly a quarter of an hour, the queen dug. Something told her she would find something here if she just kept digging. After a few minutes, others joined her. Now, nearly a dozen people were digging at once and the hole grew quickly.

"The queen set her shovel in the dirt for a moment. Her arms burned with exhaustion, but she had no intention of stopping. She would rest for a minute. Only one minute. That's when she noticed the movement." Chris hesitated. *Noticed the movement of what?* He looked over at Becky and saw her watching him with anticipation. *Come up with something now.*

"The insect was tiny," he said slowly, still reaching for inspiration, "almost too small to see. It was black as well, blending almost completely into the color of the soil. When the queen stooped to examine it, she saw that the insect was not alone. It had five or six partners marching behind it, and when the queen moved some loosened dirt, at least a dozen more emerged.

"The queen, who had a nearly encyclopedic knowledge of the species of Tamarisk, had never seen this tiny insect before. She picked one up, and the little creature stopped moving entirely, seemingly stunned. The little thing was the deepest black with a hard shell. It had four back legs and two minuscule pincers in the front. The queen was certain she was looking at something that no one in the kingdom had ever seen before."

Chris smiled awkwardly at Becky, hoping she would be prompted enough to continue because he had nothing. Becky looked upward for a moment and then picked up the story.

"Miea held the insect out for the chief scientist at the site to examine. 'Have you ever seen this before?' The scientist leaned forward and looked at the creature carefully. 'No, Your Majesty, never,' he said. Miea held the bug closer to her again. 'There's an answer here,' she said, 'I just know it.'"

Becky's eyes locked with Chris's eyes. "What's the answer?"

"Yeah, I figured you'd be wondering about that." Chris felt a little like he'd painted himself into a corner. As a scientist—even one who spent all of his time as an administrator now—he wanted his solution to the problem in Tamarisk to make sense. At the same time, though, many of the things they'd created in Tamarisk were scientifically suspect. Scientific accuracy, after all, wasn't the point. They'd taken some huge leaps in inventing the world. What was one more?

"Over the next few hours, the scientist's staff analyzed the soil around the insect colony and compared it to the soil closer to the surface. They came to a remarkable conclusion: the soil where the creatures settled was devoid of all the nutrients necessary to maintain plant life."

Chris looked over to see Becky smiling. "What?" he said.

"Now what are you going to do about it?"

He smiled back. She looked so much better than she had when she'd come into the living room less than an hour ago. "I'm going to turn it over to you."

"No chance!"

"Beck, you're about to save Tamarisk," he said with mock sweetness in his voice. "It would be selfish of me to take that from you."

"Nope, you're on a roll, Dad. I'm sure you have something brilliant in mind."

"No, really, it's all yours."

Becky's eyes narrowed. "You don't think I can handle it, do you?"

"Of course I think you can handle it. So handle it."

"Okay, I will." Becky leaned back against the pillow and didn't say anything for several minutes. Chris scrambled for a way to pick her up just in case she decided she didn't know where to go with the story.

She sat up and began. "With remarkable swiftness—" Chris laughed to himself. "With remarkable swiftness" was code for "I'm about to take a huge leap here." "—the scientists analyzed the insects and their environment. Miea contributed the expertise she had gained from working in the fields and studying at the university, and she and the large staff of scientists called to work on the project determined that the insects rose up from deep below the surface of the earth because they were starving. The solution was complicated, but with the best minds in Tamarisk working day and night, within a week they'd built machines to feed new nutrients to the insects' original homes. The insects ended their migration and quickly burrowed back where they came from, leaving the surface to the vegetation of Tamarisk.

"Almost immediately, the plants started showing signs of new life. No more than a month later, the entire kingdom was as blue and vibrant as it had ever been. A horrible crisis had been averted because of the intuition of the brilliant young queen."

Becky threw Chris a sidelong glance. *She knows how preposterous that solution sounds, but she also knows I'll let it ride.* "That Miea is one amazing person," Chris said.

"Yeah, isn't she?"

"Are we all set?"

"I think so."

"Time for the closing words?"

"Right. So ends today's saga of the land of Tamarisk." She smiled shyly at him.

Those aren't all the closing words, Beck. You're supposed to say, "Our story returns again tomorrow night."

"So, how does it feel to save an entire kingdom?" Chris said.

Becky sighed deeply. "Pretty good. Do you think we really did it?"

"I think there's a decent chance. Are you going to go back now to find out?"

"I can't. Whenever I get pulled out, I can't go back for a while afterward. Believe me, I've tried."

She's absolutely convinced this happens. I think she's got me convinced at this point, too. Geez.

"That was a great idea you had," Becky said.

"You mean the thing about the insects?"

"That was pretty good. Not your best ever, but definitely okay. I meant the thing about telling the story to make things better over there. I only hope it worked."

"Yeah, me too."

Becky looked up at the ceiling for a moment. Then she got out from under the covers, reached over, and hugged Chris. "Thanks, Dad."

"Glad I could help, babe."

///

Since Becky couldn't go back to Tamarisk, she decided that going to the movies with her father was an acceptable alternative. Chris took her to a film by a director who, less than a year ago, he'd dubbed "too dark" for her. The movie, which dealt with the themes of teen drug abuse, alienation, and active rejection of authority, received great reviews, and several of Becky's friends had seen it already. Chris wasn't entirely sure why he'd decided Becky was ready to handle this. He was even less sure why she deemed it okay to watch it with him.

"I am so glad you are not like Pauline," he said to Becky in a coffee bar afterward, referring to the heroine of the movie.

"How do you know, Dad," Becky said with a sly smile. "Maybe I have a secret life."

Chris tipped a biscotti in her direction. "I already know about your secret life. I'm guessing Pauline never once petted a hoffler."

Becky considered this for a moment. "Maybe if she had, things would have turned out differently for her."

Chris took a sip of his café au lait and admired his daughter's gleaming eyes. "Yeah, maybe."

They filled the rest of the day with window-shopping, browsing, and a walk through the park. Just passing the time. Chris didn't even mind the traffic going over the bridge, which was inevitable, even on a Sunday night.

The mood shifted instantly when he got to Polly's, though. Polly had been out when he'd picked Becky up yesterday, and he hadn't seen her since their curt phone conversation. It was immediately apparent, however, that Polly hadn't forgotten their last exchange. Chris could swear that Polly's eye sockets actually shifted closer together when she was peeved.

Polly kissed Becky on the forehead before she even got into the house. Chris thought it might be a good idea to say good-bye to Becky on the front stoop, but before he could do so, Polly said, "Did you have a nice weekend, Becky?"

"Yeah, it was great," Becky said casually.

Chris reached out to give his daughter a hug, but Polly spoke again, this time to him. "Are the two of you still playing fantasy games?"

Chris immediately felt anger bubbling. He didn't want to tangle with Polly in front of Becky, but he wasn't going to have her ridicule them, either. "We went to the movies."

Polly scowled. It dawned on him that she'd probably been working herself up for this showdown since Wednesday night. "Was that before or after you took your trip to La-La Land?"

"Mom, stop already, okay?"

Polly flicked a glance at Becky and then stared back at Chris. "Really, I want to know. How elaborate was the fantasy this time. Did you get to shake hands with a dragon, maybe?"

Chris relived the hug Becky had given him when they'd finished their Tamarisk story that morning. The contrast between that moment and this one nearly brought tears to his eyes. "Polly, don't be ridiculous."

Polly threw her eyes skyward. "Ridiculous," she said sharply.

"There are absolutely no dragons in Tamarisk. Gigantic birds, yes. Fish the size of apartment buildings, yes. Sentient globules, even. But there are no dragons."

Chris saw Becky chuckle out of the corner of his eye. He nearly smiled himself, but held his gaze on his ex-wife.

"Gigantic birds but no dragons," Polly said slowly.

"Absolutely zero dragons."

Polly tilted her head to the right. If she tilted her head to the left, that meant she was going to offer empathy or sympathy. When she tilted her head to the right, the exact opposite was coming. "Have you *been* to Tamarisk, Chris?"

Chris tilted his head involuntarily for a moment and then shifted it back. "Sadly, no, Polly. I haven't been that lucky."

Polly grinned humorlessly. "But you're saying you believe that Becky has actually been there—to this imaginary world you made up."

Chris flashed a glance at Becky. She was watching him with anticipation. *No pressure here.* Really, though, there wasn't any pressure. Becky had convinced him. Hadn't he told himself exactly that this morning? The last thing he was going to do was betray his daughter to stay out of trouble with his ex-wife. "Yeah, I believe Becky has been there. I'm sure of it."

Polly's shoulders sagged, but her gaze remained lasered to his. "Are you serious?"

Polly's controlled intensity suddenly seemed funny to him. He laughed dryly. "As serious as I can be, Polly."

He wanted to see how Becky was reacting to this, but he didn't want to implicate her by glancing in that direction. Polly took a step back, looked skyward again, and then swept a look of derision over both of them. "I'm not sure what the two of you think you're doing, but if you think I'm going to play along, you're sorely mistaken. Becky, if you continue to hallucinate this way, we're going to need to seek professional help." She looked down at the ground, shook her head, and then locked in on Chris again. "And if you continue to participate in these delusions, I'll call my lawyer."

This was the first time Polly had threatened to take him to court in years. As such, it should have had a more significant effect on Chris. The threat had surprisingly little power, though. He knew instinctively that she wouldn't try to take Becky away from him. Not now.

Interestingly, Polly didn't wait for a response from him. As soon as she finished speaking, she stalked back into the house, leaving Becky behind. Chris closed the ten feet between him and his daughter and wrapped an arm around her shoulders.

"It's gonna be ugly in there tonight, huh?"

Becky looked toward the front door and shrugged. "Nah, once we're alone, she'll let up. She's really pissed at you, though."

"How would you know the difference?"

Becky smiled. Then she put her arms around his waist and tugged. "Thanks for everything today, Dad. I love you."

"I love you, too, Beck. Sure you don't want to crash at my place tonight?"

"Yeah, that would go over really well." She hugged him again. "I'd better get inside."

Chris kissed the top of her head and let her go. As Becky got to the door, she waved to him and mouthed, "Bye." It immediately sent him back to the day he drove away for the first time.

There was a huge difference, though. This time, Becky's eyes were bright.

14

Polly was still livid about her argument with Chris the next morning. She hated getting that heated in front of Becky, but Chris had pressed every single one of her buttons. Why was she always at her worst with him? Dozens of times since the divorce she'd convinced herself that a more cordial and open relationship with her ex-husband would be best for everyone. When she saw him, though—or even talked to him on the phone—something grated and made it impossible to make even the slightest overture to him.

Now this Tamarisk thing was really beyond the pale. It had been very cute when Becky was little, and Becky and Chris certainly seemed to have a great deal of fun with it. Polly knew it distracted Becky from her illness in the early days, and for that, Polly was genuinely grateful. However, the idea of Chris using such a childish thing to try to get back into Becky's good graces was just appalling. Equally appalling was that it actually seemed to be working—enough to get Becky to fabricate stories about "traveling" to Tamarisk to show her that they had a new bond. How had Chris pulled that off? Was it possible that Polly had truly missed the signs that Becky needed more from her dad? Until a few weeks ago, she'd given every indication that just the opposite was the case.

If Chris's intention was to drive a wedge between Polly and Becky, he'd had at least temporary success. Becky had been moody and withdrawn from her the remainder of Sunday, and said very little to her before she went to school this morning.

That put a dark cast on the day, causing her to relive her battle with Chris multiple times. Meanwhile, Polly was stuck in the house waiting for the electrician to show up. She hated waiting for service people. Last night, an outlet had blown out in the family room, probably overloaded by all of Al's toys there. After that, they couldn't run the computer and the big-screen TV at the same time, and Al begged her to get it fixed before tonight's baseball game. So she was sequestered at home—doing a little seething to pass the time—until Gary arrived.

He finally showed up at a quarter to noon. Gary had done repairs on the house numerous times since Polly owned it, and she'd hoped he would have gotten there sooner. Obviously long-term customers didn't get preferential treatment from this guy, though. He went into the family room, said, "Ouch, bad one" when he saw the outlet, and then went to the basement to noodle around on the circuit breaker for a while. He finally turned the power off in the family room and came up to work on the outlet.

"Did you see that show on the Discovery Channel last night?" Gary said while he explored the damage with a little flashlight.

"The power kept blowing out in this room, so we didn't see much of anything."

"Amazing stuff. All about alternate planes of existence."

Polly winced. "What?"

"You know, parallel worlds, different versions of Earth, alien planets, that kind of thing."

"Why would I watch a show about that?"

"It was on the Discovery Channel."

Polly rubbed her forehead, feeling a potential migraine coming on. "As I said, it was hard to watch television last night."

"Open-mindedness leads to enrichment."

Polly leaned toward the electrician. "I'm sorry, I didn't get that."

"New worlds embellish existing worlds, leading to an

increase in potential."

Polly was beginning to wonder if Gary had electrocuted himself. Maybe he was having some kind of stroke or something. His speech seemed different.

"Your acknowledgement can help soothe the others," the electrician said, "make solutions possible. You have a role."

Polly felt the hairs on the back of her neck rise. How quickly could the paramedics get here if she needed them? "Gary, is there a point to these aphorisms you're spouting?"

The electrician didn't respond, simply concentrated on his work. Twice, though, he said the phrase "Acknowledgement enriches" in that phantom voice. Polly felt the need to sit down. She'd never seen someone have a psychotic experience before. She would have left the room, but she wasn't sure it was safe to leave Gary alone.

Again, Gary said, "Acknowledgement enriches." Then he reconnected a wire, clicked off his flashlight, and screwed in the faceplate. He stood, turned to her, nodded, and said, "Let's give it a try." He said it just like normal-Gary.

Gary walked right past her with minimal eye contact, went down to the basement, switched the power back on, and then returned to the family room and plugged in the television. With a flick of the remote, the TV popped on.

"You're all set," Gary said.

Polly turned off the television. "Thanks."

Gary acknowledged her with a nod and then gathered his tools.

"Gary, are you okay?"

"Yeah, I feel fine. Why?"

"What was that thing about a show on the Discovery Channel?"

Gary looked at her as though he didn't understand the question for a moment and then brightened with recognition. "Oh, right, that show about alternate planes of existence. I was channel surfing last night and I stopped on it. I don't know why; I never watch that stuff. What a crock. It made me laugh out loud. I just wondered if you saw it."

"What about the other stuff?"

"Other stuff?"

"That other stuff you were saying about being open-minded and enrichment and that kind of thing."

Polly could see from Gary's reaction that he had no idea what she meant. "I'm not following you."

She waved a hand. "Never mind."

Gary picked up his bag and headed toward the door.

"I don't believe any of that stuff about other worlds," Polly said, following him.

Gary reached for the doorknob and turned to her. "Neither do I. That's why that show made me laugh." He paused for a moment and his expression changed. His eyes seemed deeper, more thoughtful. He looked at her carefully and his attention made Polly uncomfortable. Involuntarily, she took a step back.

Then, just as quickly, Gary's old face was back. He grinned benignly and looked at the doorknob, as though he'd forgotten he'd put his hand there.

Did he really have no memory of what he'd said a few minutes earlier? He looked fine, but it was possible he really was having some kind of episode. "Do you think that maybe you should take the rest of the day off?"

His eyes narrowed and he said, "Huh?"

Polly was beginning to feel embarrassed. "Forget what I said. Just have a good day. Thanks for taking care of the outlet."

"You got it. You know, you might want to take a little rest yourself."

"Yeah, maybe I will. Now that you've fixed the television, maybe I'll just relax in front of some mindless show for a little while." She grinned embarrassedly. "Not the Discovery Channel, though."

///

For the third time that afternoon, Miea felt like a portion

of the conversation was eluding her. First, there had been the discussion with the vice chancellor of the Thorns when she confronted him about Rubus's presence at a blighted Tamariskian field. She'd expected the vice chancellor to dissemble, but his reaction was entirely unexpected. He'd claimed that his son had gone missing and then had the nerve to suggest that Miea had him kidnapped.

Shortly after this, Becky had showed up in her chambers. Her eyes moved all around the room, as though she were looking for something she'd misplaced. She walked over to a window and gazed out for a long stretch, and then, when Miea made a passing reference to an upcoming briefing on the blight, Becky suddenly got very flustered and misty-eyed. Saying nothing more than, "I need to go back," Becky disappeared, leaving Miea to wonder what had happened.

Now Dyson had showed up for his briefing, but he was offering no new information. *What were the results of the vibration study of the soil in Jonrae?* Inconclusive. *Have we learned anything from the relative heartiness of the tongass grove in the midst of Eannes Meadow?* It doesn't appear so. *What about my suggestion to deploy more analysts to Eannes?* Minister Thuja wants to give this further consideration. Dyson delivered his answers briskly and without embellishment. It almost seemed as though he were making a conscious effort to say nothing.

"Was there an actual point in your coming to make this report today?" Miea said, miffed.

For the briefest instant, Dyson's expression showed a hint of consternation. Then just as quickly, he regained his professional demeanor, looking past her rather than at her.

"You've requested these briefings on a regular schedule, Your Majesty. Therefore, I come to brief you."

"But I expect you to *say something* during these briefings. It's inconceivable that there is nothing new to report. Not under these circumstances."

"I can only bring you the information that is available, Your Majesty."

Did Dyson call her "Your Majesty" more often than anyone else in the kingdom did or did it just seem that way because the words still sounded so wrong coming from his lips? "I'm not entirely convinced that this is the case, Dyson."

Dyson's expression remained fixed. "I'm sorry, Your Majesty. I'm not sure what you mean by that."

"I'm not entirely convinced that I'm getting all the information that is available. I believe Minister Thuja is giving me the information he thinks I need."

"I don't believe that to be true, Your Majesty."

If he really didn't believe it to be true, he hadn't been paying attention when she and Thuja were in a room together. The minister's overt attempts to appear respectful while at the same time making his distrust for her youth obvious were unmistakable. Thuja didn't want to tell her everything, either because he feared she would overreact or because he wanted to control things to the point where she had virtually no decisions to make. Given the scale of this crisis, that was unacceptable.

"Does the minister take you into his confidence, Dyson?"

Dyson's eyes shifted slightly. "Excuse me, Your Majesty?"

Miea leaned forward against her desk. "I'm wondering if you discuss information with the minister when it comes in from various sources. I'm wondering if Thuja tries out different scenarios on you."

Dyson said nothing for a moment. When he spoke, he still did not look at her. "I am a member of the minister's staff. He encourages us to exchange ideas. It is part of the working environment."

"Is it safe to assume that some of the information exchanged in these conversations fails to come up in my briefings?"

"Nothing vital is left out of these briefings, Your Majesty."

"Given the confounding nature of this blight, I would think it would be difficult to determine what information is vital and what isn't. Perhaps you could let me know what some of your exchanges have been like over the past few days."

For the first time since he walked into her office that day,

Dyson looked directly into Miea's eyes. "I will not be your spy, Your Majesty."

Miea broke eye contact. "Dyson, you know how much I thrive on details."

"I know that I share with you every piece of information I am authorized to share with you. If you truly believe Minister Thuja is holding things back, you should discuss this with him. You're the queen. Order him if you think it is necessary."

Miea stood up as though launched, feeling a volatile mix of anguish and frustration. "Do you understand what is at stake here? The kingdom I love is disintegrating and I can't do anything about it. Maybe I could do something if I had access to all the raw data, if I were out in the fields, if I were working with the analysts. But we won't know whether I could or not, because the Minister—and his vaunted aide—believe I am not equipped to deal with the information."

While Miea felt her composure slip, she was amazed that Dyson was capable of maintaining his. His head tracked her movement, but his face remained calm. "Your Majesty, I again suggest that you take this subject up with Minister Thuja. If you truly believe that we are withholding anything vital, he is the only person who can assure you otherwise."

Miea closed her eyes. For some reason, she recalled the look of desperation on Becky's face when she said, "I need to go back." Miea had no idea why, but the girl was extremely upset and even flustered. Miea certainly knew how that felt. Nothing was working. They were no closer to a solution to the blight—at least to her knowledge—than they had been when they first discovered it. Thuja all but openly challenged her authority, and Dyson skewered her with formality.

With her eyes still closed, Miea felt her knees sway slightly. She didn't feel as though she was going to pass out or even stumble, but for just a second, the ground seemed the shift under her. She opened her eyes, took a moment to collect herself, and sat back at her desk.

"Are you all right?" Dyson said in a tone that she was no

longer accustomed to hearing.

Her eyes caught his and she recognized his concern. *No, I'm not all right. I'm worried. I'm frustrated. I'm alone. I'm not positive I can handle this.*

"Yes," she said, nodding slowly. "I'm fine. I'm going to call for a little argo and maybe something to eat. I didn't have time for lunch today."

"But you're okay?"

"Of course I'm okay." *What would happen if I said I wasn't? What would you do then, Dyson? Would you help me through this? Could you do that even if you wanted to?* "Thank you for this briefing."

Dyson stood and, for just a moment, Miea couldn't read his expression. He gathered himself quickly, though. "Thank you, Your Majesty."

He bowed slightly, turned, and left. Miea watched him go and continued watching for several seconds after he disappeared. Only Sorbus's arrival in her doorway brought her back to the present.

"The contingent from the Festival Committee is here, Your Majesty."

She took a deep breath and offered Sorbus a wan smile. "Send them in, please."

///

As soon as Becky was back in her bed, she regretted leaving Tamarisk so abruptly. How had she even done that? All she'd said was, "I need to go back," and she was home again. Was that all she had to do?

At the very least, she owed Miea an explanation for why she'd gotten so upset. For two days, she'd clung to the belief that the storytelling session she'd had with her father had cured the blight. When she'd traveled to Tamarisk again and learned that the crisis still existed, she'd felt like someone had knocked the air out of her. She'd felt like she was about to cry and, while she didn't have any problem with the idea of crying in front of Miea, she didn't know how to explain why she was so upset. At that moment, the only thing that seemed right was leaving.

What did Miea think about her running out, though? Was she insulted? Was she confused? Becky wouldn't be able to go back until Saturday to explain.

Meanwhile, school seemed to drone on. Distress over Tamarisk had drained Becky and she was barely listening to her teachers—all of whom seemed to have decided that today was the perfect day to lecture endlessly about some meaningless subject. By the time she got to lunch, she was ready to call it day. Unfortunately, biology, geometry, and Spanish awaited her in the afternoon. The Nestlé Toll House Bar she'd bought from the cafeteria helped a little, but she really just wanted to put her head on the table and nap for about three days.

"Did I miss out on the part where you mentioned taking a vow of silence?" Lonnie said from across the table.

Becky smiled weakly and took a sip from her water bottle. "I guess I forgot to take my fun pills this morning."

"What's going on? You seem like you're on another planet today."

Becky chuckled. "Yeah, something like that." She still hadn't mentioned her trips to Tamarisk to Lonnie. She couldn't figure out the right way to do it and she certainly wasn't going to bring the topic up in the middle of the cafeteria. "Sorry I'm such a drag."

"You didn't answer my question."

"About visiting another planet?"

"About what's going on. I can kinda tell that something's bugging you. In the old days—you know, like, yesterday—we could talk about that kind of stuff."

Becky reached across the table and squeezed Lonnie's hand. She really appreciated how well her best friend knew her—even if she didn't know everything. "Things are a little weird with Mom."

"You're kidding, right? Just at the point where you and your father are doing better you start having problems with your mom?"

"Everything balances out, huh? Actually, they're related, at least a little. I don't think Mom is totally in love with the fact that I've reconnected with my father."

"Really? That doesn't sound like her at all."

"Yeah, actually it does. Mom is amazing except when it comes to Dad. You just never got to see that part of her."

Lonnie took a little time to ponder this, her eyes angled toward the fluorescent lights. She looked back at Becky. "That really totally sucks."

Something about the way Lonnie said that set Becky off. The thing with Tamarisk last night had her completely preoccupied, but the last few days at home—since that little scene her mother created when Dad dropped her off—were awkward and even a little humiliating. Mom had that tightness in her voice that she had whenever she was disappointed in Becky, and every time they looked at each other, Becky felt like her mother was scolding her with her eyes. She had figured the skirmish with Dad was going to blow over in about a half hour. But it hadn't. Mom was still making life difficult even yesterday afternoon. If Al hadn't taken her out to dinner before Dad came—*thanks for having my back, Al*—Becky was certain there would have been another uproar and Becky would have flat-out freaked.

"Yes," Becky said sharply. "Yes, it does. It sucks big-time. Would it kill my parents to make me feel comfortable in both houses for a few days?"

"Have you spoken to her about it?"

"I can't talk to her about it. It's like she has a moat around her or something. She is being ridiculously close-minded."

"It's probably a little hard for her seeing you and your dad all lovey again."

"Why? How does that make any sense? It's not like having a better relationship with my father takes anything away from my relationship with her."

"Except for the extra time you're spending with him."

"Except for the *tiny bit* of extra time I'm spending with him.

Why are you defending her like this?"

Lonnie put her hands up. "I'm not defending her. I just think there might be some stuff you need to see from her point of view."

"I get her point of view. And I still think she's being ridiculous."

"So talk to her. Make her realize that she's wrong."

Becky could feel her frustration rising. "I *can not* talk to her," she said stiffly.

"Beck, I love you, but it sounds like you're being a little close-minded yourself."

Becky's face got warmer. Sometimes Lonnie didn't know when to let up. "You know what? You don't have all the facts, so maybe you should just keep out of this."

Lonnie leaned closer to her. She had her "reasonable" face on. That expression often made Becky laugh to herself. Today it just ticked her off. "Beck, if I don't have all the facts, maybe you should give them to me."

Becky moved forward so that their faces were as close together as possible given the presence of the table between them. "I don't want to give them to you."

Just then, Becky noticed Lonnie's expression change dramatically. She seemed frightened by something and Becky knew it had nothing to do with what she'd just said. Slowly, Lonnie wiped her hand underneath her nose. Instinctively, Becky did the same thing. When she did, she felt wetness there and she didn't have to look at her hand to know that the wetness was blood. She quickly reached for a napkin and put it to her nose.

"Let's go to the bathroom," Lonnie said softly.

Without a word, Becky stood up and followed her.

If Lonnie said anything to her while they walked, Becky didn't hear it. They went into a bathroom stall together—the same one as last time—and Becky sat down with her head leaned back and wadded-up toilet paper on her nose. After a minute, she took the paper from her nose and Lonnie handed her another wad.

"Tell me I shouldn't be worried about this," Lonnie said shakily.

Becky squeezed the paper a little tighter. "See what happens when you get me worked up?"

"Right, I knew this was my fault." Lonnie leaned a little closer and examined her face, for what, Becky couldn't imagine. "How many of these have you had lately, Beck?"

"I only have them when you're around. Maybe it really *is* your fault."

"I'm serious."

Becky pulled the paper back again. There was less blood on this one. Lonnie handed her some more toilet paper. "I'm serious, too. Not about it being your fault, but about this being only the second one. They both happened in the cafeteria and they both happened when I was excited." She rolled her eyes and tried on a grin. "This is gonna make me a really hot date in the future, huh?"

Becky's attempt to lighten things up didn't seem to have any impact on Lonnie. "When are you going to the doctor?"

"I don't remember saying anything about going to the doctor."

"Beck, you have to find out."

"It's not what you think it is."

"How do you know?"

"I would know."

"Did you know the last time?"

"I was practically an infant the last time. I didn't know anything." She lifted the paper and saw very little blood. This was passing. Lonnie handed her another wad and Becky indicated that she didn't need it.

Lonnie tossed the wad in the toilet. "What's the downside of going to the doctor and confirming that there's nothing to these nosebleeds?"

What's the downside? You're kidding, Lonnie, right? "My doctor invades my personal space."

"Almost a good enough excuse, but not quite."

A part of Becky still believed she could make this go away. A part of her even believed that there really wasn't anything to worry about. She sat forward and dabbed her nose with the toilet paper a few times. No new blood. "If it happens again, I'll go to the doctor. I promise."

"If it happens again, I'm dragging you there myself."

"You won't have to drag me; I'll go." Becky touched her best friend on the arm and summoned the resolve to look her directly in the eye. "But unless that happens, you don't mention this to anyone, okay? Especially not my mother."

Lonnie's eyes misted over instantly and she looked away for a moment. When she looked back at her, she shook her head slowly. "Okay."

They stood up together and exited the stall.

"Beck, you have to stay around for me, you know," Lonnie said softly, wrapping an arm around her shoulders. "I'd be a wreck if you weren't here."

Becky leaned her head against Lonnie's. "I'm not going anywhere," she said with all the conviction she felt. Which wasn't much.

///

Not that he ever looked forward to them, but this blind date was about the last thing Chris wanted to do tonight. He'd been edgy since the confrontation with Polly, he was in the middle of budget projections at the office (which was about as satisfying as eating air), and Becky had looked crestfallen when she'd told him this morning that their story hadn't cured Tamarisk. When he'd talked to her about an hour ago, she actually sounded worse. This blight thing was really getting to her. It would have been a great night for a high-carb dinner followed by falling asleep on the couch, but that wasn't what was on the agenda. Instead, his schedule called for a woman named Kyra.

The fact that Kyra was now more than fifteen minutes late didn't fill him with great expectation. Maybe she was going stand him up. It wouldn't be the first time. He wouldn't have minded at all.

A few minutes later, he decided to order a glass of wine. The wine and Kyra arrived at the same time. His first impression of Kyra was that she was stunning, but the waiter distracted him. He turned to thank the waiter for his drink and then looked back at the woman. She was still stunning. She was easily the most beautiful woman Lisa had ever set him up with. In fact, she was easily one of the most beautiful women he'd ever seen. What on earth was she doing here?

Kyra ordered a glass of Chianti and then turned to him. "I am so sorry I'm late. I'm working on a merger and it seems the parties are moving farther apart by the day. I just spent a half hour holding the hand of the CEO of the smaller company. If the guy was getting paid for his neuroses, he'd be a billionaire."

"Sounds like fun," Chris said sarcastically.

"I love it," Kyra said, her eyes widening. "The easy ones bore me. The challenges really get my blood going. The only problem is I have this tendency to lose track of time. Again, sorry."

"Totally okay." Kyra's hair actually shimmered. Romance novelists would call it flaxen. He was tempted to touch it to see if it emitted an electrical charge, but he restrained himself. Her drink arrived and she took a sip of it, which drew his attention to her eyes. He couldn't think of what romance novelists would call their color, but they were an almost-unearthly blue. *Oh my god, Lisa set me up with a gorgeous alien. She probably figured I'd never connect with a human woman, so she broadened her search.* "You should never have to apologize for loving anything. Even your job."

"Nicely said. And you're right; loving is a very, very good thing." She tipped her glass in his direction and took another sip.

For the next hour, the time with Kyra followed the structure of the typical blind date—light conversation, slightly probing personal question, more light conversation, slightly more probing personal question, comment about the meal, nonthreatening embarrassing admission, and more light conversation. But it didn't have the substance of one. Kyra intrigued him for any number of reasons and she had the rare ability to get him to talk about himself without his feeling self-conscious. She even mentioned that she was an avid gardener, which got him talking about plants, horticulture, and some of the work he'd done when he was an active scientist.

Had the date ended when the waiter took away their dinner plates, this would have ranked as one of the best first dates of Chris's life. Unfortunately, it didn't. The turn in the conversation began, innocuously enough, with the mention of her children.

"Oh, you have kids?" Chris said. "How old are they?"

"My son is nine and my daughter is six. They're with their father tonight."

"How long have the two of you been split?"

"Nearly five years now. The second kid really did us in, though we were wobbling even before George was born."

"Yeah, that's tough. What's it like dealing with your ex now?"

"Actually, we've gotten along considerably better since the divorce than we did during the last half-dozen years of our marriage. Parenting was just about the only thing we agreed on and we've managed to build a platonic relationship from that."

Chris chuckled cynically. "I'm sorry, could you repeat that in English, I didn't understand what you were saying."

Kyra paused as she brought her water glass to her lips. "What do you mean?"

Chris waved a hand. "Forget it; I'm just being a jerk. Let's just say I haven't had the same experience with my ex as you've had with yours."

"You have kids?"

"Kid. A fourteen-year-old daughter. She's wonderful and my former wife hates the fact that I think so."

Kyra rolled her eyes. "I find that a little hard to believe."

"No, really. I think if I had been distant to her, or distracted, or even borderline abusive, my marriage would have survived it. But loving her unconditionally and giving her every bit of my soul—that was too much for my ex to take."

Kyra's expression darkened. "That's unfortunate."

Chris felt a surge of adrenaline. After what had happened over the weekend, the very thought of Polly kicked him into fight-or-flight mode. "Yeah, it is definitely unfortunate. A household gets blown up and I lose years with my daughter not because I was a bad guy but because—catch the irony here—I was too much of a good guy. It gets better, though. Now that I've finally recaptured some of what I had with Becky, after all of that horrible time feeling tossed out onto the side of the road, Polly is trying to find a way to split us up again. It's like divorcing me once wasn't good enough."

"Wow," Kyra said thinly. "That's tough."

A part of Chris's brain registered the *can we change the subject* message Kyra was sending. It wasn't, however, the part that controlled his speech. "You know what? It's probably just as well. I mean, if it weren't Becky, something else would have killed my marriage eventually. I don't know, career issues, money issues, issues about wallpaper or pasta sauces or sitcoms. Something would have gotten us. It was preordained. Do you know why? Because romantic love always dies. Absolutely one hundred percent of the time."

Kyra seemed genuinely stunned by this statement. "Certainly not all marriages end in divorce. Some people do stay together."

"Together? Yes. In love? Absolutely not. You show me two people who have been together for any length of time and still claim to be in love and I'll show you two people who are faking it."

Kyra had the water glass in her hand through this entire tirade. Now she put it down. "You don't really believe that, do you?"

Did he really believe it? Chris gave himself a moment to consider the thought. "Yes, I do really believe it."

Kyra raised her eyebrows. "Then what are we doing here?"

she said softly, clearly hurt.

Chris realized, too late, how absurd this all must have sounded to Kyra. She didn't know him well enough to know where this eruption was coming from. She didn't know any part of his story beyond what he'd spat out in the last couple of minutes. He also realized—again, too late—that his message wasn't the kind of thing a blind date—or any kind of date for that matter—would be interested in hearing.

"I'm sorry; I've had a bad few days. I didn't mean to go off like that."

Kyra took her napkin from her lap and placed it on the table. "It sounds like this has been in your head for a little more than a couple of days."

Chris wanted to argue the point, but then realized he was just putting off the inevitable. There was nothing in his limited collection of dating skills that would help him fix this, and even if he did, things would just fall apart on the next date.

"I was having a really nice time tonight," he said, resigned. "Sorry I went postal on you."

Kyra pushed back her chair. "Feel what you're feeling, Chris. I'm just afraid that what you're feeling doesn't connect with where I'm going right now."

She stood and left the restaurant. Chris stayed, declining coffee and dessert, but ordering another glass of wine. It was a little incredible that he was capable of finding new ways to blow it with women.

Things really would have been so much better—for Kyra as well as himself—if he'd spent the night asleep on the couch instead.

15

"So, Dad, even though you don't do genetic engineering anymore, you still keep up-to-date with what's going on, right? I mean, you still read scientific journals and all that stuff, don't you?"

Chris and Becky were washing pots and pans after dinner. Feeling the need to conjure up something festive to reverse their moods, Chris had decided they would make an elaborate Mexican meal together. The food was delicious, though Becky didn't eat all that much. The downside was that it left a mountain of pots and pans.

"Yeah, of course I do. You know how I love that stuff."

Becky dried the tortilla press and put it back in the cupboard. "That means you're still pretty sharp and up-to-date and could probably call your scientific skills right back up if you had to, right?"

Chris washed a cast-iron skillet and handed it to his daughter. "Yeah, why? Have you found a new job for me?"

"Sorta."

Chris turned off the faucet and cocked an eyebrow toward Becky. He'd never discussed his unhappiness with his job with her. "Sorta?"

"Don't think I'm insane, but what would you think about coming to Tamarisk with me tonight?"

Chris's stomach fluttered. "Come to Tamarisk?"

"I don't know why I didn't think of it sooner. They're having a problem with plants and you're a plant expert. Makes sense to try, doesn't it?"

Chris laughed. "Makes sense?"

Becky looked up at the ceiling. "Okay, maybe none of this really makes sense. I actually do realize that this whole Tamarisk thing is pretty incredible. But things are really messed up over there. Who knows? Maybe you can come up with something that none of their scientists have come up with."

Becky was serious about this. "You want me to go to Tamarisk with you?"

"I think you *need* to go."

Chris allowed himself to consider the implications of what Becky was saying. She was inviting him to travel with her to another universe. It sounded so ridiculous when he thought of it that way, but wasn't there some piece of him that had been waiting for this invitation from the moment Becky mentioned her journeys there? *Magic is just science we don't understand yet.* Chris couldn't remember who'd said that, but he had never been someone who believed that physical laws were immutable. He'd always considered the possibility that remarkable—even magical—discoveries were just around the corner. Was he in the midst of participating in one?

"Is that even possible?" he said tentatively.

Becky's expression darkened. "Are you saying you don't believe I can do this?"

"I'm saying I'm wondering if *I* can do this. I don't know; I kind of assumed you were the only one with a valid passport."

Becky considered this notion. "Maybe I am. But I think we have to find out. They need you, Dad."

Chris thrilled at the words. "So how do we go about it?"

Becky laughed, as though surprised by the question. "I don't have any idea. You'll try it, though?"

Chris shrugged. His skin prickled. "Sure, why not? We didn't have anything planned for tonight anyway."

///

"We have to darken," Becky said as they sat on her bed.

"The lights?"

"The lights are already dark. We have to darken everything. You need to close your eyes and put a blanket over everything that happened today and anything else that might be on your mind."

"You do realize it's going to be a little difficult to avoid thinking about what we're doing, right?"

"Try, Dad. I don't know whether this is going to get us there or not, but I'm sure we'll never get there without it."

Chris closed his eyes. "Darkening sequence initiated."

"Traveling to Tamarisk doesn't require dorky catchphrases."

"Sorry."

Chris didn't want to let Becky down. He didn't want to let himself down. Still, closing his eyes made him think more about what they were doing, not less. He had taken a meditation class when he was in college. Maybe some of the techniques he learned then would be useful. Unfortunately, he didn't remember any of the techniques he learned then.

"You're not darkening," Becky said disapprovingly.

"Are you reading my mind?"

"I don't need to. You're fidgeting. You can't darken and fidget at the same time."

Chris took several deep breaths and tried to concentrate on the black behind his eyelids. He held both of Becky's hands so they wouldn't be separated in transit. Chris didn't want to give too much thought to what being separated could mean. Would he wind up in another part of Tamarisk? Maybe he'd wind up in another world entirely, maybe one created by some other girl and her father. For all he knew, this kind of thing happened all the time but no one talked about it.

Stop thinking. You're messing up the darkening process. Chris felt his thoughts begin to recede as the blackness got blacker. Then blacker still. Then even blacker. He felt movement now and he thought he saw something that was even blacker than black.

The motion nearly caused him to open his eyes.

With that thought, the movement stopped. *Don't think about the movement—whatever it was. Just let yourself move.* A few moments later, the blackness deepened again. Again, Chris felt a pull, but this time he darkened the thought of the pull. The sensation of movement continued for some time. Then it stopped again.

Chris felt himself suspended, as though someone had left him dangling in midair. He felt nothing other than the blackness around him. For an instant, he saw a face—no, not a face; it was a shape or a visage or something that looked like it had an expression but didn't have human features. It was there for just a moment, but when Chris searched for it, he couldn't find it.

"The journey is an arduous one."

The voice was in his head. In his skin. He didn't say the words himself, but he knew that they didn't come from outside. Unless that was the way things worked here.

"You're telling me," Chris said. Had he actually spoken or was he learning some new form of communication?

"There is no gift I can provide to make this easier other than those already provided."

"I need to do this. Help me do this."

"You don't need help. The path is open. An arduous journey awaits. Maintain your vision. Expand your vision."

Did Becky have a conversation like this every time she went to Tamarisk? Was the voice some kind of gatekeeper? Was Chris supposed to come up with some magic words to let him pass? "I don't know what that means."

"Absorb all resources. Be enriched."

As open-minded as Chris believed himself to be, this exchange was getting a little creepy. Why wasn't he moving anymore? Why couldn't he feel Becky's hands?

Suddenly the visage coalesced. It wasn't a face. It wasn't anything Chris had ever seen before and he had no words to describe it. It was will. It was energy.

And it filled him. Filled him with what, he didn't know, but all at once, Chris felt lighter and more substantial at the same time.

"Absorb this and all other resources."

Then the visage was gone, leaving only the sensation behind. Chris wasn't sure what to think, knowing only that he needed to continue to try to get to Tamarisk for Becky. He could feel her hands again. He saw the blacker-than-black path again. He felt the pull.

Again, however, the movement stopped.

What am I doing wrong? Damn, I'll bet Becky really is the only one who can do this.

"Dad, open your eyes."

Chris opened them and squeezed his daughter's hands. "Sorry, babe."

Then he looked around. At the conference room filled with brightly garbed people. At the blackish table made of some kind of stone. *Malheur. I'm nearly certain we called it malheur.* At the scaly, iridescent material covering the walls. *I don't remember that stuff at all.* At the young woman with perfect posture sitting at the head of the table staring at him intently.

He was in Tamarisk.

Chris beamed at Becky and squeezed her hands again. *This is overwhelming. I mean, I believed her, but we're* actually *here.* Becky dropped his hands and turned toward the woman he assumed to be Miea. He'd seen her face before, though he couldn't place it. She did look a little like Kiley, but that wasn't it. The video. The restaurant. What was that all about?

"Your Majesty," Becky said, "I know I didn't clear this with you, but I asked my father to come with me."

Miea nodded slowly. She didn't seem annoyed, but at the same time, she seemed both baffled and uncomfortable. "Of course your father is welcome here, Becky. I'm sure Sorbus can arrange some kind of tour for him."

"He's here to work, Your Majesty."

Chris was only half listening to this exchange. The rest of his attention focused on his surroundings. The translucent writing implements. The bluish cast of the indirect lighting. The labyrinthine weave of the carpeting. The atonal music outside that he could barely hear.

"Work, Becky?"

"My Dad's a scientist. A plant scientist."

At those words, Chris glanced over at the Miea. The queen was looking directly at him. Her gaze was serious, but there was a flicker in her eyes. "Do you think you can help us with the blight?"

Chris drew himself up. *More sightseeing later. There's a job to do now.* "I really don't know, Your Majesty. But I'm happy to give you full access to my brain."

"The brain that helped conjure Tamarisk."

Chris glanced over at the shimmering walls. "I don't think I can take much credit for that."

Miea motioned Chris and Becky to the table. "Please, come sit. The emergency council and I were just discussing the latest damage reports. To be honest, we talk about little else here these days."

Chris sat next to an elderly man, and a man and a woman much closer to Miea's age. "Can you brief me on the situation?"

The queen nodded and the woman next to Chris addressed him. "Are you familiar with blight conditions?"

"I've worked with several and studied many others."

"This one progresses in three stages. Affected plants show signs of banding for up to two weeks. Next comes a shorter period where the bands fade and the plants lose the ability to feed. Finally, necrosis and death."

"Conida?"

"The spores develop within the root system. They remain internal until the final stages of necrosis."

"Is this common for blight here?"

"Blight in itself is not common here. On the occasions where we have had any kind of localized diseases, the conida were always external. We have not had an instance of internal blight conida in nearly a decade."

Clearly botanical conditions were different in Tamarisk than they were at home. This was both good news and bad. Good in that it gave Chris reason to believe that he could provide ideas the locals would not have considered. Bad because there was an excellent chance that his ideas would have no relevance here.

For the next half hour, Chris quizzed the woman on every detail of the disease, examining samples of plants at various stages of infestation, trying to interpret data with a different set of specifications than any he was used to, and attempting to rule out as many possible causes as he could. Occasionally, the young man sitting next to the woman contributed a piece of information. Both of them obviously reported to the elderly man, but other than nodding at his colleagues once or twice, the man did not engage in this conversation. No one else, including Miea herself, participated. Every now and then, Chris would look at another person seated at the table and catch an expression both rapt and stultified.

They're probably as baffled by this experience as I am. I wonder how many of these people even knew Becky existed, and now they've seen her and her dad materialize out of thin air.

At one point, he exchanged glances with Becky. Her eyes were gleaming and her complexion shone. It dawned on him that she had been listening carefully to his exchanges and that she was impressed. Proud of him. He'd have to remember to travel to fantasy worlds with her more often.

Chris took extensive notes. Like everything else, this was a little disorienting at first because the paper felt so brittle (though it turned out to be as sturdy as twenty-four-pound bond), the pen wrote with virtually no drag, and the ink took a second or two to appear on the page. Chris acclimated to this as quickly as he could, though, because he wanted to take all of this information back with him, to study it and reference it against his texts and do further research online.

While he was writing something the woman said about the similarity between the biological makeup of the spores and that of a cyst found on a bird a few years ago in Pinzon, the pen stopped working. He shook it a few times and then reached over to borrow another. He suddenly felt heavier, as though the gravity on the planet had suddenly increased dramatically.

"Dad, we have to leave," Becky said.

"I could use a little more time."

"Not an option. Once the pull starts—"

Chris grabbed his papers. His eyes seemed to close of their own accord. He felt himself floating again and he wanted to look around to see what he was floating through. He couldn't see anything, though. Less than a minute later, gravity normalized and he looked around to find himself back in Becky's room.

He lay back on the bed and looked at his daughter with a huge smile on his face. "That was incredible."

"You sounded pretty smart in there."

"Just making stuff up."

She pushed him playfully. "Do you think you can figure out what's going on?"

"I took a million notes. I'll start looking through everything tomorrow morning—assuming I can even get to sleep tonight. Maybe I'll just get started now."

Chris sat up to look through the papers.

That's when he noticed that they hadn't made the transit with him.

///

realityjunkie: alyssa and rob have no chance of staying together. did u see the way she was talking to dillon today?

punkrockprincess: dillon rocks!!!!! alyssa would be better off with him anyway. maybe if rob didn't kiss beth at kendra's party alyssa wouldn't be looking around.

ilikepie: that kiss was totally innocent and alyssa can be pretty difficult sometimes. movies at my house friday night?

Becky often found these IM exchanges entertaining, but her head just wasn't in it today. She and her father had spent an hour Saturday night and then much of Sunday trying to reconstruct the briefing he had in Tamarisk. A lot of it was way beyond her understanding, but she was pretty good at prompting. She'd remind him that he said something that sounded like "Condoleezza" and that would jog him to write down something important about conida. By the time he dropped her back at Mom's, he'd done a decent job of recalling everything. At least he thought he had.

He said he was going to try to sneak some time on the mainframe at the office today to get a little research done. Becky knew it was hard for him to do nonwork things at work—especially since he'd been "kicked upstairs"—but he sounded like he was seriously going to try. All day at school, Becky wondered if he'd made any progress. Even now, while the discussion about whether Alyssa and Rob were going to survive the week raged on her computer screen, what she really wanted to do was call her dad.

It dawned on her that she could IM him. She'd never done that at work, even though she had him on her buddy list, because it didn't seem appropriate. Things were different now, though. She figured it was worth a shot.

questgirl14: hey, dad!

She hit send and waited. Her friends continued to chatter on (it sounded like she would be going to a Drew Barrymore film festival at Natalie's house on Friday and that Alyssa wasn't invited), but the new screen she opened remained blank for several minutes.

helichrysum: Beck? Nice surprise to see you pop up on my computer.

questgirl14: hows work goin?

helichrysum: About the same. How was school?

questgirl14: it was fine. did you have time to do any research?

helichrysum: Not as much as I wanted to do. I only got about twenty minutes on the big machine at lunchtime.

questgirl14: find anything?

helichrysum: Some of the symptoms they talked about are similar to Dothistroma Needle Blight. It affects pine trees.

questgirl14: maybe that's it!!

helichrysum: The Tamarisk blight only has SOME of the symptoms. Actually, it has a lot of them, but the cycle of the disease is different and that could mean that it's something else entirely.

questgirl14: is there a cure for this kind of blight?

helichrysum: There's a way to control it.

questgirl14: that's way better than nothing!!!!! u think they should check into it?

helichrysum: Two problems. The first is that there's no way I can be certain that it's anything like Dothistroma at this point, and if we treat the wrong thing, we could do a lot of harm. The second is that the control requires the use of copper fungicides. Might be a little tough to take barrels of the stuff with us (it's going to be tougher to transport than paper and that didn't go so well) and who knows if they have the raw materials in Tamarisk to make it there. That brings up a third thing, now that I think of it. Tamarisk is likely to be a very different ecosystem. If we introduce a fungicide from this world into it, we could wind up hurting them more than the blight has.

questgirl14: i don't know if that's possible.

helichrysum: We'll talk to them about it on Tuesday. Meanwhile, I'll try to get a lot more research done.

questgirl14: thanks dad. it's great that ur doing this. i'll let you get back to work.

helichrysum: Feel free to interrupt anytime.

questgirl14: u got it!!!!

Her dad had raised some good points about the Tamarisk ecosystem. After all, the plants were blue and the dirt was black. Who knew what that did to the makeup of stuff? Dad probably would have started working some science into the Tamarisk stories if they'd kept going with them after he split with Mom. They'd both spent a lot more time talking about the logic of the world in the months before she cut things off. Since they didn't get to the science, though, there was a definite chance that Tamarisk had significantly different physical laws. *Odds are good, Beck, since it's a different universe and is the product of your imagination.*

There weren't going to be any easy answers here. She just knew it.

punkrockprincess: hey becky, u still there???????

questgirl14: yeah, i'm still here, just thinking. I say thumbs-up drew barrymore, thumbs-down alyssarob, thumbs underground for dillon and I'll bring the popcorn on fri. the stuff we had last time tasted toxic!!!!!!!!!

///

Chris needed to pull himself away from the computer to get to his dinner date with Lisa. Once people had started to leave the office for the day, it had been much easier for him to access the mainframe without interruption or anyone questioning what he was doing. The mainframe, after all, was for *working* scientists. He felt like he was making progress, but he'd told Lisa he'd meet her at a trendy new raw food restaurant at 7:30. At 7:15, he finally shut down his computer, which meant he was going to be ten minutes late.

Lisa playfully slapped him on the wrist for making her wait and then launched into a story about her weekend. Her peripatetic boyfriend Ben had come home unexpectedly and, from what Chris could glean, they'd spent their time together trying to get through most of the Kama Sutra.

Chris listened to Lisa's R-rated narrative with as much attention as he thought was required. Presumably, it wouldn't take much to maintain the guise that he was hanging on her every word; Lisa seemed fully in the throes of her own story. Meanwhile, his thoughts could wander back to his research.

Maybe it is some form of Dothistroma—a Tamariskian form. The reason the blight doesn't act exactly the same way Dothistroma acts here is because of the differences in the ecosystem. If I can identify those differences, maybe Dothistroma will turn out to be the answer. Then I could apply what I know about the differences to identify a way to create a variation on the control . . .

"Men have gotten drinks thrown in their faces for less, sweetie," Lisa said sharply.

Chris looked into Lisa's fiery eyes. "Huh?"

"Look, Chris, maybe your problem really is that you're a eunuch. I dismissed that idea a long time ago, but if you can listen to my daffodil garden story without changing expression, then maybe you really don't have any balls. Either that or you're thinking about a much hotter story of your own."

Chris reddened. "Sorry. My mind wandered."

"You'll have to explain to me how a person's mind wanders away from what I was just talking about."

Chris arched his eyebrows. "You'll be very disappointed in me."

"Sweetie, if it hasn't happened up to now, it's likely it'll never happen."

"I was thinking about something I was doing at work."

Lisa threw up her hands. "And they said it couldn't be done."

Chris reached across the table to touch her on the forearm. "It wasn't a work thing I was doing at work."

Lisa leaned forward. "Better." She smiled devilishly. "Was it a new employee that you were doing at work?"

Chris laughed aloud. "Not exactly." Chris's relationship with Lisa was a full-disclosure one—as evidenced by the details she'd been providing during the past fifteen minutes. Was he ready to disclose this much, though? "I was working on a problem in Tamarisk."

Lisa's face clouded over. Chris's first thought was that she was having a bad reaction. Then he realized she was probably trying to remember what Tamarisk was.

"The fantasy world I created with Becky," he said to help her.

Lisa's eyes widened with recognition. Then they narrowed again.

"Except it isn't really a fantasy world," he said quickly.

"What?"

"You are not going to believe how I spent my weekend."

For the next several minutes, Chris told Lisa everything about his trip to Tamarisk, about the problems the citizens were having there, and about the work he'd done since he got back. It didn't register until he'd finished that Lisa had remained uncharacteristically silent the entire time. He took a sip of water and waited for her to say something.

"You were making up that story while I was talking because you wanted to outdo me, right?" she said slowly.

Chris smiled. "It really happened."

"Chris, I—"

Chris held up a hand. "Lisa, it really happened."

Lisa stared at him slack-jawed. *After all these years, I've finally stumped her.*

"I obviously haven't been paying enough attention to you lately," she said with a hint of sadness in her voice.

"I realize it isn't easy to comprehend."

"Nuclear physics isn't easy to comprehend. This . . . this is unfortunately much too easy to comprehend. Chris, you've gotten yourself so worked up over your relationship with Becky that you're starting to have visions."

Chris shook his head rapidly. "Don't go Polly on me here, Lisa."

"What does 'go Polly' mean?"

"It means I've already gotten the lecture about encouraging Becky's delusions."

"Becky's delusions? She thinks she can go to Tamarisk, too?"

"I just told you that a couple of minutes ago. Becky went first and I found it nearly as inconceivable as you obviously find it now. But she kept talking about it and I started to believe her. Then this weekend, I went there with her."

Lisa looked over his shoulder for several long moments. "This is *Weekly World News* stuff, you know."

"I realize it sounds that way."

Lisa laughed and then locked eyes with him. "You know, I always assumed that at least some of the crap in that rag was true. I mean, you can't make *all* of that stuff up, can you?"

She reached across the table and took his hand. Again, she didn't say anything for several moments. Chris couldn't think of a good way to break the silence.

"And you say there's a horrible blight there now?"

"No one knows how to cure it."

Lisa wrinkled her nose. "That really sucks." That was world-class empathy coming from her.

"Tell me about it."

She patted his hand. "My daffodil garden story really happened, too, you know? And I haven't even told you yet about what we did with the shower massager."

Chris chuckled. "I can hardly wait to hear."

///

The second trip to Tamarisk was less disorienting, but only slightly so. The temptation to open his eyes while he floated was strong—he wanted to know where was he traveling and how he got there—but he knew instinctually that this would be a mistake. The visage with the portentous voice didn't come along on the trip this time. Chris forgot to mention that to Becky to see if it had made an appearance her first time as well. Maybe the thing really was some kind of gatekeeper and had decided he could pass.

Once they arrived, he couldn't help glancing around the room while others spoke. So many things here seemed at once familiar and unutterably strange. Even the air felt different. It was crisper and clearer and even a normal breath seemed as cleansing as if he'd held and expelled a lungful.

We did a good job with this place, Beck. Except for that little thing about the devastating blight.

As the first time, there was a group of Tamariskian officials gathered in the conference room. Were they here all the time now? When Chris and Becky arrived, they were in the middle of a discussion about the son of the vice chancellor of the Thorns, somebody Becky had met, as it turned out. Miea suspected the Thorns had had a hand in creating the blight, but now this boy had walked into the Government Office in Tamarisk City and requested asylum. Miea ordered him held for questioning. They'd decide what to do with him after that.

When they finished that conversation, they turned to Chris to ask about what he'd learned. Unlike the first time, Thuja, the minister of agriculture was considerably more talkative, quizzing Chris on his findings over the past few days.

"Yes, it's a possibility," Chris said to a question about the Dothistroma blight. "It will be impossible to say without further analysis on this end."

"If your ecosystem is different, that would certainly be necessary."

"The real issue is that I don't know how different our ecosystems are. They could be extremely compatible or completely alien to each other. It won't be easy to determine because I can't bring any machines with me, your machines are calibrated to your world, and there's only so much you can learn by looking."

While the last point was valid, Chris longed to get outside. For one thing, he was visiting another world and yet all he'd seen so far was this room. More important, though, simply talking about the makeup of the planet was little more than an intellectual exercise. He needed to touch the plants, feel the dirt, and understand the way the wind blew and the clouds moved. Any of this could offer him clues and give him a reference point with which to work. It might never be enough without the proper machinery, but it would be something more than he had now.

A trip outside was going to have to wait, though. Thuja seemed bent on asking him dozens of different questions, all of which underscored the fact that, as far as science was concerned, they were speaking very different languages. In addition, there was the issue of time. Chris had no idea how long each visit to Tamarisk could be. Becky knew that some kind of "pull" announced the end of their stay, but she couldn't figure out how long it was before the pull came. She said that sometimes it felt as though she could stay there for hours, while on other occasions she felt like she had far less than that. Was that just a relative thing based on how she felt about what she was doing? Or did the allotted time in Tamarisk vary based on some combination of factors neither of them knew? Did those factors change now that there were two of them traveling here? Just a few simple answers would be nice to have along with all the dazzling things.

A young man seated next to Thuja leaned toward the minister. "We can charge a full team of analysts with the task of breaking down the composition of the environment in a variety of ways." He looked at Chris. "Perhaps if you can figure out a way to do the same on your end we might be able to come to some common parlance."

Chris nodded. "That will take time, but it might be worth it."

"Time is becoming a very precious commodity," Miea said. As during the first meeting, she'd said very little up to now.

"Your Majesty," Thuja said, "we have few options."

"Time is not one of them," she said sharply. "I certainly don't need to read your damage reports back to you, do I?"

Thuja looked down at his papers, but Chris could see he was glowering. Unfortunately, both of them were right. If the reports were accurate, the blight was advancing increasingly quickly. Food supplies were withering. More insects and small animals were dying off as a result. It might only be a matter of months before Tamarisk would have trouble feeding its citizens. At the same time, though, no one was offering an alternative better than an exhaustive comparative analysis of the ecosystems.

"I'll be back in four nights," Chris said. "I'll do as much as I can from my end and maybe your analysts can do the same."

"Is there any chance you could come back sooner?" Miea said.

Chris shook his head. "I'm afraid not. Becky won't be with me again until Saturday and I can't get here without her. I tried."

"You did?" Becky said, shocked. This was the first thing she'd said the entire meeting.

Chris turned to her and smiled. "Does that surprise you?"

Becky smiled back. "No, I guess not. But maybe there's a way to get you here." She turned toward Miea. "Can you, I don't know, open another door for my father?"

Miea nodded sadly. "Becky, I didn't open the first one. I'm not sure how that happened. It was providence, or a remarkable accident, or something else entirely. I do know, however, that it wasn't me who opened the door. I don't know any way to recreate this."

Chris glanced from the disappointed expression on his daughter's face to the disappointed one on the queen's. He was certain his expression looked the same as theirs. It would have been a welcome use of his nights without Becky to come to Tamarisk to help them solve their problem. Sadly, it didn't seem likely to happen.

"Chris, would it be possible for me to speak with you outside for a moment?" Miea said.

Chris got up and followed her out of the room.

"I won't pretend to understand the way things work in your world. Becky has told me a little bit about your divorce and the arrangement you have with your former wife, and she has mentioned that things are contentious between the two of you. Therefore, I realize what I have to ask is problematic, but is there any possible way you could get more days with Becky?"

"I think it might be easier for you to find another door. 'Contentious' barely begins to describe what my relationship is like with my ex-wife these days."

The queen lowered her eyes. "I'm worried that we'll never get an answer in time if you only come here twice a week."

"Your worries are justified, and I wish I could do something about them. Trust me; I would do anything to help you, especially if it meant spending more time with Becky as well. That may not be feasible, though."

Miea nodded sadly. "I understand."

She seemed incredibly vulnerable at that moment, so much more like a confused young woman than a queen. Chris wanted so badly to be able to help her. What could he say to Polly, though, to convince her to give him more nights with Becky? Was there anything in the world—especially given their last few exchanges? It was hard to imagine.

"I'll try," he said. He meant it, though he had no idea what he meant by it.

Miea looked up into his eyes and touched his arm. "It could make every difference in the world."

"I promise," he said, clasping her on the shoulder. "I'll try to the best of my ability."

16

Philip Keller's opinions were literally making Becky nauseous. The conversation about women's suffrage in history class had turned into an all-out verbal brawl after Phil announced that it was a mistake to let women have the vote. Becky took a minute to put her eyes back in her head while some of the other girls pounced on him. Predictably, the boys in the class—most of whom were nice kids one-on-one—joined in behind Phil. Except for Cam Parker, whose soul was obviously as beautiful as the rest of him, and who managed to make a good point about the need for suffrage and call Phil "a Neanderthal" in the same sentence. That was impressive.

Still, Phil persisted. He said some pre-Neanderthal stuff about "founding fathers" and women not being "properly equipped" to make decisions about government, and Becky found herself getting so worked up that she actually thought she was going to vomit. The queasiness—she'd never had this reaction to a classroom debate before—actually kept her out of the exchange. Until Phil went over the line.

"The reality is that since women have been allowed to vote, the country is in much worse shape than it was before. You do the math."

Becky sprung from her seat. The room lurched and her stomach tumbled, but she couldn't let that last comment pass. "Are you kidding me? Since women got the vote, we've had the civil rights movement, the end of communism, the information revolution—"

"—All done by men! I mean, what have women done with their votes anyway?"

Becky felt as though she was ready to leap from her body. She was so angry that she felt light-headed and had to hold on to the corner of her desk for support. "We've kept cavemen like you from blowing up the entire world—that's what we've done!"

Phil actually laughed at her. "You obviously haven't checked your facts."

Suddenly, Becky flopped back into her chair. Not because Phil Keller had bowled her over with his logic. Not because she was too worked up to continue. But because she literally couldn't stand any longer. Her head was throbbing and she felt hot and cold at the same time. She realized that what she was feeling had nothing at all to do with the classroom battle.

Becky's head rolled sideways of its own accord. She saw Lonnie kneeling next to her.

"Beck, are you okay? You're white as a ghost."

Becky tried to sit up. There were other people standing near her desk now, but she could only see the edges around them. She reached a limp hand out to her best friend.

"I'm not okay," she said with nearly all the energy she had.

Then her body gave way.

///

It was hard to believe they were talking about staff cuts again. How could the idiots in executive management have screwed this up? Chris's department had somehow escaped the layoffs four months ago, but office morale was still awful and it was about to get worse. Chris had never gone to business school, but even he knew that if you were going to downsize, it was better for the emotional health of the company to cut too deep rather than to not cut deep enough and have to cut again. The staff that survived would walk on eggshells for years after this.

Meetings such as these made him hate his job exponentially

more than he normally did. How many people could he save if he stood up right now, called the COO a blithering buffoon, and got fired? If they were doing their jobs, they'd realize they didn't need to replace him and could therefore keep some people who were truly doing something. In fact, if they really wanted to make changes that would have a permanent positive effect on the company, they could eliminate three-quarters of upper management and let the rest of the staff get on with their work.

It was times like these when he regretted turning down those other jobs. Yes, they were too far away. Yes, he would be subject to cuts such as these rather than be the one making them. At least in those jobs, though, he wouldn't feel as though he needed to spray himself with disinfectant every time he left the conference room. What made him think he'd ever be suited to this kind of career? For the hundredth time, he vowed to address this issue soon. Even if it entailed a big pay cut, he needed to get out of a management spot.

As the comptroller prattled on about "surgical precision" and outsourcing options, Chris's thoughts wandered back to Tamarisk. Miea had seemed so desperate last night. So certain that they needed a solution to the blight soon or it would be too late. She was right that progress was going to be slow if he only helped twice a week, but he still hadn't thought of any argument that would convince Polly that Becky should spend more nights with him. If he could talk his parents into coming up to visit, he'd get some extra time out of that. Polly still loved them and always let Becky be with them when they were around. That was a short-term solution at best, though. His parents had never stayed for more than four or five days and he couldn't imagine anything that would make them visit longer.

He needed to make the most of his time in Tamarisk. There had to be a way to fast-track the analysis process. He was more convinced than ever that their blight had some earthly equivalent—if not Dothistroma, then something else—and understanding the differences in the ecosystems would reveal it.

"Chris, we might need to take two people from your

department. Do you have any thoughts about how to approach that?"

He knew he wasn't going to be lucky enough to escape wielding the axe this time around. He pretended to write a note on the pad in front of him. "I'll need to take some time with that. We're running pretty lean."

Cutting two people would devastate his department and maybe even make it impossible to run. Executive management wouldn't want to hear that, though. The COO had moved to another department head to deliver more bad news when Chris's assistant opened the conference room door. She apologized for interrupting and handed Chris a note that read: *You have an urgent phone call.*

For some reason, Chris folded the paper and put it in his pocket. He made eye contact with the COO and pantomimed talking on the phone. The COO nodded and turned back to the conversation. *As long as I deliver a couple of heads on a platter, he doesn't care if I stay in this meeting or not.* Chris wondered if he could use the excuse of the phone call to skip the rest of it.

"Who's on the phone?" Chris said to his assistant as they walked down the hall.

"It's your ex-wife."

"Polly?" As the identity of the caller registered, the hairs on the back of Chris's neck rose. Polly had called him at the office to hassle him about one thing or another over the years, but she'd never pulled him out of a meeting to do so. This wasn't about anything that arbitrary.

There could only be one reason why she was on the phone.

"What's wrong?" he said as he picked up the receiver.

"Becky collapsed in school. I just got the call."

"Oh my God. What happened?"

Polly's voice was unsteady. "I don't know anything other than that she passed out in class. I'm going to the hospital right now."

"I'll meet you there."

Chris hung up the phone, closed his eyes, and tried to take

a couple of deep breaths. *She's strong. You know she's strong. This won't beat her.* Then he grabbed his jacket and headed out the door, stopping only long enough to tell his assistant that he had a family emergency.

Right after Becky had gotten sick, he'd anticipated this call nearly every day. Even after she went into remission, he still clutched when the phone rang in the office until he knew who it was. So many years had passed that he was no longer aware if he had the same reaction, but all it took was the mention of Polly's name to raise the anxiety he'd submerged. He'd convinced himself a long time ago that Becky had overcome the disease. He couldn't convince himself now, however, that there was any other explanation for why she'd passed out. He'd never been that much of an optimist.

Driving to the hospital, trying to keep his fears in check at least well enough to avoid an accident, he remembered the drive home from the doctor's office when Polly and he had first gotten the news. He'd felt so weak, he could barely turn the wheel. In the passenger seat, Polly looked catatonic, staring straight ahead, only the narrowness of her eyes betraying how devastated she felt. In his heart, Chris had truly believed that Becky was going to be fine; for some entirely unfounded reason, he had been certain she'd prevail over the leukemia. Still, she would have to endure rigors and hardships that no five-year-old should ever have to face. When he'd thought about the pain and fear she would go through, his heart cracked open. Suddenly, he couldn't drive any longer. He'd managed to get the car to the side of the road before the sobbing overtook his body. He'd reached out for Polly and they'd cried together. He'd hurt so badly for Becky, for what the next year of her life was likely to be like. Through it all, though, he'd kept thinking with absolute conviction, *she's going to be okay. Eventually, she's going to be okay.*

Why wasn't he having those thoughts now? Why did they seem artificial in his mind?

He found Polly in the emergency room. Al was already with her. He must have left from work the second Polly called him.

"What's going on?" Chris said.

"She's conscious. They're running tests. They said they'll let us see her right after they're done."

"Do the doctors have any idea what happened?"

For the briefest moment, Polly looked at him incredulously; as though she were wondering if he hadn't already come to the only conclusion conceivable. "They haven't said anything yet, but Chris . . . ," Her voice quavered and she turned into Al's embrace. Al looked at him sympathetically while he held his wife. It was obvious that even Al, who'd never known Becky when she was sick, understood the implications. This thing was so much harder to beat a second time.

A few minutes later, a nurse came out to tell them they could see Becky. Chris had been standing the entire time and was surprised at how unsteady his legs felt when he began walking. He took a couple more deep breaths as he headed toward Becky's bed. *Don't let her see you freak out.*

Becky looked surprisingly normal. She was pale and she seemed sunken in the bed, but she otherwise seemed just like herself. Chris wasn't sure what he thought he'd see when he got here, but he didn't expect her to look like she had a touch of the flu. He wasn't sure why he thought this. Certainly, he knew this kind of disease didn't transform a person instantaneously.

"I threw up on one of the doctors," Becky said when she saw them. Al took an exaggerated step back, and Becky offered him an appreciative smile. Polly kissed her and held her and then Chris pressed his lips against her forehead, holding his face next to hers for longer than he had in years.

"Have they told you anything?" Becky said.

Chris shook his head. "It takes some time for them to get the test results."

Becky nodded. "It's probably gonna get ugly again, huh?"

"Let's not jump to any conclusions before we have the information, babe."

Becky watched him carefully for a moment. The thoughts behind her expression were unmistakable. Then she lowered her eyes before glancing at her mother. Polly squeezed her hand and Chris wasn't certain he'd be able to keep up this façade for very long.

They moved Becky to a hospital room shortly thereafter. A few hours later, her doctor asked Chris, Polly, and Al to step into the hallway.

"There's no way to sugarcoat this, so I'm not going to try," the doctor said. "Becky's cancer is back. It's in several parts of her body and it appears to be spreading rapidly."

Polly clutched Al's arm and said, "Will you start treatment right away?"

"We can start treatment tomorrow morning, but I don't want to give you the wrong impression. Becky's disease is quite advanced. It's amazing she didn't show any symptoms until now. It hasn't even been a year since her last physical, but this kind of thing can move so quickly in someone this young."

The rest of the conversation came to Chris as though they held it underwater. He even participated in some of it, asking a few questions. He retained none of the answers, though. Instead, the doctor's voice looped in his head, saying, "Becky's cancer is back."

This wasn't a false alarm. And this time not even the doctor was trying to keep their hopes up.

///

Becky knew what her parents were going to say as soon as they walked into the room. Realistically, she knew what was going on long before they did. Did she actually think she could just make it go away? In truth, at least a part of her believed she could. Still, if she'd held out any hope at all, it evaporated when she saw their faces. Mom was doing everything she could to hold herself together and Dad looked like all the color had drained out of him. Even Al looked completely confused.

Mom and Dad stood on either side of the bed and took her hands. At that very moment, Becky felt butterflies in her stomach. She wanted to press the pause button. When they started speaking, this would all become real.

"It's horrible, isn't it?" she said.

Her mother held her hand to the side of her face. "The doctor is going to begin treatment tomorrow. There are things we can try."

"Is it in my blood again?" She glanced back and forth at her parents and saw them looking at each other.

Her father knelt next to her. "Beck, it's in a number of places."

Even though she'd guessed that it could be worse this time, the news hit Becky incredibly hard. How do you react to something like that any other way? Neither of them had come right out and said "Becky, you're dying," but they didn't need to. She knew what it meant that the cancer was in "a number of places." She'd read enough about it online the past few years.

She closed her eyes, but that didn't stop the tears from coming. She heard her parents crying then. She felt her father's head bobbing against the mattress. Had they been like this the last time? If they had, she didn't remember any of it. For that matter, she had no memory of crying herself last time. She remembered how horrible all the vomiting felt, how much she hated losing her hair, how much trouble she'd had sleeping, but she didn't remember crying. Maybe it was because she didn't understand what was really going on. Maybe it was because she didn't realize then what the odds were.

Opening her eyes, she put her hand on her father's head to try to comfort him. Dad got her through those early nights by filling her mind with thoughts of Tamarisk. Who knew then that they were creating something real, that they would one day travel there together? Would Tamarisk help them again now? Would it give them somewhere to go to get away from this disgusting reality?

The thought of Tamarisk reminded her of the blight for the first time since she'd passed out. When they'd met with the council last night, Miea had taken Dad outside to ask him if he could come more often. Dad and she had talked about it in the morning, though neither of them had any idea how to make that work.

She had an idea now, though. Tamarisk was sick as well, but it was possible her father could find a cure. Maybe one good thing could come from her relapse.

"I want to go home," Becky said.

Dad lifted his head. "We can't take you out yet, babe."

"I want to leave as soon as we can. I don't want to stay in the hospital any longer than I have to."

Mom patted her hand. "I'll talk to the doctors about it," she said, her voice wavering. "I'm sure they can administer the treatment on an outpatient basis."

"There's more," Becky said, watching every eye in the room lock on her. "When we get home, I want to split my time equally between your houses."

Mom started to speak. "Honey, I'm not sure that's really the best—"

"—No, Mom. There's no discussion. You never asked me what I wanted. No one ever asked me how I wanted to do this when you and Dad split up. From now on—however long that is—this is what I want."

Mom and Dad both bowed their heads. It was almost like they were praying. Al looked at her with his lips pressed together, then patted her leg and turned toward the window.

Everything was different now. When she'd woken up this morning, her biggest concern had been finding a way to get her father more days in Tamarisk. She would never have wished for this solution, but at least she had it. This would give them a chance to accomplish their mission.

And she really, really needed a mission right now.

///

Maybe it's never meant to get easier for me, Miea thought as she sat at her desk late at night after another debilitating series of meetings. *Maybe the path of my adult life is to go from horrible to difficult to extremely horrible and then to a devastating end.* Miea had always believed that the trials she'd faced after her parents died forged new strength in her, established a sense of resolve that would propel her in untold ways as she grew into her reign. After yet another session with her council regarding the blight, though, the question she could no longer avoid moved to the forefront of her mind.

Am I the last queen of Tamarisk?

They were no closer to a cure for the blight than they had been the day farmers discovered the first infested plants. Botanists ran the same tests repeatedly. Ecologists sought answers in the balance between species. Spiritualists peered into the ether for clues. Government officials interrogated the son of the vice chancellor of the Thorns while intelligence experts sought other clues about their involvement. None of this led anywhere. The brief flurry of hope that had come with the arrival of Becky's father dissipated as it became clear that he needed more time to do his work than he could spend in this world. He'd promised to try to find a way to come more often, but neither he nor Becky had appeared since. It was the longest stretch of time without Becky since her arrival. Had they abandoned Tamarisk, too heartbroken about its condition to witness the end?

Miea stood and walked to the picture of her father that sat on a shelf near the doorway. Her mother's picture was on the other side, as though the two stood sentry over the entrance to her office. Everyone told her that her father looked especially placid in this picture, at ease with his kingdom, blissfully unaware of what fate had reserved for him. Miea agreed that he exuded peace, but only she noticed the slight crinkle at the corners of his eyes. Her father had something on his mind. It might have been concern about a diplomatic tangle, it could have been thoughts about a new piece of music he'd heard the night before, or it might have been some sort of musing about his daughter's studies. Miea was certain of only one thing: whatever her father had been thinking about at that moment, it was important to him. That was the only time his face showed that crinkle.

Miea had spoken to his picture often since she had become queen. She imagined it was one of the ways she could reach him and confess her concerns to him, knowing from his expression that he considered everything she said seriously. She never knew whether the connection she felt with him in this space was real (she believed now that the meeting they'd had in the darkness the night she met Becky was something else entirely), but the conversations she had with him here had helped her on so many occasions. Nearly as much as the conversations they'd had when he was alive.

"You don't have any answers for this either, do you?" she said to the picture. One of the few true memories Miea had of the last blight was a discussion her father had had with one of his aides when he didn't realize she could hear him. There was an unfamiliar tone to his voice as he expressed frustration over his inability to do anything to find a cure.

"Tamarisk might as well not have a king for all the good I'm doing," he'd said. In that moment, Miea had understood for the first time that her father was fallible, that his strength and wisdom had limits. While he probably would have been horrified to know she'd heard him say this, it had made her love him more than ever. That night, at bedtime, she'd hugged him longer than usual when he said good night and when he pulled back he looked at her as though he understood why she did it. They never talked about that moment, but there was never any need.

"How do I prepare the kingdom for this?" she said now. "How do I let them know that we don't have a future?"

Miea closed her eyes and leaned her head against the picture. She knew her father couldn't help her with this, but she needed to feel his strength. As she allowed herself to absorb the darkness, she felt a sensation that was different from what she usually felt when doing this. She felt comforted, yes, but she'd felt that many times before. No, this was something else.

She felt consoled.

The thought made her knees weaken.

As she lifted her head, eyes still closed, Miea felt a presence in the room. Startled, she turned quickly, expecting Sorbus or one of the aides and feeling a bit embarrassed that they'd seen her doing this. Instead, she found Becky.

Instantly, she relaxed. "I'm glad you're back. I was getting a little worried."

Becky didn't smile. Becky always smiled when they met. She even did so that day she came and left quickly.

"I have something to tell you," she said. "Do you think we could sit down?"

Miea didn't like the tone of Becky's voice. *She sounds like me,* Miea thought as they walked to the sofa.

Becky sat. "I'm sorry it took me a while to get back here. I had to spend a few days at the hospital."

Miea felt a twinge of alarm. "The hospital? Are you okay?"

Becky lowered her eyes. "I'm not, no." She looked up and, as their eyes locked, Miea felt a wave of sadness she'd only experienced once before. "I'm dying," Becky said in a whisper.

Tears flooded Miea's eyes. She pulled Becky toward her and buried Becky's head in her neck. For several minutes, she felt as though she had surrendered control of her body. She couldn't speak and she couldn't raise her head. She couldn't do anything but hold Becky close to her and feel the shaking of the girl's weeping.

At last, she gathered herself enough to sit up straight. "What has happened to you?"

Becky took a deep breath and wiped her eyes. "My cancer is back. It's everywhere."

"Aren't there things your doctors can do about this? They helped you the last time."

"It was different last time. It wasn't this advanced." Becky stared off, shaking her head. "I was so stupid. I started feeling things and I tried to convince myself that I could ignore it. I should have gone to the doctor earlier."

"There's really no treatment?"

"They're trying things. Things that make me feel awful.

None of them will work, though. I'm trying to have the right attitude, but I just know that nothing will help."

This was so difficult for Miea to believe. Becky didn't look sick. She looked confused and shaken, but she didn't look sick. Then again, if one looked at the gardens of the Palace, one would never know that her kingdom was in grave danger, either.

"You need to see our doctors."

Becky looked at her inquisitively, but didn't say anything.

"Tamariskian medicine can't be exactly the same as your medicine. None of the other sciences are. Maybe our doctors can find something that yours haven't. Some solution that could be interpreted for them."

Becky nodded. "I'll try anything. I'm really scared about this."

Miea reached for Becky's hand and held it to her heart. If it were possible for Miea to transfer some of her life force to Becky, she would do it unreservedly.

Again, neither spoke for several minutes.

"Something good has come from this," Becky said.

Miea squeezed Becky's hand and then sat back.

"I told my parents that I wanted to have equal time in both houses from now on. That means my father can come here more often to find a cure for the blight."

Miea felt her eyes well up again, but she wiped the tears away before they started to run. "Becky, you need to understand something. What's happening to you probably has your father devastated. You're probably the only thing he wants to think about now. He can't be concerned with Tamarisk. How could he be?"

"Because I am," Becky said emphatically. It was the first time her voice had sounded strong since she arrived. "I am, and he knows what this means to me. Maybe your doctors can figure something out, but if they can't, I know I can't do anything to make myself better. If I can do something to make Tamarisk better, though, then I'll do it. My father will be with me the next time I'm here. I guarantee it."

"Becky, if it doesn't happen, I'll understand. If you don't want to come here anymore, I'll understand that as well."

Becky leaned forward and touched Miea's shoulder. "This is the only thing I have to look forward to," she said.

With that, they collapsed into each other's arms again.

17

Today had been Becky's first decent day. For the first time since the experimental treatments began, she didn't feel like her bones were made of rubber. She could read without feeling nauseous, and she even had a little lunch. The doctors had told her there would be many days like this; potentially a lot more if the treatments did their jobs. Even if they didn't, she still had a tiny bit of time before her body really started to break down. On days like this, it was hard for her to believe that she was as sick as they said she was. It was just like it was with the dizzy spells and bloody noses. She'd feel awful for a while and then feel better, close to normal. At this very moment, she could nearly convince herself that she was still going to be okay.

She was going to go back to school tomorrow. Mom had major issues with that, but Becky really needed to do it. What was she supposed to do, lie in bed until she wasted away? She missed her friends and some of her teachers. She missed Ray, the custodian who called her "petal," and Janet, the security guard who told her stories about her rambunctious twins while Becky waited for the bus home. She hoped it wouldn't be too weird for everyone else. People sometimes got squeamish around someone who was really sick and she knew at least one person would think that what she had was contagious. She didn't want to be a distraction and she didn't want to be a circus freak. She just wanted a tiny bit of her life back.

She was looking at a photo album in her room when Lonnie

arrived. Lonnie had been to the hospital to see her a couple of times, but this was the first time she'd come to the house since Becky got back. They hugged briefly and then Lonnie sat on the bed next to her.

"What are you looking at?" Lonnie said, pointing to the photo album.

"Last summer in Maine."

Lonnie leaned toward the album and flipped the pages. "Any pictures of Mr. Gorgeous in here?"

Becky laughed. "His name was Kyle and, no, there aren't any pictures of him in here. My mother is the one with the camera. Do you think I dragged her over to the dock and asked her to take a few shots of the first guy who ever kissed me?"

"You would have if you were really thinking." Lonnie moved away from the album. "So how are you feeling?"

"I'm okay today. Tomorrow? Who knows? I'm fine right now, though. I don't have another treatment until next week."

"That's good. I'm really glad. Everyone is asking about you."

"I'm going to school tomorrow."

Lonnie pulled away from her and twisted her face. "You are?"

"You're not going to go off on me about this the way my mother did, are you?"

"I'm not gonna go off on you, but why? I mean, if I didn't have to, I certainly wouldn't."

"I want to. I'm not going to be only a sick person for the rest of my life. I can walk, I can talk, and my brain still works. I'm going to school."

Lonnie shrugged as though she never would have had this idea. Actually, she wouldn't have. "If you say so," she said confusedly. Then she turned to Becky with concern on her face. "What if you have, you know, another episode?"

"I'll be fine. I have no intention of getting into another debate with Phil Keller."

"He felt terrible about that, you know. He thought he sent you to the hospital."

Becky rolled her eyes. "Great. So now I have to go up to one of the biggest jerks in school and make him feel better."

Lonnie waved her hand. "Nah, don't bother. In fact, when you get to class, maybe you should stagger a little when you pass his desk."

Becky laughed loudly. "That's awful."

"But a good idea, right?"

"A great idea. Even though I'm not going to do it."

"You should. He deserves it."

They both chuckled and sat back against the wall next to the bed.

"How have your parents been?" Lonnie said, the smile fading from her face.

"About how you'd expect them to be. You know my parents. Mom's trying to make things happen and Dad's trying to prop me up."

"And you're really gonna shuttle back and forth every other day?"

"It'll be fine, at least for now. Mom tried to convince me that all that 'extra traveling' was going to wear me down. I reminded her that Dad lives in Standridge, not Miami. She has to understand that this isn't open for discussion."

"I would imagine that's a little difficult for her to understand."

Becky imagined that it probably was. She didn't make this demand because she wanted to hurt her mother, even though she knew it was hard for her to hear. She did it because it was the closest she could get to the balance she had so desperately been missing since her parents split. Other than having her father move back into the house with Mom, Al, and her—now that would have been a demand—she couldn't think of anything else. Becky needed to be with her father as often as she was with her mother now. She'd missed too much with him and they'd finally gotten back to a good place. She didn't want him to get the short end of things any longer.

Of course, there was also their mission in Tamarisk. Becky refused to believe it was a coincidence that her illness kicked up to this level at the same time as Miea asked for more of her father's help. Tamarisk needed them and only something this extreme would let them get there more often. If Becky really was coming to the end of her life, she wanted this end to have some meaning. She wanted to do something more than simply die. If she could help save Tamarisk—even if the only thing she did was provide transportation for her dad—then something good would come of this.

Mom would never understand that part of it. Becky couldn't even try to explain it, considering the way Mom reacted to the very mention of Tamarisk. Becky would say something again at some point, but not now.

"Listen, Lon, there's something I haven't told you."

Lonnie's eyebrows rose. "Under normal circumstances, I'd be bracing for bad news if someone said that to me, but we kinda did the bad news part already."

Becky smiled warmly at her best friend. "This isn't bad news. You're gonna think it's pretty weird, though."

"I'm ready. I think."

"Part of the reason I need to spend more time at my dad's is because I can do something there that I can't do anywhere else. I can travel to Tamarisk."

Lonnie's jaw dropped, but it did so in slow motion.

Becky had to laugh. "You look hilarious right now."

"I'm glad I'm around to amuse you."

Becky bumped her shoulder against Lonnie's. "It's okay if you don't believe me."

"Becky, are you sure you can do this?"

"Am I sure I can do something that I've done more than a dozen times? Yeah, I'm sure."

"I mean, are you sure it's not . . . you know?"

It took Becky a moment to figure out what Lonnie's question meant. "You mean am I sure that my disease isn't making me hallucinate? One hundred percent sure. You can ask my dad about it if you want."

"Your dad knows about this?"

"All about it. He comes with me now."

Lonnie shook her head quickly and then sat up on her knees. "Your father travels with you to a fantasy place the two of you made up?"

"Well, it sounds unrealistic when you say it that way."

"Is there a way to say it where it doesn't sound unrealistic?"

Becky took both of Lonnie's hands. "Lon, it happens."

Lonnie stared at her for the longest time, as though she were trying to read her mind. "You really do this?"

"Really."

Lonnie threw herself on the bed. "That is unbelievably cool."

Becky was so glad she'd finally told Lonnie. Now that she had, she couldn't remember why she hadn't told her right away. Finally, they could talk about this the way they talked about everything else. Becky told her about Miea, and her trip on the waccasassa, and the kingdom congress, and the way everything looked, felt, smelled, and sounded. Lonnie asked lots of questions, and Becky regaled her with details. It was nearly as exciting as when she'd discovered it.

Then she told her about the blight. For some reason, she got all choked up when she did it. She totally didn't see that coming and she needed to go to the bathroom to get some tissues.

"So Tamarisk is sick, too," Lonnie said when Becky got back.

"Really sick. We're going to fix it, though. I really believe my father can do it."

Lonnie nodded and then seemed lost in her thoughts for a moment. "This is an amazing thing," she said. "I mean, it kinda changes everything, you know?"

"Yeah, it does."

They locked eyes again and Becky saw that Lonnie's were glistening. "Thanks for letting me in on this," she said with a little catch in her throat.

Becky wrapped an arm around her best friend's shoulders. "I'm so happy I can share this with you." Becky pulled her closer and Lonnie rested her head against her. "You do realize, of course, that we won't be divulging this secret to the Phil Kellers of the world, right?"

Lonnie chuckled. "My lips are totally sealed. At least until lunch tomorrow."

///

One of the first things Chris learned as a father was that being one allowed you access to previously unavailable resources. The ability to function coherently at two in the morning when a baby needed soothing, a bottle needed heating, and a diaper needed changing at the same time. The ability to navigate through a little kid's tantrum without either screaming or running away. The ability to perform the same bit of slapstick several dozen times in a row because it made your child laugh. The ability to bear up when your preteen chose a sleepover at a friend's instead of the plans you made with her the week before.

When Becky told him that she wanted him to continue to work in Tamarisk, Chris tapped as deep into this reserve as ever. He couldn't think about Tamarisk now; he could only think about what was happening to Becky. Trying to solve the problem in Tamarisk required energy, initiative, and optimism he didn't have. A part of him didn't even want to save Tamarisk. If his daughter was dying, then it didn't really matter if anything lived, did it?

Except that it mattered to Becky. She'd made that as clear to him as anything she'd ever said. Therefore, he dug into that well and convinced himself to commit to finding a cure to the blight. There was even a side benefit to it. Being in Tamarisk constituted extra time with Becky, time when she would otherwise be asleep. Every minute meant more now. The ticking clock he'd been hearing since Becky had started high school now drowned out nearly every other sound.

Today, they finally got out of the conference room and visited the vast planting fields of Ribault. This tiny agricultural town had recently celebrated an improbable victory in the kingdomwide teen speedcatch tournament. Banners congratulating the players still hung everywhere. The landscape, however, was far from celebratory. A study of ash on black. In the distance, Chris saw patches of green, but he had to remind himself that this wasn't a sign of health. Healthy foliage was a rich blue here. Green indicated the banding that precipitated necrosis.

The plan was to examine the green portion of the field. The ashen vegetation was already too far gone to provide useful data. Tamariskian botanists had erected a mobile workstation so they could analyze cuttings and provide him with data. Becky stood next to him, glancing toward the party already gathered there.

"We're going to be doing a lot of walking and bending," Chris said. "Are you sure you're up for that?"

"I'm fine. Really fine, actually." She took a deep breath. "As messed up as everything is here, it still smells so good."

Involuntarily, Chris inhaled deeply. The smell of Tamarisk was sweet, reminiscent of the chocolate and raspberries Becky loved so much. The sounds of nature here had a certain musical quality as well, though it was a discordant one, like a Philip Glass composition. As he listened, though, he heard some of the sounds harmonize, major chords against a diminished background.

"If you get tired, I want you to come back here and sit."

"Dad, I'm really fine."

She wouldn't tell me if she wasn't, Chris thought. There was no chance she'd sit around back here when all the action was out in the fields. He'd have to watch for signs of Becky wearing down.

When they arrived at the workstation, one of the botanists handed him a piece of paper. "This is the data we compiled from cuttings we took thirty minutes ago."

Chris examined the paper but could determine little from it. This was clearly a printout of some set of calculations, but the terminology associated with the calculations was foreign to him. While Becky and he had invented scores of plants and animals while creating Tamarisk, they'd spent little time talking about science. The physical laws were all in place—Becky had insisted they be very close to the ones she already knew—but the details of those laws were not. His guess was that the Tamariskians therefore invented their own approach to science (however this kind of thing worked), one that of course had a different set of criteria from any Chris knew. Was this how Tamarisk filled in all the blanks Becky and he left in its design? This place would be a remarkable study in parallel evolution. Sadly, that study would never happen. Chris could only get here with Becky, and under the most optimistic circumstances Becky's remaining visits were numbered.

He forced himself to drive these thoughts away. He was here with a specific goal, and the goal was getting farther away as Tamarisk proved more exotic. He could barely think of where to start.

He reviewed the paper again and asked the botanist a few questions in an attempt to create a common vocabulary. When this proved frustrating, Chris decided to start in a more fundamental place.

"I'd like to examine the fruiting bodies of the blight. Is there a way for me to magnify a cutting?"

The man patted an octagonal box made of some sort of crystal. "That's what this does here."

"Thanks." He turned to Becky. "Beck, can you get me a couple of fresh cuttings?"

"Sure," Becky said, getting a cutting tool from another botanist. She returned with two leafy stems.

Chris took the cuttings to the box and ran his hand over the surface of the machine. It was as smooth as plastic, but unquestionably some kind of crystal.

"Okanogan," Becky said.

"What?"

"It's made of okanogan. The crystal you can mold, remember?"

Okanogan, yes. Hearing the word was like hearing the name of an old high school friend, vague familiarity leading to a smattering of memories. Becky had come up with okanogan because she wanted the walls of Miea's room to shimmer.

"You place it in here," the botanist said. He took one of the cuttings from Chris's fingers, slid out a drawer, and lay the cutting down. "Then we view it on the other side."

One side of the octagon was a viewing screen, made up of the same okanogan as the rest of the machine. A magnified image of the cutting emerged along with a set of numbers running down the side. The botanist showed Chris how to adjust the magnification and Chris examined the fruiting bodies on the stem. This was where the blight sprouted on this individual plant, and studying them in different fields at varying stages of blight would teach him something about the way the disease progressed. He was surprised to find that the bodies had barely presented on this particular cutting. Considering the necrosis of much of the field, he'd expected a more advanced stage of the blight in all vegetation in the area. He looked out on the field. It seemed bluer up close than it had from his original perspective. If anything, he would have thought the field would seem bluer farther away. More oddities of Tamarisk.

"That's strange," the botanist said, leaning toward Chris to get a better look at the screen.

"What's that?"

"The composite figures aren't the same with this cutting as they were with the one I showed you before." The botanist retrieved the paper he'd given Chris on his arrival. "No, not the same. Similar, but perceptibly different."

"Did you take your cutting from a different portion of the field?"

The botanist shook his head. "Just a couple of plants up."

Chris considered this for a moment. "The blight could be affecting different plants along the same root system differently. That's something we'll have to examine."

The man's expression showed he wasn't satisfied with this explanation. "I hope that's it."

"What else would it be?"

The botanist touched the screen and then peered into the

machine. "We've never used an analyzer like this in the field before. We have smaller, less precise tools for that purpose. This is a laboratory machine. I just hope it isn't proving to be unreliable in the open air."

Chris sighed. This job was going to be difficult under the best circumstances. If the Tamariskian machines weren't accurate, it might prove impossible.

///

Miea no longer believed that Thuja had been editing Dyson's briefings. That was both the good news and the terrible news. Miea now conceded what she had refused to concede for so long—the minister of agriculture had no progress to report regarding the blight. Dyson's briefing was concise, and for once, Miea didn't challenge anything he said. Their business was therefore over quickly.

"Will that be all, Your Majesty?" Dyson said, seemingly a bit unsure of himself.

"I have no questions, Dyson. Thank you for your time."

Dyson rose slowly. Had he come here expecting to do battle? Had he become accustomed to that? Was he worried about what her concession meant? "Thank you, Your Majesty. I hope to bring you more news at the end of the week."

Miea nodded and Dyson held her eyes longer than usual. Did he want to say something to her? Could he read something in her demeanor this time that disturbed him or even made him worry about her? He continued to look at her and the moment became uncomfortable.

If you have something to say, say it, she thought.

For a second, Dyson looked as though he were about to speak. Instead, he bowed, turned, and headed toward the door.

Miea had had very few confidantes over the years. She shared secrets with a few childhood friends, but this became harder to do when she became a teenager and began fulfilling the diplomatic duties of a princess. For most of her teen years, she'd talked to her father about what she felt she could and left the rest unsaid.

After she met Dyson, everything changed. He never seemed to tire of hearing what was on her mind and she never tired of sharing it. Those were exciting months, liberating months, intimate months. She hadn't realized how much she missed the feeling of sharing like that until she met Becky. Now she was losing Becky as well. Maybe there was a message there. Maybe she cursed those with whom she got close.

Dyson had a hand on the doorknob when she spoke.

"Becky is seriously ill."

Dyson stopped and turned back to her. Again, he seemed confused. "What's wrong with her?"

"Cancer. Her doctors say she's dying." Unexpectedly, Miea's voice broke on the last word. She covered her mouth her hand.

Dyson took several steps back into the room. "Are they certain?"

Miea shook her head slowly. "They're trying experimental treatments. Becky doesn't seem very optimistic about them. I'm taking her to the palace physicians tomorrow."

"They might be able to make a difference. For the same reason that Becky's father might have answers about the blight."

"That's what I'm hoping. She's too young to go through something like this." Again, Miea's voice broke at the end of the sentence. She had to pull herself together.

Dyson watched her quietly for a moment, his gaze respectful, but more personal than it had been during their briefings.

"Until we know everything, miracles are always possible."

Dyson was quoting Professor Liatris again. Hearkening back to the most miraculous time of her life. Once more, Miea felt her heart breaking, for too many reasons to count. "I'm having a great deal of trouble believing that lately."

"Don't, Miea."

She glanced up at the sound of her name. Dyson looked back at her with an expression she hadn't seen in years. There was nothing she needed to see more at that moment. "I'll try,

Dyson. I'll try to convince myself that miracles are still possible."

"It's essential, Miea. Even now. Especially now."

Dyson smiled warmly and she realized she desperately wanted to take his hand, to pull him toward her and hold him if only for a minute.

She couldn't do that, though. As much as she needed the comfort, it would be a mistake to complicate her life that way, to complicate Dyson's life that way. She was the queen, he worked for one of her ministers, and the actions of everyone involved were too critical right now. Her feelings—their feelings—were secondary to their work.

The opportunity to get beyond their responsibilities—if there ever really was one—had collapsed with the Malaspina Bridge several years ago.

"Thank you, Dyson. I appreciate your compassion."

Dyson looked downward, his lips pursed. "You're welcome, Your Majesty. I'll keep Becky in my thoughts. I hope our physicians have good news."

He bowed again and went to the door, opening it this time.

"We really don't know everything, Your Majesty," he said, facing away from her. Then he continued out.

With Dyson's departure, Miea felt untethered. She had actually felt the connection between them break. For reasons too many to enumerate, a single tear ran down her cheek, perching on her chin, unwilling to fall farther. Sorbus entered and his professional mask betrayed a hint of alarm.

She couldn't feel like this. She wiped at her face and drew herself up.

"Is the minister of commerce here, Sorbus?"

"She is, Your Majesty."

"I'd like to meet with her in the small conference room. I think it's time for me to get out of the office a bit."

"Yes, Your Majesty." He didn't move from the doorway as quickly as he usually did. "Is there something I can do for you, Your Majesty?"

"I'd appreciate a cup of argo. I'm sure the minister would

like one as well."

Sorbus dipped his head deferentially. "I'll have it brought to the conference room immediately."

Sorbus left and Miea stood. It was time to get back to work. She wiped at her cheek again, but it was already dry.

18

Dad was a little concerned about the idea of Tamariskian doctors examining Becky.

"They aren't going to inject you with anything, are they?" he said severely before going off to the fields.

"I don't think so. I really don't know."

"I don't want them putting anything inside of your body. We don't know enough about the differences in our physiology."

"What are they gonna do, Dad?" Becky said flippantly. "Kill me?"

Her father looked at her like she'd slapped him in the face.

"Sorry," she said, feeling awful about it. "I won't do that again."

Entering the examining room now, though, she began to feel a little skittish. Other than a table for her to lie on, nothing else seemed familiar. Her dad and she had invented the tools of Tamariskian medicine (Miea had a little "scare" about a year after they started creating stories) but they'd done it a long time ago and the details were sketchy. In the corner were a couple of okanogan machines similar to the one her father had used in Ribault the other night. She didn't remember ever putting one of those in a story. A stand next to the table held several coils of tubing. Becky couldn't tell if there was something pulsing through the tubing or if the colors of the tubes themselves shifted in such a way that they seemed to be pulsing. Becky remembered that the tubing was made from a material known as yunque, a kind of rubber that conducted sound especially well. A different kind of yunque tubing had created the intercom system that ran throughout the palace.

Becky looked at Miea nervously. "Is this where you come for your checkups?"

"Every month."

"Every month? Is there something wrong with you?" In the stories she'd created at home, Miea's bouts of dizziness turned out to be an inconsequential thing about vitamins.

Miea smiled. "You could say that; I'm queen. One of the rules is that the queen gets a full medical examination every month."

"Ouch. So I guess you know the doctors here pretty well, huh?"

Miea put a reassuring hand on Becky's shoulder. "They do an excellent job, Becky."

Becky was sure they did. The question in her mind was *how* they did their job. While she'd remembered the important details of nearly every Tamarisk story she ever told, for some reason she couldn't remember any of the ones with the doctors.

Becky sat on the edge of the table and Miea leaned against it next to her. She didn't look like a queen just then. She looked so casual. If Becky didn't know that she had to have a million things running through her head, she'd even say Miea looked relaxed.

"Dr. Nella has bad breath," Miea said in a whisper.

"What?" Becky said with a chuckle.

Miea grinned. "It's a medical condition. You don't want to know how we learned that bit of information. Her breath is miserable, though. I thought it would be a good idea to warn you. She is, however, a very fine doctor."

As nervous as she was, Becky couldn't help but find this funny. "Anything else I should know?"

Miea leaned closer. "Her eight-year-old daughter made her necklace. It looks incredibly silly on her, but Dr. Nella wears it for sentimental reasons. You probably won't be able to take your eyes off it. If she asks you if you like it, please be nice."

"I'll tell her I love it."

"You can't do that, because she'll know you're lying. Of course, you do come from another world. Maybe hideous jewelry is normal there."

This was a very odd conversation. When Dr. Nella walked into the room, though, Miea rose up and resumed her usual stately posture. The doctor bowed to Miea and then turned to Becky. The necklace wasn't as awful as Miea had made it sound, but it definitely looked like a kid made it.

"Her Majesty has told me fascinating things about you," the doctor said.

Becky smiled at Miea. "I'm not that fascinating."

Dr. Nella barely responded to this. "She has also told me that you're seriously ill."

Becky looked downward. "I'm afraid that part is entirely true. I wish I was only as sick as I am interesting."

The doctor moved closer and put her hands on both sides of Becky's head, holding them there for long enough for Becky to become a little uncomfortable with it. Dr. Nella's hands were large and unusually warm. It was like she was applying a heat pack to Becky's face. Miea definitely wasn't joking about the doctor's breath.

Suddenly, the doctor released Becky's head and Becky lurched forward, nearly falling off the table. She caught herself and looked up at Dr. Nella, but the woman had walked over to the shelf of machines to jot some notes. She took several minutes with this, and Becky wondered how she could have learned so much from holding her head.

"I need you to lie down," the doctor said while still writing.

She certainly doesn't waste any energy on bedside manner, Becky thought as she lay back.

"Are you okay?" Miea said, taking her hand.

"I'm fine. This just takes a little getting used to."

Miea squeezed her hand. "I'm sure it does."

The queen stepped aside when Dr. Nella returned with a

cart holding a tray of instruments and a cylindrical canister made of brilliantly polished malheur. For the next several minutes, the doctor glared into her eyes and mouth, scraped under her toenails, and listened to not only her heartbeat, but also something in her forehead, her neck, her stomach, and her abdomen. Then she waved the listening device above her head and between her legs. The waving made her necklace slip around and Becky could see that some of it was held together with some kind of tape. After this, Dr. Nella ran an okanogan comb through Becky's hair repeatedly in the same spot and examined some kind of reading the comb produced.

While the doctor didn't say anything during this examination, Becky grew more comfortable with her prodding as it continued. She'd take a comb over an MRI any day of the week, and Dr. Nella's touch had a soothing quality to it that made up for the gruffness of her personality. Maybe Tamariskian doctors didn't need to be nice because they had such great hands.

"Please roll up your sleeves," Dr. Nella said abruptly.

The thought of her father's warning made Becky nervous. "I don't want you to inject me."

The doctor seemed confused by the statement. "Why would I inject you?"

"Why do you need me to roll up my sleeves?"

The doctor reached for the malheur canister. "I need to apply this directly to your skin."

Becky wasn't sure what the woman was planning to do with the canister, but she rolled up her sleeves anyway. Miea touched her on the shoulder. "Do they not have foam sensors where you come from?"

Foam sensors! Becky had completely forgotten about those. She'd invented them during Miea's medical visits in the stories because Becky had become frustrated and skittish from the dozens of blood tests she'd had during her first bout with leukemia. "No," Becky said, "we don't have them where I come from, but I remember now."

The doctor poured a thin stream of pink gel from the

canister down each forearm all the way to Becky's wrists and then worked the gel into her skin. The gel began to bubble and suck. It was a little like being tickled by a vacuum cleaner. As it did so, the gel worked itself into a pearly foam that rose several inches from her arm. The doctor busied herself with other things while Becky watched the foam sensors grow.

When the process stopped, the doctor scraped the foam into a jar, sealed it, marked it, and put it into a cabinet. She handed Becky a damp towel to clean herself.

"The foam will process for three days. To whom should I give the results?"

"Leave them with Sorbus," Miea said. "He'll give them to me and I'll discuss them with Becky and her father."

Dr. Nella bowed to Miea and then nodded in Becky's direction, departing without another word.

"I hope that didn't make you too uncomfortable," Miea said when the doctor left.

"No, not at all. It was a little weird for a while, but compared to some of the things I've been through, this was a breeze."

Miea put an arm on Becky's shoulder. "I'm glad."

"So what happens now?"

"We wait for the results."

"Do you think she has any ideas?"

"I'm sure she has some ideas. Dr. Nella is much too professional to discuss them until she has all the facts, though."

The results would be back in three days. That meant that Becky would learn about them four days from now. Was it possible that Tamariskian medicine had an answer the doctors back home didn't? She'd know soon.

///

Becky was exhausted by the time she came home from school the next day. As usual, first period was nearly a blur as she tried to get her body going, and then she felt fine for several classes after that. She got increasingly tired after lunch, though, dragged herself onto the bus, and fell asleep, nearly missing her stop. The walk to the house, probably no more than a couple of hundred yards, felt like a couple of hundred miles. She felt stupid asking her mother to pick her up from the bus stop in her car (and she definitely didn't want Mom to drive her to school), but she realized that it might come to that soon.

Mom was waiting for her at the door. "How was the day?"

"It was fine. We watched part of *Pride and Prejudice* in English today. Colin Firth is a babe."

"You were okay, though?"

Becky nodded her head vigorously. "Yeah, I was fine." She headed toward the kitchen and her mother followed.

"Do you want anything?"

"I don't think so. I'm just gonna get a glass of water."

"Sit down with me for a few minutes."

Becky could tell from the tone of her mother's voice that this wasn't an invitation to chat about her day. Mom had something serious she wanted to discuss. Becky really wanted to go to her room to rest, maybe even take another nap, but that would have to wait. She filled a glass with water and sat at the table. Her mother was already there, fingers steepled together.

"I did some more research and made some calls. I learned about a different experimental drug that I think we should try. It's called Gleevec and it's shown some success with advanced cases."

Becky shook her head slowly. The last treatment they'd tried obviously didn't do anything, but could they just switch like that? "Does Dr. Harner think I'll do better with this one?"

"We won't be going to Dr. Harner for this." Mom's face grew tighter. "I called him about it and was extremely narrow-minded. I sometimes think these doctors are like professional athletes—they only endorse products from companies that pay them. Celia put me in touch with her oncologist, but he only treats adults. He introduced me to a doctor in Bridgeport, though, and she was very encouraging. I made an appointment for noon tomorrow."

"I'll still be in school at noon."

Mom's eyes narrowed and she tilted her head to the side. "I'll come get you from school or you could just skip the day. We need to do this."

Becky had no idea how to have this conversation with her mother. How could she tell her that she believed none of these experimental drugs would work? Becky had done her own research. She knew what the odds were.

"How terrible are the side effects?"

"There are things like diarrhea, nausea, vomiting, and muscle cramps."

Great, so I'll spend the last couple of weeks I have before this disease knocks me completely on my back in the bathroom. "That doesn't sound like fun, Mom."

"I know it doesn't, honey. I know it doesn't. But we can't just do nothing. The side effects of that are worse, in case you don't realize it. This drug has gotten some great results."

Something told Becky that her only real hope lay with Dr. Nella, just as it told her that her dad was the key to solving the blight in Tamarisk. If Dr. Nella came up with some kind of treatment and she had this other drug in her system, would it screw things up? At the very least, she'd probably have to go through another battery of tests in Tamarisk.

Still, how could she explain this to her mother? Becky realized she had to try. Things were too important now. She couldn't do something that felt wrong and could dash her last hopes simply to avoid an outburst.

"Do you think we could maybe put this off until next week?" Becky said tentatively.

"Why would we do that? You know that every day matters. I tried to get the doctor to see us today."

"I'm waiting to hear back from someone."

Her mother's head snapped back and her brows folded inward. "What are you talking about? Did your father take you to see someone without discussing it with me?"

Gee, Mom, have you had a long conversation about Gleevec with him? "It wasn't Dad. It was . . ." Becky hesitated, bracing for the tirade to come. ". . . Miea."

Mom's expression was blank. "Miea?"

"The queen in Tamarisk. She took me to her doctor because their medicine is different." Becky cringed inwardly as she said this and didn't look her mother in the eye. When Mom didn't say anything right away, though, she glanced up and saw that her mother's head was bowed.

"Mom?"

Mom looked up with her face masked in sadness. "Becky, Tamarisk is something that's happening in your imagination because of your illness."

"I know you think that, Mom, but it's not."

Mom reached out and touched the side of Becky's face. "It feels real to you."

Becky clasped the hand on her face with both of hers. "It is real, Mom. I not only feel it but I can smell it and hear it and taste it and see it."

Mom put their hands to her lips and then lowered her head again.

"Come with me," Becky said. "We'll go to Dad's house tonight and I'll take you there. Then you'll see."

"Honey, don't make me do this to you," Mom said, her eyes still facing the table.

"Do what, Mom?"

Her mother took a deep breath and drew herself up. Her lips were tight, but her eyes were still soft. "I can't go to Tamarisk with you. Please don't bring that up again. And we are going to keep that appointment tomorrow. We can't give up, Becky. We just can't."

Mom stood, pulled Becky toward her, and then walked away.

Why won't she go with me? What is she afraid of? Becky watched her mother walk into the den and then went up to her room. She wanted to do her own research on Gleevec. Then she desperately needed to take a nap.

///

Nights without Becky had become borderline intolerable. The clock just kept whirring by with dizzying speed. How many more days did he have left? What would the quality of those days be as Becky's illness progressed? The fact that he was able to see her more frequently now almost mocked him, taunting him with the knowledge that this extra time came with an unbearable price. Still, the nights she was here were so much easier to take than those she spent with Polly. When Becky was with him, he could convince himself to focus on the moment—especially on days when she seemed relatively hale—and tell himself to enjoy what they had together.

Those nights also included trips to Tamarisk and the befuddling complexities of that world. Until he had a better sense of their ecosystem—the knowledge of which deftly eluded him—he couldn't attempt to devise a solution to the blight and couldn't do any meaningful work on it at home. This meant that on the days Becky was gone, he not only missed his daughter desperately, but also had nothing to divert his attention from how much he missed her.

For the first time since he'd learned that Becky was sick again, he accepted an invitation to dinner from Lisa. They spoke on the phone almost daily, but facing Lisa was tougher than speaking with her. She wanted to meet at one of her usual places, a boisterous Indian restaurant where fervent sitar music wended its way through the din of the room. Chris just simply wasn't up for that. He convinced her to meet him at a sedate New American café instead.

"It's strange to hear the sound of your fork and knife on your plate while you're eating," she said when their food arrived. "Do you really find this relaxing?"

Chris shook his head at the kind of observation only someone like Lisa would make. Then he shrugged. "I don't find anything particularly relaxing anymore."

"I know, sweetie," she said, reaching across the table to stroke his arm. "I know you don't." She kept touching him much longer than she usually did and she seemed surprisingly pensive. "You need to prepare for the future, you know," she said thoughtfully.

Chris found her change of tone irksome. "What does that even mean?"

"I know you understand this intellectually, but that isn't the point. In the near future, you're going to face a painful reality, the kind that destroys people. You can't let yourself compound the tragedy. Becky wouldn't want you to do that."

Chris looked toward the ceiling. "Why do people always say things like that in these situations?"

Lisa sat up straighter, and when she spoke, she sounded like herself again. "Just because it's a cliché doesn't mean it isn't valid. Really, think about it. Becky hated it when you hid under a rock after your divorce. You know how she feels about this."

That tone really wasn't any better. There was a reason Chris stayed home on nights without his daughter. "So, what do you think?" he said sharply. "Dancing after the funeral? Maybe we could hit some strip clubs, or go all out and spend the weekend in Vegas. If Becky really cares about me, she'll die before the height of tourist season."

Lisa's response was equally sharp. "Stop twisting my words, Chris. You know that isn't what I meant."

The room felt too quiet for this conversation. Maybe the Indian place would have been better. At a table across from them, a man smiled shyly at his female companion. It was probably an early date in their relationship and he was just beginning to understand how much he liked her. "I know that's not what you meant, but the idea of preparing for this seems ludicrous. The only thing I'm certain about is that no matter how terrible I think this is going to be, it will be a hundred times worse."

"I know you feel that way. That's why I'm worried about you. This has more potential to knock you out permanently than it does most people."

"Lisa, most people never get over the loss of a child."

"They remain functional, though. I'm seriously worried that you won't. Thank God that you have that fantasy place to go to now. Maybe if you keep traveling there after Becky's gone you won't go entirely catatonic."

Lisa accompanied the word "traveling" with air quotes. Chris didn't want to pursue what that meant. The conversation at hand was already disturbing enough. "I can only go to Tamarisk with Becky. I assume when she's gone Tamarisk will be gone as well." He'd never had that thought before and it made him suddenly and deeply sad. He washed back a sob with a sip of water, closed his eyes, and took a deep breath.

Lisa's voice softened again. "Maybe you're wrong about that, Chris. Maybe you get to keep Tamarisk."

Chris shook his head. "No. I don't."

"People need a place to go when they're grieving. Maybe this is your place."

"That was never the point of Tamarisk, Lisa. Tamarisk was always Becky's place. Maybe it was Becky's and my place. It was never meant to be only mine."

"Maybe the thing you were meant to do is keep it alive after she's gone."

Chris looked at Lisa for several seconds without saying a word. Then he looked down and returned to moving his food around his plate. Lisa couldn't understand this. No one could understand this.

Including him.

19

Becky was still up in her room when Polly heard Chris's car on the driveway. There was a time when the sound of his car door closing and Becky's barreling down the stairs to greet him were intertwined as though they were eternally connected. Polly remembered being surprised the first time Chris came to pick Becky up after the split that he made it all the way to the porch with her still in her room.

It wasn't surprising today, though. For the first time in years, Polly missed the connection between those two sounds. Hearing them united again would mean that what Becky was going through now was nothing more than a bad dream.

The doorbell rang and Polly answered it. Chris threw her the little uplift of his chin that he offered whenever she opened the door for him and she let him into the foyer. She then walked to the stairs and called up. "Honey, your father is here."

"Thanks. Two minutes."

"Do you need any help?"

"No, I'll be okay."

She turned back toward Chris. She was never sure what to do while he stood there waiting. A part of her wanted to invite him into the kitchen until Becky came down. Another part wanted simply to leave him standing there by himself. She'd done the latter countless times, but she didn't want Becky to exert herself further by seeking her out to say good-bye tonight.

Polly had talked to numerous divorced friends about the

awkwardness of pickup and drop-off. One friend actually said she looked forward to seeing her ex-husband and catching up with him. She was the decided exception, though. Most expressed feelings ranging from animosity to indifference to sorrow to discomfort. Several talked about how the experience brought back bad memories. Polly didn't get that, though. After all this time, she could barely recall the feeling of being married to Chris. Their relationship was entirely about Becky in the present day.

Of course, none of her friends had any experience dealing with what "Becky in the present day" meant now.

"How's she been?" Chris said, glancing up the stairs.

Polly closed her eyes and nodded slowly. "Not a good day."

Chris looked down at the floor. "Any reaction to the new drug?"

"Nothing extreme. She's vomited a couple of times, but the doctor said to expect that. I haven't seen any of the other possible side effects."

"But it's been a bad day?"

"Yeah. She seems . . . limp. Like she's wilting."

Chris took two steps toward the stairs and then stopped. What did he think he was going to do? He made eye contact with Polly for a second and Polly saw the frustration there. "We'll have a quiet night," he said.

"That would be good."

Chris looked defeated and Polly wished she had some strength to offer him. Did intact families handle something like this differently? Polly guessed that no one had the reserves needed to bear up well.

Polly and Chris stood in the foyer, ten feet apart, silently, for a few more minutes until she heard Becky coming down the stairs. Chris met her halfway and held her for a moment before they came down together. He walked Becky over to her, and Polly gave her daughter a long hug.

"Have a good night, honey," Polly said, stepping back.

"I will, Mom," Becky said softly.

Chris followed Becky to the door. Before he left, he turned to her and did the chin thing again. This time, Polly thought the gesture had a different meaning.

///

The meeting was as dismal as nearly every one had been since they'd first identified the blight. Miea felt physically heavier as the session wore on and she received more damage reports. This set detailed the loss of a microfarm, the devastation of one of the largest groves of plumas trees in the kingdom, and the horrifying news that diseased nuts from blight-infested bushes had poisoned an entire chorus of norbecks. Miea observed the people around the room and thought she read defeat on the faces of her advisors for the first time. She knew they'd maintained the façade of hope for her benefit, but it had become too difficult. Dyson somehow managed to survive the litany without bowing to it, but Miea knew he wasn't immune to the hurt associated with realizing that your world was slipping away.

Looking at Dyson now reminded her of their last meeting alone together. It wasn't the first time she'd thought of that conversation since it happened. For the briefest moment, she felt connected to him the way they had been at the university. She didn't need to ask herself if he'd felt it as well; his eyes confirmed it. He'd wanted to say something else that day. Maybe there was a great deal more he wanted to say. However, Miea wouldn't allow it. Couldn't allow it. Now, only a few days later, she wasn't entirely sure why. If the end was really upon them, what good did her resolve do her?

Mercifully, the meeting finished minutes later. After the cataloguing of several more casualties. After her declaration of a state of emergency in three more regions. How long would it be before she dispensed with the specifics and simply declared what everyone at the table already knew: the entire kingdom was in a state of emergency.

"Dyson, would you mind staying behind a minute?" she said

as the council filed out of the room.

"Of course, Your Majesty." Dyson said something to Thuja and the minister nodded before looking in Miea's direction and bowing gently. Not even Thuja had the heart to be brusque with her anymore. Dyson approached, but Miea said nothing as the room emptied. She turned to face the window overlooking the courtyard. A hoffler boldly stared up at her from the lawn and she offered it a tiny smile. The lizard darted away quickly.

"Is there something I can do for you, Your Majesty?"

"Trepidation is either the sign of great weakness or great wisdom," Miea said, quoting Professor Liatris as Dyson had the other day.

Dyson stood next to her now. "I took the professor at his word back then, but I've come to learn he was right."

Miea turned toward him, realizing they hadn't been this close physically in more than four years. For a moment, she couldn't utter a word as her training warred with her instincts. She could only look at Dyson's face and note how unchanged it seemed from the days when she'd memorized its every contour and line. "At the moment," she said, surprised at how slight her voice sounded, "I feel both very weak and very wise."

"You aren't weak, Miea. You have never once been weak."

She smiled joylessly and lowered her eyes. Her tears welled much too quickly for her to catch them. "But I am very, very scared."

Miea reached out and took Dyson in her arms. She held him as though he was responsible for gravity itself. It took her some time to notice that he was holding her as well, that he'd dropped his head onto hers, that her embrace had neither surprised him nor disturbed him.

It was terrible and thrilling. Just as her trip out to the fields to examine the first blighted leaves had been. Holding Dyson this way offered her rare comfort, but she never would have crossed this gulf if not for a tragedy even greater than the one that had torn them apart.

"We're losing this battle, Dyson."

"But we haven't lost it. Not yet. As long as that is true, we might never lose it."

"I don't know what to say to our people anymore. I'm supposed to speak for the kingdom, but I can't think of anything to say other than 'I'm sorry.'"

Dyson tightened his arms around her. "The people know you're doing everything you can."

"Do they?"

Dyson pulled back enough to look her in the eyes. "Of course they do. They loved you as a little girl, they loved you as a princess, and they love you now. The way you bore up after your parents' death and the way you returned a sense of celebration to the kingdom after we mourned was an incredible inspiration."

Miea chuckled softly. "I was crumbling inside and crying in private."

"We all assumed as much, and that made us love you more." He moved his head closer to her. "Even those of us you left behind."

Miea's tears returned and she buried her face in Dyson's chest. "I never left you behind. Not in my soul. The demands of the kingdom overtook me to the point where I could never do anything about it. My parents' deaths devastated me, made me want to hide in my room, and yet I had so much responsibility. Then, on top of that, there were the ongoing investigations into what killed them, the endless standoff with the Thorns, and now this crisis that has dwarfed everything else."

Dyson ran his fingers through her hair soothingly and allowed her to feel what she was feeling. To Miea, this was a remarkable luxury. For several minutes, they stood against the backdrop of the courtyard and said nothing. At last, he guided her to a sofa and sat facing her.

"I have something to tell you about what happened on the Malaspina Bridge."

The cloud around Miea's head cleared as she heard the words. "What do you mean?"

"I've been conducting my own investigation these past four years using resources available through the university, the minister's office, and some people I never thought I'd associate with."

"Why?" Miea said, stunned by this news.

"Because I knew you. I knew you wouldn't believe what the investigators told you if it didn't coincide with your assumptions. I was sure, though, even as the distance grew between us, that you would believe me. I received the definitive results from the investigation not long after Minister Thuja asked me to become your contact with Agriculture. I wanted to say something sooner, but I'm afraid our personal history got in the way."

Miea shook her head sadly. "Our personal history. I thought you despised me."

"'Despised' is definitely not the right word."

Dyson smiled at her with a warmth she hadn't seen in so long. An array of unexpected feelings raced through her. Still, she needed to know what he had discovered. "What did you learn from your investigation?"

"Your parents' deaths were accidental, Miea. It wasn't due to sabotage or an aggressive act by the Thorns or anything like that."

Miea sat up. "The investigators have said the same thing repeatedly, but bridges don't simply collapse like that. Since they could never explain how this one did, I always sent them back to find out who was responsible."

"I know you did. I followed the official investigation very closely. It was accidental, though, Miea. The bridge collapsed because it could no longer bear the stress of the entire entourage. Here's what I know that the official investigators never found—and it seems sadly ironic to tell you this today—the cause of the accident dates back to the Great Blight. The stanchions of the bridge were held together with a compound that included kootenai, a living plant organism in stasis. Kootenai has tremendous adhesive qualities and it was involved in the building of many older structures. As it was destroying many other plants in the area, the Blight killed the kootenai binding the stanchions. The official investigators never thought to look into this because the Blight had happened so long before."

"Then why didn't the bridge collapse the first time someone crossed it after the Great Blight?"

"The rest of the compound was strong enough to withstand most loads. Your parents' traveling party was too big, though. As the histories have noted, Amelan insisted that an enormous security crew accompany them. Still, they might have crossed safely if not for one other event. The lead security vehicle broke down and the entire motorcade stopped on the bridge as repairs to the vehicle were completed. The pressure proved too much for the bridge and the stanchions gave. I can show you how I recreated those events if you'd like."

Miea envisioned those final moments as her parents and the many good people who'd traveled with them realized the bridge was doomed and they had no escape. They must have been so frightened. So desperate.

As the vision played itself out in her mind, she wept for her parents again as though she'd never wept for them before. The entire time, Dyson held her, allowing her to reexperience her loss. *I wish you'd been there to hold me that day, Dyson. I should have run into your arms. I should have demanded they take you with me to the Palace. I was lost, though, and I lost you.*

At last, she looked up at him and touched his face. "Thank you. It's hard to believe any person would do this for me."

Dyson kissed her hand. "I only hope it helps a little."

"It's going to take some time for me to reconcile this, but yes, it helps. It's different knowing that no one did this deliberately. Even though it saddens me to think about how easily this could have been avoided, there's some solace in knowing no one set out to do them harm."

"It's one less burden for you to carry, Miea."

Miea looked deeply into Dyson's eyes and realized that what he said was true. The realization that there was someone in the world willing to help her this way and who understood her enough to do it filled her. She reached for the man she thought she'd let go years ago.

Although she still had burdens enough to bring herself and the entire kingdom down, they kissed, and Miea felt alive in a way she thought she never would again.

///

The difference in Becky's appearance between Tuesday night and Thursday was terrifying to Chris. On Tuesday, her spirits had been good and her complexion pink. Tonight, she was listless, her eyes cloudy, her skin tone pallid. She wasn't shutting down yet, was she? They had more time than this, didn't they?

Becky had a few bites to eat and then lay on the couch while he cleaned up after dinner. He'd bought her favorite ice cream for dessert, Stonyfield Farm Chocolate Raspberry Swirl, but it stayed in the freezer. Maybe she'd be better on Saturday and they'd have it then. When he finished in the kitchen, he sat next to her and stroked her hair.

"I'm wiped, Dad."

"I know, babe. Is there anything I can do?"

"I don't think so." She sighed. "I tried to do too much in school today. I was feeling okay, so Lonnie and I took a walk out back at lunchtime. That was stupid."

It wasn't stupid. Chris knew it was Becky's way of fighting. Even a minor victory would have been nice. "You can rest now. You'll feel better tomorrow."

"Yeah, maybe," she said vacantly. "Maybe this is just a reaction to the new drug." She drifted off for a few minutes after that, her eyes fixed on the far wall. "We're going to Mendana Island tonight to do some research, right?"

The blight had ravaged the tiny island and Chris thought he might be able to learn a great deal there, assuming the Tamariskian machines worked with some level of consistency. Becky didn't seem in any condition to travel, though. At this point, he was assuming he'd be carrying her to her bed because she would be too exhausted to walk.

"Beck, we might want to pass on Tamarisk tonight."

Becky stirred enough to turn to face him. "We can't do that."

"We may have to. We don't know what these journeys are doing to your body. They might be too stressful."

"Are you saying we shouldn't go anymore?"

This was obviously upsetting her. "I'm saying that we might need to wait until Saturday to go again. You have good days and bad days, Beck. This is a bad one."

Becky sat up, making an all-too-obvious attempt to convince him she was in better shape than he thought. "I can do it. If the journeys beat me up, I would feel it when we got there, right? I never do."

This was yet another of the many conundrums facing Chris now. Clearly going to Tamarisk was tremendously important to Becky. Yet just as clearly, she wasn't in a condition to do it. Was going there hastening her decline? If so, though, which had greater value: a limited number of days filled with wonder or a slightly less limited number of days filled with waiting for the end?

"Do you really think you're up for this the way you're feeling?"

"I really am."

Chris nodded. "Then we'll go to Mendana. Let's make it an early night, though. Okay?"

They were sitting on Becky's bed an hour later. Chris had a difficult time darkening because he couldn't stop thinking about what this trip could wind up doing to Becky. What if the effort sapped so much energy from her that she passed into a coma? As much as his battles with Polly wore on him, he didn't want to be responsible for stealing a last conversation between her and her daughter. Because he knew that Becky wanted to go to Tamarisk, he forced himself to push such worries aside, along with everything else. Becky needed to take these trips for as long as she was physically capable.

They emerged outside of the palace, where a vehicle was

waiting for them. When he opened his eyes, Chris looked to his left to see if Becky was okay. He found her gazing broadly and taking an exaggeratedly deep breath.

Becky smiled when she caught his eye. "I love the smell of this place."

Rather than debilitating her, the journey seemed to have revived Becky. *She has such an incredibly strong will,* Chris thought. *She's summoning all of her strength to show me she can still do this. If fate was even a little bit kinder, I know she could fight this disease out of her body.* Chris knew better, though. Questionable radical experiments aside, there was nothing—not even the power of optimism—that could eradicate his daughter's illness. For this moment, however, Chris would try to convince himself that Becky had found a second wind, one that would last her at least to the end of this trip.

The vehicle took them several miles to the port, where they boarded a sailboat to take them to Mendana Island. Dyson, one of the minister of agriculture's aides, joined them at the port for the half hour trip.

"Have there been any new developments in the past two days?" Chris said when the boat took sail.

"Nothing good, I'm afraid. The queen has declared a state of emergency in two more regions of the kingdom. We're evacuating everything we can from Jonrae at this point. The seapowet is literally starving to death. We've brought several dozen of them to our facilities to try to keep them alive, but I don't know how successful we'll be. The seapowet feeds on the nectar of ochoco—which grows only in Jonrae—and the ochoco fields are so devastated that the few surviving plants will wither in transport."

"We've gotta do something, Dad," Becky said.

"I know we do, babe. I wish we had more time and more information." Chris turned to Dyson. "Have you been able to figure out why we're getting discrepancies in the calibrations?"

"I'm afraid that has turned out to be nearly as confusing as everything else associated with this blight. We took several readings yesterday at various times and all the calibrations were consistent."

"Maybe the machines have adjusted to the environmental changes."

"We can only hope so. We'll see what we learn today. A crew has been working at our Mendana outpost for several hours already."

Chris saw the island come into view. From the middle distance, it seemed sparsely vegetated, but as they got closer, Chris realized that what he'd mistaken for dirt (what he first perceived as black he now saw as dark ash) was actually huge patches of plants in the last stages of necrosis. This was the worst case he'd seen yet, and it was much closer to the palace than the other fields he'd visited, even if this one was surrounded by water. Was the disease that was extinguishing this island currently riding the waves back to the city that was Tamarisk's beating heart?

They debarked and rode another vehicle toward the center of the island. The trees were barren here, pale multihued branches lay naked. Slim flowers occasionally peeked up from blue leaves, but the vegetation that remained alive was mostly unadorned.

"The tongass is gone," Dyson said mournfully. "There are other places in the kingdom where the tongass has withstood the blight. I thought we could learn something from that. It has been devastated here, though."

Chris understood the sense of loss in Dyson's voice all too well. When the vehicle stopped near the crew that arrived that morning, Chris exited slowly, heavyhearted.

"It's so upsetting, isn't it?" Becky said. "Do you remember this place from the stories?"

"The name seems familiar, but I couldn't think of why I knew it."

"The Rainbow Fair."

"This is that place?" Chris glanced around him with a new sense of distress. The story they'd created about this island came vividly to mind now. It was about the event that turned this lightly populated spot into the hottest destination in Tamarisk one weekend a year—a festival that set itself against the natural splendor of hundreds of varieties of flowers in full bloom displaying the full spectrum of the Tamariskian rainbow. There would be no Rainbow Fair this year. "We need to get to work."

He examined cuttings with the botanists' machinery, reading reports and trying to put them into context. As before, Becky helped him in whatever way she could. Even though there were many other people available to do the same thing, she seemed revived by the work, and Chris wanted her to be as involved as possible. The Becky he saw now was far different from the sallow girl he'd sat with less than an hour ago. She pitched in diligently, and when he asked her if she needed to take a break, she scoffed at the absurdity of the question.

There seemed to be new problems with the calibrations, though. Dyson quizzed the staff on their earlier findings and each swore that the readings had been consistent all day. There had been heavy cloud cover until shortly before his arrival, and it was possible that clear sunshine had made an appreciable difference on the plants, even those as diseased as these.

Chris pondered this. It had been very sunny on Chris's first day out in the fields, but overcast the second when the readings showed fewer discrepancies. Was there a way for them to simulate the effects of the sun and maybe combat the blight with this artificial nourishment? It was something else to consider.

While he studied a screen, he heard Becky squeal. Instantly alarmed, he pivoted to the sound only to realize that her exclamation was one of joy. She'd knelt down to pet a rotund, furry, biped animal no more than two feet high.

"It's a chestatee," Becky said. "Remember them, Dad? He seems a little confused."

Chris guessed the chestatee was likely very confused. He remembered the docile animals well from their stories. They lived in trees and fed off the vegetation on the branches. This little guy was probably wondering why he was hungry all the time now.

Becky sat on the ground to pet the chestatee and it climbed into her lap, making a deep rumbling sound. For the first time, Chris noted the particular music of this island, bass-heavy and monotone. Because it was closest, he heard this particular chestatee distinctly, but he was certain others of its kind were contributing to the island's aural backdrop.

The animal climbed Becky's chest and licked at her chin. Becky laughed in surprise and tipped over backward. She snuggled the chestatee close to her and then playfully pawed at it, causing the chestatee to wave a paw at her as well. The two lay together playing for several minutes as Chris reveled in the pleasure on his daughter's face. Her laugh was melodious, her eyes radiant. It was such a contrast to how she appeared in the apartment that he nearly wept over the fact that Tamarisk—even in the midst of its own crisis—could give her moments like this.

Eventually, Becky stood up and brushed herself off. The chestatee sauntered away, probably in search of food. Chris barely noticed them, though. His eyes instead went to the spot the two of them had vacated.

The withered plants upon which Becky and the animal had lain were now a brilliant blue.

20

Chris was still puzzling over the strange occurrence in Mendana two days later when Becky and he returned to Tamarisk. They took cuttings from the refreshed plants immediately and found the samples to be hearty and strong. Readings elsewhere fluctuated throughout the day. Chris and some of the Tamariskian scientists tried to find another chestatee, wondering if the animal, or perhaps the animal's interaction with Becky had some bearing on the blight, but none were around. It was yet another mystery that left him feeling both closer to and farther from a solution.

Today, Becky and he were planning to go to another blighted region of Tamarisk where chestatees lived. There was no scientific reason to believe the animals had a healing effect on the ecosystem, but it was foolish to ignore even wild speculation at this point.

Becky seemed a little better tonight. Chris marveled at how she'd rallied herself the last time they were in Tamarisk; the image of her wrestling playfully with the chestatee was nearly as incongruous as the mark they'd left on the ground. When they had gotten home that night, she fell asleep in mid-sentence and had trouble getting up to go to school the next morning. Tonight, though, she ate a little more for dinner and even felt strong enough for a board game before they made their trip. Chris knew there would be far more nights like Thursday in Becky's future than there would be nights like tonight, but he was thankful for any grace.

As with the last time they visited Tamarisk, they arrived outside of the castle, expecting a vehicle to be waiting for them. So many things still confused him about these transits (beyond the obvious, of course). How, for instance, did they know when and where Becky and he would show up? Did they simply have greeters posted everywhere?

No vehicle was here this time, though. Instead, they found one of Miea's aides who informed Chris that the queen wished to see him alone. Chris thought it was odd that Miea would exclude Becky from any conversation, but Becky reminded him that the test results were due from the Tamariskian doctor.

"She must have bad news, Dad," Becky said, resigned. Becky hadn't mentioned the test results all day, but obviously she'd pinned more hopes on them than Chris had anticipated.

"We don't know that, babe. This could have nothing to do with that. Maybe she wants to talk to me privately about what happened in Mendana and then she'll call you in to talk about the results." This made no sense to Chris, and he doubted he'd convinced Becky with such shallow reasoning, but it was the best he could offer in an attempt to reassure her.

Sorbus pulled Miea out of a meeting the moment Chris arrived. The queen asked him to follow her to her chambers and requested argo from her aide for both of them. Chris sat on a sofa and Miea sat across from him in a high-backed chair. It was obvious Miea had something important to tell him, but she waited until they sat to get to it.

"Dr. Nella delivered her report on Becky a few hours ago."

Chris instantly felt nervous. He'd convinced himself not to place any hopes on this. He'd even tried to put it out of his mind entirely. Now he realized he'd failed to do either. "Can she help?"

"She found nothing."

Chris's heart sank. "So there's nothing you can do, either." Yet another potential miracle cure had turned out to be pure fancy.

"No, Chris, you're misunderstanding me. I'm not saying that she couldn't find anything that would help Becky. I'm saying that she couldn't find anything at all. Becky doesn't have cancer here. Becky doesn't have *any* illness here."

Chris leaned closer to Miea, as though he wasn't sure he'd heard her correctly. "She's not sick?"

Miea smiled. "I have no way to say what she's like in Connecticut, but she's not sick when she's here."

Chris wasn't sure how to react. "Maybe it's the machines. We've been getting all kinds of inconsistent readings out in the fields."

"It isn't the machines. Dr. Nella knew what to look for. We have a great deal of experience here with this kind of disease."

Of course they would. In the early stories Becky created about Tamarisk, the subject had come up on numerous occasions. "But how can she possibly not be sick here?"

Miea sat up in her chair. Her eyes were brighter than Chris had ever seen them. "I don't think anyone can answer that question. I have a guess, though. Becky told me that Tamarisk was your idea."

Chris held up a hand. "Tamarisk was definitely Becky's idea."

"It was your idea to create a world for bedtime stories, though."

"Yes, it was."

"Which you did to take Becky's mind off of her cancer treatments."

Chris nodded slowly. "That's how it started, yes."

Miea stood up and moved next to him on the sofa. She was practically vibrating with energy. Was this the same woman who'd spoken in such a dire way about her home during their last meeting?

"This is my theory: I think Tamarisk became real because of Becky's illness. The two of you weren't just telling stories to ease Becky's mind. You were creating a world where she would never be sick."

The revelation hit Chris all at once. He saw himself in Becky's room in those early days after her illness, fully convinced that she would get better. He'd intended the stories to help with the transition. Instead, though, Becky's body only managed to force the cancer into retreat. As it turned out, it had been an un-winnable fight from the very beginning. Was it possible that the stories really did have another purpose? Could Miea be right about this? Were they creating a world where Becky was okay? If so, then this was a greater fantasy that he ever imagined it to be.

The stories—the time together creating them, the imagination they unlocked, the special language they allowed Chris and Becky to speak together—had always been precious to him. Until now, though, sitting in Tamarisk and hearing this remarkable news, he'd only begun to realize how precious they were.

The images were too much for him to handle. Becky's little-girl voice telling the first of the Tamarisk tales. Her more mature voice whispering in his ear that Tamarisk was real. Her expression when she learned that her illness was back. Her rolling on the ground without a care with the chestatee.

A sob wracked his body and he covered his face with his hands. He cried uncontrollably for several minutes, the flood releasing a wide variety of emotions at once.

At some point, Sorbus arrived with the argo. Miea touched him gently on the shoulder and asked him if he wanted a cup. Chris nodded and lifted his head, taking the carved wooden tumbler filled with effervescent brew. He sipped slowly, allowing the bubbles to play over his face, then breathed deeply and looked up at Miea.

"Are you all right?" she said.

"I have no idea."

"There's more. At least I believe there is. Dyson told me about what happened with Becky and the chestatee out on Mendana Island the other day."

"I've been trying to make sense of that."

"I believe I already have. Again, this is just a theory, but I think it is a very sound one. The discrepancies in the readings when Becky and you are in the fields ties in with this. I think the news we received from Dr. Nella and the revival of those plants shows definitively that Becky and Tamarisk have a symbiotic relationship."

Chris put his cup on the table. His head was clearing. "Are you saying that the blight and Becky's cancer are related?"

"I'm saying they're the same thing. Becky is healthier here than she is in your world, and our world is healthier when she's here. The difference is simply a matter of scale."

That made sense to the degree that any of this made sense. What were the implications, though? What did it matter? "Still, at the end of the day, Becky is very sick at home, with no hope of a solution, and I suppose that means there is no solution available for Tamarisk, either."

"Except if Becky lives here permanently."

Chris startled at the sound of those words. "Is that even possible?"

"I think it was always meant to be."

"But she gets yanked back into our world at entirely unexpected moments. She doesn't have any control over it. How could she possibly stay?"

"The night Becky and I met I'd been meditating on the troubles we were having here. As I did, I found myself speaking to someone who looked like my father but didn't speak like my father. That led to the path opening between Tamarisk and Becky. Last night, after speaking with Dr. Nella, I meditated in the same way, hoping to meet that presence again. It came to me this time without the guise of my father. To tell you the truth, I don't know what it looked like. It spoke in phrases I didn't completely understand, but then I felt a powerful sense of energy coming from it and into me, and it said, 'Read the signs.'"

"I met that thing," Chris said dazedly.

"You did?"

"The first time I came here. It juiced me, too, and it said a number of baffling things. 'Absorb this and all other resources.'

I've been trying to figure out what that meant since I heard it. It has to do with what we're talking about now, doesn't it?"

"Maybe it does. I've spent most of the day trying to 'read the signs' and I think I have something. I believe if she truly decided she wanted to stay, Becky could do so—but only if she decided that she would stay here permanently. That's what the signs mean about her health and her effect on our ecosystem. The biggest sign was that she was even able to get here at all. I think she goes home because she thinks of Connecticut as home. Maybe it isn't. Maybe *here* is home and if she acknowledges that she'll stay."

"And she would remain healthy here?"

"I think she'd be as healthy as she is here right now. Certainly, she would not have cancer. Read the signs."

Chris wanted desperately to believe Miea's theory, even though he knew she had no way of testing it. While her suppositions were hardly scientific, they made sense. Becky wasn't sick here. Her contact with Tamariskian plants made the plants healthier. She even made hungry chestatees playful. Could she really live here, though? Nothing that he knew suggested it was possible.

Yet it was the only choice Becky could make. Her time back home was ticking down fast. Here—if she could really stay here—she would be free of illness, of pain, and of fear of death. If Miea was right, Becky only needed to make the decision to stay here forever and her cancer would disappear.

"Can I stay here with her?" Chris said impulsively. He hadn't really thought it through, but how much thinking was required? The most important thing in his world would be here, and Tamarisk would offer endless opportunities to discover. Nothing at home rivaled that.

Miea tipped her head sympathetically and shook it slowly. "That's not what the signs suggest. This is Becky's world, Chris. It was created for her—you said so yourself. You can't get here on your own. I believe that means you can't choose to stay here, either."

"You don't know that for certain," he said sharply.

Miea looked at him carefully. "I don't know *any* of this for certain. What I'm saying to you now is the result of speculation and meditation. None of this can be proven ahead of time, Chris. I believe it, though. As strongly as I've ever believed anything."

"What if Becky chooses to keep me here?"

Miea's expression clouded. "I don't believe daughters can make that choice."

That means I lose her either way. Of course, there were huge differences.

"Where would she live?"

"Right here in the palace with me." Miea smiled softly, almost as though she were trying to spare his feelings. "We would be like sisters."

Miea's eyes were gleaming when she said this. *She's been thinking about this all day.* Chris had no doubt that Miea would love and care for Becky. He'd never be with his daughter again, but he would know that she lived a life of comfort and wonder. Could he—or any parent—wish for more?

Of course I could. I could wish that I could share it with her.

This wasn't like sending her off to college. Not long ago, he'd lamented the fact that once she went away to school, she would only be a visitor when he saw her. Now there wouldn't even be the visits. If Miea was right, though—and when it came down to it, he really had little choice but to believe along with her—she would live. She would live a remarkable life. A life even she never would have dreamed.

"I guess we should go tell her," he said, a little unsteadily.

Miea put a hand on his. "Give yourself a chance to get used to it first, Chris. Tell her when you get back home. I have another idea for how to spend our time together today."

///

While she waited for her father and Miea, Becky explored the courtyard. Even now, when the kingdom was facing so many problems, she seemed to find something new wherever she looked. As she bent to examine a nearly translucent flower, her eyes fell on a tiny blue-orange-silver bird with a topknot of dark feathers. It hopped toward her first on one leg and then the other, twisting its head quickly from side to side. When Becky took a step in its direction, the bird emitted a loud call, something between a chirp and a bark. The volume of the sound so completely surprised Becky that she tumbled over and landed on her butt. Becky laughed, and the bird—she remembered now that it was called a hobcaw—took a peck out of the sole of her sneaker before flying off.

Becky didn't get up immediately. She enjoyed running her hands through the tufted blue grass, inhaling the chocolatey smells of the Tamariskian soil. From this level, things even sounded different, as though the insects had their own music. Becky laid back and breathed deeply. She always felt so good here. She felt lighter, almost as though the gravity was different in this place, even though she knew it wasn't. At this moment, it was nearly impossible for her to believe that things were going terribly wrong all around and inside of her.

Dad had been in with Miea for a while now. What were they talking about? It had to have something to do with Dr. Nella's examination, and since Miea didn't want her involved, it definitely couldn't be good news. Maybe they were taking so long because Dad was having a tough time dealing with it. Becky knew how hard he was taking everything, even though he was trying not to show it. It was a little bit like when he and Mom got divorced.

No, actually, it was entirely different.

She rolled over and laid her cheek on the cool grass. The sensation comforted her. She knew one day soon she would no longer be able to visit Tamarisk and she wanted to memorize these feelings to hold on to for however long she had left after that.

What were those last days going to be like? No one wanted to talk to her about that part, but Becky knew they were going to be ugly. If she was lucky—if you could call it that—she'd fall into a coma before the worst of it.

She'd avoided thinking about this because it was so unbelievably scary. Dying wasn't bad enough. It had to be a painful death, too. Becky didn't want to die. And even with how she'd been feeling at home lately, it was so surreal to consider that it was just around the corner. In her heart, she believed that she still had so much life left. She had so many things she wanted to accomplish, so many things she thought she was *supposed to* accomplish. It was hard to imagine—especially now, lying here, enjoying this as much as she did—that she was about to be shut off, cut down.

She shuddered and sat up. *Don't do this. Don't torture yourself. It doesn't make anything better.* Becky tried to get her head back to where it had been just moments ago, but the music she heard in the air now seemed to be out of tune. A couple of distinct, flat notes disrupted the rich harmonies of the birds and animals. She shook her head, but the sounds remained.

"Beck, are you okay?" her father said from a distance. She stood up and turned toward his voice. Miea was walking with him.

"Yeah, I'm fine. I was just checking some stuff out."

She went toward them and tried to read their expressions. It was obvious that her father had a lot on his mind, but he didn't look upset exactly. Miea, on the other hand, seemed happy. Even more surprisingly, she hugged Becky and kissed her on the cheek when they met up.

"You've heard from Dr. Nella?" Becky said, her eyes flitting between Miea and her father. Dad seemed about to say something, but Miea spoke up.

"There was a problem with one of the reports. It seems that several of our machines have become unreliable lately. We'll have everything for your next visit."

"Does the 'problem with one of the reports' mean it says something bad and you're making sure?"

"No, nothing like that. Nothing like that at all."

Miea didn't sound like herself and this made Becky suspicious. "If you say so."

"Becky, really. There is nothing in the reports for you to worry about. We just need a little more time."

"Babe, it's okay," Dad said. "It really is."

There was definitely more going on here than they were saying, but she was pretty sure at this point that her father wouldn't have been able to hide it from her if this was a disaster, so she let it go. "How come you were in there so long?"

"Miea and I had a number of details to talk about. Especially after that thing that happened in Mendana on Thursday. We should have come out to get you, but we got caught up in speculation."

Becky nodded. Though the timing was weird, her father could have been telling her the truth. She could imagine Dad and Miea getting into all kinds of theories about what had happened with her and the chestatee. She had a few thoughts about that herself.

"Well, we should really get out in the fields. You kinda used up a lot of our time in there. Who knows how much we have left now."

"Your father and you aren't going out to the fields today, Becky," Miea said.

"What do you mean? We might be on to something with this chestatee thing."

"I realize that. I also realize that we've all been searching endlessly for a cure to the blight. I think the best thing for all of us is to take a break today. It might give us some perspective."

Becky looked at her father and he just shrugged. She turned back to Miea. "I'm a little worried that we're running out of time. I mean all of us."

Miea pulled her close again. Something was definitely off here. "I know you are. I need you to trust me on this, though. We've all been acting nonstop. We need to take the time to clear our thoughts."

"Miea's right, babe," Dad said. "And I really wouldn't mind

getting a chance to just enjoy this place a little."

"Okay," Becky said slowly, looking at both of them strangely. "If you really think this is a good idea, I'll go along with it. What did you have in mind?"

"I want to take you to the university," Miea said. "My waccasassa is waiting for us."

///

Chris is a good man, Miea thought as they flew. *He's had to maintain a brave face for his daughter so often in the past, and now I've turned his world upside down yet again.* She was sure that his first ride in a waccasassa was fascinating to him, but the joy he showed must have required some work. He was doing that for Becky's benefit, to prevent her from seeing that his emotions were roiling. They had to be. Dr. Nella had provided the revelation that would save both Becky and Tamarisk. Chris was right when he said Miea's theory wasn't a fact, but the facts they had fit, and Miea's time in the darkness last night had given her further reason to believe.

The solution, though, meant Chris would never get to see Becky again. Even if it was greatly preferable to Becky's other fate, Chris had to feel a profound sense of loss from this.

The bird landed in the open field behind the Humanities Center. Of course, there were no such things as casual visits where a queen was concerned, and a team had flown on ahead to prepare the school for her arrival. Dean Sambucus—looking a little grayer than Miea remembered—and a large coterie of students were waiting when Miea's party touched down.

"It's very good to see you again, Your Majesty," the dean said when she stepped off the waccasassa.

"Thank you, Dean. It has been a long time."

"A very long time, Your Majesty. I hope you'll grace us with more frequent visits in the future."

Miea glanced over at Becky. "I look forward to that."

Miea attempted to dispense with formalities quickly. The

purpose of this visit wasn't to bestow official greetings on the university. It was to show Becky and Chris a part of her life. Fortunately, Dean Sambucus and the others in his party seemed to understand and they left the three of them as alone as Miea could ever be in a public place.

The foliage around the campus was in full bloom. The university was a botanical paradise, displaying every species of Tamariskian flora the climate allowed. The School of Botanical Studies—from which both Dyson and Thuja had graduated—was the finest in the kingdom, with an elite staff of professors and research scientists, many of whom were on call elsewhere during the current crisis. This region of Tamarisk had been spared the worst of the blight up to now and, given what Miea had learned today, would likely be spared forever. Miea realized there was a possibility that Becky would decide not to live in Tamarisk permanently, but she considered that possibility remote. How could Becky think of turning this down when death awaited her at home?

The first stop on their tour was Menziesii Hall, the ornately decorated auditorium built via a donation from her great-great-great-grandparents. Constructed from huge slabs of malheur, the building was carved by dozens of artisans over the course of years. At the time of its construction, artists considered work on a portion of the hall to be the most prestigious commission available, competed aggressively for the honor, and contributed some of their most passionate pieces.

"This place is incredible," Becky said, running her hand over a carving of the hills of Custis.

"The detail is extraordinary," Chris said. "So many artistic styles blended so seamlessly."

Miea was delighted they were so impressed. "It's even more of a masterwork than it appears. Each carving was 'tuned' by engineers so that the sound is consistent in every seat in the hall."

"Wow," Becky said, placing her ear against a wall, "I wish there was a concert playing here right now."

Miea tossed a quick look to Chris. "Maybe the next time you're here."

The stop after this was Miea's old dormitory. It was constructed, like many of the buildings around the campus, from sturdy uinta, a crimsonochre variety mined in a quarry only a few miles south. Compared to the architectural magic of Menziesii Hall, the dormitories were plain—simple structures with clean lines. They represented Miea's first, and only, attempt at living on her own, however, and as such held a very special place in her heart.

"I wonder if we can get into my old room," Miea said, entering a building.

"You stayed in a regular dormitory?" Chris said.

Miea smiled. "Yes, I did, though it required a significant amount of negotiation. You wouldn't believe the suite they had planned for me."

Becky seemed fascinated with even these modest surroundings. "So you got to live here totally on your own?"

"Along with a roommate and a couple hundred other students."

"This is very cool."

They continued to the room itself, and Miea knocked on the door. She heard scurrying and then a harried-looking woman quickly opened the door.

"I know I'm late, I'm sorr—" The woman stopped abruptly. She had clearly been expecting someone else.

"I lived here once," Miea said. "Do you mind if we come in for a moment?"

The woman didn't move and didn't say a word, staring confusedly. At last, she said, "Your Majesty?" very softly.

"I realize I have no right to impose on you. This trip was something of a whim. Would you mind if we took a look for just a minute?"

The woman stepped out of the doorway. "No, no, of course. Come right in." She hurriedly began picking up food, clothing, and loose papers.

"My guess is that this room looked considerably neater when you lived here," Chris said in a whisper.

"It didn't, actually."

Becky tugged on her arm. "You were a slob when you were a teenager?"

Miea rolled her eyes. "I'm still a slob. You just can't tell because people pick up after me immediately."

Becky threw a playful slap at her father's chest. "See, Dad. There's something royal about being sloppy."

"Thanks, Miea," Chris said sternly. He was smiling, though. This trip seemed to be relaxing him. Maybe he'd begun to reconcile the conversation they'd had earlier.

The woman who lived in the room now was obviously uncomfortable having the queen here. She'd stopped picking up, but stood nervously in a corner. Miea walked over to the window to view the rolling meadow and its shimmering rainbow of wildflowers. Dyson and she had picnicked in that very meadow when she was last here. She never had the opportunity to return to her room that day.

"It's a wonderful view, isn't it?" she said to the woman. The view was the one concession she gave to special treatment. The position of this window afforded the best vista in the entire building.

The woman took a step forward. "I sometimes spend hours glancing out at that meadow. Your Majesty, no one ever told me that this room had once been yours. I would have taken better care of it if I'd known."

"Don't be silly. It's your room now and you should live in it the way you want to live in it. I certainly did." Miea glanced out the window for another long moment. She'd lost so much since she'd last stood here. For the first time in a long time, though—maybe even the first time since that day—she had reason to believe that good things were coming. Even Dyson had returned to her.

She turned and smiled at the woman. "You're late and I'm keeping you. We'll go now."

They left the dormitory and walked toward the center of campus. On the common, people read, ate, laid on blankets, and conversed with friends. Several of them stood and bowed when she passed, and Miea waved politely. A collection of students followed her at a distance, probably thinking she hadn't noticed that they were doing so. Though she'd never blended into the crowd here, she had been far less conspicuous when she was a member of the class.

A group was playing poledisk, with the launcher throwing the disk at unpredictable distances and three others trying desperately to catch it on their poles, laughing and exchanging insults with the launcher as they did.

"I love this game," Becky said as she stopped and watched.

"Do you have poledisk where you come from?"

"No, I made it up. But I got a chance to play it on one of my trips. I even scored!"

"That's very impressive for someone with no experience."

"Yeah," Becky said proudly, then turned to admire the participants' antics. "Do you think they'd let me play?"

Miea smiled. "Something tells me they might." They walked a little closer and she called to the launcher. "Excuse me?"

The launcher threw the disk dozens of yards away from his cohorts and then turned to her, chuckling over what he'd done. When he recognized Miea, though, his expression sobered and he bowed awkwardly. One player retrieved the disk and then all four bowed together.

"I'm sorry to interrupt you, but I wonder if my friend could join you for a few minutes."

The four rose from their bows and looked at one another, exchanging something she couldn't hear. "Of course, Your Majesty," said one of the players with a pole, walking toward Miea. Becky met him along the way and took the pole from him.

"Dad, watch," she said. "I'm really good at this."

Play resumed with the launcher making several easy throws to Becky and glancing back in Miea's direction. After a few of these, Becky said, "You can throw harder. I know what I'm doing," and the game resumed at a somewhat less frenetic pace than when Miea had originally broken in.

Miea turned to Chris, who cheered as Becky made a difficult catch. "She's really enjoying herself."

"You have no idea how hard I've wished to see her like this again."

"I know you must feel overwhelmed by what you've learned today, Chris, but keep this image in your head. This is what Becky can be like all the time. Maybe this is what Becky was always meant to be like."

///

The disk spiraled in the air far to Becky's left. She sprinted after it, pole raised high. She knew she could get it if she ran as hard as she could. She reached for the disk—and suddenly felt like a train had hit her. The pole flew from her hand and she tumbled hard to the ground. Only after she landed did she see the boy who had slammed into her. She was dazed, but she was pretty sure she was all right.

The boy scrambled to his feet quickly and came to her side. "I'm so sorry. Are you okay?"

Becky stood up and dusted herself off. She waved back her father, who'd started jogging in her direction with a concerned look on his face. "Yeah, I'm fine. I should have paid more attention to where I was going. Are you okay?"

"Of course, of course." The boy ran to get her pole and handed it to her gently. "Is the queen going to have me arrested?" he said nervously.

Becky laughed loudly. "I'll bet I can get you a reduced sentence."

The boy seemed worried. "I really didn't do it intentionally."

"I'm joking. The queen is cool."

The boy looked toward Miea and then back at Becky. "How do you know her? Are you her cousin or something?"

"I think you would call us distant relatives."

"Are you thinking of coming to school here?"

Becky glanced out at the campus and sighed. "I wish I could, but I live really far away. This is probably the only chance I'll ever get to visit."

"That's really too bad." The launcher gestured to the boy and he gestured back. "Do you want to take a few more throws? I promise to keep my eyes open."

"Yeah, that would be great."

The game resumed with the launcher making a few lame throws that Becky could have caught lying down. Again, Becky needed to push him to play harder. The effects of the crash hadn't bothered her at all.

///

If Chris had any doubts regarding Miea's claims about Becky's health, Becky's response to the collision had eliminated them. Sick kids didn't bounce up like that. As far as he knew, he was in good shape, but if someone ran into him the way that kid ran into Becky, Chris probably would have stayed on the ground a while.

He would talk to Becky about living in Tamarisk when they got home. Of course, there was no choice. Even if Miea's theory proved false, they were no worse off than they were already. Seeing Becky this vibrant, though, made him want to believe that Miea had uncovered the answer to keeping her this way.

For now, he just wanted to watch her play, to sear her vitality into his memory. He wanted to think of her this way always.

Miea seemed to delight in watching Becky nearly as much as he did. She'd said they'd be like sisters living here. As they walked away from the common and continued their tour of the campus, Miea wrapped an arm around Becky's shoulders. Exactly the way a big sister might.

They approached the School of Technology, another handsomely constructed building made from the same orangish stone as many others, when Chris felt some resistance to his steps.

"Did you feel that, Beck?" he said.

"Yeah. I was kinda hoping the pull would forget about us for a while."

The pull was more intense than usual. Maybe it just seemed that way now because of what he knew. How could Becky fight a force like this by simply deciding to do so?

Miea hugged Becky and then reached for Chris. Before they could touch, though, Chris felt himself slip away.

He opened his eyes to find himself seated on Becky's bed. She was slumped against him, her head on his chest, sleeping and breathing softly.

She'd had a wonderful adventure tonight, certainly the most lighthearted time she'd spent in weeks. There had been a physical toll, however. As he settled her under her covers, Becky didn't stir at all.

Chris watched her still form for several minutes. She was no longer the boundless vision he'd seen running only a short while ago. She would never be that person in this world again.

No, there was no choice at all, regardless of his doubts.

In the morning, he would let Becky know what Miea had told him.

21

Chris was up by six the next morning after a fitful sleep. He'd been thinking about what he needed to say to Becky the entire night. How did one prepare for a conversation like this?

Waiting for her to awaken, he tried reading the paper and then some of a new novel he'd started, but he couldn't concentrate. He tried watching television, but there was little more than infomercials at this time on a Sunday. He thought about pulling out the home movie DVDs again, but even he realized how ridiculously maudlin that would be. This wasn't a time to wallow. All wallowing had been temporarily—maybe permanently—suspended. He'd allowed melancholy to seduce him for the last time.

Eventually he sat back on the couch and watched the ceiling, a meditative exercise that managed to prove more restorative than hours of tossing in bed.

Becky came into the room around nine thirty. "Is there something interesting up there?" she said. He sat up and beckoned her to sit next to him. Her eyes looked sunken and her skin sallow. He wished he could see her play poledisk again.

"Babe, I have something serious to talk to you about."

Becky slumped against the couch. "I knew it. I knew Miea had horrible news and didn't want to tell me last night."

"She did have news, Beck, but it isn't horrible. It's remarkable. I mean, utterly remarkable. On every level."

He proceeded to tell her everything Miea told him about

Dr. Nella's findings and about the connection between her and Tamarisk.

"I can live there?" Becky said when he finished.

"You can live *well* there. With nothing at all wrong with you."

"That's why I could run around so much last night. I couldn't figure out how that was happening."

"You'll have all the energy of a very, very healthy fourteen-year-old."

Becky stared at the middle distance, obviously trying to assimilate this. She looked back at him. "Can people come to visit me?"

Chris felt tears coming to his eyes and he fought them back. "I'm afraid not, babe."

"Can I come back here sometimes?"

"Not unless Miea is reading the signs wrong. It's a one-way ticket, Beck."

Becky seemed to capture these words very slowly. Chris could see her thinking, imagining a future without the people who'd always surrounded her. Whose face flashed in her head? Polly's? Lonnie's? Some guy she'd never told him about? His?

"So if I go there, I go there alone. Forever."

Chris exhorted himself to bear up. He needed all the strength he possessed. This could not be about him in any way. "That's how it would have to be."

Becky lowered her eyes. "I don't know that I could do that."

Chris took both of her hands in his and squeezed them tightly. "Think about the alternative, babe. How is that even an option now that we know this? You just got an amazing new lease on life. You can live unimpaired in a spectacular place. Think of our best vacation ever, quintuple that, and you're talking about a bad day in Tamarisk."

Becky held his gaze for a long moment and then looked away. "This is just so permanent."

"So is the decision not to go."

Becky looked at him again through eyes that bore layers of confusion, illness, and innocence. "You want me to do this."

"No," he said with a dry laugh. "I want the third option where I get to go with you or at least come to visit several times a week. Unfortunately, that doesn't seem to be one of the choices."

Becky leaned toward him and he pulled her close. She felt so substantial to him. Chris knew he needed to memorize this feeling. For several minutes neither spoke. Then Becky sat back against the couch, Chris's arm behind her.

"If I go, the blight is over?"

"You make Tamarisk better every time you're there. If you stayed there permanently, the blight would disappear."

"This is so incredible."

"You can believe it, Beck. Think about what it felt like at the university last night. You weren't sick. You were completely better. A big college kid slammed into you, and you bounced right up."

Now it was Becky's turn to stare at the ceiling. "How do we tell Mom?"

"We'll figure something out."

Becky leaned forward. "Dad, she doesn't believe any of this."

"We'll figure something out. That can't be an impediment at this point."

"It is, though, Dad."

Chris understood—even better than Becky did—how Polly's resistance could feel like a huge obstacle. He wouldn't let her get in the way this time, though.

"I'll deal with your mother," he said, knowing he hadn't effectively "dealt with" Polly in years. That didn't matter. Their history meant nothing now.

"We can't just shove this down her throat. I couldn't live with that. If I didn't have her blessing, I wouldn't be able to live with myself. I can't live a happy life in Tamarisk if I know she's here mourning my death."

Chris hadn't anticipated this particular complication. He should have realized that Becky would want both Polly and him to make peace with this, but he wasn't thinking that way. All he understood was that Tamarisk was an immense gift. You didn't turn down gifts like that.

"Then we'll get her blessing."

"It's not gonna be easy, Dad. She'll just think both of us have lost our minds."

"We'll talk to her this afternoon when I bring you back."

Absorb this and all other resources, Chris thought, repeating the words from that otherworldly voice, as he often did these days.

///

It turned out that optimism was an easily recalled sense, even though Miea had employed it so infrequently the past few years. She had awoken this morning feeling even more refreshed than she felt after Dr. Nella's news. Her world would live. Becky would live. There was a future again—a future that held genuine promise. On top of that, Dyson was coming to have lunch with her today, the first time since their reunion that he would be here on non-state business. She'd spoken with him last night and told him everything, and he was nearly as overjoyed as she was. Today they would close the door to her chambers, she'd insist on no interruptions (she'd cancelled a meeting with the minister of transportation to make room for the lunch), and they would talk about anything other than the blight.

"You needed me, Your Majesty?" Sorbus said, entering her office.

Miea stood from her desk and approached her closest aide. "We have some planning to do, Sorbus. We need to get a construction crew and a decorator in here immediately."

"Absolutely, Your Majesty. Can I give them some idea of their task before they arrive?"

"We're going to be doing some renovation to the residence. To the suite next to my own."

"Your old rooms, Your Majesty?"

"Yes. I no longer require the files, studies, and models that are in there. We can put those in storage. No, we can dispose of them entirely—I think; let me get back to you about that. I want that area to be a living space again. I want to knock down a few walls to make it more open. I want a door that goes directly out onto the courtyard. I want bigger windows . . . and a skylight in the bedroom."

"I'll let the construction people know."

"Tell the decorator to think of creative ways to use payette. Seney as well. She seemed to be very fond of that fabric."

"'She,' Your Majesty?"

Miea smiled broadly. She'd been so preoccupied gesturing and imagining ways to improve the space that she'd forgotten to tell Sorbus why she wanted any of this. "We're building these rooms for Becky."

Sorbus nodded. "It's very gracious of you to give her a place to settle during her visits."

"Soon she won't be visiting any longer. Becky is coming here to live."

"But I thought—"

"Nothing is exactly what any of us thought, Sorbus. And that is a very good thing."

///

They'd spent the last few hours on the couch. Becky had felt strong enough to sit outside for a little while in the morning, but her strength waned quickly and she could barely make it back up to the apartment. They'd watched television with Becky's head on Chris's lap the rest of the day.

Chris hadn't brought up their conversation about Tamarisk again. Had he added another weight to her already heavy load? A cure for Becky's illness was available, but it carried with it additional compromises and issues, including one Chris had managed not to consider—Polly. How ironic would it be if his imagination had helped generate a new life for his sick daughter and his ex-wife's lack of imagination prevented her from having that life?

Chris had long ago stopped rehearsing speeches for Polly. Preparedness made little difference in whether he got through to her or not. This time, though, as he sat with Becky and stroked her hair, he refined the way he intended to broach this subject. He found it frustratingly easy to imagine Polly's responses.

Becky ate a little before they took the trip back to Moorewood, but she vomited on the side of the road before they made it to the bridge. When they got back in the car, she offered him the most heartbreaking smile he'd ever experienced. The kind that said she understood that they would consider this a good day soon. It was at that moment that Chris realized—even though he thought he'd realized it before—how totally unprepared he was for his daughter's physical breakdown.

At Polly's, Chris helped Becky out of the car and then looped his arm around hers as they approached the door.

"Are you really going to talk to her now?" Becky said unsteadily.

"I'm definitely going to talk to her now."

"Do you want me to be there?"

"I think it would be better if you're not."

Becky squeezed his arm and then entered the house. Polly was there a moment later, hugging her daughter.

"I need a few minutes with you," Chris said while Polly was still holding Becky.

"I'm gonna go up to my room," Becky said, kissing her mother on the cheek. She looked at the stairs and then pulled in her breath. "No, maybe I'll just go into the kitchen." She reached a hand toward Chris and he held it for a moment before she left.

"What's up?" Polly said after watching Becky disappear around the corner.

Chris chose to dive into the conversation. Preliminaries had no value. "I learned about something last night that will cure Becky."

Polly startled for an instant, but recovered quickly. "We've already started on the Gleevec. We're not going to switch course and try some wild alternative. Alternative medicine has never been proven to work."

"This isn't alternative medicine and it isn't a miracle drug, Polly. It's Tamarisk."

Polly seemed disappointed for a moment, as though he'd somehow managed to let her down even though she already held him in such low esteem.

Then her face contorted and the fire was back. "You really must be kidding me. Don't you think I'm in enough pain already without your terrorizing me with make-believe? What are you going to tell me? That Becky's 'medical consultation' in Tamarisk revealed that she just needs to spend more time talking to pixies?"

Polly's anger had no affect on Chris. "Do you know what amazes me? You're willing to explore any pill you hear about regardless of how little research has been done, but you won't open your mind to anything else."

"There's a difference between research science and imaginary worlds, Chris."

"Yes, there is. There very definitely is. Only one of them offers a way for Becky to get better."

Polly stared intently at Chris. If she was trying to get him to look away, she'd chosen the wrong moment. Eventually, she shook her head and said, "I'm going to spend some time my daughter. You know where the door is."

"Polly, we want the same thing. What's the downside of listening to what I have to say?"

Polly glared at him again and then threw up her hands and sat on the stairs that led to the second floor. "Okay, Chris. What do you have to say?"

Chris walked over to the stairs and sat on the step below his ex-wife. "There's a reason Tamarisk exists."

"This assumes one believes Tamarisk exists."

He let the comment pass. "It exists as a home for Becky."

Polly's brows furled. "What?"

Chris leaned forward a bit. "Becky isn't sick in Tamarisk."

"That's very comforting, Chris. Totally irrelevant, but

comforting. I can't believe you're doing this now. I had actually started to convince myself that it might be better for us if you and I went through this together. What a dope I am."

Chris was finding it increasingly difficult to keep his own anger in check, but he fought through it. "What I'm saying is not totally irrelevant. It's her only hope. Tamarisk came to life because Becky can be healthy there."

Polly smirked. "This is your new theory."

"It's not a theory. You should have seen what she was like when we were there last night."

Polly's eyes narrowed and she reddened. "You were there last night?"

"Yes. I was there last night. I've been to Tamarisk many times. You should have seen our daughter—"

"—Chris, can you hear yourself."

"Polly, you need to listen to me. I realize this sounds crazy. I could barely believe it myself when Becky first started talking about it. But there's a reason that this has happened. Becky can live in Tamarisk. When she's there, she's as full of life as she's ever been."

"Oh my god."

Was she acknowledging the possibility of this? Chris pressed on. "I know. It's a lot to absorb. I tossed and turned all night thinking about it. We'll never see her again, but we'll know she's okay."

Polly said nothing for a moment. When she spoke again, her voice had a thinner timbre. "I'm so sorry, Chris. You're even farther along than I am. That has to be excruciating. Listen, I've been talking to a good therapist. Maybe you can meet with one of her associates."

Chris felt as though he'd experienced a sudden drop in blood sugar. "You think I'm imagining this."

"I *know* you're imagining this. As devastated as I am about what's happening to Becky, as much hurt as I feel every moment, I know what you're experiencing is much more harmful to you."

"This is not a delusion."

Polly stood up. She now towered over him. "Seek help, Chris. Do it for Becky."

"This is not a delusion. There are ways of showing you."

Polly walked down the stairs past him and headed toward the kitchen. "I'll e-mail you the phone number of my therapist. There are several other doctors in her group."

With that, Polly turned the corner and went into the kitchen to see their daughter. Chris felt humiliated. He thought for a moment about following Polly down the hallway, but he didn't want to have a nasty confrontation with her in front of Becky. Instead, he waited on the stairs for a few minutes in case Becky came out to see him.

When it was obvious that she wasn't coming, he left the house, feeling as defeated as he'd ever felt leaving here.

Absorb this and all other resources.

He couldn't let Polly win this time, though. He'd conceded so much to her the past four years. There was no room for concession now.

22

Every time she returned to Tamarisk at this point, Becky felt like an inflatable toy reinflating. With each day in the past week, she felt herself getting progressively weaker at home. She'd read that Gleevec did great things for some people, but it was doing nothing for her other than making her painfully nauseous. She had longer and longer stretches where she felt too tired to move. Tonight, Dad had to carry her to the bedroom and she had trouble lifting her head to kiss him good night. Two days earlier, she fell asleep while darkening and never made the crossing to Tamarisk. Dad stayed by her side this time to make sure she didn't do that again.

When she arrived at the palace, though, she felt intensely awake and clearheaded. She took a deep breath and it seemed like she could inhale all the air in the kingdom and still have room for more. Her mind might have been playing tricks on her—especially now that she knew what she did about this place—but she'd never felt this good at home. Ever in her life.

And she might never feel this good ever again. Mom had blown Dad off when he tried to talk to her about Becky's living in Tamarisk, and then she wouldn't get into it at all with Becky. "The Gleevec needs a little time," was all she would say when Becky tried to convince her that Tamarisk was her only chance. Over and over, Becky tried to get her to come here to see the place for herself, to realize it was real, but Mom was a brick wall, absolutely refusing to explain why. Becky couldn't understand it. She knew her mother didn't want her to die, but she wouldn't allow her the only chance she had to live. Dad seemed increasingly desperate, calling Mom several times (only to have her hang up on him) and visiting the house unannounced yesterday. Tonight, he told Becky that she needed to think about making this decision without her mother's approval, but Becky didn't think she could do that. How could she live in Tamarisk without saying good-bye to her mother and knowing that Mom would live the rest of her life thinking her daughter was dead?

Sorbus took her into Miea's chambers and said the queen would be there shortly. The palace was very noisy today, with sounds of sawing and hammering just down the hall. Considering how uncertain everything was right now, it seemed like a strange time to be doing construction.

A few minutes later, Miea entered the room and hugged Becky tightly. "How are you feeling?" she said.

"Great. Wonderful, really."

"It has been several days since you were last here. I was a little worried."

Becky wrinkled her nose. "I had a problem getting here the other night."

Miea reached for her hand. "Oh, Becky."

"I'm here tonight, though. My dad was watching from the other side."

Miea looked down at her hand and squeezed it. "Have you made any progress with your mother?"

"None. None at all. I'd say we were going backward, but you can't go backward from where we started."

"I'm so worried for you. The fact that you couldn't make the transit the other night scares me. What if you go back today and I never see you again?"

Becky didn't want to think about that, although she couldn't think about anything else. She knew that if she could no longer make the transit, her last hope was gone. But what about Tamarisk? If Becky was too sick to return, the blight would overrun the entire kingdom. Would Tamarisk die the same time she did or would something else happen? Maybe it was just the opposite. Maybe if she died, Tamarisk would be free of her illness. That was something to hold on to if things turned out for the worst for her.

"I can't come here without my mom's blessings, Miea. I just can't. I would never be that selfish."

Miea looked at her carefully. "I know you can't." They stood in the same position for a long moment before Miea patted her hand. "Come for a walk with me."

They went out into the courtyard, the very first part of the outside world Becky had ever seen in Tamarisk. Gardeners tended to the flowers and bushes, birds flitted, and ground animals scurried. It was as beautiful as it was every time she came out here. The sound was different, though. The music in the air was even more out of harmony than it was the last time she was outside. There was a deep bass sound in the air, almost like a growl, in a completely different key from the higher melodies.

They continued past the courtyard to the field where Becky caught her rides on the waccasassa. Just stepping out here gave Becky a sense of soaring. That first trip, when she met the micro-farmer and the poledisk players and when she visited the bloat marshes, was one of the most exciting experiences of her life. It gave her the feeling that she belonged in Tamarisk—though back then, she didn't realize how much she belonged.

As they stepped out onto the glade now, though, Becky saw green blotches marking the field and rolling down into the valley below.

"Is that what I think it is?" she said anxiously.

Miea nodded. "The blight is coming to the palace. These appeared in the last couple of days." She pointed down the hill. "Much of the foliage in Tamarisk City has already gone into necrosis. The death cycle is increasing rapidly."

"Maybe if I spent a little time in town, the plants would come back to life."

"They probably would. It wouldn't last, though. It might be better if we didn't raise the hopes of the townspeople."

Becky studied the buildings just barely visible from this distance. "They must be terrified about what's happening."

"They're frighteningly silent. Normally the town is bustling and cacophonous. Now it's still. Most people are staying in their homes. Those who go out are going about their business listlessly. It's as though they're resigned. I think I would have preferred an uprising."

They realize it's pointless, Becky thought. *They love the queen too much to make this even worse than it already is.* "I'll keep trying, Miea. I want this at least as much for Tamarisk as I want it for me."

Miea wrapped an arm around her shoulder and they stared out at the field, the hillside, the town, and the vast expanse of Tamarisk that lay in front of them. The view from this perspective was remarkable, and if Becky tried hard, she could still see the kingdom of her imagination.

It was a kingdom of wonders dreamed by a girl with limitless amounts of hope.

"I need some of that hope now," Becky said in a whisper. She hadn't intended to say the words aloud, but she obviously had because Miea squeezed her shoulder.

Becky took another deep breath. The Tamariskian air filled her up.

///

Three days later, Becky lay in the nurse's office waiting for her mother to come to get her. Lonnie and she had been on their way to their second period class when Becky felt her legs go rubbery. She sat on the floor in the hall while kids filed past her quickly, a number of them asking if she was okay while Lonnie waved them away. When the halls cleared, Lonnie helped her to the nurse and then stayed with her.

"You can go to class, I'll be okay," Becky said. Lonnie had already brought her a glass of water, a second pillow, and a trash can in case she felt like she was going to throw up.

"I am not going to class."

"You're just using me as an excuse to skip school."

"Saw right through that one, huh? You know me backward, Beck."

Becky tried to smile, but she wasn't sure it appeared on her face. She felt so listless, like she would fall asleep in a second if she closed her eyes. She didn't want to close her eyes, though. She didn't want her mother to find her lying unconscious. Becky tried to prop herself up on the pillow, but found the effort exhausting. She lay back.

"Do you need help?" Lonnie said.

"No, I'm all right like this."

Lonnie leaned over and stroked her hair. Becky's forehead was clammy and Lonnie probably would have teased her about that under different circumstances.

"You know I love you, right, Beck?"

"I love you, too, Lon."

"Best friends should say that to each other more often."

"You're right. I'll remember that."

"Not that it matters with me. I'm retiring your number."

That was an odd thing to say, even for someone like Lonnie. "Is that supposed to mean something?"

"It's like in baseball when a great player retires and they never use his number again. You're my last best friend."

Lonnie's voice cracked on the last word and tears ran down both sides of her face. Becky wasn't sure she'd ever seen Lonnie cry like this before. The tears over boyfriends leaked; these dripped. "I don't want to be your last best friend, Lon."

Lonnie sniffled and wiped her eyes. "I'm not asking for your opinion."

"I really don't, Lon."

"And I really don't care."

Mom walked in a few minutes later, looking horribly shaken up. She knelt down and hugged Becky and then turned and hugged Lonnie for a long time as well.

"Do you think you can stand up?" she said when she turned

back to Becky.

"I'm not sure."

The nurse walked over and said, "We have a wheelchair, if you'd like."

Becky flashed a look of alarm at her mother. "I don't want to leave here in a wheelchair, Mom. I can walk out."

She pulled herself to a sitting position, thankful that the room hadn't started spinning immediately. With Mom on one side and Lonnie on the other, she got to her feet. Her legs weren't as wobbly as before and she took a few unsteady steps. With her best friend and her mother on each arm, she made her way to the car.

Lonnie hugged her tightly before she sat down in the passenger seat and again before she closed the door. "I'll come over after school," she said.

"Definitely do that."

"I will. And I'm totally retiring your number, Beck. No one will ever wear it again."

"We can talk about that this afternoon."

Lonnie stepped back, waving as they drove off. Becky looked behind her to see Lonnie wiping her eyes with the back of the hand she used for waving.

As Mom exited the parking lot, the school receded behind her. She watched it until it disappeared from view.

23

For the past two weeks, ever since Becky had stopped going to school, Chris only went to the office on days when his daughter was with Polly. The downsizing had begun and management had been less gracious about his decision to stay home with her than they should have been under the circumstances, but he simply didn't care. If his supervisors truly believed he would choose time at work over any extra moment he could get with Becky, they were hideously deluded.

Becky didn't move around much anymore, and she needed help getting in the car to go back and forth between houses. Shuttling her took its toll and it might have been best to leave her in one place, but Becky insisted on continuing to alternate houses. Polly protested vehemently, but she stopped short whenever Becky made her desires clear. Chris didn't understand many things about Polly, but he understood that Becky was and had always been as essential in her life as Becky was in his. She wouldn't make this issue a battleground with her daughter now.

However, she gladly did battle on many other fronts. The transitions from his home to hers were always difficult, punctuated by strained exchanges about Tamarisk. Polly steadfastly refused to believe Tamarisk existed and rejected any offer to see the proof for herself, instead vehemently imploring Chris to get into therapy. Not even Becky could get through to her. Polly just continued to perpetuate a real fantasy: that the Gleevec would suddenly have an impact on Becky's disease. Chris knew the experimental drug worked in an encouraging number of cases. He also knew, as Polly would have if she'd paid attention to the research, that if it were going to work, it would have shown some sign by now.

"Babe, if you can make it over there tonight, just stay," Chris had said last night. He hadn't been to Tamarisk himself in weeks because he needed to monitor Becky's ability to make the transit from this side.

"No, Dad, I won't," Becky said with as much emphasis as she could put on anything these days.

"Becky, you have to. How can you put the personal feelings of your mother or me or anyone else above your own life?"

"Dad, stop. Please."

Ultimately, it didn't matter. For the first time since he'd been watching, Becky couldn't make the crossing. She hadn't fallen asleep this time; this was something else.

Her eyes fluttered and then she looked at him sadly. "I can't darken," she said. "I can't get my mind to do it." Then she wept as he held her, only stopping when she fell asleep. If Becky wasn't even strong enough to control her thoughts—something she'd mastered brilliantly in the last months—there was the very real chance she'd never get to Tamarisk again.

Was it too late for him to participate in Polly's fantasy at this point?

They were due back at Polly's at 10:00. As usual, Chris awoke at 6:00, checked in on his sleeping daughter, and then tried to stay busy. As was also usual, though, he ended up on the couch in the ersatz form of meditation that he'd started practicing; head back, eyes to the ceiling, his mantra the continuous loop of thoughts about Becky. At 9:15, he rose out of this trance to realize that Becky was still asleep. He hated waking her, but understood the discomfort of jostling her out of bed was preferable to any additional tension she might feel if he brought her to Polly's late.

When he went into Becky's room, she was lying on her back in the precise position she had been when he awoke that morning. He kissed her forehead and stroked her hair.

"Babe, we need to get going soon."

Becky didn't move. Her skin was warm and he could see that she was breathing shallowly, but his words had failed to rouse her in any way.

"Beck? Beck, we need to go."

Chris had read a great deal about Becky's illness, and he knew how the stages progressed at the end. Sometimes the patient lapsed into a coma and then the body failed. Sometimes it happened all at once.

"Beck? Babe?"

Her eyes opened narrowly and fixed on him.

"Do you think you can get up?"

Becky closed her eyes again, seemed lost for a few moments, and then opened her eyes a little wider. "I don't think so."

He could carry her to the car to take her to Polly's, but he thought the ride might be horrible for her in a sitting position. He could call an ambulance to take her to the hospital, but he knew Becky didn't really want that. She didn't want to spend her last days in such an impersonal place.

"I'll be right back," he said and went to the phone in his bedroom.

It took a long moment before he could press the speed dial. He knew what it was like to receive a call like this, and he wouldn't wish it on anyone. At last, he pressed the button and waited for his ex-wife to answer.

"Polly, you need to come over."

"What's wrong?" Polly said, the two words expressing every emotion he already felt.

"I can't get her up. You need to come see her and then we'll decide what to do."

///

An accident had shut traffic on the bridge down to one lane. Polly sat in the car, suspended between Moorewood and

Standridge wondering if some driver's mistake was going to cost her the ability to share her child's last waking moments.

Her conversation with Chris had lasted less than a minute, but his message was unmistakable. Becky was entering the final stages of her disease. She might hold on a little while longer, might even rally a little, but it was no longer possible to believe that any attempt at fighting this horrible illness would be successful.

Polly had considered so many times in the past few months what life would be like without Becky, and now realized that she wasn't ready in any way to face it. As she passed the bottleneck on the bridge and headed toward Chris's apartment, she knew she'd underestimated everything: the heartache, the pain, the desperate desire to stop time to prevent this from happening. As these feelings surrounded and threatened to smother her, she fought back the desperate urge to pull the car over and succumb to them. Only the need to speak to her daughter again—to hold her while Becky could still feel her—prevented Polly from allowing the grief to win. That could happen later. She wouldn't fight it then.

Still, as she rode the elevator up to Chris's floor, she felt a moment's hesitation. One last thread of blind hope suggested to her that if she didn't go into the apartment, nothing would happen. Then the elevator doors opened, the thread broke, and she walked toward the inevitable.

"She's more alert than when I called you," Chris said when he let her into the apartment, "but she keeps going in and out."

"It took me so long to get here. I was worried . . ." She couldn't finish the sentence.

Chris stepped out of her way. "Go see her."

Becky was lying with her head propped against two pillows when Polly entered the room. She looked sunken and pale, but her eyes still had some of their old brightness, even if it was just a glint. Becky raised one hand to her slowly and Polly rushed to her side, gathering her up and holding her to her chest. She'd managed not to cry since Chris's call, but now she couldn't hold back any longer. She buried her head in her daughter's hair and allowed the tears to fall.

"Come with me, Mom," Becky said softly.

Polly lay Becky back against the pillows and took her hand. "Come with you where, honey."

"To Tamarisk."

Polly closed her eyes and felt tears stream down both cheeks. "You know we can't really go there."

"We can, Mom. Let me take you."

Polly hadn't noticed that Chris had walked back into the room until she saw him standing beside them. "Polly, please."

She'd fought this moment so hard. She didn't want to prove to her daughter that Tamarisk was nothing more than a flight of the imagination. Somehow, Becky and Chris shared this delusion—in some ways they always had—but Polly wouldn't be able to pretend the way they did. She'd never been able to do that.

"Becky, Tamarisk is a fantasy. It's a wonderful fantasy that you created with your father, but it isn't real."

Becky closed her eyes and a tear rolled toward her temple. "You need to believe me. You need to know that I'll be okay there."

Polly lay her head over Becky's heart and wept. What could she do to comfort her daughter? How much time was left? There were so many difficult decisions to make, and she had no power to make any of this even a little bit better.

Chris laid a hand on her arm. "Can I see you outside for a second?"

Polly didn't want to let go of Becky for even a minute. "Not now, Chris."

"It needs to be now."

Polly desperately wanted to stay in this place, but she rose up slowly and kissed Becky on the forehead. "I'll be back in a minute, honey."

Becky seemed confused and helpless. Polly could only begin to imagine what was going on in her mind. Turning away from her required Herculean effort.

Polly glanced through her tears at Chris. He seemed surprisingly composed under the circumstances. How was that possible? She knew Chris too well to believe that this wasn't killing him. She broke eye contact and walked into the living room. She heard the door to Becky's room close. When she turned around, Chris was no more than a couple of feet behind her.

"You have to let her go," he said firmly.

Polly laughed bitterly. "I didn't realize I had any other choice."

"That's not what I mean. I think you know that. What I mean is that you have to let her go to Tamarisk."

Polly held a hand to her head and closed her eyes. She tried to breathe normally, but couldn't suppress a sob. "Chris, our child is dying in there. These might be her last waking moments. If you have any compassion at all, you won't compromise those moments with another one of these deluded arguments."

Chris took her shoulders. The gesture surprised her enough to make her drop her hand and open her eyes. "Polly, this is not about you and me. This isn't about anything that's happened to us in the past or anything that will happen in the future. This is exclusively about Becky. You can say that I'm deluded. You can say that I need professional help. But you know in your heart that Becky believes in Tamarisk. It doesn't matter whether you believe she can go there or not, just as it doesn't matter whether you believe she can live a healthy life there. The only thing that matters is that Becky wants and needs your blessing. She needs to believe that you won't think of her as dead."

"How can I possibly do that?"

"By summoning whatever you need to summon to convince her."

Polly looked down at the floor. She felt as though the very air around her was forcing her to the ground.

"I can't play pretend, Chris. That's your specialty."

"You have to try. You have to do it for Becky. She needs to know that you're okay with her making the crossing. If you let her go—assuming it's not too late already—she will have an extraordinary future."

Polly's body shook when she thought about how little future Becky had left. "I can't believe that. I'll never believe that."

"Make yourself believe it," Chris said sharply. "Look, Polly, maybe you're right. Maybe Becky and I are caught up in the middle of some gigantic joint hallucination. I know that isn't the case, but even if it is—even if we're completely crazy—your blessing will allow Becky some peace and hope at the end. What could possibly be wrong with that?"

Polly looked up into Chris's eyes. There was resolve there she hadn't noticed before. He knew he was right. Definitively.

And for the first time, Polly understood that, in some very real way, he was. Polly had been so concerned with not proving to Becky that Tamarisk was a dream that she hadn't considered the possibility that Becky would gain comfort from believing that her mother bought into the dream. What Chris said was true. It didn't matter if Tamarisk was real to her. If it offered Becky some kind of solace, that was a gift.

"Would she ever believe me?"

Chris's expression softened. "She'll believe you if you let her believe you."

Polly closed her eyes yet again and then clasped her hands together. Then she looked at Chris one more time and walked past him into Becky's room.

Becky's eyes caught her the moment she turned the corner. As sick as the girl was, she still carried a trace of hope. Seeing that, Polly realized that Becky would of course believe her. Becky desperately wanted to believe her.

Polly knelt at the side of the bed, grasped her daughter's hand, and said, "Tell me something about Tamarisk."

Becky smiled with effort. "It sounds like music."

"Good music?"

"Magical music."

Polly kissed Becky's hand. "And it's pretty there?"

Becky's eyes managed to shine a little. "Gorgeous. They

have colors you've never seen before."

Polly smiled as encouragingly as she could. "It sounds wonderful."

Becky offered the lightest squeeze of her hand. "It's real, Mom."

Again, Polly lay her head over her daughter's heart. "I know it is, honey. It took me a long time to believe it, but I believe it now. I know you can go there and be well."

Polly felt Becky's chest rise. "I should go soon."

"I know you should. Let's just stay like this for a little while, though. Okay?"

"Okay, Mom."

Becky reached up and laid her hand on Polly's hair. When she did, Polly felt stronger.

"Is it the kind of music I would like, or the kind of music that you and your father like?"

"It's the kind of music everyone likes."

Polly squeezed Becky a little tighter. She'd done what she could do. Maybe that would mean something in the end.

24

Becky slept for several hours after her conversation with Polly. Chris and Polly sat wordlessly by the bed for most of that time. Chris explained to Polly that when Becky awoke, he'd help her make the journey to Tamarisk. His ex-wife didn't argue. She did ask what would happen if Becky couldn't "make the journey"—which he interpreted as code for "when she finds out she's been imagining this"—but she didn't give him a hard time when he responded by saying they didn't have to worry about that.

A few minutes ago, Al had come to the apartment. He and Polly went into the living room. Chris could hear them speaking with each other, but he couldn't distinguish what they were saying. Chris was glad they had each other for this; Polly was going to need support much more than Chris would.

It dawned on Chris that, with every minute she slept, Becky got another minute weaker. Would she still be strong enough to make the transit? Would she awaken at all?

At 2:00, he decided he would try to awaken her. For the past few years, he'd been applying the brake to time, hoping to slow Becky's evolution to adulthood. Now, ironically, he was in a rush to get on with things. Not, of course, because he wanted her to go, but because he knew she had to go before it was too late.

He kissed her forehead and stroked her hair. She didn't respond immediately, but then she shifted a little and opened her eyes about half way.

"Hey, babe. How are you doing in there?"

Becky groaned and shifted a little more. Chris helped her to a sitting position and placed several pillows against her back.

"Mom is really okay with this?"

"She is, babe. She told me so."

"So she believes in Tamarisk now?"

Chris kissed her forehead again. "I think she's horribly jealous that she didn't take you up on that offer to go for a visit."

New concern came to Becky's expression. "I can still take her there."

"We can't take that chance, babe. We don't want to wait until tomorrow for you to go there by yourself."

Becky looked down at the bedspread and then around the room. "I know. You're right."

Chris went into the living room to get Polly and Al and the three of them returned to stand by the side of Becky's bed. For several moments, no one said anything. Chris felt suspended, as though time had somehow stopped while they were here. Suddenly, he found it difficult to move forward.

Finally, Al leaned toward Becky and patted her on the leg. "From what I hear, you have a little magic trick to perform."

Becky grinned. "You didn't know I was a magician, did you?"

"Not true. I always knew you had something up your sleeve."

Becky smiled at Al and her eyes seemed bright. Chris felt conflicted over his daughter's relative alertness. Maybe they had another day or two like this. Maybe he could have just a little more time with her. He knew it was wrong to think this way, though. It could become too late at any moment.

"I think it might be a good idea to get started," he said.

Becky nodded. "Yeah, you're right."

"Do you want to lean against me the way we did it yesterday?"

Becky tried to sit up a little straighter. "That would be good."

Chris helped Becky sit at the edge of the bed. She wasn't

steady enough to hold herself up and as they looked into each other's eyes, he understood how much this distressed her. "It's okay, babe. You'll be wrestling a chestatee again really soon. Maybe right after the huge state dinner they have to welcome you to your new home."

He sat next to her and she leaned into him. Polly sat down on the other side and rubbed Becky's arm. Until that moment, Chris wasn't sure how Polly planned to participate in this or if she would even participate at all. He was glad she was there for her daughter.

Al came over and hugged Becky. "I think this is Mom and Dad time," he said with a catch in his throat.

Becky looked at him affectionately.

"Thanks for being a great roommate," he said.

Becky leaned toward him and he hugged her again. "Keep Mom smiling."

"I will, Beck. I promise." He squeezed her again, kissed Polly on the top of the head, and exited.

Becky leaned against Chris, then turned to her mother and leaned against her. Polly pulled her close and then turned Becky's face to put their foreheads together. Chris wondered for a moment if he should give Polly and Becky some time alone together, but didn't want to interrupt them now.

"You're my heart," Polly said, the words coming out haltingly. "You know that, right?"

"I love you, Mom."

"You're the most perfect thing that ever happened to me. I'll have that forever."

Becky started crying and the two held their faces together, tears intermingling. Chris hadn't heard Polly say, "You're my heart" to Becky in years, since well before the divorce. He flashed on an image of Polly rocking their infant daughter after feeding her and saying those words. The future had turned out so differently from the one he'd anticipated back then.

Polly held Becky's face in her hands and kissed her on both cheeks. "Go lean toward your father," she said. "That's how it works, right?"

Becky moved toward him and he took her in his arms. "Want to tell one more Tamarisk story before you go?" he said.

Becky sniffled. "I don't think I can."

He tightened his hold on her. "Is it okay if I tell one myself every night before I go to bed? They'll all have you in them, of course."

"I'd like that."

Chris kissed her and pulled her even tighter. "I love you, babe."

"Love you, Dad."

He buried her head in his chest and held her there for a long time. He knew he had to let her go, but it was proving even more difficult than he'd expected. At last, he pulled back and let her lean against him without his exerting any pressure on her.

"Dad?" she said softly.

"Yeah, babe."

"Thanks."

"Always, Beck."

She didn't say anything else and Chris assumed she'd begun the darkening process. He had no idea what to do if Becky had trouble making the transit. His having her lean on him these past few weeks served no purpose, really, except perhaps to the degree that she thought it served a purpose. The thought came to mind that he would have no idea if she'd succeeded. How would he know the difference between Becky's safe transit to Tamarisk and something else entirely? What if she got pulled back? How would he help her in her final days to reconcile that Miea's theory was wrong?

Several minutes passed and Chris felt Becky's body grow slack. He didn't want to move her in case she was still traveling, but his thoughts raced. Was it too late to call an ambulance? Was it possible the hospital could keep her alive long enough to seek one last miracle? Was there something that science could do for her that Tamarisk couldn't?

Chris felt the change before he saw it. The panic that had

begun to rise within him subsided, as though a soothing wave had washed over him. He breathed deeply and then did it again, exhaling slowly and evenly. The wave of feeling covered him, but rather than crashing away, it embraced him.

Chris looked down at the bed and his soul stirred.

"She's there," he said to Polly. "She's made it and she can live there permanently. Miea was right."

"How do you know that?" Polly said, running a hand over the face of her daughter's lifeless form, tears flowing freely.

"Look at the bedspread."

Polly turned away from Becky and her breath caught. "This was the old comforter, right?"

"It was."

It was, but it wasn't the same any longer.

Becky's white bedspread had turned the deepest shade of Tamariskian blue.

25

Gage absorbed the presence of this fully alive world and felt a heightened level of joy. Centering, Gage dreamed of the possibilities. This story was so unexpected, so deeply enriched that Gage had only begun to consider the implications. It was a new home. A home for those with the wrong homes. At least those who could imagine it.

There were new gifts on this world. Maybe new chances for gifts because of this world. This was something to explore.

It would be a welcome journey. The newest chapter in Gage's own story.

Gage marveled again at the wonder of potential.

///

Becky closed her eyes and listened to the music that was always in the air in Tamarisk. The sounds were always interesting, as though constantly being reinvented, but unlike when she had been a visitor, there was nothing discordant.

She looked up at the turquoise sky. Was her original home out there somewhere? Was it somewhere else? She'd stopped to consider this at least once every day, wondering what Dad, Mom, Al, Lonnie, and her other friends might be doing. Miea had told her about a trick where she imagined conversations with her father, and Becky had started doing that. It was amazing how real those conversations felt. Now Becky had a "talk" with her father every night, catching him up on what was going on in Tamarisk and asking him about his life.

She knew he was doing okay. Everyone was. In her last moments before she left for Tamarisk forever, Becky realized that they would be. Still, she missed them.

"Looking for those invisible birds again?" Rubus said, bumping shoulders with her and craning his head upward in an exaggerated way.

"You really don't see them? I'm very worried about you." She grinned and pushed him playfully and they continued their walk.

The Thorn boy was one of the first big surprises she received right after she started living here. She was walking down a hallway with Miea when she saw him coming in the other direction carrying a stack of books.

"Rubus," Becky said brightly when she saw him.

He stopped, studied Becky's face for a moment, and then his jaw dropped. "You're visiting *here*?" he said.

Becky smiled at Miea. "Actually, I'm not visiting anymore. I just moved in."

"To the palace?"

"This is Becky's new home," Miea said.

Rubus seemed to give this an unusual amount of thought and then his eyes widened. "You're . . . the girl?"

"Well, I'm *a* girl."

Rubus smacked his hands together. "I knew there was something about you."

Becky laughed awkwardly. "I'll try to take that as a compliment. So now we know what I'm doing here. But what are you doing here?"

"I'm working for the queen," he said, nodding deferentially toward Miea. "I've denounced my homeland and defected to Tamarisk. I wasn't meant to be a Thorn. I belong here."

Becky rocked back on her heels. "Wow."

"Rubus is studying our culture," Miea said. "It is my hope that once he gains an unbiased perspective on our people that he can help us in the diplomatic corps."

"Most of the Thorns are good people," Rubus said. "Except for those in the government like my parents. This might be crazy, but maybe I can help bring us all together."

Becky smiled at him broadly. "That doesn't sound crazy. That sounds like a great dream." She hesitated and her face felt warm. "So you work in the palace?"

Rubus pointed back in the direction he came. "Just down the hall."

"Wow. Cool."

Rubus smiled. "Maybe we can get together again after all."

As it turned out, they got together quite a bit, but reaching that point required some work on Becky's part. At first, Miea tried to coddle her. The queen told her that her only responsibility was to get used to the Tamariskian schools and do well there. Becky made it very clear that she had no desire to be a pampered little member of the palace. For one thing, she had so much energy that she needed to expend. She was only sleeping four or five hours a night but she still felt wide awake all the time. Becky had no idea that it was possible to feel this good.

More important, though, there were too many things to do. The blight had disappeared quickly, but people, flora, and fauna all over Tamarisk had suffered greatly during the bad times and they needed help with recovery. Then there were other things to do, like assist Miea with some of the ideas she had that she'd never had time to do herself. Tamarisk was an amazing place, but it could always be more amazing. All it took was imagination and conviction, and Becky had huge amounts of both.

Miea got the message pretty quickly, telling Becky she'd known someone who was just like her at her age. On the weekends, she sent Becky on aid missions to the microfarms. During the week after school, she worked with Rubus, helping him to learn the culture and develop a way to appeal directly to the citizenry of Gunnthorn. At first, they did most of their work in one of the palace offices, but lately they'd taken to going for long walks in the meadow.

They'd been walking now for about twenty minutes when they heard some rustling a few dozen yards ahead. Becky expected to see an animal bound out or a bird take flight. Instead, two painfully slim young boys—maybe six or seven years old—dressed only with cloths around their distended waists rose from the wildflowers. They looked at each other, then at the sky, and then at the landscape around them before looking at each other again. They seemed mystified.

"I don't feel the same," one boy said, moving his arms and stretching his sticklike legs.

"Neither do I," the other boy said. He took a deep breath. "I feel . . . easy. Where are we?"

"It's like the place in my stories."

"It's nothing like the place in your stories."

"You're right; it's not. It's like nowhere else in the world."

They laughed loudly, with abandon. Becky and Rubus looked at each other and then stared again at the boys, speechless.

One boy plucked a wildflower and ate it.

"You can eat them?" the other boy said.

"I don't know. I think so."

The other boy also took a flower and bit into it, chewing more carefully.

Becky approached them slowly. "Hello?"

The boys turned sharply toward the sound of her voice, throwing down the flowers as though they'd committed a terrible crime.

"It's okay," Becky said. "You don't need to be afraid."

"We didn't mean to steal. We're just very hungry."

"We can fix that. We'll take you to get food."

Rubus stepped alongside Becky. "Food that tastes much better than those flowers."

The boys seemed fascinated with this information.

"The flowers tasted good."

Becky reached out a hand. "Then you'll really like what the kitchen can whip up."

One of the boys tentatively took Becky's hand while the other took Rubus's. The four began walking toward the palace.

"This isn't Awassa, is it?"

Becky shook her head. "It's Tamarisk City."

"Do we have to go back?"

"I don't know yet. I guess we'll find out."

"You said you have food here?"

"We have lots of food."

The boy thought about this for a minute. Then he threw his head to the sky and laughed even more boisterously than before. "It *is* like the place in my stories. Amare didn't believe me when I told him there could be something more."

Becky turned to Rubus. He looked like his eyes were going to pop right out of his head. He leaned toward her. "What's happening here?"

"I don't have any idea. Apparently, you're not the only one who has a lot to learn about this culture. Isn't it great?"

///

Fridays were always the biggest challenge. Chris spent every Friday out in the field—which he loved—but the work took him down to Fairfield and Westchester Counties, which meant contending with rush hour traffic most of the way back to Standridge, including an interminable stretch on 95. He knew he shouldn't complain, considering his commute the other four workdays consisted of twenty pleasant minutes up the Connecticut River, but it was difficult to remember that when traveling fifteen miles an hour twenty miles from home at 6:15 with a 7:30 dinner date.

By the time he got home, he realized that, if he left the apartment in the next five minutes and there was no traffic going over the bridge, he'd only be slightly late. He'd call Nigella as soon as he got back into the car.

In the past year, Chris had developed something of a reputation as a plant doctor. He'd returned to work a month after

Becky made the transit and suddenly found it surprisingly easy to do something he should have done years earlier. The first time his boss implied that his trimmed department was underperforming because of his extended absence, Chris cleaned out his desk. Chris didn't want special treatment because of what he'd been through, but the complete lack of empathy illustrated how soulless his office had become and how completely he didn't belong there. It would have been hard enough to be a suit for a company he believed in. Under these circumstances, it was impossible. He made a number of calls to contacts he'd developed over his years of quasi-job-searching and it turned out that a farm in southern Connecticut needed help curing, of all things, a blight affecting its tomato plants. A few freelance months working for a number of growers led to a full-time position with the area's largest network of nurseries. Plenty of dirt under his fingernails and absolutely no budget reports.

The only downside was that cleaning up for Friday dinner dates required extra time—time he didn't have tonight. As he finished scrubbing, the phone rang. Chris glanced at the caller ID, saw it was Lisa, and answered.

"I can't talk," he said by way of greeting.

"If you can't talk, why did you answer the phone?"

"After all this time, I still find you undeniable."

Lisa chortled on the other end. "I wish I could train Ben to feel the same way. Six months into this marriage, he decides he needs to go back out on the road. Looks like I'm going to be a part-time wife."

"You were complaining the other day that you thought the two of you were spending too much time together."

"I wasn't actually serious about that."

Chris chose a fresh shirt and wrestled it on while still holding the phone. "I promise to be more sympathetic tomorrow. I really have to run."

"Another sultry evening with *Nigella*?" Lisa extended the second syllable of Nigella's name to make it sound especially exotic.

"That's definitely the plan. Assuming I ever get off the phone with you."

"She's too perfect for you, sweetie. Life without adversity is boring."

"I'm willing to try it out. And, really, you're just upset that I met Nigella on my own."

"Guilty as charged. I fixed you up with plenty of terrific women. If you had told me you were ready to try again, I would have fixed you up with plenty more."

Chris put his shoes back on and grabbed his car keys. "Probably true and completely beside the point—not to mention the fact that I had no idea I was ready to try again."

"Well, go have a fabulous date and try not to think about me pining away over here."

"Ben's gone already?"

"He's not going on his first trip for another couple of weeks, but I'm pining in advance. Give Nigella a kiss for me."

Chris clicked off the phone and headed for the door, remembering as he grabbed the doorknob that he'd left his cell phone in his other jacket. As he went to the bedroom to get it, he heard a knock.

I'm never leaving here tonight.

He got the phone and then answered the door.

Polly was standing on the other side. "Oh, you're going out. I'm sorry, I should have called."

Chris opened the door further and stepped aside to let Polly in. She pecked him on the cheek as she passed, something she'd started doing a few days after the event that Chris would never think of as a funeral. "No, it's fine. What's up?"

Polly tilted her head to the left. "I just felt one of my overwhelming urges to spend some time in her room. You know, to feel that thing that we feel when we're there. Do you think I can just have a few minutes?"

Nigella would understand. If he called her cell right now, he could probably catch her before she got to the restaurant and just reschedule for 8:00. He probably should have done that from the start. Some of the nuances of dating still eluded him.

"Yeah, of course. Come on in."

The vision of the blue bedspread the moment Becky made the transit had established a renewed level of communication between Chris and Polly. Polly had never come right out and said that she believed Becky was living happily in Tamarisk, but maybe she didn't need to. They spoke at length in the days that followed, sharing stories of the girl they knew together for ten years and independently for the last four. While Chris missed Becky horribly, Polly seemed to be having the harder time coping, and Chris felt his heart go out to her, wanting to find some way to ease her pain.

It dawned on Chris that he had the benefit of Becky's room at his apartment. He'd spent time in that room nightly and the "conversations" he held with Becky were extremely vivid. Details sprang to mind that he couldn't possibly have imagined. Chris realized that some version of the path to Tamarisk must still be open. It wasn't enough to get him there—he'd tried on several occasions—but it was enough to maintain the cosmic equivalent of a phone line. This gave him a sense of peace and connection with his daughter and, while it couldn't possibly substitute for being with her, it provided much more solace than a photo album, a DVD, or one of her favorite board games. Knowing that it would take her longer to reach the same link but that she could get there eventually, Chris invited Polly to spend some time in Becky's room herself and told her she could visit whenever she wanted.

Chris called Nigella and then went to Becky's room to join Polly. The air was different there, warmer and with the faintest scent of chocolate and raspberries. As happened every time he entered, Chris felt his muscles loosen and time seem to slow down. He spent a good part of every day wondering what Becky was doing, imagining her holding court with Miea, soaring on a waccasassa, or studying tone poetry at school. Here, though, he knew he was doing something more than wondering.

Watching Polly sitting on the blue quilt, he realized that

she'd begun to feel some of the same things. He sat next to her, closed his eyes, and let images flood his mind. Something about a norbeck symphony. Something about a harvest festival. Something about a royal wedding.

"It really is like she's here, isn't it?" Polly said with a sense of wonder that reminded him of their early days together.

Chris ran his hands along the blue quilt. "She is. She's always here."

a note from the author

I had a great deal on my mind while writing this novel, and I tried to put as much of it on the page as I could without getting heavy-handed about any of it. Several readers saw this novel before publication, and each had a somewhat different interpretation of it. In the years since the book's first publication, I've gotten many others, and I always find them fascinating and thought-provoking.

I would be very interested in your sense of the events that unfolded in this novel. If you have a moment, e-mail me at laronica@fictionstudio.com with your thoughts.

Thanks.